HOUSE OF LIES

DETECTIVE KAREN HART SERIES

D.S. BUTLER

THOMAS & MERCER

Text copyright © 2020 by D. S. Butler
All rights reserved.

Published by Thomas & Mercer, Seattle

www.apub.com

Amazon, the Amazon logo, and Thomas & Mercer are trademarks of Amazon.com, Inc., or its affiliates.

ISBN-13: 9781542017572
ISBN-10: 1542017572

Cover design by @blacksheep-uk.com

Printed in the United States of America

HOUSE
OF
LIES

ALSO BY
D. S. BUTLER

Lost Child
Her Missing Daughter

DS Karen Hart Series:

Bring Them Home
Where Secrets Lie
Don't Turn Back

DS Jack Mackinnon Crime Series:

Deadly Obsession
Deadly Motive
Deadly Revenge
Deadly Justice
Deadly Ritual
Deadly Payback
Deadly Game
Deadly Intent

East End Series:

East End Trouble
East End Diamond
East End Retribution

Harper Grant Mystery Series:

HOUSE
OF
LIES

PROLOGUE

Alison King swallowed nervously as she looked around the wood-panelled hall. Oil paintings covered the walls. On her first day at Chidlow House, she'd made the mistake of taking a close look at the artwork. It was disturbing. The hunting scenes were violent, and the portraits were odd. Stern-faced men and miserable women were scattered among the bloodthirsty canvases.

She shuddered. It was just a house. A big, grand, empty house, but a house all the same. The Chidlow family had a long, chequered history, which delighted the teenage students Alison was teaching. At lunchtime she'd overheard them sharing ghost stories about the Drowned Lady. Of course, she didn't believe in ghosts. She was a grown-up, not a naive, pliable teenager. But there was something about this house . . .

Giving herself a mental shake, she squared her shoulders and walked on. The smells of old wood and dust from the thick curtains hung in the air as she walked past a large window which looked out on to the extensive gardens. It had a large windowsill with a cushioned seat, in theory a perfect reading nook. Somewhere to curl up and disappear into a novel. In daylight, the house didn't seem nearly as scary. The sun streamed in through the large pane of glass and the view across the lawns to the lake was undoubtedly beautiful. But when the shadows began to lengthen and the creaks and groans of the old house took on an ominous tone, it was the last place Alison wanted to read. No, she couldn't imagine curling up and reading in a spot like this. Alison hadn't read more than a couple of pages since she'd arrived. She hadn't been able to relax enough to enter a fictional world, because that meant letting her guard down and she couldn't do that. Not here.

The house was oppressive. Malevolent.

Where had that thought come from? A house couldn't do any harm. The people in it, on the other hand . . .

She paused and turned in a circle, confused, sure she'd heard something – dripping water, a whisper. She stood still, her ears straining against the silence, but heard nothing. She was alone.

This place was making her hypersensitive. It wasn't like her to be so skittish. Once she made it to her room, she could bolt the door and feel safe. But she couldn't go to her room yet. She had some important information for the director of the study programme.

Last night she'd heard water trickling in the old pipes and scratching behind the walls. The scratching had probably been mice. Rodents creeping in through cracks and crevices wouldn't be unusual in a house of this age and size. That was the logical explanation. But at night, her mind played fanciful tricks, and though she didn't believe in spirits or otherworldly beings, the noises meant she'd stayed awake most of the night.

A house she'd shared in her student days had had a rodent problem. They'd been nesting in the loft insulation and chewed through various wires, causing untold damage.

She was annoyed at herself for getting spooked. When the students spoke about the haunting of Chidlow House they did so in awed, thrilled whispers. They weren't scared of the Drowned Lady. If a group of teenagers could get through a week in the old house without having a panic attack, surely she could do the same. After all, she was the one who was supposed to be responsible for their welfare.

Earlier two of the students had asked if she'd heard the sound of dripping water and whispering last night.

She hadn't been able to reply at first. Then she'd stammered something about how the gurgling of the pipes was the most logical reason for the odd noises. The students accepted her explanation readily enough, but she hadn't really convinced herself.

It could be one of the students playing a practical joke. She wouldn't be surprised. Teenage boys often made very odd efforts to gain attention from their female peers. Or her first guess could be correct – gurgling pipes. Air trapped within them could cause knocking or other unusual sounds. Perhaps the noise was from an animal? They could make all sorts of strange noises. She'd read that foxes could make a sound like a baby crying.

With a sigh of relief she realised she'd reached the corridor leading to Graham Doyle's suite. She needed to talk to the programme director as soon as possible. Though she would have liked to leave the matter until morning, it really couldn't wait. Handling the problem was way above her pay grade. Doyle could do it. He was immensely proud of holding the study week at Chidlow House and would want to know if there was a chance something could tarnish the programme's reputation.

Only a few days left, Alison told herself as she walked along the narrow hallway. She could cope with a few more days. She would never do this again though, no matter how good the money was. The stress simply wasn't worth it.

She'd only taken a few steps when a flash of something white streaked across the end of the corridor, in front of the window.

Her limbs froze and she couldn't even take a breath, let alone call for help.

What was that? It was no mouse or gurgling pipes. She'd definitely seen something, a figure in white racing along the hall.

She turned around desperately, looking for someone else who could have seen the apparition. Doyle's room was only a few feet away. But her legs refused to move. Her feet felt like they were bolted to the floor.

She forced herself to take a breath, clenched her fists in her pockets.

No, she wouldn't ask Doyle for help. When she'd mentioned the noises to him earlier, he'd looked at her as though she'd lost her marbles and then patronisingly patted her hand.

Don't panic. Think logically. There's no such thing as ghosts so it must be a student messing about.

'Who's there?' she called. She was trying to make her voice sound authoritative, but it came out reedy and weak, and she sounded exactly how she felt – scared.

Gathering all her courage, she rushed forward just as all the lights went off.

Plunged into darkness, she stopped, paralysed by fear. Something moved past her. There wasn't enough light from the window to see anything, but she felt the rush of air as it passed.

'What? Who was that?' She didn't even try to hide the fear in her voice this time.

A second later, the lights came back on. Alison took a breath. Then she heard the whispering again. A door opened.

She felt sick.

It had to be a student playing a practical joke. That was the only explanation that made sense. Her fear ebbed away and was replaced by anger. It really wasn't funny. Turning off the lights like that could have resulted in someone getting hurt. The carpet along the hallway was threadbare in parts and crumpled in others. Definitely a tripping hazard. Especially in the dark.

At the end of the corridor was a rickety old staircase that would have been used by the servants more than a hundred years ago. What if someone had taken a wrong turn in the dark and tumbled down the stairs?

She walked quickly to the door, which had been left ajar. It led to the roof. Alison smiled. They clearly weren't as clever as they thought. This was the only entrance and exit to the roof.

She'd been up there several times, sneaking a cigarette, as Doyle had banned the students and teachers smoking anywhere near Chidlow House. She climbed the narrow staircase, determined to locate the practical joker.

She pushed open the upper door, struggling as the wind was ferocious up here. She staggered outside as the blustery wind whipped her hair around her face. Scanning the area, she quickly ruled out the possibility of someone hiding on the pitched portion of the roof. It was far too steep and the slate tiles were too slippery.

The flatter section of the roof was smaller and not completely flat, but there weren't many places to hide. She walked towards the edge – holding on to a stone gargoyle to steady herself.

For a moment she was distracted by the view. Lights glittered from farmhouses nestled snug between fields, and small villages sparkled like jewels partially hidden by trees. She took a deep breath of cold night air and felt invigorated. On the roof she felt free of the dread that crept around her when she was inside Chidlow House.

A muffled clunk made her spin around. There was no one there, but the door to the staircase was now closed. Had the wind blown it shut? Or had her practical joker taken the opportunity to scurry away? She sighed and ran a hand through her hair, which had become tangled thanks to the bracing wind.

At least now she knew it was a student, and not the Drowned Lady. There wasn't a ghost singling her out. She took one more look at the spectacular view, then peered down at the dark gardens. The view from the roof was the only thing she liked about Chidlow House.

With a shake of her head, she decided to go back to find Doyle. She'd speak to the students tomorrow and make sure they understood that practical jokes like this weren't acceptable, and she would make it clear she'd be talking to their parents if this behaviour continued.

They weren't a bad lot, really. Spoiled, but that was to be expected with their rich and powerful parents. They'd never had to want for anything in their lives. But they were good at heart. She'd explain it in a way that didn't embarrass them, but made sure they knew not to do anything like it again.

She even managed to smile at her earlier fright and was just turning away from the edge of the roof when her breath caught in her throat.

'What are you doing up here?' she asked as her thumping heart slowly returned to its normal rhythm.

But the only response to her question was a hard and definite shove. Two hands pushed against her chest and Alison King tumbled backwards into the darkness.

CHAPTER ONE

It was Thursday night, and Natasha Layton was getting ready to go out with her friend, Cressida.

Students weren't supposed to leave Chidlow House unsupervised. But they did plenty of things that they weren't supposed to. Sneaking out was Natasha's way of rebelling against her strict parents. She'd managed to creep out unnoticed four times so far.

She was good at rebelling in secret. But not so good at standing up to her orthopaedic surgeon father. And terrible at openly defying her mother, a lecturer in history at Lincoln University.

Natasha slumped into the seat at her desk and pushed the textbooks away with a sigh. It wasn't that she hadn't tried. She had. Multiple times. But whenever she attempted to have a rational conversation with her parents and explain how she felt, she ended up sulking like a five-year-old. She couldn't help it. It happened every time. To be fair, it was her mother who had a special way of frustrating every argument Natasha put forward. Her father did little more than raise his bushy eyebrows and look at her disapprovingly when she brought up the subject of having more freedom.

She was seventeen, after all, and not a child. Though her mother clearly didn't think so. Natasha wasn't allowed to do anything alone. She had to be driven to socially approved events and collected at a respectable time.

Her mother certainly wouldn't have approved of visits to the local pub, which was where Natasha was intending to go tonight with Cressida.

Natasha opened up her compact and studied her face in the mirror. Then she picked up an ink-black liquid eyeliner and added an upward flick to each eye. She grinned at her reflection. That was better. Now she looked like someone going out to have a good time.

Of course, her mother would have been appalled. She liked the no-makeup look. That was a joke. The no-makeup look took her forty minutes to apply every morning.

Natasha scoffed under her breath and rummaged in her makeup bag, taking out a hot-pink lip gloss and applying a thick, shiny layer to her lips. It might have been a little over the top for a visit to the local pub, but Natasha liked to make the most of her opportunities.

Her mother preferred to dress conservatively even on nights out. 'Elegant yet understated' was her catchphrase. If she'd seen what Natasha was wearing tonight, she would have been horrified.

Natasha tugged the green stretchy top a little lower, pleased at how the tight material hugged her curves. Then she caught another glimpse of herself in the mirror and frowned. Her eyebrows were far too bushy – she had her father to thank for those – but she didn't dare pluck them. That was another thing her mother would pitch a fit about.

She frowned. Her eyebrows almost joined together! She swore softly under her breath and grabbed the tweezers. Plucking a few hairs from the middle of her brow line, Natasha swore a little louder. It hurt so much! It made her eyes water.

She glanced at the time on her phone. Cressida was supposed to be here in about five minutes. Did she have everything she needed? Money – which wasn't as easy to come by as you would think. Her mother and father both came from wealthy families but they kept a tight grip on the purse strings. Natasha didn't have as much money as most of the other teenagers on the study week. She'd only managed to gather change here and there – from occasions when her mother had given her cash to go and buy a cup of coffee when they'd been out.

Fortunately, Cressida's parents were far more generous. Cressida had an allowance and was not shy in sharing her wealth. Still, Natasha didn't like to go out without her own money as insurance. She didn't want to get stuck in the middle of nowhere without being able to get a taxi. As her mother constantly told her, it was a dangerous world out there for a young woman.

Natasha rolled her eyes. If her mother had her way, Natasha would never see anything of the real world. Her parents expected her to be either a surgeon like her father or a lecturer like her mother. They'd gone to Oxford – in fact, that was where they'd met – and they took it for granted that Natasha would do the same. Hence the intensive study programme before her second year of chemistry, biology and maths A levels.

She'd really wanted to study English, but her mother hadn't felt that was appropriate.

When Natasha had complained, she'd said, 'Darling, there's nothing stopping you reading books as a hobby, but it's hardly a career, is it?'

Natasha tried to argue her point, but Imogen Layton had pinched the bridge of her nose as though the subject pained her. Whenever Natasha tried to talk about her plans for the future, it brought on one of her mother's headaches.

Another thing that brought on her mother's headaches was the mere mention of boys. If she so much as suggested going to a party where there would be members of the opposite sex, that would almost certainly bring on a nasty migraine and her mother would need to lie in a dark room to recover.

Natasha rolled her eyes again and grabbed her coat. It was a sensible garment – tailored wool – and it hardly went with tonight's outfit, but then her mother would never sanction buying something fashionable. She liked black, grey and beige. Nothing bright or exciting.

She reached for a pair of clip-on earrings, held them up to her earlobe and then put them back down in disgust. They looked horrid and clunky. Seventeen years old and she wasn't even allowed her ears pierced, for goodness' sake. How ridiculous was that?

They were halfway through the study week now, which meant only a few more days of relative freedom. She was determined to make the most of it. Though they weren't supposed to leave Chidlow House, no one was monitoring their movements now, except the programme director, Graham Doyle, who felt it was beneath him to interact with students anyway. The other teachers went home at seven. They were supposed to be supervised overnight by two adults – Doyle and a young teacher called Alison King. But Miss King had fallen from the roof.

Natasha shivered. That had been awful. The police had been called and everyone was talking about it. Some of the students had treated the whole affair as an opportunity to gossip and spread rumours. Had she jumped or had the Drowned Lady of Chidlow House pushed her off the edge? It was childish. Only kids were scared of ghosts.

It was a shame; Natasha had liked Miss King. She had to admit her death meant . . . but no, she wouldn't think about that now. Tonight she was supposed to be having fun.

The ghost rumours were daft, but inevitable really. According to some of the other students, Miss King had told Graham Doyle she'd heard dripping water and whispering in the hallways at night.

Of course, that set all the boys off. They made up more stories about the Drowned Lady, trying to frighten anyone who'd listen. Natasha and Cressida were far too mature to fall for that nonsense, but there was something about this old, creepy house that made her almost believe the stories could be true. She'd never admit that though. Cressida would think she was a baby.

She heard a noise outside the door and assumed it was Cressida. With a wide smile she flung it open, but there was nobody there.

She frowned and looked up and down the hall. Empty. Then she noticed the note. Her name was scrawled in blue biro on the piece of lined A4 paper, which was folded into quarters.

Someone must have shoved it under the door and run off. No doubt one of the immature boys on the course.

Natasha leaned down, snatched it up and skimmed the jerky writing. When she'd finished reading, she scrunched the paper up into a ball and then chucked it into the wastepaper bin under her desk.

'Stuff and nonsense,' she muttered, and then realised she sounded exactly like her mother.

There was a knock at the door. This time it really was Cressida.

Her friend's eyes were bright. Her long, shimmering blonde hair fell almost to her waist. She smiled, showing off dimples. 'Well, are you ready?'

'Of course. Can't wait to get out of here.' Natasha tossed her hair, wishing it shone as prettily as her friend's.

After locking her door, she linked her arm through Cressida's and they set off along the corridor.

When they reached the main staircase, they saw Ethan. He was a police officer's son, and Natasha found him creepy. His eyes were close-set and he was . . . watchful. Every time she glanced his way, he was looking at her. And even when she didn't look at him, she could feel his eyes on her.

'Where are you off to?' he asked.

'None of your business,' Cressida said, and shared a smirk with Natasha.

'If you're going to the pub, I could come,' Ethan said. He constantly tried to tag along. Yesterday he'd sat, uninvited, at their table for lunch. Today he'd lingered behind them in the library, burying his head in a copy of *The History of Chidlow House* when they'd noticed him.

Cressida said he was sad and desperate. That didn't stop her using him though. She'd copied his answers from the algebra assignment, made him run errands and given him little tasks. Cressida was right. He was desperate. Desperate to impress.

'I really don't think so,' Cressida said, and pulled Natasha along.

Before they passed him, Natasha saw Ethan's cheeks flush a deep red. For a split second Natasha felt bad but then pushed the guilt away. She shouldn't care so much about other people. Cressida was always saying it was about time she put herself first. Natasha worried too much about what other people thought of her, especially her mother.

Cressida often told her to stop being such a boring goody-goody.

A secret smile played on Natasha's lips as she hugged her arms to her chest. She turned away so Cressida wouldn't see. She didn't want her friend to suspect anything, and there were some things she couldn't talk about. Especially with Cressida.

Cressida unlocked the French windows, then pushed them open before stepping out on to the patio. Natasha followed, trying not to look at the stone slabs beneath her feet. Miss King had landed on the patio. The area had been cleaned, but Natasha still didn't want to look down.

The moon was huge in the sky, and in the distance, the surface of the lake – home to the Drowned Lady – shimmered through the trees. The grounds were beautiful and looked after by the gardener, Mike. He was a bit odd, but all the girls on the course had a crush on him. He was the dark and brooding type. An interesting man, not a silly little boy like Ethan.

Mike used a stick to get around and rumours swirled about how he'd injured his leg. Ethan said he'd heard the gardener had been wounded when he'd been in the army, but Cressida reckoned he'd been born with a twisted, deformed leg. Ella said she was positive he'd hurt his leg in a car accident. But none of them knew for sure. And he wasn't the type of man you could just ask about that sort of thing. He wasn't friendly. A shouted hello and a wave might get you a nod if you were lucky. He was secretive and silent, and the air of mystery around him only made him more interesting.

Even Cressida was fascinated by him, though she wouldn't admit it. Natasha suspected it was because he'd ignored her when she'd tried to flirt with him. She hadn't liked that at all.

The air was cold, making Natasha's eyes water and her nose run. She sniffed as they headed across the lawns.

'Are we still going to the pub?' she asked, surprised at the route they were taking.

'We're going to meet someone first,' Cressida said with a grin. Her face fell into shadow as a cloud drifted over the moon.

Natasha blinked in surprise. 'Who?'

But Cressida just laughed and said, 'It's a surprise.'

They were heading in the general direction of the gardener's cottage. Natasha's mouth was dry. She felt a flutter in her stomach – a mixture of anticipation and fear. It was one thing to watch Mike roam the grounds during the day. Then he seemed fascinating, like an angry, misunderstood hero from a romance novel. But now, in the dark, as the shadows shifted around them, the gardener was less appealing. What was thrilling and exciting during daylight now felt dangerous and threatening.

Once they reached the cover of the trees to the right of the lawn, Cressida said, 'Did you know Lord Chidlow's staying at home this week?'

'The owner?' Natasha had seen a portrait of him somewhere in the house. She couldn't remember where. Perhaps the dining hall. He looked intimidating, with piercing eyes and a long sharp nose, greying hair and jowly cheeks.

'Yes. And he's super rich. I thought I might try to seek him out tomorrow. Maybe accidentally stumble into his private quarters.' She winked.

Natasha pulled a face. 'But why? He's ancient.'

Cressida shrugged. 'I'm into older men.'

There was older and then there was *older*. Natasha stared after her friend, but Cressida was moving quickly along the tree line towards the lake. Natasha hurried after her. She was pretty sure Cressida was just trying to sound mature and impressive. But with Cressida, you never really knew.

CHAPTER TWO

At seven forty-five on Friday morning, Karen Hart got out of the shower after another sleepless night. She wrapped herself in a towel and ran a hand through her short, dark hair. Despite taking the same route from the bathroom to the bedroom every day for years, today she managed to stub her toe on the bathroom cabinet.

A string of curse words left her lips and she put a fist to her mouth to smother them. She limped down the hallway to the bedroom with gritted teeth.

She had just finished buttoning her blouse when her mobile phone rang. She snatched it up from the nightstand.

'DS Karen Hart.'

There was a pause and then, 'Karen? Is everything all right?'

It was her boss, DI Scott Morgan. She wasn't surprised at the concern in his voice. She knew she sounded angry, and her bad temper wasn't only down to the pain in her foot.

It was now October, and despite efforts by Internal Affairs, DI Freeman still hadn't been charged over his involvement with the Cooks, a local family who'd been trafficking vulnerable people. Every day, Karen tried and failed to put the matter behind her. The idea that Freeman might get away with everything he'd done was sickening, and Karen's fury made it hard to concentrate on anything else.

'I'm fine. I just stubbed my toe coming out of the bathroom. What is it?'

'Two missing kids,' he said, pausing to let his words sink in.

'Again?' Karen's grip tightened on the phone. A previous investigation, when two schoolgirls went missing in Heighington, was still fresh in her mind. It had been the first important case they'd worked on together.

If there was one thing guaranteed to take her mind off her own problems, it was working on a time-sensitive case. She didn't know where she'd be without her work and the rest of her team.

'This one's different. They're seventeen-year-old, female A-level students. They attend Markham but have been taking part in an intensive study week at Chidlow House, in Harmston.'

Karen grabbed her suit jacket and left the bedroom with her phone tucked between her chin and shoulder. 'How long have they been missing?'

'No one's sure. One of the other students saw them leaving at nine p.m. last night, and no one saw them return. Their absence was only noticed when they didn't turn up for breakfast this morning.'

Karen frowned as she made her way downstairs. 'And we're already on the case?'

'Yes, the superintendent called me directly. She wants us to act quickly on this one.'

'I understand,' Karen said. But she didn't understand, not really.

Two teenagers sneaking out at night wasn't unusual. The fact they hadn't returned was worrying, but it wasn't yet eight a.m. Not much time had passed since it was noticed the girls were missing. Karen liked to think her team was conscientious and quick to act in cases like this, but that was pretty fast even for them. What was behind this eager response? Were either of the girls known to be a high-risk target for abduction? Children of diplomats and heirs to foreign thrones were known to attend Markham School for Young Ladies.

Karen shook her head. The school sounded like a relic from a previous century!

'They could have gone to a party, stayed out all night and crashed at a friend's house,' Morgan suggested. 'With any luck they'll turn up soon looking sheepish.'

'But the super wants us to investigate straightaway? Talk to the parents, check local CCTV?'

'Actually, she wants us to get to Chidlow House ASAP. There's a lot of pressure on this case.'

'Why?'

'I'm not sure yet, but I'm sure we'll soon find out.'

Karen marched through the kitchen looking for her handbag and eyeing the coffee machine sadly. She wouldn't have time to get her usual fix before leaving today.

'I take it the parents have been informed and the youngsters haven't just got sick of studying and gone back home?'

'Correct. Both sets of parents are coming to Harmston. They live locally so they might be there before us.'

'All right, I'll meet you there.'

After she hung up, Karen grabbed her bag and car keys and headed for the door, hoping this was a case where she could really make a difference. She needed something to get her teeth into and to take her mind off the failing investigation into DI Freeman's corruption.

She returned her neighbour's wave before getting into her Honda Civic, but didn't pause for a chat. She was growing tired of explaining to Christine that there were no new updates on the corruption investigation and of seeing her own disappointment mirrored on her friend's face.

A few months ago, the team had come across a criminal network paying off members of Lincolnshire Police. Although two traffic officers had been kicked off the force for their role in bungling the investigation into the accident that had killed Karen's husband and daughter, their informant had also named DI Freeman, an officer who Karen had been very close to and trusted, as the man behind the cover-up. He had been taken off active duty but hadn't been punished in any other way. It was bad enough that he wasn't behind bars; the idea of him returning to active duty made Karen furious.

Last month, Karen had made an appointment with the assistant chief constable, Kenneth Fry, to ask that he pay particular attention to the case. But he hadn't seemed particularly responsive. Though his face was a mask of pity as they talked, Karen couldn't help thinking he was putting it on. His sympathy was an act, and not a particularly good one. All he really wanted was to make the right noises, tick the correct boxes and get Karen out of his office.

During the meeting, Karen had calmly stated her case, but the ACC hadn't seemed interested, and when she'd pushed him, asking for actions rather than words, his faux sympathy had slid away, revealing his irritation.

'I can assure you, DS Hart, that procedures are in place and followed to the letter,' Fry had said. 'We can't simply take the word of a criminal informant against one of our officers, who I might add has never made a single misstep in the past. How would you like it if an accusation was levelled at you and we acted before a thorough investigation?'

Karen had only just managed to keep her temper. 'I'm not asking you to act without one. I'm asking you to make sure there *is* one.'

'I realise you have suffered a terrible tragedy, but this is starting to feel like a witch hunt against DI Freeman, which I can't condone.

I know it's extremely difficult for you, but I must ask you to be patient while we conduct the inquiry.'

Patient! It had been months and they seemed to be no further on.

The superintendent had been kind enough to keep Karen updated, but there weren't many updates to be had. As time drew on, she began to feel that DI Freeman was going to get away with his part in covering up the story behind her husband and daughter's deaths, and it made her blood boil.

The rain hammered down as Karen drove into Harmston. The small village sat on the Lincoln Cliff. Though Lincolnshire was well known as a flat county, it certainly had a few steep hills scattered here and there.

Wet brown and yellow leaves carpeted the sides of the road, impairing drainage, and the heavy rain made it hard to see more than a few feet ahead. The windscreen wipers clunked rhythmically from side to side. She was impatient to get there but knew in this weather she had to take it slowly.

Chidlow House was one of two grand houses in Harmston; the other was Harmston Hall. Both houses had been constructed along the cliff line, overlooking the countryside for miles and boasting a view of the Derbyshire Hills on a good day. Though she doubted anyone could have seen more than a few metres in this rain and visibility.

Finally locating the turnoff at the gatehouse for Chidlow House, Karen indicated and then stopped at the police barrier. Tape had been set up and a policeman in a waterproof coat and hat stood miserably beside the stone gatepost.

He shuffled over to the car as she lowered the window.

'DS Karen Hart.'

The officer held up his notepad to make a note and then re-covered it with a waterproof top sheet. 'Doesn't look like there's much chance of it clearing up.' He nodded up at the heavy grey clouds.

'No, forecast says it will be like this all day.'

He nodded again, looking even more despondent.

Karen thought of the evidence. If this was a crime scene, vital information could be washed away, making it much harder for them to do their job.

The police officer hunched his shoulders and returned to his sentry position after lowering the police tape.

Karen drove along the winding lane leading up to the property. A flurry of leaves swirled around the car as she turned the final corner and got a proper view of the house.

It was an impressive sight. Perhaps even more impressive than Harmston Hall. She didn't know too much about Chidlow House, and identifying the owners would be a top priority. Many of these old ancestral homes weren't in private use anymore, but rather used for hotels or conference centres. The upkeep of such huge buildings took its toll on even the richest members of society. Karen imagined the heating bill alone would make her eyes water. The front was imposing. The building was constructed from local stone, and a parapet, decorated with gargoyles, gave the impression of a mostly flat roof, though some green slate was just visible.

Karen understood that Harmston Hall, which was less than a mile away, had once been used as a home for the 'mentally defective'. A chilling term, and a reminder of how a lack of understanding had led to people being incarcerated for years with no hope of ever getting out. As far as she knew, however, Chidlow House had always been privately owned. Times must have been hard if the owners had taken to letting it out for a study week.

She pulled up at the front of the building, parking between a marked police vehicle and DI Morgan's car. Then she took a moment to take in her surroundings. There was a grand portico entrance, with stone steps leading up to it. On the left she could make out a terraced area looking out on to fading flowerbeds and lush green lawns leading to a wooded area. The heavy rain made it difficult to see any further.

Glancing up at the house, she judged it to be three storeys, unless there were more rooms in the attic. In one of the upper-storey windows she saw a flash of movement. Someone was watching.

CHAPTER THREE

Karen lifted the hood of her raincoat and got out of the car. Within seconds, the bottoms of her trousers were soaked.

She made her way to the top of the stone steps and the uniformed officer standing there.

She tugged her ID out of her pocket, holding it up for him. 'DS Karen Hart. Is DI Morgan about?'

This officer had definitely got the better end of the deal. Though he had to stand guard, he was under cover.

'He is, ma'am. I saw him just a moment ago. I think he's still in the entrance hall.' He pointed through the large oak doors.

Karen walked inside, her heels clicking on the marble floor. She lowered her hood, thankful to be out of the rain.

The entrance hall was large with a small, modern reception desk located on the left side. Above the desk was a huge portrait of a haughty, hawkish man with fair hair, probably one of the Chidlows. Stone flooring and wood-panelled walls made the area dark and, in Karen's opinion, a bit gloomy. A huge chandelier dominated the ceiling but hadn't been switched on. In the centre of the hall was a large curved staircase with an ornate banister decorated with carved swirls and flourishes in the wood.

Directly ahead she saw DI Morgan talking to a short, balding man. Dark hair fringed his collar, and he moved in a jerky way – stress, probably.

Karen walked up to join them. Morgan caught her eye and smiled.

'This is DS Hart,' he said, introducing her to the man beside him. 'Graham Doyle is the programme director for the intensive study week that's being held here at Chidlow House. He's the one who reported the two young women missing. Natasha Layton and Cressida Blake.'

Neither name sounded familiar to Karen. They certainly didn't sound like foreign royalty. She gave Graham Doyle a brief smile. 'Please continue. I'll catch up.'

Doyle nodded. 'Yes, as I was saying, I didn't realise they were missing until this morning. Their parents pay handsomely for this study week and I like to make sure they get value for money. Lessons start at eight every morning and breakfast is served at seven. When neither girl showed up for breakfast and they weren't in their rooms, I called the police.'

'And what can you tell us about the two girls?' Morgan asked. 'Do you have any reason to believe they were planning to leave the course early?'

'It's highly likely if you ask me,' Doyle said, looking around shiftily to make sure no one could overhear. 'They were rather excitable young women, and if they sneaked off to get out of extra classes, it wouldn't surprise me. I'm afraid their parents probably didn't know what they were up to.'

'Who was responsible for their welfare while they were staying here?' Karen asked.

'Well . . .' Doyle rubbed his nose nervously. 'That would be me. I'm staying on site. We did have another teacher here too, but an unfortunate incident occurred. She fell from the roof. Died instantly. It was a bit too late to get another guardian at this stage, and I thought I'd be sufficient. Of course I wasn't expecting anyone to run off. It's most upsetting. This is the first time we've run the programme here and, well, it's not exactly good for the course's reputation.'

'No, I can see it wouldn't be very good for your reputation,' Karen said dryly, thinking that he didn't seem particularly worried about the students' safety. 'When did the teacher fall?'

'Tuesday night.'

'What was she doing up there?'

'I really don't know. She shouldn't have been up there.'

'Did she fall or jump?'

Doyle sighed heavily. 'Maybe things got too much for her. I didn't know her well. I think the police spoke to her family.'

They'd need to speak to whoever had been in charge of the investigation. Karen made a mental note to ask Rick to follow up on that.

'When were the students last seen?' Morgan asked.

'Natasha and Cressida were spotted leaving by Ethan, a fellow student.' Doyle treated them to a knowing smile that only served to confuse Karen. 'Obviously I've informed the parents of the missing young ladies, but I'm hoping the other parents won't have to know.'

'Well, our priority, of course, is locating the young women and making sure they're safe.'

'Of course, and I'll cooperate fully. Whatever you want to know. I'm an open book.'

'We'll need to talk to Ethan if he was the last person at Chidlow House to see them,' Morgan said.

'Ethan said he thought they were heading to the local pub, but they didn't want him to tag along. He doesn't know if they were meeting anyone. I'm sure you'll get more out of him, but that's the basic gist of things. They were all dressed up, lots of makeup, that sort of thing.' He paused, then sighed again. 'It really is most unfortunate.'

'We'll need to talk to the owner of the property,' Karen said.

'Oh, I see. We've only just managed to persuade Lord Chidlow to open up his amazing venue to us. I'm not sure he'll want to continue at Christmas now. We had another week of intensive study planned then.'

'Lord Chidlow is the owner,' Morgan clarified for Karen's benefit.

'Yes, that's right. Lord Edward Chidlow. His family have owned the house since the fifteenth century, or at least the land the house is now built on. Of course, it's changed quite considerably over the years.' Doyle gestured around. 'The current house was constructed in 1712. Some of it was pulled down in the 1890s but renovated in the same style as the original.'

'And is Lord Chidlow here?' Karen asked.

'He is. I'd prefer we didn't disturb him, or at least minimally if that's at all possible.'

'We will need to talk to him, Mr Doyle,' Morgan said.

'I fully appreciate that. It's just, well . . . he's a busy man – an important man – and I'd really like this whole mess to disrupt things as little as possible.'

'I'm sure you would, but as we've already said, our priority is locating the girls – and to do that we're going to have to talk to everybody who was here last night,' Karen said, losing patience with Graham Doyle.

She didn't care about the profitability of the programme. Two seventeen-year-olds could be in trouble and they had been missing for ten hours before anyone noticed.

Doyle looked at Karen as though she'd asked him to walk into a lion's den. His face screwed up, and he pressed a hand to his forehead. Why was he so reluctant for them to talk to the owner of the house? Was Edward Chidlow some kind of tyrant?

'Perhaps you could talk to him later, after I . . . I've had time to explain things to him,' Doyle said, stuttering. 'I think he's very busy at the moment.'

Karen narrowed her eyes. 'Actually, I'd prefer we spoke to him right now please, Mr Doyle.'

He was clearly worried about the future of his course, and probably rightly so. Would anyone want to send their teenagers on another study course when two previous attendees had gone missing and a teacher had died? She doubted Chidlow would like the publicity, either.

Doyle's shoulders slumped. 'Very well. We can go and see him now. I think he's in his study. Although don't blame me if he's upset at being disturbed.'

'We won't,' Morgan said curtly.

They followed him along a dark wood-panelled hallway. Karen looked up and noticed the intricate plaster patterns on the ceiling were crumbling in places. In the past this must have been a very grand house indeed. And at first appearances it was still breathtaking. But on closer inspection, the signs of wear and tear and a general lack of upkeep were clear to see. It must cost a fortune to keep the place going.

'I've asked DC Sophie Jones to do a background check on all the adults who've been working at Chidlow House this week,' Morgan said to Karen.

'She find anything?'

'Not yet.'

'She won't,' Doyle said with a sniff. 'I can assure you all staff had criminal record checks before they were employed.'

Karen sent a message to Sophie, asking her to check social media accounts for both young women and start the procedure to request their phone records.

Doyle stopped beside a door which had angels carved into the decorative panels. He rapped on the wood. A muffled voice sounded from within, and Karen assumed the person had said to enter because Doyle took a deep breath and opened the door.

A man she assumed to be Edward Chidlow was sitting behind the desk. The portrait hanging in the entrance hall was a good likeness. Even seated, he looked tall. He had a long narrow nose and close-set eyes, reminding Karen of a bird of prey. His slim build suited his expensive clothes. He probably had his own tailor. His thick white shirt showed no sign of creases.

Karen stood a little straighter and smoothed the crumpled front of her jacket.

Chidlow watched them with an impassive expression. His fair hair, lightly flecked with grey, was brushed back from his long face. His sharp blue eyes fixed on Karen as both she and Morgan approached the desk.

'I'm very sorry to trouble you, Lord Chidlow,' Graham Doyle began, pressing his hands together as though begging forgiveness. 'The police officers insisted they speak to you. I'm afraid it's about the two teenagers who've gone missing.'

Chidlow eased back in his chair and said in a bored tone, 'The course is being held at my property, but I've never met either girl.'

He bowed his head, looking back at the paperwork on his desk, effectively dismissing them.

Morgan moved closer, leaning over the desk and looking down at Chidlow. 'We have a few questions for you, sir.'

Chidlow looked up again, annoyance showing on his face. 'I really don't see how I can help you.'

'I told them it was nothing to do with you but . . .' Doyle trailed off.

'Very well.' Chidlow stood up with a sigh and moved to the French windows, gesturing for them to take a seat beside the small table in front of the floor-to-ceiling bookcase. He remained standing beside the window.

Karen knew the type. Selfish and shallow, Chidlow thought the world revolved around him. From his point of view, the police weren't here to help, but to make his life difficult.

The windows were large, but the heavy velvet drapes and grey sky outside made the room dark and oppressive. A small lamp sat on Chidlow's desk, and there was a fire behind his chair, but it was unlit.

Chidlow tugged absently at one sleeve of his shirt. Karen took a seat beside the small ladder attached to the bookcase. She scanned the books. They were leather-bound and in dark colours – burgundies, navy blues and forest greens – nothing like the brightly coloured paperbacks Karen had at home.

Morgan began the questioning by asking Chidlow about the course. Chidlow looked at Doyle, who was hovering next to the door looking increasingly uneasy.

'To be honest, I have nothing to do with the course. It wasn't even my idea, rather my accountant's suggestion. It's expensive to run a house like this and he thought it would bring in some extra funds. If I'd known the trouble it was going to cause, I'd never have agreed to it.'

'The teacher who died, Alison King—' Morgan began.

Chidlow cut him off. 'An absolute nuisance. Why she had to pick my roof to jump off, I don't know.'

Karen raised an eyebrow. She wanted to remark on his callousness, but he was already being difficult, and if he decided not to cooperate, he could make their investigation very challenging. 'Was it suicide rather than an accident?' she asked, overlooking his cold comment.

'Why are you asking me?' His eyes narrowed and he looked down his hawkish nose at Karen. 'You lot investigated. You'd know more than me.'

'By "you lot" I take it you're referring to Lincolnshire Police?'

'Yes, they were swarming all over the place after the teacher died and now this . . .' He flung up his hands.

'And this is the first time a course for students has been held here?' Morgan asked.

Doyle interrupted. 'Yes, I told you that already.'

Morgan turned to face Doyle. 'Thank you for your help, Mr Doyle. That will be all. We'll talk to Lord Chidlow on his own.'

The little dark-haired man's face flushed scarlet. He hesitated for a moment before spinning on his heel and stalking out of the room.

After the door slammed, Chidlow chuckled. 'You've made an enemy for life there.'

'Perhaps,' Morgan said dryly.

Karen knew Morgan wasn't in the business of trying to make friends during an investigation. He only wanted to get to the truth.

'This is the first time we've had school students here, but there have been a few business courses held here over the past two years. The adults were far less trouble.'

Morgan asked for more details and made a note of the previous courses.

'I hope you don't mind me saying,' Chidlow said, 'but you seem to be taking this very seriously. They are seventeen years old, after all, and they've only been missing overnight.'

'That's true,' Morgan said.

'Do you suspect foul play?'

'We're keeping an open mind at the moment.'

'I thought they'd probably gone off to a party somewhere last night, and they'll turn up nursing hangovers later today.' Chidlow shrugged.

'I hope they do,' Karen said.

Her first impression of Chidlow was that the man was arrogant and used to being surrounded by flatterers and sycophants like

Doyle, but he was right about one thing. This investigation had been fast-tracked for some reason. There was no evidence that the young women had been abducted or were in danger.

'Do you have any background details on the students?' Karen asked.

Chidlow shook his head. 'I'm afraid you'll have to ask Mr Doyle about that. I really don't know. I don't even know the number of students off the top of my head. I simply know that they've commandeered three of the big rooms downstairs – the old drawing room, the dining hall and the main library – leaving me crammed into this little room.' He looked around his study, which in Karen's opinion was actually rather large, with a sneer. 'And they've booked out fifteen of the bedrooms, over two floors. I believe two of the rooms were occupied by staff, so by deduction there are probably thirteen students here.' He raised an eyebrow. 'An unlucky number if you believe that sort of thing.'

'And how much are they charged for the course? Any scholarships?' Karen asked, wondering if all the students were from privileged backgrounds.

'Again, I don't know the details. My accountant can tell you how much I'm getting paid by Doyle's company to host the course here, but I couldn't tell you what he charges.'

He was right. It was a question better suited for Doyle. This wasn't the type of course an average comprehensive student would be attending to swot up for their A levels. This would be expensive, exclusive. Perhaps Chidlow moved in the same social circles as the students' parents.

'Do you know any of the students' parents?' Karen asked.

Chidlow shook his head. 'No, and I have no interest in any of them. I'm afraid my involvement here is purely financial. Needs must. I wish I didn't have to do it. I'd prefer to generate the money needed for the house in some other way, but . . .' Chidlow seemed distracted. He trailed off, looking out of the window.

Karen leaned forward to get a better view. The rain was drumming against the French windows, trickling down the glass, which made it hard to see.

There was a figure walking on the lawn, heading to the terrace. 'Who's that?' she asked.

'Oh, that's just the groundsman, Mike Harrington.'

As he got closer, Karen got a better look at him. She guessed he was about her age. He was wearing a long, dark coat, collar raised. He had a slight limp and leaned on a stick as he walked. Despite the limp, he looked strong and moved with purpose.

'Has he worked here long?'

'A few years. Quiet chap. Keeps to himself, but a good worker. I've had no complaints.' Chidlow sounded bored. His well-groomed appearance was a contrast to the groundsman.

'Does he live locally?'

'He lives on the property, actually. There's a cottage on the other side of the lake over there.'

Karen stood and peered out of the French windows. The rain was so heavy it obscured most of the view. 'There's a lake?'

'Yes,' Chidlow said. 'It's hard to see today but it's not much further than that crop of trees just there.'

She would have to take Chidlow's word on that. She could only just make out the trees.

'Do you live alone here in the house?' Morgan asked.

'I don't see what that has to do with anything.'

Morgan said nothing but watched him expectantly until Chidlow finally answered.

He huffed out a breath. 'Yes.'

'Not married?' Karen asked.

'No, not anymore. I've got a flat in London and spend most of my time there, but I do try to get back to Chidlow House regularly. I wanted to be here during the course to make sure they weren't wrecking the place.' He frowned. 'I suspected it was a bad idea, and I've been proved right. Teenagers are more trouble than they're worth.'

'So you won't be holding the course again?'

'I doubt it. Maybe business conferences but no more kids.'

There was something shifty about Chidlow. He took his time answering their questions, carefully choosing his words. And he was very keen to distance himself from the course and the students.

'Mr Doyle was kind enough to give us a list of students who were attending the study week,' Morgan said. 'If I run through their names, you can tell me if you recognise any of them.'

Chidlow frowned. 'I assure you, Detective, I'm a man of my word. I told you I don't know any of the students, and I didn't meet either of the missing girls. I can't help you.' He turned his back on them as though the matter was ended.

Karen couldn't help thinking that this was a strong reaction for an innocent man. It didn't mean he had anything to do with the disappearances, but she suspected Edward Chidlow was a man with something to hide.

Chidlow sat back down at his desk and tapped his long, tapered fingers on the old-fashioned blotter. 'Are we done?'

Karen was about to tell him that no, they weren't done, and they would have more questions for him in due course, but there was a knock and Graham Doyle poked his head around the door.

He no longer looked angry, but nervous.

'What is it?' Chidlow snapped.

But Doyle was so preoccupied he forgot to be deferential and polite to Chidlow and ignored him. Instead, he looked at Morgan and Karen. 'Detective, the parents are here.'

CHAPTER FOUR

Doyle led them to the library, where the missing girls' parents were waiting. It was larger than Chidlow's study. Three walls were lined with bookcases, containing the same expensive-looking leather-bound books. French windows led out on to a terrace. A log fire in the large grate gave out welcome heat. The bottoms of Karen's trousers were still damp, and she hadn't been able to shake off the chill that seemed to pervade Chidlow House.

There were three narrow sofas in the room as well as a number of armchairs. Despite all the available seating, the three adults in the room remained standing, tense. All three looked up expectantly as Doyle and the police officers entered the room.

'This is Mrs Layton and Mr and Mrs Blake,' Doyle said. He turned, nodding at the parents. 'DI Morgan and DS Hart are the detectives I told you about.'

Mr Blake stepped forward. He had a youthful appearance and tanned skin, dark hair and bright eyes. He was only a couple of inches taller than Karen. He'd loosened his tie and taken off his suit jacket. He'd probably been heading to work when he got the news.

He thrust out his hand and said, 'Ryan Blake. I'm Cressida's father, and this is my wife, Jasmine.' He gestured to the tall woman beside him. She had long, dark hair and an oddly blank expression.

She wore a dark red shift dress and black cardigan, probably cashmere and expensive.

Unlike Ryan, whose face was animated and clearly showed his distress at the situation, his wife's face appeared impassive. Her skin was smooth and unlined, and it occurred to Karen that could be due to cosmetic surgery rather than a true lack of emotion.

'And I'm Imogen Layton.' The other woman who had been standing by the fire strode over to them.

'Yes, Mrs Layton is an historian at the university,' Doyle said, gazing at her with admiration.

Imogen barely spared him a glance. She was tall with chin-length brown hair. A silk scarf in muted colours was tied around her neck. 'Elegant' was the first word that came to Karen's mind as she assessed the woman.

'Can you tell us what's going on?' Imogen asked, looking directly at Morgan. 'All we know is that Mr Doyle here somehow seems to have lost our daughters.'

'I wouldn't put it quite like that, Mrs Layton,' Doyle said with a nervous, spluttering cough. 'They're teenagers. They probably went out last night, forgot the time and couldn't get a taxi back. The weather *has* been awful.'

All three parents glanced at the French windows, which were being lashed with rain – probably imagining their daughters out there alone, unsheltered.

Graham Doyle could be right. In most of these cases the youngsters did turn up unharmed within a few hours. Though Karen had been a police officer too long to rule out other possibilities.

'I can tell you what we know so far,' Morgan said. 'Cressida and Natasha went out together last night at nine p.m. Mr Doyle raised the alarm when they didn't show up for breakfast at seven a.m. this morning.'

'Yes, we got a call,' Imogen said. 'He told us to stay at home, but of course we couldn't.'

'And Natasha's father? Has he been informed?' Morgan asked.

'He's on his way. He was needed in surgery this morning.'

'Would you like us to wait until he gets here?'

'No, you can ask me any questions you have. Then I'd like you to get on with finding our daughters.'

There was a click. Graham Doyle had left the room and shut the door behind him.

'Let's sit down,' Morgan said.

Jasmine was the first to gracefully sit on one of the sofas, and then Ryan, who'd been running his hand repeatedly through his dark hair, sat beside her. Imogen sat opposite them and Morgan and Karen sat in the wing-backed armchairs closest to the fire.

'Were any of you aware that Cressida and Natasha had intended to go out last night?'

'No,' Imogen said. 'Natasha was supposed to be studying. I would not have approved of an outing.'

'No,' Ryan agreed, his voice a little hoarse. 'I don't believe they're supposed to be going out at all while they're here. It's a study week. They're meant to remain on the premises.'

'All right. And Cressida and Natasha were good friends?' Karen asked.

'Yes, they were close,' Jasmine said, speaking for the first time.

'Well, I don't know how close they were,' Ryan said. 'But they were friends, certainly.'

Imogen said nothing but Karen noted the way her facial features tightened, and she filed it away for later. Did she not approve of the friendship between Cressida and Natasha?

'What about boyfriends? Was either girl seeing anyone?' Karen asked.

35

'Not Natasha,' Imogen said without hesitation. 'She knows she's here to study. This is an important year for her, and there's plenty of time for boys later.'

Karen was surprised. Did Imogen really think that her seventeen-year-old daughter had no interest in romance and would be content to dedicate herself solely to academic study? That seemed unlikely from what Karen knew of teenagers. Still, they would talk to the young woman's peers and get a fuller view of Natasha's character.

Morgan directed the next question to the Blakes. 'How about Cressida?'

'Not as far as I know,' Ryan said, running his fingers through his thick thatch of hair again.

Jasmine looked down at her hands, clutched together in her lap. 'She wasn't seeing anyone at the moment.'

'Do they have friends close by?' DI Morgan asked.

'Not very close. Most of Cressida's friends are based in Grantham and Newark,' Jasmine replied.

'Same with Natasha,' Imogen said. 'She doesn't know anyone in Harmston.'

'And they both attend Markham?' Morgan asked.

'Yes, both girls go to Markham School for Young Ladies,' Imogen said. 'It's a private all-girls school near Grantham.'

If they'd returned to the Grantham area, they would have needed a taxi or a lift from a friend, unless they were hitchhiking. The area wasn't well served with public transport. 'We'll check locally, see if anyone has spotted them in the last twenty-four hours. If you could contact their friends . . .'

'Yes, I've made a start on that already,' Imogen said, impatiently tapping her foot.

'We'll talk to the other students on the course. With your permission, we'd like to search Cressida's and Natasha's rooms. We might find something that tells us where they've gone,' Morgan said.

'I really think you should be out there searching for them. That would be a better use of your time. You are planning a search, I take it?' Imogen demanded, then turned to look out of the window.

A search party in the pouring rain was not an inviting prospect. If a crime had been committed, it was likely some of the evidence had been washed away. But they weren't at that stage yet. It was too early.

'Right now, our priority is speaking to friends and family so we can build up a picture of Natasha and Cressida, understand their state of mind.'

'State of mind? They're teenagers. They were probably just trying to escape studying for a few hours, wanted to have some fun. They could be hurt, lying in a ditch somewhere. You should be searching for them,' Ryan said, jabbing a finger in the direction of the window. 'I have to agree with Imogen on that.'

'I understand you're worried, Mr Blake, but first we need to—'

'You need to be out there looking for them,' Ryan said, stabbing his finger at the window again and cutting Morgan off. 'If you don't go out there and start searching, then I will.'

'We will organise a search, but we need to talk to the other students and teachers on the course to make sure we're not missing something obvious first.'

'But this is very out of character. Natasha wouldn't just stay out all night. She knows I would be worried,' Imogen insisted, gripping her hands together.

'We will instigate a search in the next few hours if we haven't found them before then, but on most occasions, missing teenagers do turn up. I know it's a very worrying time,' Karen said.

Imogen pursed her lips together and turned her head towards the fire. Ryan Blake clenched his fists, and then folded his arms over his chest.

'Do we have your permission to search their rooms?' Morgan asked.

'I really don't see why—' Ryan began, but Jasmine put a hand on her husband's knee. 'Of course you have our permission. We're wasting time here arguing about it. Please do everything you need to do to find them.'

Karen nodded. 'We will.'

Morgan was asking a few more background questions when the door to the library creaked open and Graham Doyle appeared, looking very smug.

'Detectives, I'm sorry to interrupt, but your boss is here.'

Their boss? Who did he mean? Superintendent Murray?

This was proceeding much faster than any missing persons case Karen had worked on. Why was the disappearance of these particular students being prioritised? Karen couldn't understand why the superintendent needed to be on site. This was certainly unusual.

'I'm glad to hear it,' Ryan said, standing up at the same time as Morgan and Karen. 'I hope your boss will get the search underway. We're all wasting time sitting around here chatting.'

With a broad and, in Karen's opinion, inappropriate smile, Graham Doyle led them from the library back to the entrance hall.

CHAPTER FIVE

At first Karen didn't recognise the bulky man standing near the front door. He wore a brown raincoat and water dripped from the hem. His short, grey hair was bristly and damp. He was talking to a teenage boy whose hunched shoulders and bowed head made his discomfort clear.

At the sound of their footsteps the man turned around. Karen recognised him. It was the chief constable. Why was he here? What was it about this case that needed the presence of the chief constable?

Karen wondered if she might get a chance to talk to him about the Freeman case. She'd been unable to get a meeting with him; Assistant Chief Constable Fry was the best she'd managed, and he'd been as much help as a chocolate teapot. If she could just get the chief constable on her side, it would make a huge difference. If he pushed the investigation, elevated its importance, they'd have a much better chance of tracking down the individuals involved in the corruption. But then, how could she be sure she could trust him?

Was he here because he was connected to Lord Chidlow in some way? The thought made Karen's stomach clench.

The chief constable smiled, the skin around his eyes crinkling. 'Detectives.' He held out his hand to Morgan first.

'Chief Constable John Grayson,' he said, shaking Morgan's hand.

'DI Morgan, sir. And this is DS Hart,' Morgan said as Karen held out her own hand.

The chief constable shook it heartily and said, 'Good, good. I asked the superintendent to put her two best detectives on this case, so I'm expecting good things.'

He'd asked the superintendent?

Things were slowly sliding into place. The chief constable definitely had a personal interest in this case. Was he going to order them to go easy on Chidlow?

'And this is my son Ethan,' Grayson said, slapping the boy on the shoulder.

The final piece of the puzzle. Now the quick response time made sense. Ethan had been attending the study week, and Grayson was eager to get the situation resolved. Perhaps a little underhanded to use his position, but two kids were missing, the same age as his own son. He'd want the matter cleared up as soon as possible.

She held out her hand. 'Hi, Ethan. You've been studying here this week, have you?'

Ethan, who'd been staring at the floor, managed to raise his gaze to meet Karen's. 'Uh, yeah.'

'Did you know Natasha and Cressida?' Morgan asked.

'Not well. I mean . . . I knew them from this study programme, but we didn't go to the same school or anything like that.'

'You hadn't met them before this week?' Morgan asked.

The boy risked a quick glance at his father and then shook his head.

'Did they tell you where they were going last night?' Karen asked.

Ethan's gaze slid to the floor again. 'No. I was the one who saw them when they left, and I thought they might be going to the local pub. I asked them, but they didn't want to tell me.'

'They didn't invite you to join them?' DI Morgan asked.

Ethan gave a wry smile. 'No. They were popular, you know. They didn't want to be seen hanging around with someone like me. It was different if Cressida wanted me to do something for her.'

Chief Constable Grayson frowned. 'What do you mean, Ethan? You're popular. You're on the rugby team at school. You've got plenty of friends.'

Ethan's cheeks coloured. 'Not like them. They thought a lot of themselves, at least Cressida did. Reckoned I was immature. Said she wouldn't be seen dead with someone her own age.'

'She said that last night?' Karen asked.

'No, a couple of days ago. Last night she didn't say much. Just something like "I don't think so" when I asked if I could tag along.'

'Cressida was seeing older men?' Morgan asked.

Ethan nodded. 'I think so. I don't know names or anything, but Cressida said she didn't waste time with boys.'

'What did you mean when you said it was different if Cressida wanted you to do something for her?' Karen asked.

He shuffled from foot to foot. 'Oh, nothing really. Just if she needed help with a maths problem or something, then she'd pay attention to me.'

Karen looked at John Grayson. His concern for his son was obvious. She'd been wrong. He was here for Ethan, not as a corrupt favour to Lord Chidlow.

She needed to keep her mind on the case but couldn't help wondering when she'd get a chance to speak to the chief constable alone. She couldn't pass up this opportunity. But perhaps it was better to wait until after they'd spoken to Ethan and the other students.

Morgan continued to talk to Ethan using questions that weren't pressing or accusatory, but the kid looked uncomfortable. Every now and again he raised his hand to cover his mouth, shooting a nervous glance at his father. Was he seeking reassurance? Or worrying he might say too much?

'Would you prefer to go somewhere quiet to talk, Ethan?' Karen asked, aware of the PC standing in the doorway and Doyle sitting at the reception desk, holding a phone to his ear but not talking. She was pretty sure he was trying to listen in.

Without waiting for his son's reply, Grayson slapped a hand on Ethan's shoulder again. 'Good idea. Yes, let's do that.'

Karen walked over to the desk where Doyle was sitting pretending to be on the phone. 'Is there somewhere we could talk to the chief constable and Ethan in private?'

Doyle put a hand over the mouthpiece and gave an exaggerated sigh. 'I'm actually in the middle of a phone call, Detective.'

'No, you're not.'

Doyle's jaw dropped, but he kept the headset clamped to the side of his head. 'What do you mean?'

'You're not on the phone to anyone,' Karen said, pointing at the display on the telephone, which showed the date and time and nothing else. She had a similar handset, and if a call was active, the telephone number was displayed on the small screen. The date and time were only visible when a call wasn't connected.

Doyle slowly replaced the handset. 'Well, I *was* on the phone. It's just been disconnected.' He stood up and huffed, 'Follow me.'

He led them along the right of the entrance hall and then into another corridor, very similar to the one on the left that led to Chidlow's study and the library.

He opened the door to a small office. 'This is the room I've been using. You can use it . . . for now.'

He left, closing the door behind him.

Grayson sat on a padded computer chair, and Ethan removed a cream-coloured paperback with a red title from the back pocket of his jeans and put it face down on the floor, before sitting on a stool. There were no other chairs. Karen considered going to look for some but decided they couldn't afford to waste time. She leaned against the large windowsill, and Morgan remained standing. It wasn't the ideal way to question Ethan. He was already nervous, and having Morgan tower over him while asking questions wasn't going to put him at ease.

'Can you tell me in your own words exactly what happened last night when you saw Cressida and Natasha?' Karen asked.

'I was bored. I was hanging around the house, looking for something to do, and I heard them coming downstairs. They were talking and laughing. I didn't hear what they were talking about, but I noticed they were dressed up and wondered where they were going.'

'Can you recall exactly what they were wearing? That could be helpful,' Karen said, getting ready to make a note on her phone.

'Um . . .' Ethan looked up at the ceiling and chewed on his lip for a moment before answering. 'Cressida was wearing blue jeans and a coat. It was black or maybe brown, a dark colour anyway. I think she was wearing a white top underneath.'

'And how did she have her hair?'

'It was, um, I don't really remember.' His forehead creased in concentration. 'I don't think she had it tied up . . .'

'Okay. And Natasha?'

'She wore her hair loose. It's curly and comes to about here.' Ethan pointed at a spot below his shoulders. 'She had on a green fitted top and a black wool coat over the top. Black jeans and black boots with a low heel. She had pink lipstick on, silver earrings and a silver chain. She didn't have a bag with her.'

'That's a fantastic description,' Karen said. 'Very helpful.'

Ethan smiled shyly.

'I couldn't help noticing your description of Natasha was more detailed. Why is that, Ethan?'

Ethan's cheeks flushed. 'I . . . I'm not sure. I suppose I just noticed Natasha more.'

'Do you like Natasha?'

'Yes, she's nice. I mean, she takes the time to talk to me in class, but Cressida is always around and she doesn't like me as much.'

'Would you say you had a crush on Natasha?' Karen asked.

'A crush? That's ridiculous,' Grayson said quickly. He'd remained silent up until now. 'Don't be silly, Ethan,' he snapped at his son.

His reaction was understandable. They were looking into the disappearance of two young women, and having a romantic interest in Natasha would lead to them viewing Ethan as a suspect. Grayson didn't want that for his son.

Ethan looked even more uncomfortable. 'I, uh, not really. I just . . . she's just nice, you know?'

Morgan took over. 'Any ideas as to where they were going?'

'Maybe the pub.'

'The one in Harmston?'

'Yeah. I don't know for sure. I just heard them talking about it.'

'Last night?'

'No, a couple of days ago.'

'And had they gone out like this before?'

Ethan nodded. 'Yeah, a couple of times this week.'

'And students aren't supposed to leave Chidlow House, are they?'

Ethan swallowed and looked at his father before answering. 'No, but, you know, since that teacher fell off the roof, it's only Mr Doyle keeping an eye on us now, so it's easy to sneak out if you want to.'

'Did any of the other students go out last night?'

'I'm not sure,' Ethan said.

'Were you aware of Natasha or Cressida being particularly friendly with anyone else on the course? Are they close to anyone?'

'Not really. I don't think they hang out with anyone else. I mean, I know Cressida and Natasha go to school with another girl who's on the course, but I don't think they're friends.'

'And what's the girl's name?'

'Ella. Ella Seaton.'

Karen made a note. She'd be high up on the list of students they needed to question.

'Is there anything else you want to tell us, Ethan?' Morgan asked. 'Anything you can think of that might be important.'

Ethan shook his head. 'I don't think so.'

When they'd finished questioning Ethan, he asked if he could leave. Morgan gave his permission and the chief constable's son practically ran out of the room.

Odd behaviour? Or just a kid with awkward social skills? Being interviewed by police officers could be a nerve-wracking experience, even for a chief constable's son. His reaction was a bit extreme, but understandable, wasn't it?

Karen was sure Ethan had a crush on Natasha and that could be important to their investigation.

'So, what do you think so far?' Grayson asked, slapping his hands together and looking at Karen and Morgan.

'It's early days, sir,' Morgan said. 'We've spoken to the parents and they're keen for us to start the search.'

Grayson groaned. 'It's not come to that yet, has it?'

'It might be a bit premature,' Karen agreed. 'Especially in this weather.'

Morgan said, 'We're going to talk to the students first, and search Natasha and Cressida's rooms. If, after speaking to the students, we haven't any answers, then we'll start a search of the grounds and go into the local village, the pub and talk to locals.'

45

'Right,' Grayson said, stroking his chin.

'Unless you have any comments or recommendations, sir?' Morgan asked.

'No, no. I have full confidence in you. The superintendent told me you were her best. I'm sure you'll track them down. They're young. Probably went out for the evening and didn't think of the pandemonium that would ensue when they didn't turn up for their cornflakes this morning.' His words were jovial, but his expression was tense.

He stood.

'Right, I'll let you get to work. Keep me updated,' Grayson said.

'I'll find Mr Doyle and get the keys to Natasha and Cressida's rooms,' Morgan said, as Karen hung back.

'Sir, I wanted to have a quick word if that's possible?' Karen asked Grayson when Morgan had left the room.

'Of course. What is it?'

'It's actually nothing to do with this case. It's about the internal investigation into DI Freeman's corruption. You're aware of it, sir.'

'Yes,' the chief constable said slowly, carefully. 'I am aware of it, DS Hart.'

'I've been trying to get an appointment to see you but it's been nigh on impossible.'

'I've been very busy. I believe you spoke to Assistant Chief Constable Fry.'

'I did, sir. But I found it hard to convey how important this investigation is, not just to me personally but to the force. I don't believe the corruption starts and ends with DI Freeman.'

'I'm well aware of your thoughts, DS Hart. I believe you shared all this with the assistant chief constable a few weeks ago.'

'I did, sir, but since then nothing has happened, and quite frankly, I'm losing hope in the system.'

'The system is in place for a reason, DS Hart. The investigation is ongoing. There are two young women missing. If you can't give this case your full attention, then perhaps I should ask the superintendent to assign another officer.'

Karen clenched her teeth and took a deep breath before replying. 'That won't be necessary, sir. I'll give this investigation my whole focus. I just wanted to make sure that you hadn't forgotten about it.'

'Of course I haven't forgotten. I'm hardly likely to forget a corruption investigation,' he said in an annoyed whisper as he buttoned his coat.

After he left the room, Karen took a moment to collect her thoughts. That hadn't gone well but perhaps it was her fault. She hadn't chosen the best time to approach him.

Trying to push all thoughts of corruption aside, she headed out to find Morgan. Chief Constable Grayson was right – Natasha and Cressida deserved her full attention. As much as it pained her to admit it, Freeman and the corruption investigation would have to wait.

CHAPTER SIX

Karen found Morgan talking to Graham Doyle in the entrance hall. Doyle had a set of keys clutched in his hand.

'Mr Doyle has the master set,' Morgan explained as Karen approached. 'He's going to take us up to the rooms.'

'Thank you,' Karen said to Doyle, stepping back for him to lead the way.

Doyle gave a snooty sniff and strode across the entrance hall. They walked along the corridor, passing the drawing room and the closed door to Chidlow's study, to the rear of the house where there was another large, sweeping staircase.

It was even darker there. The wood panelling covered every wall and the floor-length curtains let in very little light from the window in front of the stairs. Portraits of women in old-fashioned clothes were hung along the staircase.

As they began to climb the stairs, Karen asked, 'Was this the set of stairs where Ethan saw Natasha and Cressida leaving last night?'

'Yes, actually, it was,' Doyle replied.

'The teacher who fell from the roof . . .' Karen began.

'A very unfortunate incident.'

'What's your gut reaction? Do you think it was an accidental fall?'

Doyle paused before replying. 'I really couldn't say.'

The wood creaked beneath their feet as they continued in silence.

When they reached the first-floor landing, Doyle turned to Karen. 'She didn't seem depressed to me. There'll be an inquest, I expect. One thing was a little odd, though.'

'What was odd?'

'Well, she didn't like this house very much. Got a fancy into her head it was really haunted. Silly, I know.' He smiled and shrugged, playing with the set of keys, passing them from hand to hand. 'She said she'd heard noises.'

'What kind of noises?'

'I don't know. I think she'd been spooked by the ghost stories.'

'Ghost stories?' Morgan asked.

'Well, they say Chidlow House is haunted by the Drowned Lady, one of Lord Chidlow's ancestors who drowned in the lake. All nonsense, of course, and I didn't really think Alison, Miss King, was the flighty type. She was a good teacher. Obviously something had scared her. I wondered if she'd dreamed the noises. Perhaps she'd been sleepwalking when she fell from the roof.'

'Did she have a history of sleepwalking?'

'I don't know. It's pure speculation on my part.'

'She fell at night and no one saw anything?' Karen asked. She would need to follow this up and get the official incident report.

'Yes. They think it happened at night, but no one saw or heard anything. She wasn't found until the next morning, when the groundsman discovered her body on the patio. Thankfully I was able to stop the students seeing the body.' He turned and pointed to the next set of stairs. 'The boys sleep on the second floor, but Cressida and Natasha's rooms are on this level.'

'How many girls are there on the course?' Morgan asked.

'Six girls, and seven lads,' Doyle said. 'I've been fielding calls this morning. I'm sure all the parents are going to want to take their children home today, so if you want to speak to them, I suggest you do it pretty quick.'

'I'd appreciate it if you would make sure that none of the students leave before we talk to them, please, Mr Doyle,' Morgan said.

'I'm not sure how I can stop the parents taking their own children home.' Doyle sniffed.

'Do your best. Tell them the police have asked the students to remain on the premises until after we've told them they can leave.'

Doyle sighed as though he had the weight of the world upon his shoulders. 'I can't believe this is happening. This course has been one disaster after another.'

He put a key in the lock of the first door they came to. 'This is Natasha's room.'

The room was small with a single bed pushed against the wall. The decor was similar to the rest of the house. The lower half of the wall was covered in wood panels; above it was a section wallpapered with a grey-and-white damask pattern, faded with age.

There was a brass and crystal light fitting in the centre of the ceiling, too big and grand for such a small area. A tall mahogany chest of drawers was set back against one wall, with an oval mirror sitting on top. Karen walked towards the small desk and fragile-looking chair which sat under the large window.

The rain had let up a fraction. Though it was still coming down heavily, visibility was better now, and she got a glimpse of the lake. It was steel grey, a reflection of the sky. The view from Natasha's room was impressive. On another occasion, Karen might have described it as beautiful, but today it looked ominous.

As Doyle prepared to leave them to their search, there was a noise outside that caught Karen's attention. It sounded like whispering.

'What is that?' Karen said, walking towards the door.

'Oh, it's the pipes. Old houses like this one make funny noises sometimes.'

Karen frowned. It didn't sound much like gurgling pipework to her. Was this the odd sound Alison King claimed to have heard?

Before Doyle left, he handed them the master set of keys. 'This one,' he said, pointing to the one labelled *10*, 'is Cressida's room. When you're done, I'll be down in my office.'

They put on gloves, then searched Natasha's room carefully. Karen went through the wardrobe first and found an empty wheeled suitcase at the bottom. She examined the clothes and found only staid, sensible outfits. The type of thing she'd expect a business-woman in her thirties or forties to wear, not a seventeen-year-old student. *Interesting*, she thought, filing the knowledge away. The clothes Natasha had been wearing on Thursday night, according to Ethan's description, hadn't been like the rest of the items in her wardrobe.

Perhaps Natasha wasn't as sensible as her mother believed. There was a collection of lipsticks on one corner of the chest of drawers, next to a large bottle of Ghost perfume and a big red makeup bag. Karen picked up the bag. There was foundation, con-cealer, a shimmer highlighter, two types of mascara, three eyelin-ers, bronzer, blusher and various brushes. All items that suggested Natasha took great care over her appearance. Quite a large collec-tion of makeup to take to a study week.

Morgan searched the chest of drawers.

'Anything?' Karen asked.

'Nothing unusual. Underwear, T-shirts and a few jumpers.'

As he moved to the nightstand, Karen walked over to the desk. It was scattered with study materials and textbooks. An A4 pad sat in the centre of the desk next to a battered copy of *Anne of Green Gables*. Karen smiled as she turned the book over in her hands. She'd read it many times herself over the years. She'd just set it down beside the maths textbook when a movement outside caught her eye.

'It's him again,' she said.

'Who?' Morgan asked, moving to her side.

'The groundsman, Mike Harrington.'

'Well, he is the groundsman. He's supposed to be tending the gardens.'

'In this weather?'

'We'll have a word with him later. He might have seen something.'

There was something about Mike Harrington that didn't seem quite right, but Karen wasn't sure what it was. Was it simply that he was out in the rain? But then a groundsman would have to do his job in all weathers. He walked fast for a man with a limp, his stick stabbing into the ground with each step. A spaniel, bedraggled thanks to the rain, trotted beside him. Surely there would be something he could do inside during weather like this, especially if the grounds turned out to be a crime scene and he was trampling all over it.

He had a strong jawline. He rubbed a hand over his unshaven chin as the wind buffeted against him, opening his unzipped coat. Underneath he wore an olive-green polo shirt and brown cargo trousers. His hair looked black, but it was hard to tell if it would be lighter when dry.

'So, what did you think of Chidlow?' Morgan asked.

'Bit of a snob, though that doesn't mean he had anything to do with the girls disappearing.'

'No,' Morgan said. 'I didn't really warm to him either. What about the parents? Hiding anything?'

'Too early to say.' Karen flicked through a textbook hoping to find something helpful inside, but found nothing. 'Uptight, but you'd expect that as their daughters are missing. Ryan Blake's interesting.'

'Interesting?'

'Wouldn't look me directly in the eye when I spoke to him.'

Morgan nodded as he pulled open another drawer. 'I noticed that too. It concerns me we haven't seen Mr Layton yet.'

'Yes; do you think he really is performing surgery?'

'Stupid to lie about it. We can easily check.'

Karen nodded. It wasn't a pleasant prospect to consider the parents being behind their own child's disappearance. But it was a necessity.

Everyone knew about the danger of abductions and the need to keep your children safe and close to home. But, for some, the danger lurked at home. They couldn't discount any of the parents as suspects if something had happened to the students. Teenagers pushed boundaries. Mix that with a parent with a temper problem and the worst could happen.

'Now we know why we're taking this case at a hundred miles an hour,' Morgan said dryly.

'Yes, the chief constable's son.'

'What did you think of Ethan?'

'He seemed a bit browbeaten to me. I'm sure he had some feelings for Natasha. You don't describe someone like that and notice what they're wearing in such great detail otherwise,' Karen said.

'I'll try talking to him again when his father's not there,' Morgan said. 'That might get him to open up.'

'I'm not sure Grayson would like that. He shut down any talk of Ethan having a crush on Natasha.'

'It's only normal for him to be protective of his son.'

Karen nodded and opened a drawer, wondering how protective she'd have been of Tilly if her daughter had reached her teenage years. Josh would have found it hard when she developed an interest in boys. Karen liked to think she'd have been the one Tilly would have confided in. But she'd never know, thanks to Charlie Cook, and Freeman and his network of corrupt officers.

Karen slammed the drawer shut. 'I've been wanting to talk to the chief constable for ages and suddenly he appears on one of my cases.'

'You wanted to talk to him about Freeman?' Morgan asked.

'Yes, I want to know what the hold-up is. I want to know why everything is taking so long and nobody's pushing for a resolution.'

'Internal investigations do take a long time, Karen,' Morgan said.

She knew Morgan was only being reasonable, but right now his reasonableness annoyed her. Besides, there was taking time and making progress and there was coming to a dead standstill, which is what had really happened.

'Well, it doesn't hurt to keep an eye on things and encourage the inquiry to focus on the facts,' she said, flipping through another textbook.

'No, of course not. I don't mean . . .' Morgan broke off.

He was kneeling next to the wastepaper bin, going through the contents.

'What is it?' Karen asked, crouching beside him.

Morgan flattened out a piece of screwed-up paper. On it were two handwritten words.

Somebody knows.

'Somebody knows what?' Karen said. 'Do you think Natasha wrote that? Here, let's compare it to the handwriting in her study notes.'

Morgan placed the sheet of paper on the desk. 'Looks similar in style. Was it the start of a note to someone? Or the discarded beginnings of an essay?'

'Maybe she was planning to send a note to someone and thought better of it.'

They searched every inch of Natasha's room, but found nothing to indicate where she'd gone last night: no messages, no secret diary hidden under the bed.

Then they made their way to Cressida's room. It was decorated in a very similar style to Natasha's, although much messier. Clothes were scattered on the floor, and scrunched-up pieces of paper were left on the desk. They were all study notes – nothing helpful.

They took their time going through the room methodically, but finally Morgan shook his head. 'No luck with the rooms. That note worries me. I'll ask Rick to speak to the staff at the pub in the village but I think we're going to have to start the search, don't you?'

Karen nodded slowly, her gaze magnetically drawn to the window. The view of the lake was almost obscured by trees. 'Yes. I don't know what we're going to find in this weather, but there's a chance one of the girls could be hurt – injured somewhere.'

'Possibly, if it was just one of them, but two makes it unlikely. The other would have gone for help, wouldn't they? But I think we should get a search underway. We need to make the most of the daylight hours.' He checked his watch. 'Right. I'll get on to Sophie, ask her if she's got anything from the local hospitals or accident reports, and I'll ask Rick to follow up on the teacher who fell from the roof. What was her name? Alison?'

Karen checked the notes app on her phone. 'Yes, Alison King.'

'Probably nothing but it's a bit of a coincidence it happened the same week, so I'll get him to talk to the investigating officer.'

'Good idea.'

'If you can track down the other students and arrange somewhere for us to interview them, I'll get the search party organised.'

Karen nodded. 'Will do. Do you think we should get family liaison officers assigned for the Blakes and the Laytons?'

'Yes, I do. Let's get that sorted first.'

Karen pulled out her mobile phone and dialled as she looked out of the window. As she waited for the call to be picked up, she stared down at the patio below. As the rain hit the stones, it rebounded with force. Puddles pooled on the slabs. From this distance, the lawn looked lush and green, but the ground would be saturated and soggy. She hoped the rain would let up soon.

CHAPTER SEVEN

When they made it back to the entrance hall, they were met by a buzz of activity. The hall was filled with parents. The police constable who had been standing on the door was desperately trying to keep them contained in one area as they demanded to know where their children were.

Graham Doyle sat at the reception desk, his head in his hands.

He looked up as Morgan and Karen stopped beside the desk. 'Detectives, please tell me you're going to allow the students to go home with their parents now.'

'I'm afraid not,' Morgan said.

This response was greeted by angry exclamations from some of the parents who'd gathered to form a ring around the desk, and a groan from Doyle.

'We need to speak to every student before they go home,' Morgan continued, raising his voice so all the parents in the hall would hear him. His voice was calm but carried well, and eventually everyone fell silent to listen to him. 'I know this is very inconvenient and you're all worried for your children's safety, but I promise we'll get through the questioning as quickly as possible and you should be able to take your children home later today.' He turned to Doyle and added, in a quieter voice, 'We'd like to speak to Ella Seaton first.'

Doyle frowned. 'Well, I suppose you could, but it would be more helpful if you chose one of the other students to kick things off. You see, Ella's parents are away in Africa. They're not going to be able to pick her up today, so she'll be here overnight anyway. Perhaps Stuart Blythe would be a better choice. He's quite anxious to return home. His parents are Lord and Lady Blythe—'

Morgan cut him off. 'No, we need to speak to Ella Seaton first because she knew both the girls. Unless Stuart Blythe is close to them?'

Doyle thought for a moment. 'No, I don't think he is.'

'Then we need to speak to Ella first, please.'

Doyle's shoulders slumped as he sighed in defeat. 'Very well. I'll get her. The students have their meals in the dining room. It's slightly smaller than the dining hall but should be a sufficient size to keep everyone together. Shall I ask the students and their parents to wait there until you're ready to question them? The other teachers are already there.'

'Yes, that's fine.'

Doyle got to his feet, grumbling, 'I don't know what I'll do at lunchtime. There's certainly not enough sandwiches to go around.'

'I'm sure they can sort themselves out,' Morgan said. 'The parents don't have to stay. There's nothing stopping them going out for lunch.'

Chidlow appeared at the back of the hall and barked at Doyle to keep the noise down. His face was red, and he waved his fist as he spoke.

'V . . . very sorry, Lord Chidlow,' Doyle stammered, trying to smooth his thinning hair. 'I really couldn't have anticipated this. All the parents have shown up to take their children home and—'

'I really don't care, Doyle,' Chidlow growled. 'I didn't sign up for this. The whole thing's an inconvenience I could do without.'

Chidlow caught sight of Karen watching him. He scowled and then retreated back along the corridor towards his study. A few seconds later, the door slammed.

Two young women were missing but Chidlow only seemed to care about the inconvenience and the disruption to his everyday life.

They settled in Doyle's office after grabbing two extra chairs from the room next door, and waited for the programme director to bring Ella Seaton to them.

'I'm anticipating some problems with these interviews,' Morgan said as he quickly checked his phone for messages.

'You think the students will be difficult?'

'No, it's the parents I'm worried about. Money means power, and I suspect most of the parents out there are used to getting their own way. They didn't like being told they can't take their children home.'

'Well, there's no way around it,' Karen said. 'We need to talk to them. We can't just let them leave – they're not all local. We'd be driving around the country for interviews if we let them go home now. There's only eleven of them. It won't take us too long.'

Morgan nodded. 'We've spoken to Ethan, so that just leaves ten.'

'Let's hope we get something out of Ella Seaton. We might not even need to speak to the others,' Karen said.

There was a knock on the door. Doyle entered, with a shy-looking girl trailing behind him. The girl had a mass of frizzy, mousey hair that shot out from her scalp in all directions. It must have been quite difficult to manage but the haircut she had certainly didn't help. If anything, it made her hair appear even bushier.

Self-consciously, Ella tried to smooth her hair. As she shuffled towards a chair, she kept her head bowed. She wore baggy jeans and an oversized cream jumper. The cuffs of the jumper reached her fingertips.

Karen gave her a reassuring smile as she sat down. 'We just want a quick chat. There's nothing to worry about. You're not in any trouble.'

The girl raised her head and gave Karen a quick smile in return. Her skin was pale, and her eyebrows and eyelashes were so sparse they gave her face a bare, unfinished appearance.

Ella sat meekly in the chair, waiting for the first question as Doyle picked up the master set of keys from the desk, nodded and then left the room.

'We're told you know Cressida and Natasha,' Morgan began, his tone warm and friendly.

Ella clasped her hands together, resting them on her lap, and nodded. 'Yes, that's right. We go to the same school, Markham in Grantham.'

'Do you get on well?' Karen asked.

Ella bit down on her lower lip. 'Well, I wouldn't say we're great friends or anything, but we aren't enemies either.'

Enemies? That was a funny choice of word. 'How long have you known them?' Karen asked.

'Well, I've known Cressida since we were quite small, maybe six or so. We went to the same ballet class in Grantham. I didn't meet Natasha until we started secondary school, so I've known her since I was eleven. But like I say, we're not particularly close.'

'Different circles?' Karen asked.

A frown puckered Ella's pale face. 'What do you mean, "different circles"?'

'You move in different social circles. You've got different groups of friends.'

'Oh, I see. Yes, I suppose so. Well, they've got friends, tons of them. I'm not exactly Miss Popular at school. I've got my parents to thank for that.'

'Your parents? Why?'

'Because they have decided not to spoil me.' She rolled her eyes. 'I'm not allowed to buy my own clothes, no jewellery. I can't even have my ears pierced until I'm eighteen, and they won't let me have a mobile phone. So you can see why I don't fit in. Girls like Natasha and Cressida get everything they want from their parents.'

'I can see how that might be difficult. Do you know where they were going last night? They left around nine p.m., we think.'

Ella shook her head. 'I'm sorry, I don't know. They didn't really confide in me about things like that.'

'Do you know if either of them had a boyfriend?'

Ella tugged at the sleeve of her jumper, pulling a strand of wool free at the hem. 'I'm not sure exactly. I think Cressida did. I mean, she was always talking about different men she was seeing, but she didn't tell me exactly. I just overheard her conversations with Natasha.'

'And were the men her own age?'

'No, I don't think so. In fact, she was saying only yesterday that she preferred older men. She even said Edward Chidlow was her type.' Ella raised her pale eyebrows in emphasis.

Karen moved smoothly on to the next question, trying not to react, but mentally filed the information away. Edward Chidlow, Cressida's type? He was a great deal older than her – twenty-five years, minimum.

'And what about Natasha?' Karen asked.

'I don't think she was seeing anyone. She didn't really talk about it like Cressida did. She was a bit more private I suppose.'

They continued to question Ella about the staff and the other students and their relationships with Cressida and Natasha.

When Ella was more relaxed, Karen returned to the subject of Edward Chidlow. 'Did Cressida spend much time with Edward Chidlow?'

Ella's jaw dropped. 'No, sorry. I didn't mean to imply they were together or anything. She just happened to mention him. I don't think she was serious. She just likes to shock people, you know, to sound impressive.'

Morgan nodded.

'I didn't mean to get anyone in trouble,' Ella said, her gaze flicking between Morgan and Karen.

'You haven't, Ella, don't worry,' Karen said. 'We just want to know anything about Natasha or Cressida that could be important. It doesn't matter if you get it wrong or it turns out not to be relevant to their disappearance. Sometimes minor things can be crucial.'

'I do want to help. I know we weren't the best of friends or anything, but I don't like to think anything bad has happened to them.'

'We hope they turn up safe and sound soon. But just in case they don't, we need to ask a few more questions,' Morgan said.

He continued to question Ella, and Karen took the opportunity to study the young woman.

Ella's shoulders were hunched and her spine curved, as though she wanted to curl into a ball and disappear. Although it was obvious from her posture that she was painfully shy, she answered all their questions with a clear and sharp voice, projecting a confidence that contradicted her body language. Life at private school had taught her that, Karen thought.

When Morgan had asked his last question, Karen changed tack. 'Ella, could you tell me what you know about Ethan Grayson and Natasha.'

'Ethan and Natasha?' Ella's eyes widened. 'I don't think there was anything going on between them if that's what you mean. Not that I noticed anyway. We only met Ethan this week.'

'When was the last time you saw Natasha or Cressida?'

Ella tapped a finger against her chin. 'I saw them at dinner and then we were in the library for a while. The fire had been lit, thank goodness, because it's so cold at night. The central heating is terrible. I was reading and they were chatting with the other students. And then I went up to bed about eight. I got a bit bored with them all really. I prefer my own space.' She shrugged. 'I didn't see them again after that. I didn't know anything had happened until they didn't turn up for breakfast and Mr Doyle started to panic.'

'What do you know about the teacher who fell from the roof?'

'Oh, that was horrible,' Ella said. 'Miss King was really nice. She did modern languages. I'm doing French A level, so I spent quite a lot of time with her this week. She didn't like the house much. Said it gave her the creeps.'

'Why'd she say that?'

'I think the stories of the Drowned Lady got to her. She heard trickling water and the pipes banging at night, and she wasn't really used to an old draughty house like this. None of us are. I can't say I'm very keen myself.'

Karen had to agree. The place was freezing and must be even colder at night.

'I suppose we're used to modern heating systems these days.' She smiled at Ella. 'It is very cold.'

'Yes, and would you believe this place doesn't even have en-suites. Not quite what we're used to at Markham. If I need to use the bathroom at night, I have to put on my coat and run there and back.' Ella flushed as she caught Morgan's eye. 'Sorry, not very ladylike talk for a girl from Markham. I'm always getting told off for that.'

Morgan laughed. 'It sounds like a very sensible strategy if you ask me.'

'You've been really helpful, Ella,' Karen said. 'Is there anything else you'd like to tell us?'

Ella thought for a moment. 'I suppose you might be interested in any men who'd taken an interest in Cressida.'

Karen leaned forward. 'Yes, we would.'

'Well, I'm not saying anything was going on exactly, but Cressida was boasting to some of the boys. She said the gardener had made a move on her, but she'd had to let him down gently because he was only a gardener and really not her type.'

'Gardener?' Karen asked.

'Yes. He lurks around the place looking miserable. He's got a limp and walks with a stick. Nice dog, though.'

The groundsman, Mike Harrington, jumped several places on Karen's mental list of suspicious characters.

Morgan asked, 'When did this happen?'

'Um, I don't know when he made his move, but she was talking about it two nights ago. To be honest, knowing Cressida, she could have made the whole thing up. He doesn't really seem the type to bother with someone like her. He's quite handsome in an odd, brooding way. Reminds me of Heathcliff in *Wuthering Heights*. We're studying that for A-level English.'

Karen smiled. 'We'll have a word with him. Ella, you've been a great help.'

Morgan was opening the door for Ella to leave when they heard a commotion outside. Morgan and Karen both left the office, heading towards the shouting as Ella scurried off towards the dining room.

'What are you doing to find my daughter?' A tall man with broad shoulders and a protruding stomach stood in the entrance hall, towering over Graham Doyle.

He had large bushy eyebrows and a look of fury on his face as he prodded Doyle's chest.

Doyle spotted Morgan and Karen. 'Detectives, this is Todd Layton, Natasha's father.'

But the man didn't turn. He didn't even acknowledge them. 'I hope you have good insurance, Mr Doyle, because you're going to need it.'

'Of course I have insurance, and I understand that you're quite upset, but really I've done everything I can—'

'Mr Layton, I'm DI Morgan. This is my colleague DS Hart. We're looking for your daughter.'

'You are? Then what are you doing standing in front of me? You're not going to find her here,' Layton said in a low rumbling voice.

Morgan ignored the sarcasm. 'We've been talking to other students on the course. There will be a search of the land around Chidlow House this afternoon. We're still hopeful that Cressida and Natasha went out last night of their own accord and will return safely.'

Todd Layton's anger ebbed away, and he raked a hand through his auburn hair. His bushy eyebrows knitted together. 'I don't think so. Not Natasha. She's so quiet and well behaved. This just isn't like her. Something must have happened.'

'We're going to do our best to find her,' Karen said.

'Maybe I was wrong,' Layton said, narrowing his eyes and looking past Karen. 'I think you're probably looking in the right place after all.'

'What do you mean?'

Layton pointed at the large oil painting of Edward Chidlow that hung behind the reception desk. 'You've heard about Chidlow's reputation, haven't you?'

'His reputation?' Karen looked at the painting, which emphasised Chidlow's close-set eyes and hawkish nose. There was something sinister about this old house, but the uneasy feeling it gave Karen had more to do with its owner than its ghost.

CHAPTER EIGHT

DC Rick Cooper made his way along the corridor on the third floor of Nettleham headquarters. He'd just been speaking to DI Harry Bolt, the officer in charge of the Alison King investigation. Karen had asked him to find out what he could about the details surrounding her death, but so far Harry hadn't unearthed anything suspicious.

Twenty-seven-year-old Alison King had been in a positive frame of mind according to her family and friends, with no history of mental illness. The investigating team had found a few cigarette ends on the roof, and it looked like Alison may have sneaked up there to smoke and lost her footing in the dark, falling over the small parapet.

That was only their working theory, though. Rick didn't have much concrete information to report back to Karen.

He jogged down the stairs. A trip up to the third floor was about all the excitement he got these days. Not exactly a thrill a minute, but it was nice to get out of the open-plan main office for a short time. Sitting at his desk doing paperwork made his mind drift to things he didn't necessarily want to focus on.

A few months back, he'd taken some time off work for a trip to Mablethorpe with his mum. She and his dad had taken Rick there with his sister, Lauren, when they were tots, and he had many fond memories of the place.

Despite her dementia, she'd been particularly lucid in the weeks leading up to the holiday, so Rick had high hopes they would have a smashing time. But it hadn't quite worked out the way he'd planned. In fact, his mother had been very disturbed at the change in her routine. She hadn't understood where she was or who she was with, and on the second day of the holiday, she'd woken up bewildered and hadn't even recognised Rick.

She'd forgotten people before, of course. But never him. On a few occasions over the past year, she'd failed to recognise Lauren and had accused her of being an interloper or a fraud. So Rick had known it was coming. He had seen how it affected his sister, how it hurt her, but he'd never been on the receiving end. And though he'd been expecting it, knowing that eventually the day would come when his mother looked at his face and saw a stranger, he hadn't expected the pain to be so intense. He thought he'd been prepared. So why, even now, did it feel like somebody had punched a hole in his stomach and clamped his guts in a vice when he remembered the blank look on his mum's face?

All the hopes Rick had held for the holiday evaporated on the second day. He hadn't wanted to continue the holiday after that. His first reaction was to pack up the car and take his mum straight home, but Priya, his mum's carer, had been there, and she'd persuaded Rick to stick it out for a little longer.

The following day, his mother had seemed more settled and she hadn't blanked on him again. She knew who he was, even though she thought he was still a kid. She'd got times and years mixed up a lot recently.

They did the things he'd planned – visited the arcades, had fish and chips, walked along the beach, stopped for a cuppa at the same place they always used to stop for tea and toasted teacakes. But it felt like he was trying too hard, forcing it. His mother wasn't laughing, enjoying the trip down memory lane as he'd hoped. Instead she wore a confused smile all the time, as though she didn't know quite what was going on but wanted to make Rick happy, so she kept a smile on her face.

Since they'd got back from the holiday, things had only got worse. The doctor had changed his mum's medication, which hadn't helped. There was always a bedding-in period as she got used to the new drugs, but Rick couldn't help thinking that maybe this was it now. There wouldn't be many more times when they could share a memory or a laugh. Soon those memories would be Rick's alone.

Before heading back to the office, Rick nipped to the canteen and bought himself a ham and cheese sandwich. He sat at a table near the window. The rain was still coming down steadily and the wind had picked up now, moving the branches of the trees opposite the car park.

Patches of floodwater dotted the fields. There were flood warnings in force all over Lincolnshire and had been for the past two weeks. He hoped the two missing students hadn't been caught up in the bad weather. In Derbyshire, a woman had been swept away by the floodwaters, but in Lincolnshire, thankfully, the damage had been to property and industry rather than a threat to life.

There had been no reports of young women matching Natasha's or Cressida's description at any of the local hospitals.

When his phone vibrated in his pocket, he hastily swallowed a mouthful of his sandwich and reached in his pocket to retrieve it. It was Karen.

'Hello, Sarge.'

'Rick, what did you find out about Alison King?'

'Not a great deal I'm afraid. Harry reckons she went up to the roof for a cigarette and fell. No indication she was depressed or wanted to end her own life.'

'Right. It's probably got nothing to do with the students' disappearance, but I thought it was worth checking out.'

'Absolutely. Any news your end?' Rick asked.

'Nothing much, but I would like you to look into Graham Doyle's company. I'd also like you to speak to all the teachers who were working here this week, and I'm particularly interested in Edward Chidlow's background.'

'Chidlow's a person of interest, is he?'

'Possibly,' Karen said. 'I'm not sure yet, but we need to look at him and anyone who's been in contact with these students this week. Chidlow's interesting because, according to Todd Layton – Natasha's father – Chidlow has quite the reputation.'

'What sort of reputation?'

'Layton said, according to the local rumour mill, Chidlow likes younger women.'

'How much younger?'

'That's what I need you to look into, Rick.'

'All right, Sarge. I'll see what I can find out.'

After hanging up, Rick polished off his sandwich in two final bites, and took one last look out of the window. Yes, England was a green and pleasant land thanks to all the rain they had, but it could be really depressing. He could do with seeing the sun break through the clouds for a moment or two.

He stood, and with a sigh he threw the sandwich wrapper in the bin before heading back to the office. The background work was important, but sometimes he found it difficult to connect to a case when he hadn't actually met any of the suspects. But he had to admit it was easier to do the background searches here, with access to all the databases.

Maybe later he'd go to Chidlow House and check in with Karen in person. But first he needed to do some digging into Edward Chidlow's character.

While DI Morgan took a call from Superintendent Murray, Karen stood in Doyle's office, looking out at the lawns and the woods in the distance. The heavy rain had reduced to a fine drizzle, giving the grounds a misty, eerie feel.

The search was underway. Grey figures fanned out across the Chidlow property. They'd started close to the house but were now slowly moving further afield.

Lord Chidlow had not been happy when Karen informed him that they'd need to search the house too.

He'd come close to throwing a tantrum, declaring he didn't want police officers clomping around in his home. 'The missing students are hardly likely to still be here, are they?'

'We don't know, sir. That's why we need to look into all the rooms,' Karen had said.

He'd flung up his hands. 'Fine. You can do the search but I'm not having anyone going through my personal possessions. Stay out of my study.'

His unhelpful reaction was irritating, but he was well within his rights to refuse them access. They could get a warrant but that would take time. It made sense to humour him, for now. Karen agreed it was unlikely the girls were still in the house, but they might find something that indicated where they'd gone or who had taken them.

When Morgan finished his call with the superintendent and put his mobile back in his pocket, Karen said, 'Are you ready for the next student?'

DI Morgan nodded. 'Yes, I think we should probably talk to Stuart Blythe first. Doyle said his parents are making quite a fuss about getting him home.'

Karen stood up. 'I'll go and get him.'

'Thanks,' DI Morgan said. 'I think we'll be able to cover more ground if I question the students alone and you start looking around the house.'

'You don't think they could still be here, do you? It is a big house.'

Morgan shook his head. 'I doubt it. They could be trapped somewhere, but surely we'd have heard them calling for help. I think it's more likely we'll find out something from one of the students, but we still need to do the search.'

'No problem. I'll get Stuart and then make a start.'

She left Doyle's office and headed to the library. The dining room, where Doyle had wanted to keep the parents and students, had proved too uncomfortable. After a multitude of complaints about the hard chairs and canteen-like long table, he'd moved them to the large library.

Karen stopped by the door. Though it was a big room, it seemed crowded with so many people inside. Everyone was talking at once and no one seemed to notice her standing there, which gave her time to watch and observe.

Every student was sitting with at least one parent and looking at their mobiles, except Ella Seaton and Ethan Grayson.

The chief constable had gone back to work, leaving his son alone. Karen wondered where Ethan's mother was. She didn't know much about the chief constable's personal life. Why would she?

Ethan sat on a high-backed chair and looked forlorn and isolated. Not that the other families were chatting happily. The tones of the voices in the room were angry and irritable.

When Karen had commented on the obnoxious behaviour of some of the parents, who'd demanded to be seen first so they could get back to their important lives, Morgan had said it was only to be expected. They were rich and used to getting their own way. He believed they were only thinking of themselves and not the two missing students, but Karen wasn't sure that was true. She thought they were concerned about Natasha and Cressida. They were disturbed by the girls' disappearance and they were scared.

They knew it could just as easily have been their child. Their pushy behaviour and rudeness stemmed from their fear.

Natasha's and Cressida's parents had gone home. They'd be kept up to date by the family liaison officers but would be spared the stress of the investigation and the search.

Karen started to approach Stuart Blythe and his parents when she noticed Ella was watching someone intently. Sat in the corner of the room alone, her wide pale eyes were focused on Ethan. Was there a romantic involvement there, at least on Ella's part?

But the way Ella was watching Ethan didn't make Karen think she had a crush. It was more like Ella was looking at a specimen under a microscope. She wasn't gazing adoringly at him. She was observing. The thought gave Karen a chill, but she wasn't sure why.

She forced her attention away from Ella and moved towards Stuart, who was sitting in the opposite corner of the room with his parents. As she approached him, she passed Ethan and took a moment to pause by his chair.

'Are you okay?' she asked.

Ethan jerked his chin up and glared at her. 'Of course.'

'You look a bit upset. Is there anything else you wanted to talk about?'

Now that Karen had walked into the centre of the library, the parents and other students noticed her. A hush fell over the room and most people turned to look. One lad sitting a few feet away straightened in his chair and pulled nervously at his collar.

Colour rose in Ethan's cheeks. 'I've already told you everything,' he said in a loud voice. 'There's nothing else. Why don't you leave me alone?' He thrust up from the chair and stormed out of the library.

Karen watched him calmly. Was that a show for his fellow students or did the police presence here make him uneasy? If he was nervous, the question was: why? Was he scared he'd be caught out or was he simply upset about Natasha and Cressida's disappearance?

She headed over to Stuart. 'We'd like to talk to you next, Stuart, if that's okay?' She smiled at Lord and Lady Blythe and was met with stony expressions.

'About time,' Stuart's father grumbled. 'We really need to get back before rush hour.'

Karen didn't respond but looked expectantly at Stuart, who got to his feet.

His mother grabbed his hand. 'Would you like us to come in with you, darling?'

'No, thank you, Mother. I'll be fine on my own.' Stuart gave a stiff nod, which seemed an unusually formal way to respond to a parent.

'Don't worry, darling. We're here if you need anything.' She patted his hand.

He followed Karen out of the library, and as soon as they were through the door and into the corridor, he turned to her. 'I'm so glad you picked me next, Detective.'

Karen nodded as she led him to Doyle's office. 'Yes, I know. Your parents are very eager to get you home.'

'No, that's not what I meant at all. I'm glad you picked me because I've got something to tell you about Cressida and Natasha.'

CHAPTER NINE

Karen slowed and turned to look at Stuart Blythe. In the dim light, the shadows under his eyes and cheekbones made him look gaunt, older. 'What do you have to tell us, Stuart?'

Stuart looked over his shoulder, agitated. 'I'd prefer to wait until we're inside the office to talk if you don't mind. I don't want to be overheard.'

Karen was intrigued. 'All right. No problem.'

She ushered him along to Doyle's office, then shut the door behind them.

Morgan looked up, surprised that Karen was staying for the interview and not going ahead and starting to search the house as they'd previously discussed. But the search could wait for now. Karen wanted to know what Stuart could tell them.

She pulled out a chair for him in front of the desk and then sat down beside him. Morgan remained sitting behind the desk.

'Stuart has some information for us,' she said.

'I see,' Morgan said. 'And what's that, Stuart?'

Stuart licked his lips and looked directly at Morgan. His freckled face flushed.

'They were taking drugs,' he said.

Both Karen and Morgan paused while they digested this information. There had been no indication that either girl had been taking drugs, especially not Natasha. Her parents seemed very strict and kept an eye on her.

'What sort of drugs?' Karen asked.

'I saw them smoking weed just this week,' he said in a disapproving tone.

'Was it only weed or something harder?' Morgan asked.

'I don't know. I only saw them smoking weed.'

'Do you know who they got it from? Was it another student on the course?' Karen asked.

Stuart folded his arms across his chest. 'No; I'm not sure. They thought a lot of themselves though. They brought it down to the library and got some of the other students to go outside with them to smoke it. They thought it was funny, doing it under Doyle's nose.'

'Who were the other students with them?' Karen asked.

'I'd rather not say,' Stuart said. 'I mean, I'm only telling you this because it could be important, but I don't want to get anyone else into trouble.'

'This is a serious situation, Stuart. We need to know who the other students were, so we can speak to them and find out if they know where Cressida and Natasha got the weed.'

Stuart thought about that for a minute.

Neither Karen nor Morgan pushed. They needed him to feel like he was in control – that he was volunteering information. If they pressed too hard, he might clam up. Perhaps Natasha and Cressida had been selling the weed to others. Rich students were ideal customers. If they'd been supplying other drugs, perhaps they'd got mixed up in something. Maybe they'd crossed a dealer who wasn't keen on two posh girls encroaching on his turf.

But if they were just smoking some weed, it could be a false lead. It wasn't unusual for teenagers to experiment. Still, they couldn't ignore it.

Finally, Stuart spoke again. 'I think it was Robert Carthey and Ethan Grayson.'

Morgan raised an eyebrow. 'Ethan Grayson. The chief constable's son?'

Well, that certainly complicated things.

Stuart nodded. 'Yes, that's right. You won't tell them I said anything, will you? I don't approve of it, but I don't want them to think I'm a snitch.'

'We'll do our best to keep your name out of it, Stuart,' Karen said. 'We're going to search Chidlow House. Do I have your permission to search your room?'

Stuart gave the same oddly formal, stiff nod he'd given to his mother earlier. 'Of course, I have nothing to hide.'

'Thank you. I'll leave you with DI Morgan now.'

After Karen left the room she went in search of Doyle and the master keys. She had Stuart and Ella's permission to search their rooms, so she'd start with them.

She couldn't find Doyle anywhere, but the master keys were lying on the reception desk. She picked them up and asked the PC on the door to let Doyle know she'd taken them when he returned.

Heading up the sweeping wooden staircase, she noted how quiet it was on this side of the house, away from the hustle and bustle of the library and the angry voices. The steps creaked beneath her feet. The portraits on the walls made her feel as though she were being watched. Their beady eyes seemed to follow her.

Chidlow House was the perfect setting for a ghost story. Karen understood why Alison King would have been spooked.

She glanced at the portraits as she passed, trying to spot a family resemblance to Chidlow. Most of the male subjects in the paintings were bloated and overweight, probably due to an excess of good living. All had proud and haughty expressions, so she supposed they had that in common with Edward Chidlow. The women were different: slender to the point of illness. Hollow-cheeked and pale with dark circles beneath their eyes. Their faces looked haunted, not helped by the cold palette of colours used and the harsh brushstrokes. The painters could have displayed the females in a more flattering light.

She made it up to the first floor and tried to remember which one was Ella Seaton's room. She was pretty sure Doyle had said it was room seven, the one next to the shared bathroom. She found the bathroom easily enough because it had an image of a brass lady in old-fashioned clothes on the door.

Inside, the bathroom was huge and draughty. There were three toilet cubicles on the left of the room. The toilets had elevated cisterns and chain flushes. There was a separate shower enclosure, which looked more modern than the other fittings, and a large enamel bath in the centre of the room. On the right, there was an old-fashioned washstand with a large mirror attached to the wall tiles.

A big free-standing cupboard stood near the window, but it was locked. None of the keys on Doyle's set fitted the small lock. It was probably full of supplies: toilet rolls, cleaning products, nothing of any importance. But she'd need to find the key eventually if she wanted to complete a thorough search.

Karen shut the door and prepared to move on to the next room. Number seven was on the left of the bathroom, but on the other side was a door with no number. It was the only one in the hallway without one. Karen was intrigued. She tested each and every key on the keyring, but none fitted. She gave a frustrated sigh. She really wasn't having much luck with locks today.

She moved on to room seven, Ella's room. This time she found the key helpfully labelled and it turned smoothly in the lock.

Ella's room was neat and tidy. She had the same style of desk beneath the window as in Natasha and Cressida's rooms. Her notebooks and textbooks were carefully stacked in piles, an elegant, silver fountain pen beside them. The pen and a red pencil case were the only personal things visible in the room. There was no jewellery or makeup.

Karen put the large bunch of keys on top of the dresser, pulled on gloves and made her way around the room. She found a bible in the top drawer of the nightstand and flicked through it looking for hidden notes or receipts, but found nothing. The wardrobe contained only one pair of brown slip-on shoes, one long black coat and a variety of baggy jumpers and loose-fitting shirts. The lower drawers in the dresser contained folded jeans and a pair of fleece pyjamas decorated with penguins. The top drawer contained underwear and nothing else.

Karen checked beneath the mattress and under the bed and pulled out a small suitcase and a carryall that had been stashed away from sight. Feeling hopeful, she opened them, but both were empty. She wasn't sure what she was expecting to find but there was something about Ella Seaton that made Karen think there was more to the girl than met the eye. She came across as very shy and unassuming, but when they'd talked to her, she'd spoken confidently and formally, an unusual combination for a teenage girl.

Karen stood up, brushed some fluff from her trousers and turned towards the window. A movement outside caught her eye. At first, she thought it was someone from the search party but then realised it was a man approaching the house. She moved closer, leaning on the desk to get a better view, and saw it was the groundsman again.

She was about to pull back when he looked straight up, directly at her. The rain was only a fine mist, so she could see him clearly, and could have sworn he was scowling at her.

'Not exactly a cheerful chap,' she murmured, wondering whether Rick or Sophie had unearthed any information on the staff at Chidlow House.

She was particularly interested to see what they dug up on Mike Harrington.

As she shifted away from the window, her foot caught the dark pink velvet drape. The drapes were heavy, but this one seemed even weightier than usual and there was a clunk as it moved back. It wasn't the sound of soft velvet brushing against the wall, but something hard, something solid.

Karen kneeled down, feeling the bottom of the material. Her fingers located something thin, rectangular and hard. Turning the drape she saw the hem had been unpicked, leaving loose threads and a little pocket. She put her hand inside and located something cold and metallic.

She pulled it from its hiding place. It was a phone. Karen frowned. How strange. Why would Ella hide her phone here? Why wouldn't she have it on her like all the other students? They'd all had their electronic devices gripped in their hands when Karen had entered the library, as had most of the parents. But Ella hadn't been holding a phone. She'd been sitting, hands in her lap, watching Ethan.

And why did she tell Karen she didn't have one? Had she gone behind her parents' backs to get it? Or did the phone belong to someone else?

Karen tapped the phone and the screen lit up. Ella's face was on the home screen, but it was locked with a code so Karen couldn't access anything.

Ella was pulling a goofy face in the picture, and it made Karen smile and remember that though these students tried so hard to be seen as grown-ups, underneath it all they still had very childish tendencies.

The snap reminded Karen of her own daughter. She'd had a tendency to pull faces when Karen tried to take a photo. She didn't have many of Tilly just smiling. Most of them were shots of her with her tongue poking out or pulling a silly face. They were Karen's favourite pictures, though. The ones that showed the true Tilly. Videos were even better. She had one stored on her phone, just a short clip of Tilly talking to her teddy bear. She'd read some-where that one of the first memories to fade was the sound of a loved one's voice. Karen couldn't bear the thought of that.

She realised she was gripping the phone so tightly the button on the side was digging into her palm. She relaxed her hand and put the phone back where she'd found it, still wondering why Ella had kept it there. Perhaps she was worried about the phone being stolen.

She decided to ask Ella about it later and pushed to her feet. Then she froze. She could hear whispering, coming from outside. Karen moved swiftly, grabbing the key ring as she passed the dresser and heading out into the corridor. The noises were louder there – definite whispering, and was that the sound of dripping water?

The whispers were unnerving enough, but the steady dripping noise made Karen's throat grow dry. She pulled Ella's door shut, locked it and then turned right.

'Is anyone there?'

At the end of the corridor, she saw a blur of colour. Someone was there, moving quickly towards the stairs.

Karen followed, turning the corner, but when she reached the staircase it was empty. There was no one on this floor. Unless they'd gone into one of the bedrooms. She turned around in a circle, staring at the row of doors. She hadn't heard a door open or shut.

She was still staring back at the hallway when the sound of creaking on the stairs made her jump and whirl around. She peered over the banister.

Her heart was thumping. She could easily see why the students referred to the house as haunted and why Alison King had found the place creepy.

But there was no ghostly apparition, just the solid figure of Graham Doyle climbing the stairs from the ground floor.

'Do you hear that?' Karen asked, but the sounds had stopped.

Doyle paused, cocked his head to one side, listening. 'Hear what?'

Karen let out a long breath. 'It doesn't matter.'

'Oh, don't tell me you're hearing the noises as well. That doesn't bode well . . .'

'What do you mean?' Karen asked.

'Well, Miss King heard the noises. Legend has it that Edward Chidlow's great-great-grandmother drowned herself in the lake and her spirit haunts the house. If you hear or see her, it's very bad luck. As poor Miss King discovered.'

'Nonsense.' Karen eyed him with suspicion.

He flushed. 'I don't believe it, of course. I was just telling you about how the ghost story came about.'

Karen held up the bunch of keys. 'I took the keys from the reception desk. I'm planning to search all the student rooms now. I've just done Ella Seaton's. I'm going to head upstairs and do the boys' floor next. Can you inform the parents and get their permission?'

Doyle closed his eyes. 'That's just how I wanted to spend my afternoon,' he said sarcastically. 'I'm sure the parents will be thrilled.'

'Just tell them it could help find Natasha and Cressida. That's all that matters at the moment.'

'I hope they see it like that,' Doyle said, turning around to go back downstairs.

'Which number is Robert Carthey's room?'

'Oh.' He rubbed his chin. 'Number twenty-two, I think.'

'Thanks. Did I interrupt you?' Karen asked.

'What?' He turned.

'You were coming upstairs.'

'Oh . . . I . . . I forgot what I was going upstairs for, actually. Can't have been important.'

He gave her a nervous smile before continuing his descent.

CHAPTER TEN

Karen wanted to check the room used by Robert Carthey, the lad who'd been smoking weed with Ethan, Natasha and Cressida, next. She suspected Robert was the young man who'd been nervously yanking his collar and sending worried glances her way when she'd spoken to Ethan earlier.

She liked to think she was good at reading people, particularly picking up on the small signs people displayed when they were trying to hide something, but in this case, anyone would have picked up on his unease. Robert definitely wouldn't make a good poker player.

She waited by the locked door of room twenty-two, listening for more of the whispering, but the hallway was quiet. The only sound was the rasping and gurgling of the old heating system kicking in.

Karen unlocked the door. It creaked open, and she was immediately greeted by the green, ripe smell of cannabis. It was faint but definitely noticeable, lingering in the air.

She didn't know if Robert had hidden the weed in his room, but someone had definitely been smoking in there recently. She put the set of keys down on the dresser, pulled on gloves and looked around.

Now, if I was a teenage boy, where would I hide my stash? she wondered as she walked slowly around the bed.

She checked the bedside cabinet first but found only a small red bible. Next, she turned her attention to the large chest of drawers. The top drawers contained underwear and T-shirts. The drawer beneath that contained wool jumpers and then . . . jackpot!

Karen's fingers closed around a small plastic bag. She pulled it out and smiled. One small bag of weed.

She began to remove the jumpers one at a time from the drawer, to make sure she didn't miss anything else. And there, right at the back, tucked under a green cashmere jumper, was a ready-rolled spliff. She plucked that out of the drawer and set it beside the bag of weed on top of the dresser.

Before she could remove another item of clothing from the drawer, there was a knock at the door. She opened it to find Doyle standing there, along with the young lad and his parents. Robert looked terrified, his parents looked angry and Doyle looked distressed.

'I'm sorry, Detective, but Robert's parents aren't happy for you to look through his belongings. They say it's an invasion of his privacy, and you need to speak to their lawyer before you perform any kind of search.'

Karen looked at Robert. 'Worried I might find something?'

Robert shook his head. 'Um . . . no . . . nothing like that. I just . . . I don't want you snooping.'

'In case I find this?' Karen enquired, gesturing and opening the door wider so they could all see the bag of weed and the spliff sitting on top of the dresser.

'Stupid boy!' Robert's father yelled, and his mother covered her face with her hands and groaned.

'It just helps me relax. Gets me in the zone to study,' Robert protested. 'It's only for personal use. It should be legal anyway. It is in Amsterdam.'

'But we're not in Amsterdam at the moment, Robert,' Karen said. 'Tell me, did you share this with Cressida and Natasha?'

Robert's jaw dropped open. 'Well, I—'

'Don't answer the question, you stupid boy,' his father said, grabbing Robert by the shoulders and giving him a stern shake.

'He didn't mean it,' Mrs Carthey said, looking at Karen pleadingly. 'He's easily led. Surely you can turn a blind eye just this once? This could ruin his future!'

'The police won't be taking this any further, will you?' Mr Carthey said coldly, letting go of Robert. 'He's just a boy. Made a stupid mistake, of course, but I mean you can hardly press charges when he's been smoking with the chief constable's son, can you?'

Mr Carthey stared at Karen with a nasty gleam in his eyes and a smug smile on his face.

Karen understood parents would always try to protect their children, but this was going too far, and she particularly hated the point he made about the chief constable. She wanted John Grayson to be incorruptible. The fact that his son was involved shouldn't matter. Both boys should be reprimanded, though their punishment would be little more than a black mark against their names for possession. It would serve as a warning for the future and teach them they couldn't break the law and expect to get away with it.

Robert looked miserably down at his feet.

It would be easy to agree to forget about the drugs. It was only weed, and lots of kids dabbled in softer drugs and didn't get hooked or end up on the streets. But could she live with herself if she did that? She wanted to root out corruption in the Lincolnshire force and yet here she was considering letting this lad off with a warning to save complications.

There was also a chance this could have something to do with Cressida and Natasha's disappearance. So Karen would have to include this in the official report, even if she made an enemy of the chief constable.

'Can you tell me where you got the drugs from?'

Robert turned to his father. 'Do I have to tell her that?'

'No, you don't have to say anything.'

'If you don't, then perhaps I'll have to look on you as the one who's been supplying the drugs to your fellow students. Dealing drugs is seen very differently to possession in the eyes of the law.'

Robert paled. 'But I . . . I just let them have a smoke because we're friends. I wasn't selling it to them. I'm not a drug dealer.'

'Well, it sounds to me like you are, unless you can tell me who supplied the drugs.'

'It was my brother,' he said. 'I don't know where he got them, just someone at his university.'

His father bellowed in outrage and ordered Robert to keep quiet. The boy lowered his head.

'Please, Detective,' Robert's mother said. 'I know he's been an idiot, but he's not a bad lad really, and I know he hasn't got anything to do with the girls' disappearance. If he had he would tell you, wouldn't you, Robert?'

Robert nodded solemnly. 'I would. I really don't know what happened to them. I wish I did. They were nice. I liked them. We had a laugh.'

'Did you know them before the course?' Karen asked.

He shook his head. 'No, we met here.'

'And Ethan?'

'I met him here as well. I didn't know anyone here before. I had to come because my grades have been so bad, and my mum wants me to go to the same university as my brother.'

'Did you see them leave last night?'

He shook his head. 'No, I didn't. I was up here.'

'What were you doing?'

'Trying to study,' he said. 'None of this stuff makes sense to me. It seems like it takes me twice as long as everyone else to soak up the material. And that's why I was smoking, you know. It helps me retain information.'

'That's odd. I think most scientific studies on cannabis show the opposite effect,' Karen said.

Robert flushed again. 'All right. It's just because it helps me relax. It's so stressful feeling like an idiot all the time. Everybody else catches on much quicker than I do. I'm not really academic.'

'Yes, you are, Robert. You just need to knuckle down and concentrate,' his mother said.

'Yeah, right.' He rolled his eyes.

'Let's go downstairs and you can talk to Detective Inspector Morgan about this,' Karen said.

'Will that be the end of the incident?' Mr Carthey asked hopefully.

'I doubt it,' Karen said.

'Well, if Robert is charged then I'm going to make sure the chief constable's son is as well,' he said irritably, and stomped out of Robert's room.

Morgan hung up the phone and frowned. He'd just been speaking to the superintendent.

Usually she was content with phone updates from Morgan during an investigation, but she'd asked for Karen to return to the station as soon as possible to brief her on developments – and that was odd.

In the past, they'd followed the normal chain of command, and Morgan liaised with the superintendent directly. He wondered why she wanted to speak to Karen in person. Was it simply that she wanted to be brought up to date, or was there more to it?

Only a few minutes ago, he'd finished his interview with Robert Carthey. So far, he couldn't see any links between Robert and Natasha or Cressida, other than the fact they'd shared a joint a couple of times during the study week. Robert insisted he'd got his weed from his brother, and neither girl had asked him where he'd got it from or met his brother or his brother's dealer. It had seemed like a promising lead at first, but it was rapidly fizzling out.

It amazed Morgan that someone with so much money, so many opportunities, would risk their future.

People didn't see cannabis as a serious drug. He knew a couple of his fellow officers had partaken in an occasional joint before joining the force. It had been shown to improve symptoms for a number of medical conditions, so it was understandable people took a lenient view.

But when Robert had admitted his brother wasn't only using weed, Morgan had warned Robert of the risks involved, the possibility that cannabis could lead to harder drugs and that a criminal record could ruin his prospects. He wasn't sure if his well-worn speech had connected with Robert, but the boy did seem genuinely remorseful.

Despite all his advantages and money, at the end of the day he was still a teenager, trying to find his way in life and more often than not messing things up.

Morgan stood up and put his mobile in his pocket, intending to look for Karen. She'd returned to the second floor to carry on searching, so he should be able to find her up there. He walked towards the back of the house and the large staircase that led up to the students' rooms.

Chidlow House was rich with history and oil paintings were everywhere he looked. Hunting scenes were obviously a favourite.

Men wearing red jackets and white breeches, perched on large horses, were delicately painted in front of lush countryside. There were lots of pictures of hunting dogs too, as well as the usual family portraits.

He walked up the stairs, and on reaching the top of the first flight, he stopped short. Ella Seaton was standing in front of him, pale as a ghost.

She gasped and put her hand to her chest. 'Oh, you scared me!'

She reached out a hand to grip the banister.

Morgan apologised and stepped aside. 'I thought you were supposed to be in the library, Ella.'

'Oh, yes, I am. I just wanted to go to my room . . . for something.'

Her cheeks flushed and she put her hands against her pockets, as though trying to stop Morgan seeing inside, but he couldn't very well order her to empty out her pockets here on the staircase, not without good reason.

'Well, why don't you join the others?' he said.

He preferred all the students and parents to be in one place where he could keep tabs on them, as well as making sure they stayed safe. He didn't want any other students going missing.

Ella nodded meekly.

'Did you see DS Hart up here?' Morgan asked.

'No, sorry.' She gave him an apologetic smile and then nimbly made her way down the stairs.

Morgan turned and climbed the second flight. She was an odd girl, definitely a little nervous and jumpy.

The wind was howling outside, and a sudden squall directed raindrops hard against the windowpanes at the end of the corridor, sounding like a hundred tiny hands tapping on the glass. He felt a sudden chill as he walked across the deep red carpet.

The doors were all made of oak, old and battered with age, yet they had an old-world charm. The brass doorknobs matched the brass numbers on the doors.

He paused for a moment, listening, trying to detect which room Karen was in, but couldn't hear anything.

Deciding to knock on each door in turn, he rapped on the wood of number twenty, then suddenly stopped when he heard a whispering voice. He couldn't decipher what it was saying.

He turned sharply but there was no one in the corridor with him and it definitely hadn't sounded like Karen. It sounded younger, like a girl but slightly distorted by an echo.

The hairs on the back of his neck stood up and his skin prickled. Then the sound came again.

'Who's there?' he called out, but there was no response.

A door opened near the end of the corridor. It was Karen.

'Looking for me?' she asked.

Morgan frowned. 'Did you hear that?' He fell silent listening again for the noise, but there was nothing.

'No. What was it?' Karen asked.

'Whispering.'

Karen's frown matched his. 'I didn't hear it just now, but I did hear it earlier, yes.'

Morgan thought back to meeting Ella on the stairs. Could it be her? Was she playing tricks on them? It was a childish thing to do, but who else could it be? Everyone else was supposed to be downstairs in the library.

'Is something wrong?' Karen asked.

'I came up to tell you the superintendent wants you to go back to the station. She wants an update.'

'From me?' Karen asked, surprised.

'Yes, she asked for you specifically, and in person.'

'Why?' Karen asked.

'I don't know. It struck me as odd, but she insisted. I gave her an update over the phone, thinking that would be enough, but she asked for you to come back as soon as possible.'

Karen sighed and looked back regretfully over her shoulder at the room she'd been searching. 'It's going to put us behind. Did you tell her I was looking through the rooms?'

'I did, but she still asked for you to return to the station and said she'd send some bodies to help with the indoor search.'

'Who? I'd prefer to oversee the search myself.'

'I'll keep an eye on things.' Morgan knew Karen had trouble delegating tasks to officers outside their immediate team. Her trust issues were understandable. She'd been betrayed by officers she'd relied on in the past, and it would take time to build up that trust again. 'It must be important. I can't see why she would ask otherwise.'

Karen nodded slowly. 'I suppose you're right, but it's a pain.' She walked back into the room, grabbed the keys and then locked the door before handing the key ring to Morgan. 'What about Chidlow? He's not going to like it if we bring more officers into his house.'

'I'll deal with him,' Morgan said.

They walked back downstairs together.

'I'll probably be at least an hour,' Karen said. 'Do you want me to ask Rick or Sophie to come down?'

'No, I think it's better they work on the background at the station. It's easier to access everything there.'

'Right,' Karen said. 'Well, good luck. I'll see you in about an hour.'

DI Morgan watched her leave, wondering again what was so important that the superintendent needed to see Karen in person.

CHAPTER ELEVEN

Although there was a break in the rain, the journey back to the station wasn't easy, as many of the smaller roads were flooded. As Karen navigated the country lanes, her car tyres sent waves of water on to the grass verges.

Karen, reluctant to be away from the case any longer than she had to be, rushed straight to the superintendent's office without stopping to catch up with Sophie and Rick.

Pamela, Superintendent Murray's assistant, told her she could go into the office straightaway. Karen did so and was surprised to see that the superintendent wasn't alone. Sitting beside her desk, making himself comfortable, was Chief Constable John Grayson. They'd been eating chocolate digestives and drinking coffee.

'Ma'am,' Karen said. 'You wanted an update.'

'That's right, Karen,' the superintendent said, smiling. 'Come in, take a seat. Chief Constable Grayson is very keen to hear about your progress, too.'

'Right,' Karen said, taking a seat and shaking her head when the superintendent offered her coffee. 'I think DI Morgan has already given you an update?'

'Yes,' Murray said. 'I heard you found some cannabis.'

Karen nodded. 'That's right, but I'm not convinced it's related to the girls' disappearance.'

'I'm glad to hear it,' the chief constable said. 'I was very disappointed to hear that Ethan may be involved.'

'Another student reported Ethan smoking, but he wasn't the one who supplied the drugs to Cressida or Natasha,' Karen said.

'That's something I suppose, but I can't help thinking I've let him down.' Grayson looked down at his wedding ring. 'It's just me and Ethan, you see, since Kath died. It's not easy bringing up a teenage boy on your own.'

'I wasn't aware your wife had died, sir,' Karen said. 'I'm very sorry.'

Grayson met Karen's gaze. 'Thank you. It's not easy.'

He looked pained. Karen knew what it was like to deal with loss. The death of Ethan's mother probably went some way to explaining the teenager's behaviour too.

Superintendent Murray stood up. 'Excuse me. I need to talk to Pamela. I'll be back in a moment.'

She left the room, shutting the door behind her.

'I'm glad it's you and DI Morgan on the case,' Grayson said. 'I can trust you, I'm sure of it.'

'We'll do our best to find the girls, sir,' Karen said, unsure where this conversation was heading. She sympathised with the loss of the chief constable's wife, but couldn't help feeling this was some sort of ambush.

The superintendent suddenly leaving the room and the chief constable being so friendly? It smelled like a set-up.

'I'm sure you will. I've been impressed with your career so far, Karen.'

Karen frowned. She wasn't aware she was on Grayson's radar. And she was pretty sure Assistant Chief Constable Fry hadn't known her name until she made a nuisance of herself over the corruption investigation.

'Thank you, sir,' she said, shifting awkwardly in her seat.

'I don't want you to think I'm not taking the investigation into DI Freeman seriously, Karen. I've been thinking about it since we spoke, and I'm sure I can do something to encourage the inquiry team to continue on the right track. These investigations have a habit of getting dropped.'

'They were thinking of stopping the case against him?' Karen asked, outraged.

'I'm afraid it was heading in that direction. It's not easy to find people to testify against a police officer. And without evidence or testimony, any charges we bring against him won't stick. I'm afraid they tend to think of it as a cost problem.'

Karen balled her fists. The idea that the death of her family was being viewed in financial terms didn't sit well with her at all. 'But Charlie Cook said—'

'The word of a criminal doesn't hold much weight. We need more.'

Karen's mouth was dry. She wished she'd taken the superintendent up on the offer of coffee. If it was evidence they needed, then Karen would find it. Somehow. There was still Alice Price, who'd accused some of her fellow Lincolnshire officers of corruption. Alice was slightly unbalanced, admittedly, but maybe she knew something that could lead to the truth. Karen would keep digging until she got the answers she needed.

'I didn't say all this to upset you,' Grayson continued. 'You can rest assured I won't let them drop the case. Not until they've exhausted all avenues. I can promise you that.'

'Oh, well, thank you. I appreciate that,' Karen said hesitantly, uncomfortably aware of what could be behind this sudden change of attitude.

'Of course, I'd like you to keep me up to date on this case. I don't need to tell you that having a drug charge against Ethan would adversely affect his future. That concerns me.'

Karen narrowed her eyes. Was Grayson offering his support in exchange for omitting Ethan's drug use in her reports? She couldn't accept that.

'I can't leave Ethan's involvement out of the report, sir.'

'Of course not. I would never ask you to do that.'

No, you're too clever to ask directly, Karen thought, but she caught the heavy implication behind his words.

The superintendent came back into her office. 'Sorry about that. There was something I forgot to ask Pamela to do for me earlier. Thank you for the update, Karen.'

'Is that all, ma'am?' Karen asked.

'Yes.'

'I'll get back to Chidlow House then.'

'Yes, very good,' the superintendent said. 'Morgan asked for more officers to help with the internal search, so I've sent a couple of extra people along to him. That should help you out.'

'Thank you,' Karen said, imagining Lord Chidlow's reaction when he saw the extra officers appear at the house. He would not be very happy about that development at all.

She stood up, said her goodbyes and left the office even more confused than when she'd arrived. Had Grayson been implying that he'd help her with the investigation into Freeman only if she overlooked his son's bad behaviour? Surely not. He couldn't be offering to help her with a corruption inquiry in exchange for her breaking the rules.

The irony was too much.

After a treacherous journey back through the flooded country lanes, Karen parked outside Chidlow House. The rain fell in fat drops against the windscreen.

Great. More rain; just what they didn't need. Karen groaned as she cut the engine and grabbed her raincoat. Luckily for her, she wasn't one of the officers trying to search the grounds.

As she locked the car, she caught sight of the groundsman in the distance walking across the lawn. He had the spaniel beside him again. Karen shoved her arms into her jacket then made her way towards them. She called out twice, but the wind snatched her words away before they reached him. He took long strides despite his limp, and Karen had to jog to catch up with him, calling out as she did so.

'Hey, can you wait a minute? I want a word with you,' she said.

He carried on walking. His steps only hesitated once, but Karen was convinced he'd heard her. Even if he was hard of hearing, the dog's reaction beside him must have alerted him to her presence.

She called out again. 'I said, can you stop? I want to talk to you.'

Finally, he came to a halt and turned around with a surly expression on his face. His eyes narrowed but he said nothing, just stared at her. He'd be quite good-looking if he stopped frowning.

'You're the groundsman, aren't you? Mike, isn't it?'

He took a long time to answer, but finally nodded. 'Mike Harrington.'

'DS Karen Hart. And who's this?' she said, smiling at the dog.

The question threw him for a moment. He frowned and then said gruffly, 'Sandy.'

'You know we're investigating the disappearance of two female students from the study programme at Chidlow House . . .' Karen began.

'I don't know anything about it.'

'You didn't see them or speak to them while they were here?'

He shook his head. 'Not that I remember.'

'Do you have much interaction with the students?'

'No, not if I can help it,' he said, and ordered Sandy to stay still. The spaniel was full of gleeful energy, quite a contrast to the sullen groundsman.

'Maybe I could show you a picture of Natasha and Cressida? You might have seen them and not realised who they were,' Karen said, digging through her bag to pull out the file.

He gave a long, drawn-out sigh and took a step closer to look at the pictures, leaning on his cane.

He shrugged. 'I think I may have seen them about.'

'Did you speak to either of them?'

'I don't think so. I just do my job and keep to myself.'

'They're pretty young women. You would have remembered if you'd spoken to them, wouldn't you?'

He stared at her for a long moment and then said, 'Look, I really do have work to be getting on with.'

Karen put the file back in her bag. 'Fine. I'll walk with you and we can talk as we go.'

With an irritated huff, he began to walk, and Karen fell into step beside him. 'What do you know about Lord Chidlow?'

'He's my boss.'

'Yes, but do you know him personally? Friends?'

'Not really, no.'

'Does he have many visitors to the estate during the year? Parties?'

'I keep my nose out of other people's business. I find life's easier that way.'

'Someone mentioned Chidlow had quite the reputation around here.'

'I wouldn't know anything about that.'

'This is the first time there's been a study week at the house for students?'

'Yes.'

'You're not very talkative, are you?'

He turned, looking at Karen, and she thought she saw a smile tug at his lips. But it soon vanished and was replaced by the sullen expression again. 'I like my own company. I'm not one for chatter.'

I'd noticed, thought Karen.

'We think the girls left the house at nine p.m. last night. Probably left by the French windows at the side.' She pointed back at the house and was surprised at how far they'd walked.

He didn't say anything.

'Well?' Karen prompted.

'Well, what? You didn't ask me a question.'

'Well, did you see anything last night or hear anything?'

'No.'

'Where were you last night?'

'At home.'

'You live on the estate. Is that right?'

'Yes. I stay in the cottage on the other side of the lake. It's quite a way from the house so it's not surprising I didn't hear anything.'

'Must be lonely over there on your own. Quite cut off.'

'I like it.'

'I wonder if Sandy heard anything,' Karen said, leaning down to stroke the dog, much to Sandy's delight. 'She didn't react strangely to anything last night? No barking?'

'No,' he said. 'And you shouldn't pet her like that. She's a working dog.'

Karen frowned. 'Surely even working dogs like a bit of affection now and then.' She straightened. 'Well, thank you for your time.'

'You'd better get back to the house. The rain is getting heavier.' He looked up at the dark clouds.

'I will,' Karen said, but before the words left her mouth, he was marching off towards the woods with Sandy at his heels.

CHAPTER TWELVE

Karen kept her head down and quickened her step as the rain began to fall more heavily. When she got closer to the house, she noticed that some members of the search party were standing out on the patio.

'Sarge?' a familiar voice said. Karen turned to see DC Farzana Shah waving at her from the French windows. 'Come in. You're getting soaked. I've only just got here myself. The super asked me to come down and help with the search of the house.'

Karen stepped inside, wiping her feet on the rug, then shivered. There was a large fire in the grate. She moved closer to it. 'What's going on out there? Have they found something?'

Farzana nodded. 'They found one of the girls.'

'Which girl?' Karen asked.

'Cressida.'

'Alive?'

'Yes. I mean, she's traumatised, looks like she's been out all night.'

'Where is she?'

'They've put her in the front parlour, part of Chidlow's private residence. DI Morgan is talking to her now. We've called her parents. She's just through here,' Farzana said, leading the way.

Karen shrugged off her wet raincoat as she stepped into the room. Morgan stood beside the sofa where Cressida was sitting, huddled in a blanket. She was wearing the same clothes described by Ethan – a white shirt and jeans. But there was no sign of her coat. She still wore her jewellery – an expensive-looking charm bracelet, made from white gold or silver, shone on her wrist as she lifted her arm.

Her jeans were soaked, and through a gap in the blanket Karen could see her shirt was also wet. Cressida sat trembling, looking down at her lap.

DI Morgan was explaining in a calm voice that they would need to take her clothes for forensics, and she would be seen by a doctor shortly.

As Karen approached them, he shot her a thankful look.

'This is Karen, one of my fellow detectives,' Morgan said. Then, in a lower voice, he said to Karen, 'She's not talking. In shock, I think.'

'Any news on Natasha?' Karen asked.

Morgan shook his head.

Karen put her coat and bag on the floor beside the sofa and sat next to the terrified young woman.

'Cressida, my name's Karen. I'm a detective with Lincolnshire Police, and I'm one of the officers who's been looking for you and Natasha. We're going to get you checked out by a doctor and then take you back to the station where you'll be safe. We've contacted your parents so they'll be here soon. Do you think you could answer a couple of questions for me now?'

Cressida said nothing, just continued to stare down at her lap, shivering.

'Do you know where Natasha is?'

No answer.

'What happened to you?'

Karen wanted to ask if she'd got lost, if she'd been picked up or hurt by someone, but she knew better than to use leading questions at this stage.

Still Cressida didn't answer. She lifted her head, and Karen saw a long scratch on her cheek.

'Can you tell me where you've been, Cressida?'

No response.

'I want you to know that you're safe now. We're here to help you, but as Natasha is still missing, we really need your help to find her. So, is there anything you can tell me?'

Cressida clutched at the blanket over her shoulders, took a shaky breath and turned, looking at Karen for the first time. Her eyes were bright blue and watery, and her flaxen blonde hair hung in wet strands over the blanket. 'N . . . Natasha,' she managed to say.

'Yes, that's right. Do you know where Natasha is?' Karen asked again.

Cressida opened her mouth, but no sound came out.

'We really need to find her. Were you with her last night?'

Cressida took another breath. 'I d . . . don't know. I can't remember.' And then she clutched at her throat. 'I can't breathe.'

Karen felt a jolt of adrenaline as she loosened the collar of the girl's shirt, but Cressida clawed at her throat as though there was something constricting her neck.

'It's okay. You're safe,' Karen said again.

Was this some kind of panic attack, or was there something really wrong with the girl's throat? She was wheezing now.

Morgan was beside her. 'Okay, Cressida. Try to breathe out.' Then, to Karen: 'I think she's hyperventilating.'

After a worrying few moments, Cressida's breathing became less erratic. She put her head forward, resting it on her knees, and Karen stroked her back, speaking softly.

'It's going to be all right. Your mum and dad are coming. They'll be here really soon. Try to relax.'

Eventually Cressida got her breathing under control. When she straightened, Karen looked into her eyes. They seemed empty. No fear, no panic, just nothingness.

Ryan Blake exploded into the room first, closely followed by his wife, Jasmine.

'Cressida!' He rushed to her, kneeling and wrapping his arms around her, but she was unresponsive.

Her mother flew to her other side, kissing her daughter's cheek, pushing back the damp strands of hair from her forehead. 'Darling, we've been so worried. You're okay, aren't you? Tell me you're okay.'

But Cressida was silent.

'Cressida's going to be examined by a doctor,' Morgan explained. 'We're going to need her clothes too.'

Ryan gave him an angry look. 'Hasn't she been through enough without you fussing over her? Give her some space,' he snapped, waving a hand to make Morgan step back.

'I understand you'd like Cressida to be given some space, sir, but Natasha is still missing. We need to examine her clothes.'

Jasmine gasped as the significance of what Morgan was saying sank in. Her eyes were wide. 'You think she was . . . Oh no. You think someone did something to her.' Jasmine paled and put her hand up to her mouth. 'I'm going to be sick,' she said, and rushed out of the room.

Ryan turned to look at Karen, his eyes red. 'You suspect she's been . . . interfered with?'

'We need to consider all possibilities,' Karen said.

Ryan put a fist to his mouth, choking back a sob. Then he hugged his daughter. 'You're all right, darling. Daddy's here now. You're safe. I promise.'

With her chin resting on her father's shoulder, Cressida's blue eyes stared straight ahead. It reminded Karen of the portraits on the stairs of the haunted young women. She suspected it would be quite some time before Cressida felt safe again.

At Nettleham station, DC Sophie Jones was focusing on her computer screen, trying to fight the niggling worry she was being left out. She would much prefer to be on the scene at Chidlow House but had to be satisfied with background research.

She'd volunteered to be one of the family liaison officers but they'd given the roles to Siobhan and Lydia – not surprising really as Sophie had only just finished her training.

Rick sat at the desk opposite chatting animatedly on the phone. He was looking into the teachers who'd been working at the study course. No one they'd looked into had come up in a criminal record search, which was hardly unusual, because to work at these institutions you needed a criminal record check.

They'd not found much about Edward Chidlow at all yet, which was a disappointment considering Karen had said there were rumours about him.

Sophie stared at the blue-tinted screen, trying to tune out the buzz of the open office, chattering voices and clacking keys. She reached for her mug and breathed in the scent of the green tea and lemon. She'd been using herbal teas to try to cut down on caffeine, but Rick had cheerfully informed her this morning that it was in green tea. Maybe she'd move on to raspberry and cranberry next week.

She took a sip of the hot tea and put it down on her desk, then scrolled back through the data she'd gathered so far, but there were no red flags for Chidlow. And Doyle had a very strait-laced, boring background.

Doyle had never married. He had been a teacher for over twenty-five years at various private schools around the country before setting up his own study programme. There had been no complaints recorded against him. She'd spoken to two of his previous employers, and they'd sung his praises.

She was about to log off her search and go and get something to eat when she had an idea. She closed down the database and opened up the internet browser, logging on to *The Hilt* magazine. It wasn't really her type of reading material these days, but she was familiar with it. She'd gone through a phase in her teenage years of not being able to get enough of magazines. Now it seemed a bit silly to care what colour lip gloss the latest B-list celebrity wore.

The Hilt was slightly different to the normal gossip rags. Instead of celebrities and TV stars, it was full of minor royals, lords and ladies – a kind of gossip magazine for the upper classes.

There weren't many articles on the actual website, but there was a search bar for past issues, so she searched for the name 'Lord Edward Chidlow' and leaned forward, resting her chin on her hand as she scanned the results.

There were three hits. The first two were quite boring, describing Chidlow attending society weddings. But the third one looked like it could be juicy. A Chidlow scandal. Unfortunately, when Sophie tried to click the link it went to a screen that said the article she'd requested was unavailable. She made a note of the date of the article and the title, then entered it into the internet search bar and clicked on 'Image search'.

A few headshots appeared – some of Chidlow himself, and a couple of him with a woman about his age. His first wife, Sophie suspected. Then, she had some good luck. Someone had uploaded a scan of the magazine article.

She clicked on the image to open it up and started to read. The article was full of salacious gossip. Quite how much was true, Sophie wasn't sure, but it certainly was interesting. Apparently, Chidlow had run off and left his wife for a much younger woman. Sophie sipped her tea. Maybe this was the reason for the rumours.

So he had an interest in younger women. That didn't mean he'd be interested in seventeen-year-old A-level students though, did it?

There was no mention of the name of the young woman he'd run off with, but maybe she could get more information from Edward Chidlow's ex-wife.

If the split wasn't amicable – as Sophie suspected was likely, since Chidlow had left his wife for a woman half her age – then the ex–Lady Chidlow might be prepared to give them some information.

After a quick search through the police database, she acquired a number for Chidlow's former wife.

The call seemed to take forever to connect.

'Yah,' a posh female voice answered.

'Hello. Is that Lady Chidlow?'

'No, it isn't. I'm her assistant. Who's this?'

'This is DC Sophie Jones of the Lincolnshire Police. I was hoping to speak to Lady Chidlow.'

'Police.' Suddenly the voice on the other end of the line sounded interested. The woman smacked her lips. It sounded like she was chewing gum. 'Why do the police want to talk to her?'

'I'm afraid that's confidential,' Sophie said. 'Would you mind putting her on the line?'

'Oh, I can't, sorry. She's out today. Spa day, and I'm under strict instructions she can't be disturbed.'

'I see. Could I have your name?'

'Jessica, her PA. I'll let her know you called.'

'Thank you.' Sophie gave Jessica her number.

'Are you sure you can't tell me what it's about?'

'No, I'm afraid I can't,' Sophie said and hung up.

She glanced over at Rick. He was still chatting away on the phone. With any luck they'd be able to go out and speak to some of the teachers soon, rather than spending all their time in the office. It did get quite tedious sitting in front of the computer all day. She preferred in-person interviews.

Sophie looked back down at her notepad. There was one other person Karen wanted them to look into and that was the groundsman. Sophie checked through her notes. Mike Harrington.

She did the usual criminal record checks. Nothing. Then she flipped through the personnel files that Doyle and Chidlow had handed over to Karen. She skimmed the contents of Harrington's file, then entered his name and date of birth into the database. When the results came back, she frowned.

As soon as Rick hung up the phone, she called him over. 'I think you should have a look at this. It seems the groundsman has a surprising history.'

CHAPTER THIRTEEN

At five thirty they were preparing to take Cressida back to the station for an interview. She'd told them nothing to indicate what had happened, where she'd been or, more importantly, where Natasha was. Karen thought they might get more out of her when they got her away from Chidlow House. She was traumatised, and a safe, neutral space would hopefully make her feel more secure.

The PC who'd been standing at the front door all day came into the parlour to let Karen know the car was ready to take Cressida back to the station. Farzana had taken over searching Chidlow House, and Morgan had almost finished questioning the students. Most had been allowed to go home.

Karen was about to tell Cressida and her parents they were due to leave for the station when Inspector Grant, the officer who'd been leading the search team, approached her. He was a large man with a bulbous nose.

'DS Hart.' As he spoke, his gaze flickered down to the bottom of Cressida's jeans, which were coated in dark red mud.

'Have you found anything?' Karen asked.

'I just wanted to mention something I'd noticed. The mud . . .' he said, lowering his voice to a whisper, ' . . . on her jeans. It's quite distinctive.'

Karen nodded. 'Yes, it is.'

'This red mud is around the shore of the lake. I haven't seen it anywhere else on the grounds.'

Karen took a deep breath. She knew what he was getting at. He wanted to know if it was time to dredge the lake.

The mud was a definite sign that Cressida had been near the lake at some point. Had there been some kind of accident? Was that where they'd find Natasha?

'It's not going to be easy to search the lake in the dark,' Karen said, and the inspector nodded, 'but I think we should probably ready the aquatic team for a search tomorrow.'

Grant nodded. 'How long do you want us to keep searching around the grounds?'

'Keep going for now. I know once it gets dark it's going to be nigh on impossible, but keep at it. Cressida managed to get back to the house, so the chances are Natasha could be close.'

Karen had already spoken to Morgan and they'd agreed that he would finish up at Chidlow House while Karen went to the station with Cressida.

When Karen approached Cressida and her mother, Jasmine Blake looked up through tearful eyes. 'I really do think she should get out of these wet things. She's going to catch a cold.'

'I know it seems cruel to keep Cressida in those clothes, but it's what's best for forensics. It won't be long now. We'll get her back to the station, and she'll be able to change just as soon as a doctor's seen her. Perhaps you could bring her some clean clothes to the station?'

Karen glanced at Ryan Blake, who had his head in his hands. He looked up and nodded once.

Karen's mobile rang. 'Excuse me,' she said, turning around, pulling the phone out of her pocket and glancing at the screen.

It was Alice Price.

Karen wanted to talk to her again. A couple of years ago, Alice had accused senior officers of corruption and then been persuaded to leave the police service after she'd had a breakdown. Karen suspected she'd been bullied out, though it was hard to get the truth from Alice. She was in a manic state and suffering from anxiety and wasn't a reliable source.

Karen hesitated, wanting to pick up the call, but now was not a good time. She pressed the red button to send Alice's call to voicemail and then turned back to Cressida. 'Are you ready to go? You can bring the blanket with you.'

Cressida said nothing but got stiffly to her feet, the blanket clasped around her shoulders. They walked slowly, Cressida shuffling beside Karen as they left the parlour and walked slowly down to the entrance hall.

'The car is just outside,' Karen said. 'We'll soon have you warm, changed and back at home, okay?'

Cressida didn't even look at her.

Karen led the trembling young woman outside and down the stone steps towards the marked car.

The ground was covered with soggy red and yellow leaves. There was a rush of wind, cold against Karen's cheeks, as they got closer to the car. Behind them, a glow of light came from Chidlow's study. Karen turned. He was watching them through the windows. The groundsman and his dog were in there with him. She wondered what they were talking about.

Outside the French windows leading to Chidlow's study, leaning against the wall, was the groundsman's walking stick.

Sandy barked, a muffled sound from inside the study, and Cressida turned back, looking towards the house. Karen tried to guide her to the car but she was rigid. Karen looked at her, confused.

Suddenly Cressida recoiled, snatching her hand away from Karen and trying to pull back. Her mother grabbed her arms as Karen tried to reassure her.

'Everything's okay, Cressida. We're just going to take you to the station. Your mum's coming with us.'

Cressida let out a high-pitched scream and began to tremble violently. Tears rolled down her cheeks. It took minutes of gentle persuasion to calm her. They finally managed to get her to sit in the back of the squad car with her mother.

Karen had just opened the door on the front passenger side when Morgan put a hand on her shoulder. 'I heard the scream,' he said. 'What was that about? The car? Do you think she got into a car last night?'

Karen shook her head. 'I don't think it was the car.'

She nodded to the window, where Chidlow stood, hands behind his back, looking directly at them.

'You think she was reacting to Chidlow?' Morgan asked.

'Possibly.'

Morgan left to finish up the interviews, and Karen got into the car and nodded to the officer in the driver's seat.

As they pulled away, Karen looked back at Chidlow's study. Was Cressida reacting to him? The groundsman, Mike Harrington, had been in the study too. Not as easy to see him from the car, but his walking stick was propped up against the wall. Cressida could have seen that when she'd looked back at the house.

Maybe it wasn't Chidlow she was scared of after all.

Karen glanced at the clock as the seconds ticked by. She was waiting for Cressida. She'd prepared one of the family rooms, which was different to the interview rooms. It had brightly coloured sofas and abstract prints on the wall. An attempt to make the surroundings appear less official.

When traumatised victims or witnesses were interviewed, it helped to have a more relaxed atmosphere, although Karen wasn't sure how much of a difference comfy cushions and padded seats would make in Cressida's case. During the journey to the station she'd whimpered and trembled in her mother's arms.

This was a part of the job that Karen didn't enjoy. The young woman only wanted to go home. She wanted to feel safe with her parents and stop thinking about whatever had happened to her last night.

But Karen couldn't let her do that. Because it was looking more and more likely that Cressida and Natasha had been abducted and held against their will. And if that was the case, then they needed to find the perpetrator, and more urgently they needed to find Natasha. The longer she was out there, the less chance they had of getting her back unharmed.

Tomorrow they'd dredge the lake, and the thought made Karen's stomach churn.

She looked at the clock again. It had been nearly an hour since Cressida had arrived at the station. She'd been processed, her clothes taken, her body examined and photographed. Then she'd had to go through the indignity of a rape exam. After all the tests were finished, she would finally be allowed to shower and put on fresh clothes. By Karen's estimation, she should be ready to be interviewed soon.

Karen pulled out her mobile to see if there was any news from Morgan and remembered the call from Alice. She had a voicemail.

'DS Hart, this is Alice Price. I don't know if you remember me. We spoke in the summer. Anyway, my husband is not very keen for me to revisit the past, as I'm sure you can understand, but I can't let it go. A name keeps coming back to me. I think you should look into him. His name is DCI Churchill. I don't know if he's tied up in whatever it was Freeman was up to, but I think there could be a connection. If you ever want to talk, you can reach me on this number. I know what it's like when no one else believes you.'

Karen lowered the phone and stared at the screen. DCI Churchill? The name rang a bell, but she hadn't worked with him personally. Why hadn't Alice mentioned him before?

She'd look back through her notes later. Karen had put together a file containing information on Freeman and his relationship with the Cooks. She was sure the corruption went deeper, much deeper than Freeman himself. But it wasn't easy investigating on your own. Morgan had been helping, using his downtime to go through the files and trying to link officers to cases where the outcomes had been suspicious – focusing on cases where the Cook family had been investigated but charges were dropped, reports lost.

But it was hard to gather the evidence needed to untangle the web of corruption around Freeman. If Chief Constable Grayson lent his support to the inquiry, that could lead to a breakthrough.

If there was corruption, there had to be evidence somewhere. And if they kept looking, they would eventually find it. But if they threw in the towel at this stage, blamed everything on Freeman and then let him off with early retirement, then this would all be for nothing. Karen couldn't live with that outcome.

The door opened and Karen put the mobile back in her pocket, trying to turn her focus back to the current case. But it wasn't Cressida and her mother. It was the officer who'd taken the girl's clothes for processing.

'Is everything all right?' Karen asked. 'Did it go smoothly?'

'She was compliant, poor thing. Absolutely terrified, but she did everything asked of her. We got fingernail scrapes, got her clothes all bagged up and sent to the lab. Hopefully it will give you something to go on.'

111

Karen nodded. 'Did she say anything about Natasha?'

'Is that the other young woman who's missing?'

'Yes.'

The officer shook her head. 'No, she barely spoke. Not even giving a yes or no to some questions. I think she's in shock.'

'Any clues to indicate what happened to her?'

'No, but she'll be ready for her interview soon. She's had a shower and I left her getting dressed with her mother.'

'Thanks for letting me know,' Karen said, and the woman stepped out of the room only to step back in again. 'In fact, they're coming along now.'

She opened the door wider so Cressida and her mother could enter the room.

Karen stayed where she was. She didn't want to crowd the young woman. 'Come in and take a seat, Cressida. Mrs Blake.' She nodded at Cressida's mother.

Both women sat on the red sofa, and Karen sat on a bright blue chair. The primary colours were a bit OTT, but the decor was designed to appeal to children.

'You've done very well so far, Cressida. Now, I know you want to go home, but I've just got to ask you a few questions first. Is that okay?'

Cressida didn't say anything. Her mother reached over, squeezed her hand and said, 'That's okay, isn't it, Cressida? The detective wants to help you.'

Karen leaned forward, resting her elbows on her knees, trying to make eye contact with Cressida, who seemed determined to stare down at her lap.

'Just a few questions. You can have a drink first if you like. I've got some Coke or water here.'

Both Cressida and her mother shook their heads.

'All right. Now, you know we're very concerned about Natasha. Did you go out together last night?'

Cressida didn't say anything, just stared unblinking down at her hands.

'Ethan said he saw you leaving the house together at about nine o'clock last night.'

Cressida hugged her arms around her middle.

'I don't think she remembers,' Jasmine said. 'I think she's blanked it all out.'

'Anything you can remember, anything at all, Cressida, would help us. I'm sure you're worried about Natasha too, aren't you?' Cressida lifted her head and her watery blue eyes met Karen's. 'We really need to find her as soon as possible. Did you go to the pub last night or meet up with friends?'

'I don't remember,' Cressida said in a quiet voice.

'All right, why don't you just tell me what you do remember.'

There was a long pause and then Cressida spoke in a whisper. 'I don't remember anything, except being cold and wet and scared.'

'Do you recall how you got the scratch on your cheek?'

Cressida pressed a hand to her cheek and shook her head.

Despite Karen's patient questioning, they got nowhere. In response to every question about last night, Cressida said she couldn't remember.

'Okay, I know this is really difficult for you. When we were leaving to come to the station, you had to get in the police car, and you got very upset. Can you tell me what upset you?'

Cressida began to tremble again.

'We came outside, walked towards the car and there were police officers around,' Karen said, watching Cressida's reaction carefully. 'Behind us, Edward Chidlow's office was lit up. Have you spoken to him before, Cressida?'

Cressida tightened her arms around her stomach but still didn't say anything.

'And I noticed the groundsman's stick outside. Mike Harrington was there.'

Cressida's breath hitched and tears began to trickle down her face. She brushed her wet cheeks with the back of her hand, shivering despite the warmth of the room.

'Please, she's distressed. That's enough. She's told you she doesn't know. She can't remember. I want to take her home. If she remembers something, you'll be the first to know,' Jasmine Blake insisted, putting her arm around her daughter's shoulders.

It was late and this was hard on Cressida, but could Karen really let her go home when Natasha was still out there?

Questioning Cressida was their best hope. Without her, the chances of finding Natasha were fading fast.

CHAPTER FOURTEEN

It was eight p.m. and Sophie was considering calling it a night. Nothing untoward had come up on any of the background searches for the staff working at Chidlow House. It was all very boring and normal, apart from the groundsman. Now he did have an interesting past.

Sophie stretched and then flicked back through the files on her desk. Mike Harrington was an ex-copper and dog handler and had left the force in a hurry more than three years ago. As far as she could tell from the records, there was no scandal attached to his departure and nothing to indicate he should be a suspect.

She had also followed up with his old boss, who had told her Harrington was one of the best handlers he'd ever worked with, but that he'd fallen apart after the death of his son, jacked in his job and cut off contact with his old friends and colleagues after his divorce. A sad story, but again, no reason to think Harrington would be important to their investigation.

CCTV from business and private residences in the surrounding villages had been a disappointment too. At one stage, Sophie had had her hopes lifted when Mrs Claire Jackson from Harmston reported seeing the girls. Sophie had raced to the woman's large property, thrilled to finally have something to go on. Her excitement started to ebb when she realised the woman had poor eyesight.

Mrs Jackson was eighty-two. On Monday afternoon, she'd gone outside to rake some leaves in her driveway and had taken a tumble. Two girls, who were walking up the hill, stopped to help her back inside and made her a cup of tea.

'They were angels. I could have been on the ground for hours if they hadn't stopped to help.' Mrs Jackson had looked down at her bandaged ankle. 'Twisted, not broken, but I didn't know that at the time.'

'You're sure it was the students we're looking for?' Sophie had asked, pushing two photographs across the table.

'Oh, yes, absolutely. They made me a cup of tea at two p.m. I know because I asked them the time. Wondered how long I'd been out there.'

But the way she'd leaned over the photographs and squinted hadn't given Sophie much cause to share the woman's confidence.

Mrs Jackson had reached for a custard cream and asked Sophie to pour more tea. She was enjoying the company, poor thing, Sophie had thought. Had to be lonely in that huge house.

'Is there anyone helping you get around?' Sophie had asked.

'My sister pops in every day. It's a shame it happened now really. My son is normally in the annexe, but he's currently on a six-month sabbatical in Australia.'

'Oh, you have an annexe?'

'Yes, in the back garden. It gives him some privacy and it's nice for me to have him so close.'

Sophie had stood and peered out of the kitchen window. A small square building, a tiny bungalow, was nestled under the trees. A good idea, really. House prices were going up and up and things weren't easy for first-time buyers. If her parents had the space, Sophie might have ended up doing something like that.

'Could I take a look inside?' It was a long shot, but they were checking outbuildings, so why not an annexe?

'Well, you could but I seem to have misplaced the key. I'm sure it must be around here somewhere.'

She'd started to get to her feet, but Sophie stopped her. 'Don't worry. Do you know where the girls had been going when they found you on Monday?'

'They said they were going back to Chidlow House. Asked me not to tell anyone I'd seen them because they were supposed to be studying.' Her smile faded. 'I said I wouldn't, but if it helps find them . . .'

'You've done the right thing.'

'Oh, I almost forgot,' she'd said, wincing as she got to her feet. 'I've got one of those daft doorbell thingybobs.'

'Sorry?'

'You know, they record people when they come to the door. My son fitted it a few months back.'

'You have video footage of the girls?'

'Pass me my phone, dear.'

Sophie had done as she'd asked and waited impatiently for Mrs Jackson to access the video.

Finally, Mrs Jackson had passed the phone to Sophie. 'Here, you do it. I can never work the blasted thing.'

Sophie had quickly accessed the footage from Monday afternoon at two p.m. and held her breath as Natasha and Cressida appeared on the screen. They walked either side of Mrs Jackson, gently supporting the old woman as they helped her into the house. There was sound too. Sophie found it sad to hear them talking with no idea what would happen later in the week. Mrs Jackson had been telling them about her son and how she was looking forward to him coming home because she felt so much safer when he was living in the annexe in the garden.

When Sophie looked up, she noticed Mrs Jackson's eyes had filled with tears.

'I really do hope you find them.'

Sophie had gone back through all the recordings from the doorbell camera but hadn't seen the young women again.

'Why do the recordings stop on Monday?' Sophie had asked, puzzled. 'Were there no alerts?' She found it hard to believe there had been nothing, not even false alarms triggering the camera.

'Battery ran out. I'm not sure how to charge it.'

Sophie had to help the old woman put the battery on charge before she returned to the station, feeling frustrated at her lack of progress.

Now, Sophie had put down the files and picked up her mug, intending to wash it before going home, when the phone on her desk rang. She picked it up. 'DC Jones.'

'Oh, hello. This is Mr Clark. I spoke to you earlier. I'm the owner of the restaurant in Harmston.'

A flicker of hope. Sophie sat back down. 'Yes, Mr Clark. Did you remember something?'

'Actually, yes. Like I told you, I checked the CCTV camera from outside and there was no sign of either girl last night or in the early hours of the morning. But there was something about the photograph you showed me that rang a bell.'

'Go on.' Sophie picked up a pen and pulled the pad towards her.

'I was sure I recognised one of them, you see, but I couldn't remember from where or when. So I went back through the CCTV from inside the restaurant and I was right. One of the students had dinner here on Monday evening.'

'Which one?'

'The one with brown hair. Natasha, wasn't it?'

'Yes, that's right. Natasha. Was she alone?'

'She was having dinner with a man. Anyway, I haven't taken a really good look at the recording yet. I think they were here for an hour or so. I thought you'd want to know straightaway.'

'Thank you. Are you open now if I come around? Can I take a copy of the video?'

'Yes, pop around whenever you like. We don't shut until ten and it's as dead as a doornail in here unfortunately.'

'That's a shame,' Sophie commiserated, but her mind was jumping ahead with the excitement of having a lead. She shut down her computer as she talked to him. 'Was anyone else with them? Or just the two of them?'

'I can't remember if anyone else joined them. I haven't watched all the footage yet.'

'Okay, not a problem. I can do that. I should be with you in about twenty minutes.'

'Right. See you then.'

Sophie quickly shrugged on her coat. Though she knew Rick was still at work because his mobile was sitting next to his computer and his computer was still switched on, he was nowhere to be seen.

Sophie scrawled him a quick note, grabbed her handbag and left the station.

It was wet and dark, and the roads were still flooded. She parked outside the restaurant, which was on Harmston High Street. It had only been open since the summer. Harmston was a quiet village with few amenities. So the restaurant, which served Italian food – pasta and pizza – was a welcome addition.

She walked into the restaurant and her mouth watered at the smell of cooking. There was only one couple in there, sitting near the window. Mr Clark had been right. It was very quiet. The man she guessed was the owner was standing miserably at the back of the restaurant, arms folded over his chest, but he brightened when he saw Sophie.

'Ah, we can talk in the office,' Mr Clark said quietly after the introductions were out of the way, and he asked another member of staff to keep an eye on the front of house.

119

He led Sophie through the kitchen and into a small room at the back of the restaurant. He pulled out a chair for her at the desk and nudged the mouse to make the computer screen come alive.

There she was – Natasha, smiling, almost glowing with happiness at the table by the window that Sophie had just walked past.

She was sitting opposite a man. Unfortunately he had his back to the camera, and the camera only caught about a third of his head. He wore a blue jumper with a blue checked shirt underneath and had dark hair, but apart from that it was hard to get any more information.

He was sitting down, but Sophie judged he was only an inch or two taller than Natasha.

She leaned forward. 'This is great. Can I play it?'

'Absolutely,' Mr Clark said, and he showed Sophie the controls. 'Can I get you something to drink? Maybe something to eat. Some pasta?'

'Oh no, really. I don't want to put you out,' Sophie said. 'I'll be fine.'

'You'll be doing me a favour. I've just made a fresh batch of tomato and basil sauce and I'm not exactly run off my feet tonight. Go on. What do you say? Just a small bowl?'

'Okay, that would be lovely, thanks,' Sophie said, tempted by the smell of garlic.

After Mr Clark left, Sophie began to watch the footage. Natasha was animated and clearly not in distress. In fact, she seemed really happy. Sophie waited for the man to turn around, but he didn't. At one point he reached over and filled up Natasha's wine glass. Sophie raised an eyebrow. Natasha was only seventeen.

When Mr Clark came back with a bowl of pasta and a glass of water, Sophie thanked him.

'I thought maybe it was her father with her at first,' he said, looking at the screen. 'He's a bit older than her, don't you think?'

Sophie nodded, but it was hard to tell how old the man was with only this view to go on, and she knew Mr Layton, Natasha's father, had auburn hair.

The man sitting opposite Natasha most definitely wasn't her father.

With her eyes fixed on the screen, Sophie sampled the pasta. It was delicious. 'Lovely,' she said. 'You deserve to be much busier than you are.'

'Well, spread the word,' he said. 'Let your friends know.'

Sophie smiled. 'I will do.' She was now twenty minutes through the footage, and the man still hadn't turned around. There was no way she'd be able to identify him from this.

'Do you have any other angles from inside the restaurant that would give us a better view?' Sophie asked.

Mr Clark shook his head sadly. 'I'm afraid not. We've only got one camera inside. I set it up myself, trying to save money.'

'What about when they entered or left the restaurant?'

'No. I mean, we do have a CCTV camera outside, as you know, but unfortunately that gets overwritten every forty-eight hours. I didn't think there'd be a reason to keep it any longer than that. And the more data you store, the more expensive it is on the cloud plan I've signed up to. That's why I installed the internal one myself, to save a bit of money and use a hard drive to store the recordings.'

'I understand. Do you remember how they paid? Can I see the card receipts for Monday night?'

He gave her a regretful look. 'You can, but I remember he paid cash. It stuck in my mind because it was unusual. Most people pay by card these days.'

Sophie stabbed a piece of fusilli with her fork. 'Shame,' she said. 'It's not going to be very easy to identify him.'

Mr Clark looked sympathetic. 'No, I don't envy you that job. But could I tempt you with a bit of garlic bread to go with that pasta?'

Sophie shook her head. 'No, really. You've been kind enough.' And as she stared at the footage, she forgot about Mr Clark lingering by her shoulder and instead focused on all the details of the man on the screen. Was there anything unusual about him? Any birthmarks? Tattoos? Nothing she could see.

Natasha looked normal, happy. Had this man hurt her? Was he the one who had taken Natasha and Cressida? Sophie rubbed her eyes and sighed. Even if they couldn't identify him from the footage, it might help jog Cressida's memory.

Sophie called Karen from the car when she'd finished viewing the footage.

'So you can't see his face at all?' Karen asked.

'No, it's going to be very hard to identify him.'

'Right. I think we need to go and see the Laytons. Did you take screenshots?'

'I did, yes. None of them are very clear, although they are very good images of Natasha.'

'All right. Well, it's going to be difficult, but I think we need to see them in person. Let's see if Natasha's parents can identify him or if they know who she was going out with on Monday night.'

'Do you want to meet me there?' Sophie asked.

'Yes, I'm going to leave Chidlow House now. They've stopped the search.'

Sophie couldn't miss the sadness in Karen's tone. 'Oh, I'm sorry,' Sophie said. 'It's so difficult when everyone wants to keep searching, but there's not much point when it's this dark.'

'No. They'll start up again tomorrow at first light. We're going to dredge the lake.' Karen paused and then added, 'I can meet you at the Laytons' in about ten minutes. Do you have their address?'

Sophie confirmed she did before hanging up.

The heavy despondency in Karen's tone really hit home. It wasn't often Karen got that way. She was usually the one driving forward for answers, ever the optimist. Believing they were always just one step away from a breakthrough.

But now that they'd found Cressida so traumatised, it didn't bode well for Natasha. Sophie didn't have as much experience as Karen, but even she knew that.

Karen's Honda Civic looked tiny in the enormous driveway. She was standing beside the fountain close to the entrance, gazing up at the Laytons' property.

It was certainly a beautiful house. A large, red-brick, detached home with steps up to the entrance and a Virginia creeper winding its way over the walls, showing off its beautiful red leaves.

She parked her car beside Karen's.

'Have you been here long?' Sophie asked, walking over to Karen.

'No, I've only just got here myself. Ready?'

Sophie nodded. She had the screenshots on her phone. There hadn't been time to print them out.

They knocked on the front door and waited. As the doorbell chimed inside, Karen said, 'I spoke to the family liaison officer. It's Siobhan. She knows we're coming.'

Before Sophie could reply, Siobhan opened the door. 'Hello,' she said. 'Mr and Mrs Layton are expecting you. They're in the kitchen.'

Sophie walked behind Siobhan and Karen into a sleek, modern kitchen. Everything was white. The tiles on the floor, the units, the sink and even the taps. The effect was dazzling.

Huge sliding glass doors lined one wall, looking out on to the garden. A large white sofa sat in front of the glass, and to its left was a seating area and a dining table for ten.

Imogen Layton stood beside the kitchen counter, leaning on it. 'Detectives,' she said in a strained voice. 'Can I offer you a cup of tea, coffee?'

Todd Layton rose from the dining table, where he'd been sitting with his head in his hands. 'Forget tea or coffee,' he said. 'Have you found her?'

'We haven't found her yet,' Karen said quickly. 'As you know, we've found Cressida, and we're trying to find out if she knows where Natasha is.'

'Why isn't she talking?' Imogen pushed her hair back from her face. 'Surely she can just tell you where Natasha is.'

'She says she doesn't know.'

'But that makes no sense,' Mr Layton said. 'She was with Natasha. They left together last night.'

'I know, sir,' Karen said, 'but Cressida says she can't remember what happened.'

'She has to remember,' he said, raking a hand through his thick auburn hair. 'That's just ridiculous. How can she not know what happened? She was *with* Natasha.'

The man's pain was clear to see, and Sophie awkwardly clutched the files to her chest. From his point of view, they should have carried on questioning Cressida through the night until she remembered. That's what anyone would want the police to do for their daughter, but they couldn't.

If Cressida said she didn't know what had happened to Natasha, they had to respect that. There was a chance that they'd left the house together and then separated, though it was unlikely. The most logical scenario, in Sophie's opinion, was that the girls had gone somewhere together. Something terrible had happened, and in an attempt to protect herself, Cressida had blocked it out.

She understood Todd Layton's pain. If it had been her, if someone in her family was missing, she'd want Cressida questioned over and over again until she remembered, as cruel as that might be.

'They've got something to show you,' Siobhan said. 'Here.' She put her hand on Imogen's forearm. 'Why don't I make us all a cup of tea. You can sit at the table and the detectives can tell you what they've found.'

Imogen remained frozen to the spot. 'You found something?' She looked horrified, as though she expected them to say they'd found something of Natasha's, something that might indicate that her daughter was dead.

'It's CCTV footage,' Sophie said quickly. 'We want you to have a look at it. It's Natasha in the company of a man we would like to identify.'

'With a *man*?' Todd Layton said. 'Who? She wouldn't be with a man. You mean one of the teachers from the course?'

'I don't think so,' Sophie replied. 'We can't rule it out though. We hoped you could have a look at the images and see if you recognise him. It's not the best angle, I'm afraid.'

She walked to the dining table, put her phone down and accessed the images as Todd and Imogen stood either side of her.

Karen pulled out a chair. 'Why don't we all sit down,' she said.

Imogen picked up the phone first and flipped through the screenshots, shaking her head. 'Is this all you've got? There's no shots of his face at all.'

'I know,' Sophie said. 'That's down to the angle of the camera, unfortunately.'

'When was this taken?' Mr Layton asked, taking the phone from his wife.

'Monday evening, seven thirty p.m.'

'This Monday just gone?' Imogen asked.

Sophie nodded.

'That makes no sense. I spoke to Natasha at six o'clock on Monday. She told me she was going to spend the evening studying. She said the place was a total bore because there was nothing to do, so she may as well study.' She shook her head, pressing a hand to her forehead. 'I don't understand.'

'Is there an actual video of this?' Mr Layton asked. 'I want to see it.'

'There is, but we haven't got it with us at the moment, sir,' Sophie said. 'This is the best view of the man who was with Natasha that night.'

He frowned. 'In this picture he's got his hand on hers.' He looked up angrily at Sophie. 'Who is this man? Surely you must be able to use some kind of recognition software or something, in this day and age?'

'We won't be able to do that from this footage,' Karen said. 'We'd hoped you would know who Natasha was out with on Monday evening. Any names you can think of could be helpful.'

He shook his head. 'Natasha wouldn't, she couldn't . . .' He trailed off.

'I know it's a bit of a shock,' Karen said, 'but if you do have any ideas . . . If anything comes to you later, then please tell Siobhan and she'll pass it on to us. We'll keep you updated. Siobhan's staying here tonight – is that right?'

Siobhan nodded. 'Right.'

'If there are any developments overnight, Siobhan will wake you.'

'I don't think I'll get any sleep tonight,' Imogen said.

Mr Layton grabbed the phone again and stared at the image of his daughter. 'I'd like to get my hands on this man.'

'We need to identify the man and talk to him, but we don't yet know if this man took Natasha, or even if Natasha is with him now,' Karen said.

'I'm not an idiot, Detective,' Todd Layton snarled. 'I'm well aware that it's very likely I'm looking at the man who's taken my daughter.'

CHAPTER FIFTEEN

Karen got into her car and checked the time. Quarter to ten, and she felt bone-weary. She craved a glass of wine, but the Co-op in Branston would be shut by the time she got there, and she didn't have any wine at home.

She drove away from the Laytons' huge house and a short distance away pulled into a lay-by, where she sent text messages to Morgan and Rick letting them know the Laytons hadn't been able to identify the man with Natasha on Monday night.

It was too late to phone Alice and ask for more information on DCI Churchill. She'd have to return her call tomorrow.

Despite the fact that she felt tired enough to drop off while she was standing up, she knew she wouldn't sleep well tonight. She needed someone to talk to.

The logical choice was to call in on Anthony, her old boss. She could ask him what he knew about DCI Churchill, but it was too late to visit him. Anthony was retired, happy with his slippers and his crossword. He'd probably be tucked up in bed by now.

So Karen called the person she'd come to rely on over the past few months.

It took a while for Morgan to answer. 'Karen, everything all right?'

'Yes, it's not about the case,' she said hurriedly, knowing he'd assume she was calling about Cressida or Natasha. She told him about Alice's voicemail. 'Do you know DCI Churchill?'

'No, but then I haven't been in Lincolnshire as long as you have. I take it he's an officer from the Lincolnshire force?'

'I think so,' Karen said. 'I've heard of him, but I haven't worked with him. I was going to head home, maybe check through some of the old files to see if I could find any mention of him in the cases Freeman worked, try to work out if there's any connection between the two men.'

'That's a good idea,' Morgan said, but he didn't volunteer to join her, which surprised Karen.

'I could bring the files to you if you fancy going over them with me for an hour. I mean, unless you're busy . . .' She trailed off.

He didn't answer straightaway.

Morgan was a night owl, usually not going to bed before midnight, but he sounded preoccupied tonight. She wondered if he'd dozed off and her call had woken him.

'You could come to my house, but I haven't got any wine,' Karen said, 'and I could really do with a glass of red.'

'I'm sorry, Karen,' Morgan said. 'I'm actually busy at the moment. Jill's here. We've just had dinner.'

'Oh, I'm sorry,' Karen said, sitting up straighter in the driver's seat and pressing her hand to her forehead. She hadn't even considered the possibility he'd be seeing someone tonight. Jill was new on the scene.

'So it's still going well between you two? That's good,' Karen said. 'Sorry to disturb you. I'll see you tomorrow.'

'It's fine. You didn't disturb us. It's just that's why I can't go through the files tonight,' Morgan explained.

'Of course, yes. It was stupid of me to call anyway. It's late. I'll let you go. Give my regards to Jill.' Then Karen hung up.

She'd completely forgotten about Jill. How had that happened? Was she really so focused on herself and her own problems she didn't consider anyone else actually having a personal life? Just because her life began and ended with work didn't mean that was the case for everyone else.

He'd told Karen about his date with Jill a few weeks ago, but had Morgan mentioned her again since? She couldn't remember. No, he couldn't have done. She would have remembered if he had. She wasn't that self-involved, was she?

They hadn't been seeing each other long. If she remembered correctly, Jill was a cousin of Lisa in admin, and Lisa had decided they'd make a great couple.

That was a few weeks ago now, so Karen guessed they must have hit it off. *Good for him*, she thought.

She meant it. She was glad he'd found someone. Morgan deserved to be happy, didn't he? So why did she suddenly feel so alone?

She'd come to depend on Morgan. They hadn't done much more than pore over the files together, but having someone there, trying to help, even if they hadn't got very far, had made her feel better. Knowing someone was on her side, someone who wanted justice for her and her family, had been invaluable.

She shoved her mobile back in her bag and drove towards Branston. It was just after ten when she got home, and instead of going inside after she parked the car, she walked along the main road and then turned on to the long driveway leading to Branston Hall. The bar would still be open.

The trees rustled in the wind. Almost-bare branches reached up to the dark, cloudy sky. Thank goodness it wasn't still raining. She headed inside, through the stone-pillared entrance, walking on the soft red carpet. She was lucky, having this place just across the road.

The bar and restaurant were mainly for residents of the hotel, but she knew a couple of locals who used the bar. Though they probably wouldn't be here at this time. She scanned the bar to see if Paul, one of the regulars, was about, but there was no sign of him. Shame. She would have liked to see a friendly face and had a chat to pass the time, take her mind off the day.

The bar was quiet. They'd stopped serving food and the tables were empty. A couple sat huddled together on the sofa in front of the huge fire, but there were no other customers in the bar area.

The chap behind the bar looked up as Karen walked towards him. 'Quiet tonight?' she asked.

'It is now; we were busy earlier and there's a big group in the restaurant,' he said. 'What can I get you?'

'I'll have a glass of red, please,' she said, and he poured her a glass of Shiraz. 'I'll pay now,' she added, not wanting to be tempted into a second glass.

After she paid, she took a seat beside the palms at the window. It was cooler there than in the more comfortable seating area by the fire, but she wanted to give the couple some privacy. Besides, being around loved-up people wasn't an attractive proposition at the moment.

She could see the tops of the flames from where she sat. She loved that fire, the huge cosiness of it, blasting out heat. The Hall had a very different feel to Chidlow House, she thought as she sipped her wine. Branston Hall felt comfortable, lived in and loved, even though it was a hotel now. She wondered whether the echoes of the past made a difference to how people viewed places. Not the house itself, because that was obviously just raw materials – bricks and mortar – but how the stories and history of a place might influence opinions. The portraits of the sad women on the staircase had probably influenced how Karen felt about Chidlow House.

There were many big old houses concentrated in this small area. Branston Hall, of course. Washingborough Hall wasn't far away. Then there was Hainton House, which was near the pub in the village. Hainton, a former rectory, had been converted into flats; Washingborough Hall, like Branston, was a hotel; and some of the other larger family homes had been converted into nursing homes. Large houses weren't often privately owned these days, for good reason. It cost a fortune to keep up with repairs.

As she sipped her wine, she scrolled through her phone looking back at the reports Sophie and Rick had filed that day. None of the teachers had backgrounds that would warrant suspicion. Even so, she'd ask Sophie or Rick to follow up with them in person tomorrow. It was easier to read people when they were sitting in front of you. Not so easy when you were talking on the phone and you couldn't see their facial expressions.

She looked at her half-finished glass of wine and felt a pang of guilt. It seemed wrong to stop working, to relax, when Natasha was still missing. Logically Karen knew that she couldn't work twenty-four hours a day, and there was no point continuing the search when darkness fell. And there were only so many times she could ask a traumatised teenager the same questions before having to let her go home.

Her phone pinged with an incoming email. It was from Farzana. She and Rick were working late tonight. She reported that the interior of the house had been searched except Chidlow's study, the room beside the bathroom on the girls' floor and the cupboard in the bathroom. Chidlow had told Farzana he'd been unable to find the keys for the locked room and cupboard. He'd insisted both were only used for storage.

Tomorrow she would make sure Chidlow found the missing keys or she'd get a locksmith in to open them. You didn't solve cases if you weren't thorough.

Karen's stomach rumbled. She would have bought some crisps to go with her wine, but they only sold vegetable crisps, which Karen didn't like and enjoyed even less when they were three pounds a packet.

She selected the Home Curries app on her phone and put in an order for chicken tikka masala and mushroom rice. Probably not the healthiest choice for dinner, but she loved curry, and the food from the small Branston takeaway was excellent.

She finished her wine, then carried her empty glass back to the bar and thanked Steve for her drink. She walked along the cut-through by the village hall to pick up her curry. There were deep puddles along the path, and by the time she got to the curry house her boots were covered in mud.

Once home, she plated her dinner up in the kitchen and poured herself a glass of fizzy water. Then she walked across to the sideboard, lifted her glass in a toast and, gazing at the photograph of her husband, said, 'Happy anniversary, Josh.'

Time had made it easier. She could look at his photograph without tears springing to her eyes now. But she still had the burning need to find out who was responsible for covering up the truth behind his and Tilly's deaths.

She now knew who'd been driving the car that had forced him off the road. Technically Charlie Cook had killed her family, but it was all tied into the corruption in the force. Freeman had covered up for the Cooks and made the crash look like an accident.

Her husband and daughter had perished, and Freeman had sidled up to her offering comfort and false pity. It made Karen's blood boil to think how easily she'd been taken in.

She turned away from the photograph, grabbed a fork from the cutlery drawer and took her plate to the table. She wouldn't think about it now. She couldn't. Tomorrow she'd phone Alice Price.

Tonight she'd look through the files for an hour or so and see what she could find on DCI Churchill.

She didn't make it to the full hour. After thirty minutes of flipping through the paperwork she'd accumulated, her eyelids were drooping shut so she headed up to bed.

In bed, she stared at the ceiling, trying to push away thoughts about the corruption inquiry and her current case, but she kept thinking about Morgan and Jill. Would it be awkward tomorrow? Had Morgan been getting fed up of her relying on him so much but been too polite to say so?

She gave up trying to fall asleep and began to listen to an audiobook on her phone. An hour later, with the gentle tones of David Suchet's voice reading *Dead Man's Folly* filling her ears, she finally managed to drift off.

CHAPTER SIXTEEN

By eleven p.m. Morgan had been scrolling through work files on his laptop. He'd been tired but had a feeling he'd missed something.

Guilt niggled away at him. He'd only spent an hour with Jill tonight, just enough time to cook and eat some pasta. He hadn't wanted to cancel their arrangement and let her down, but he'd been preoccupied and definitely not the best company. Of course, she'd quickly noticed something was bothering him.

After Karen's call, he'd tried to concentrate on what Jill was saying, to take part in the conversation, but he'd found it hard to focus on anything other than the case. It was unfair of him. Jill deserved better, but he couldn't stop worrying about Karen. He didn't want to leave her to deal with the situation alone. This investigation was a tough one for all of them, but it was especially hard for Karen. Cases involving kids always were, and she was still struggling to come to terms with Freeman's betrayal.

The meal tonight had been the fourth evening he'd spent time with Jill. She worked at the university as an administrator. She was unattached, attractive and had a way of chatting and telling stories that put Morgan at ease. She was a talker, he wasn't. He preferred to sit back and listen.

Definitely an introvert to her extrovert, but he liked her. She made him feel comfortable. He didn't feel like he had to pretend to be something he wasn't to keep her interested.

They'd got on so well he'd started to think that this might develop into something meaningful. But then work had encroached, filling his head so full of theories and what-ifs that he couldn't concentrate on anything else.

He really needed an off switch. Other people managed it, didn't they? Why couldn't he?

There were plenty of police officers who were happily married with kids. They must have found a way to balance home life with work. To leave cases at the door when they returned to their families. But he found it impossible. How was he supposed to stop thinking about the missing young woman?

He'd checked in with Farzana, who was still at the station looking at yet more CCTV footage as they'd widened the search parameters, but there were no new developments.

He'd made a plan for the next day. At first light, the search team would return to the Chidlow property. He'd asked the superintendent for more bodies and intended on expanding the search deeper into the surrounding woodland that encircled Chidlow's land.

He'd also organised the underwater team to dredge the lake. It wasn't a huge area and he thought they'd be able to complete the job within a day. He hoped they wouldn't find anything, but they had to check. The mud on Cressida's jeans indicated she'd been near the shore of the lake at some point.

The reddish mud was distinctive, although perhaps not unique. It was possible she'd got the mud on her jeans from somewhere else. Goodness knows – with all the rain they'd been having, there was no shortage of mud. They'd know more once Forensics had finished with her clothes.

As he clicked on the next folder, he remembered Jill's face as she'd left. One thing he liked about her was that she was easy to read. He didn't have to puzzle over what she was thinking. Tonight she had looked disappointed and confused, which was understandable. He'd gone from being attentive and interested in what she had to say to being monosyllabic and distracted while she chatted to him.

Every time she'd tried a different subject, his mind had returned to the current case. In the end she'd taken the hint, and though he'd felt bad, he'd been relieved when she left.

'I can see you're not quite here tonight,' she'd said with a regretful smile. 'Why don't I go home? Maybe we can meet up next weekend for dinner.'

Morgan had agreed. At least she hadn't written him off completely. Hopefully by next weekend the case would be solved, and his mind would be clear. Sure, he'd have other cases to deal with, but nothing this major.

He rubbed his eyes and stretched, thinking how tired he was. He'd have an early start tomorrow. Yes, plans were in place and the inspector in charge of the search knew what he was doing, but as SIO, Morgan was determined to be there before the team got started.

He walked through to the kitchen to finish stacking the dishwasher, and as he stood by the sink, he glanced out as a sudden squall of wind blew leaves against the kitchen window.

He hoped Natasha was safe, warm and dry somewhere, but he had a bad feeling about this case.

He shook his head. *A bad feeling.* He was starting to sound like Rick with his superstitions. All that nonsense about the haunting of Chidlow House must have got to him. Morgan was a practical man and he dealt with facts, not emotions. All the same, when another gust of wind shook more leaves from the trees outside, he shivered.

◆ ◆ ◆

Early the following morning, Karen stood in the library and stared out over Chidlow's property towards the grey, choppy lake. The underwater search team would be here soon. Now that all the students had gone home, except Ella Seaton, the house was oddly quiet. Karen found the stillness unnerving.

Chidlow had allowed them to use his library as a temporary incident room. Doyle had provided the usual, very weak coffee. This morning he hadn't even bothered with biscuits. As her stomach rumbled, Karen wished she hadn't missed breakfast. She must have eaten a thousand calories for dinner last night, so why was she so hungry this morning?

'Everything all right?'

Karen turned and saw Morgan entering the library. He smiled and she smiled back, pretending everything was fine and not awkward at all. It shouldn't be. She didn't know why she felt uncomfortable. She'd mentioned going over the files last night, but he was busy. That was all there was to it. It wasn't a snub. They were still friends. He was still her boss. It didn't change their working relationship at all.

'The underwater search unit hasn't arrived yet,' Karen said, nodding at the lake. 'They should be here soon though.'

Morgan nodded. 'Inspector Grant is leading the main search team through the woodland on the north-east side of the property this morning.'

'The area behind the lake?'

Morgan nodded, but before he could say anything else, the door opened and PC Smith appeared.

'Here they are,' Smith said, turning to smile at Sophie, who was standing behind him. She carried a cardboard tray of takeaway coffee cups and a paper bag.

She held them up. 'Pastries and strong coffee. I thought you might need it.'

Morgan beamed at her. 'Good thinking.'

Sophie put the tray down on the table and they helped themselves to coffee.

Karen sighed with pleasure. It was a million times better than the stuff Doyle had provided. 'Where's Rick?'

'I left him out front. He's just taking a phone call, following up a reference from one of the teachers. He should be here in a minute.'

Karen nodded. Sophie and Rick had worked their way through all the teachers who'd taught on the study course, but had found nothing suggesting the staff were involved in the disappearance of the students.

'This place is spooky. Have you seen those paintings?' Rick asked as he walked into the library, heading straight for the bag of pastries and selecting a pain au chocolat.

'The portraits?' Karen asked.

'Yes, and the hunting ones. Not sure why anyone would want to look at pictures like that day after day.' He shuddered. 'Not very cheerful. Have they started searching the lake yet?' he asked, then bit into the pastry.

'Not yet. But the team should be here soon,' Karen said.

There was a knock at the open door. Lord Chidlow stood on the threshold.

'Good morning,' Karen said.

'Good morning,' he replied, looking down his hawkish nose at her. 'I see you've brought in some supplies.' He eyed the pastries.

'Yes, help yourself,' Sophie said, and Karen was surprised he did so, selecting a croissant.

'Have there been any developments?' Chidlow asked, closely inspecting the croissant before taking a small bite.

'Nothing new since yesterday,' Rick said. 'I've heard local stories about the haunting of this place. What can you tell us?'

Karen wondered whether to shut the conversation down and direct Rick's focus back to the plan for the day. They had a lot to get through, but she supposed an informal chat with Chidlow over pastries gave her a chance to observe the man. Maybe he'd lower his guard. There was no denying Cressida had reacted very strongly last night when they'd left the property and Chidlow had been standing by the window. And hadn't Ella Seaton said Cressida was interested in older men?

'Yes, that's right. One of the most haunted houses in Britain,' Chidlow said with pride.

Karen doubted that. She'd never heard the ghost story and she'd lived locally for years.

'It's a sad tale,' Chidlow continued. 'My grandmother told it to me. The story was passed down over generations. There were three women in the Chidlow family, including my great-great-grandmother, who drowned themselves in the lake.'

'How awful,' Sophie said.

Chidlow nodded. 'It was a long time ago now, but one of the women is said to haunt the house, whispering her torment as water drips from her gown.'

'Have you ever heard her?' Sophie asked.

Chidlow smiled and shook his head. 'It's said that only sensitive souls can hear her. Those who are mentally fragile themselves.'

Karen frowned. 'What a load of codswallop.'

'You heard the whispering, didn't you?' Doyle said.

He was standing behind Karen. She hadn't realised the man had come into the room until he spoke. He moved so quietly around the house – creepily so.

Karen said nothing.

'I'm sure you did,' Doyle insisted. 'Just yesterday you asked me about it. You came out of the room you'd been searching and you said you'd heard something.'

'Oh, you should be careful,' Edward Chidlow said, tearing off a piece of croissant with his long, tapered fingers. 'It's supposed to be a warning if you hear the ghost of Chidlow House.'

Karen managed not to roll her eyes. 'I'll keep my guard up,' she said dryly.

'Yes, you should be careful,' Doyle said. 'The last person who heard the whispering and sound of dripping water was Miss King.'

'The teacher who fell off the roof?' Rick asked, giving Karen a worried look.

'For goodness' sake,' Karen said irritably. 'I didn't hear a ghost.'

'Then what did you hear?' Doyle asked.

'Most likely a leak and students whispering somewhere. Or the house could have one of those old calling devices used to communicate with servants. What were they called? Voice pipes? Sound could travel in unusual ways in a house like this.'

'I'm not aware of Chidlow House ever having any speaking tubes,' Edward Chidlow said. 'I could be wrong, I suppose.'

Rick was still staring at Karen, wide-eyed. 'Can't hurt to be careful, Sarge.'

Karen gave him a withering look. 'Right. That's enough ghost stories for one morning. Rick, you're with me. Let's get down to the lake so we're ready to meet the search team. Sophie, I want you to contact the family liaison officers, please. We need to check on Cressida. She could have remembered something that could help us track down Natasha.'

'Yes, Sarge,' Sophie said, putting down her coffee and pulling out her mobile phone.

As she turned to leave, Karen caught the expression on Morgan's face. He was frowning, looked preoccupied.

She paused, about to ask if he was okay, when PC Smith appeared at the door again. 'Sarge,' he said, looking at Karen and then glancing over to Morgan. 'The underwater search team is here.'

CHAPTER SEVENTEEN

Rick and Karen stood by the edge of the lake, watching the team unload its equipment. In the distance, there were calls from the search party heading into the woods. The lake's surface was still now that the wind had died down. An old blue rowboat with peeling paint and battered oars was pulled up on the shore. Lord Chidlow said it hadn't been used in years.

The team had brought a small vessel on a trailer pulled by a Land Rover. Lord Chidlow had not been pleased when he realised they were going to drive across his pristine lawn, especially after all the rain. Deep tracks of mud had been churned up by the wheels, but it couldn't be helped.

Jed Morris, the head of the underwater search team, explained the procedure to Rick and Karen. 'First we'll take the boat around and see if there's anything visible from the surface. If not, that's when we'll start to send the divers down. We'll do it section by section, fanning out so we don't miss anything. It's not a huge area so we should be done by the end of today.'

'Don't you have scanning equipment?' Karen asked. 'I thought you'd be able to use that to locate any unexpected objects on the bottom of the lake.'

'We do, but unfortunately the scanning equipment is being used by another team this morning. We could have put off the search, but I understand you're keen to get started.'

'Yes. We've got a missing girl and we're worried that she could be . . .' Karen trailed off, looking at the lake.

'Of course, yes. We'll cover every inch of the lake. You don't need to worry. If she's there, we'll find her.'

'Is it going to take longer without the scanning equipment?' Karen asked.

Jed nodded. 'Yes, but like I said it's not a large area.'

'All right. Thanks,' Karen said.

As Jed walked away, Rick turned to her and said, 'Seems a bit daft having a diving team but not the scanning equipment to go with it.'

'Cutbacks,' she said.

Rick lifted his collar as the wind picked up again, sending ripples over the surface of the lake. They stood in silence as they watched the vessel do a slow loop around the lake. There was a cluster of weeds in the centre that looked like a miniature green island.

'Right,' Karen said. 'Rick, you can stay here, see if they find anything. I'm going to walk back.'

Rick frowned as Karen started to head off in the opposite direction to the house. 'Where are you going, Sarge? It's that way,' he said, jerking his thumb towards Chidlow House.

'I want to call in at the groundsman's cottage first,' Karen said. 'I think we should talk to him again today. Officially. Bring him up to the house.'

'Then why don't you just call him on his mobile and get him to meet you there?'

'He doesn't have a mobile,' Karen said.

Rick looked aghast. 'I thought everyone had a mobile these days.'

'Most people do. I guess he takes this living-off-the-grid thing seriously. Anyway, the cottage isn't far. Just on the other side of these trees, according to Chidlow. I'll see you back at the house.'

'You really want me to stand here until the search is finished?' Rick asked.

Karen kept her tone serious. 'Absolutely. If they find something, I want to be the first to know.'

Rick sighed, folding his arms over his chest. 'You spoil me, Sarge. I get all the best jobs.'

'I'm just messing with you. Stay here to see if they spot anything from the surface. If not, then head back. DI Morgan's got a long list of tasks waiting.'

As Karen walked into the woods, rain started to fall again. It was only a light mist at first, tiny drops settling on her hair and coat. She trudged through the damp leaves, thinking how much quieter it was as she walked between the trees.

The groundsman was odd. No doubt about it. But Sophie had filled her in on his background, and Karen knew what losing a child did to a person. It changed you. If living out here like a hermit made him feel better, helped him cope, then who was she to judge?

But in this case, he had been in the vicinity when the young women went missing. A single man living alone. She'd be a fool to rule him out as a suspect. When the two students had left Chidlow House on Thursday evening, he could have run into them out here. Karen looked around at the tall trees, the wet leaves. It was so quiet. No one would hear. No one would have seen.

She walked further into the woods, looking through the gaps between the trees for the cottage that Lord Chidlow had told her was close.

But there was no sign of a building, and the rain was starting to fall more heavily now. Karen hunched her shoulders and walked faster. Then, to her right, she noticed a movement between the trunks of two hazel trees. She froze. Only the caw of a crow broke the silence.

She waited, then heard the crack of a twig. Her heart was pounding, her mouth dry.

Ridiculous. It was probably just an animal.

'Is anyone there?' she called out.

Maybe it was the groundsman out for a walk. But no, his dog would be barking now, alerting him to her presence. She raked a hand through her wet hair and scanned the surrounding trees. Everything looked the same. She walked a little further, called out again.

Another caw from a crow made her jump. She pressed a hand to her chest as the rain pattered around her. This was stupid. It was all that talk of ghosts earlier that had set her on edge. Why be afraid of a ghost? It was people in the here and now that could hurt you, as she well knew.

Karen thought the idea of malevolent spirits was odd. If there was such a thing as ghosts, wouldn't it be the people who loved you most who'd come back? Those that loved so deeply they couldn't bear to leave? Surely that emotion would be more powerful than any malicious intent.

Water was trickling down the back of her neck now, and she shivered, turning around in a circle, disoriented. All the trees looked the same. She'd been a fool to walk so far into the woods. It was easy to see how someone could get lost. She looked up at the sky, looking for the sun, trying to work out her position in respect to the lake and the house. But the sun was firmly hidden behind grey clouds.

She walked up to a large oak tree, touching her hand to the wet bark. Moss was growing on the right side of the tree. She was tempted to turn around and walk back to the lake. But she'd come this far, and she really did want to speak to the groundsman.

She carried on walking, and after a moment noticed a curl of smoke above the trees. Heartened by the sight, Karen moved faster, the rain hammering down now.

She stepped into a clearing, and the cottage appeared in front of her like something out of a fairy tale. She rushed up to the small covered porch. The cottage was constructed of pale stone and looked like it had been there for centuries, now almost sinking into the earth. On the right of the door were sandbags stacked up beside a wheelbarrow.

She hammered on the door. Would he be walking the grounds in this weather? He had to be home, didn't he? The fire was lit.

But he had been out in the rain before. She'd seen him.

She heard barks from inside and then the door opened. He was even taller than she remembered, and he stood there blocking the doorway, glowering at her, an unwelcome visitor.

'Mr Harrington,' Karen said, 'I'd like a word.'

His expression didn't change, but he stepped back and gestured for her to come inside.

'I thought we would go back to the house for an interview, actually,' Karen said.

'In this weather?' He shook his head and walked back inside the cottage.

Karen hesitated before following him and shutting the door.

Sandy padded up to greet Karen, delightedly wagging her tail, tilting her head and thoroughly enjoying Karen scratching behind her ears.

'That's enough. Back to your basket,' Harrington ordered the dog, and then he glowered again at Karen. 'She's a working dog. She's normally very well behaved.'

He narrowed his eyes as though Sandy's friendliness was Karen's fault.

Karen took in the interior of the cottage. It was as tiny as it looked from the outside. There was a small kitchen area, then a sofa in front of the fire. A well-used, round oak table with one dining chair sat under the stairs. Brown cardboard boxes were piled up by the back door. Despite its small size, the place appeared comfortable and cosy, and Karen had a sudden urge to stand beside the fire and warm her hands. Instead, she looked up at Mike Harrington. 'Are you free to answer some questions now?'

He looked beyond her, out of the small window, as the rain fell so heavily it obscured even the view of the trees. 'I can't really say no, can I?'

'Well, you can, actually, though it will make you look guilty if you do.'

He shrugged. 'What do you want to ask?'

'Like I said, it would be better to do this at the house.'

Karen noticed that Harrington had moved so that his bulky frame was blocking the front door. She was also aware that the back door beside the staircase was blocked by the cardboard boxes. She felt cornered, trapped, and she didn't like it.

'I don't mind walking to the house if that's what you really want, but you don't seem dressed for it,' he said, looking her up and down.

Karen frowned down at her clothes. She was wearing a waterproof mac, but it ended mid-thigh, which meant the bottoms of her trousers were saturated. Her leather boots were more suited to the office than walks through the woods. She ran a hand through her wet hair.

'Look,' he said, 'stand by the fire, dry off a bit. I'll even make you a cup of tea.'

Karen considered insisting they go back to the house, but he was right. The rain was very heavy. Besides, maybe he'd open up more at home.

As she stood beside the fire, she noticed that there were no personal effects in the cottage other than one small silver-framed photograph on top of the mantelpiece. She tilted it towards her. A small boy missing one of his front teeth smiled up at her.

'Don't touch that,' Harrington said, glaring at her with the kettle in his hand.

'Sorry. Your son?' Karen asked, putting it back.

He grunted but didn't answer.

'You know,' Karen called out as he filled the kettle at the sink, 'those boxes blocking the back door aren't a good idea. What if there's a fire?'

He didn't bother to turn this time. 'Then I'd climb out of the window.'

'How long have they been there? Since you moved?' she asked, walking towards them.

'Yes.'

'Why haven't you unpacked?'

'They're part of my old life,' he said, tensing as she got closer to the boxes.

She reached for one.

'Would you just stop it? That's incredibly rude you know.' He slammed the kettle on to the hob.

'Sorry,' Karen said, putting her hands in her pockets instead. It occurred to her that maybe they were things he couldn't bear to be parted with, but at the same time were too painful to look at every day. Perhaps his son's possessions.

'You know, it must take a special kind of person to do your job, digging into things that don't concern you,' Harrington said.

'Thanks,' Karen replied with false cheer, because she knew he didn't mean it as a compliment.

He glared at her again as the kettle whistled to a boil.

'Anyway,' Karen said. 'You'd probably know quite a bit about my job since you were an officer yourself.' She saw him tense. 'Why didn't you mention it before?'

'Didn't seem important.'

'You must have known we'd look into your background.'

'So I suppose you know all about me now, do you?' His words were harsh and hostile, but when he turned, he didn't look angry. He looked broken.

Karen suddenly felt claustrophobic. She wanted to be outside. She wanted to get out of this cottage even if it was raining. Was it because Harrington was doing his best to seem intimidating, or was it that his grief was so obvious here that it threatened to overwhelm her?

'Forget about the tea,' Karen said. 'Look, the rain's eased up. Let's go back to the house.'

He looked at her as though she'd gone mad but she walked purposefully towards the door, and to Harrington's obvious annoyance Sandy got out of her basket and trotted up to Karen expectantly.

'What's got into you?' he grumbled, shaking his head at the dog.

As they walked together through the trees, Karen tried to shake off the uncomfortable feeling she'd experienced in the cottage.

'Any news on the other girl?'

It took her a moment to realise Harrington had asked her a question. 'Not yet. We've got a team searching the lake this morning.'

His face slackened. 'You think she's dead?'

'We're searching the lake,' Karen said, not wanting to commit to anything more.

Distracted, Harrington ran a hand through his hair. 'Poor kid,' he said in a low voice, so quietly Karen only just caught it.

CHAPTER EIGHTEEN

Karen walked back to the house with Mike Harrington, their shoulders hunched against the light but steady rain. The search of the lake was well underway now. She nodded at Rick as they went past.

Sandy scampered happily at Harrington's heels.

'How old is she?' asked Karen, nodding at the spaniel.

'Eleven.'

'She's still got the energy of a puppy.'

'That's the breed, I think. Believe it or not, she had even more energy when she was younger.'

'She was your service dog, right?'

He nodded. 'Yes. A detection dog, but she's retired now, just like me.'

'After all that training they let the dog go?' Karen asked.

'Dogs tend to have one handler. It's unusual for them to be passed around. So when I left the force, Sandy did as well.'

'So, one dog, one owner.'

'That's right. We're partners,' Harrington said, looking fondly at the dog.

It was the first time Karen had seen a real change to his surly expression. Could this man really be a suspect?

He ticked a lot of boxes – single, living alone, brooding, and the people around him thought he was a bit odd. But he obviously cared deeply about Sandy, and Karen couldn't help empathising with his situation. He'd lost his child, after all, and she knew how that turned your life upside down. At one point, she'd wished she could go off somewhere, lock herself away from everyone else and forget about the world for a while.

She focused on Chidlow House as they approached. It dominated the landscape. Grey, angry clouds moved swiftly in the sky above. The gargoyles looked like no more than lumps of stone from this distance. Had Alison King reached to grab one of those, to save herself, before falling to her death?

Karen shivered.

She glanced at Harrington and decided she'd ask Morgan to talk to him further. Was she a professional? Yes, but there was a part of her that felt sorry for the ill-tempered man walking beside her, and she didn't want that to get in the way of the interview.

Morgan would be precise, thorough and wouldn't let feelings get in the way. He'd be better placed to do the questioning.

She left Harrington and Sandy in Doyle's office and went to locate Morgan. Before she found him, Sophie caught her in the hallway.

'Can I have a quick word, Sarge?' Sophie asked.

'Sure.'

'Cressida is here.'

Karen frowned. 'At the house?'

That was a surprise. She hadn't thought the young woman would want to come back after her severe reaction last night.

'Yes,' Sophie said. 'She's with her mum and dad. They're waiting in Chidlow's parlour. She said she came back because she wants to help. She's worried about her friend.'

That was promising. 'Maybe she's remembered something about Thursday night.'

Sophie shook her head. 'She still says she can't recall much but hoped that being back here would jog her memory. Her mum and

151

dad aren't too happy about her being here, but apparently Cressida begged them.'

'All right. I'll have a quick word with Cressida now. I've put Mike Harrington in Doyle's office. If Morgan's free, he can interview him now.'

'I think the boss is around somewhere,' Sophie said. 'I'll try to find him.'

'Thanks.'

'Harrington's a bit odd, isn't he?' Sophie said. 'From what his old DI said, he sounds like a recluse, a bit of an oddball. Do you think he's someone we should look at closely?'

Karen shrugged. 'He likes to keep to himself, that's for sure, but he lost a child a few years ago, and that changes a person.'

'Oh yes, of course it does. Sorry,' Sophie said hurriedly. 'I really put my foot in my mouth there, didn't I?'

'No, not at all. Don't worry about it,' Karen said. 'I'll go and talk to Cressida and her parents.'

Karen left Sophie and made her way to the parlour. She found Mr and Mrs Blake sitting on a small sofa beside the fire with Graham Doyle standing over them, simpering.

'The girl is a credit to you,' he was saying. 'Shows such strength after all she's been through.'

Jasmine Blake smiled politely. She sat with her legs crossed, hands on her lap, poised, more like a model posing than a real person.

Karen quickly scanned the room but Cressida wasn't in the parlour with her parents. 'Mr and Mrs Blake,' she said. 'It's a surprise to see you here this morning.'

'It was a surprise to us too,' Ryan Blake grumbled. He, too, looked like a model on a shoot. A white open-necked shirt, tan trousers and expensive shoes, with a heavy splash of aftershave. They both clearly took care over their appearance.

Jasmine shot her husband a chastising look and said, 'Yes, it was Cressida's idea. I wasn't sure it was a good one at first, but she really wants to help Natasha and thought being back here might help her remember something.'

'It might,' Karen said. 'Has she remembered anything at all about Thursday night or Friday before she returned?'

Ryan Blake shook his head. 'No, nothing.'

'I was just about to get some coffee for Mr and Mrs Blake,' Doyle said, wearing a sickly sweet smile. 'Would you like some, DS Hart?'

'That's kind of you, but no, thank you. Where is Cressida now?' she asked, turning to the Blakes.

'She's gone upstairs,' Jasmine said, fiddling with the pearls at her throat. 'She wanted to see her friend Ella. I was amazed the girl is still here. I thought all the students had gone home.'

'Most of them have,' Karen said. 'They went home after questioning last night, but Ella's parents are out of the country at the moment, so she's staying here until tomorrow.'

'Oh, quite brave of her,' Jasmine said, pushing her glossy hair back from her face. 'I'm not sure I'd like to stay here after everything that's happened.'

'Well, really, it's a most unfortunate situation, but it's nothing to do with Chidlow House,' Doyle said. 'I assure you that Ella is perfectly safe. I'm still staying here, and I keep a close eye on things.'

'You were supposed to keep a close eye on things before,' Ryan Blake said, 'and yet my daughter and her friend went missing and you haven't found the other girl yet.'

'Natasha,' Karen said, feeling the need to give the young woman's name rather than refer to her as 'the other girl'.

'Yes, of course,' Ryan said, turning away from Karen and looking at the fire.

He had a long nose, a Roman profile. When she'd first met him, Karen had thought he looked young for his age, but now he looked every day of his forty-two years. His dark hair had some kind of product on it that glistened. The flickering light from the fire cast odd shadows on his face.

'Right. I'll find Cressida and see if she wants to have a chat. We'll try to gently jog her memory. Anything she remembers about Thursday night could be important.'

Karen left Doyle apologising profusely and offering various long-winded explanations to the Blakes.

As she made her way to the back of the house and the staircase leading to the student rooms, she came across Morgan talking to DC Farzana Shah. They both looked up as Karen approached.

'Did Sophie find you?' Karen asked.

Morgan shook his head. 'Why was she looking for me?'

'Mike Harrington is here. I hoped you could talk to him. He's in Doyle's office.'

'Okay.'

He'd paused before speaking but didn't ask why Karen wanted to avoid questioning the groundskeeper herself.

'How's the search going?' she asked. 'Has Chidlow found the missing keys?'

'No,' Farzana said. 'Yesterday he said he's sure they're around somewhere but couldn't find them. He was supposed to look for them last night. Now, I can't find him. According to Doyle, he's walking the grounds somewhere.'

'We really need to search every room. It's unlikely Natasha's hiding out in there, or there's anything in there that will tell us where she is, but we can't do a half-hearted search of the property. What about Chidlow's study?'

'We're planning to search Chidlow's own study later today. He'd asked me yesterday to hold back because he had some important paperwork to get finished. I said that was okay. I hope that was all right?'

'No. He's stalling. We should search his study ASAP,' Morgan said.

Farzana nodded. 'Okay.'

'What about the cellars?' Karen asked.

'Nothing down there apart from old bottles of wine and some casks of port.'

'If I recall correctly, PC Smith used to be a locksmith,' Morgan said, thoughtfully. 'I'll ask him to take a look at the cupboard and the locked room to see if he can get access without causing any damage.'

There were footsteps behind them.

Karen turned and to her annoyance saw Mike Harrington standing there. 'I thought you were waiting for me in Doyle's office.'

'I was,' he said, 'but I got bored. You've been ages. I couldn't help overhearing you need to open a lock. I've got some tools.'

Karen was momentarily thrown by a suspect offering to assist them. But PC Smith couldn't tackle the lock without tools.

'That would be helpful. Thank you. Where's Sandy?' Karen asked.

'Sandy?' Morgan raised an eyebrow.

'Mike's dog,' Karen explained.

'She's still in Graham Doyle's office, curled up by the fire. For an ex-working dog, she sure likes her home comforts these days,' he said dryly. 'Shall I go and get those tools?'

Karen looked at Morgan. 'Did you want to question him first?'

'No, get the tools,' Morgan said. 'We'll open everything up so it can be searched, and I can talk to Mr Harrington afterwards.'

'Suits me.' Harrington turned and strolled off, presumably to get the tools.

'I'm going to find Cressida,' Karen said. 'Apparently she's gone to talk to Ella Seaton.'

'I didn't know they were good friends,' Farzana commented.

'I'm not sure they are,' Karen said, 'but I suppose they've got a common bond at the moment. They're surrounded by adults – parents, teachers and police officers – so they'll probably gain some comfort talking to each other.'

As Karen made her way up the creaking staircase she kept her eyes averted from the portraits. She wouldn't describe them as spooky, as Rick had, but they were disturbing. The women looked so sad, so hopeless.

Keeping her gaze focused straight ahead, she marched up the steps. When she got to the girls' floor, she paused, trying to remember which one was Ella's room. *Number seven*, she thought, and began to walk towards it, only to freeze halfway down the corridor when she heard the strange sounds again.

Distant, muffled whispers. She held her breath so she could hear better. The sound of dripping water was faint but most definitely there.

She followed the noise. It was coming from the door with no number, next to the bathroom. Karen reached for the doorknob and turned it, but found it still locked.

She pressed her ear to the smooth wood and listened. There it was again – dripping water and whispering. The combination was disturbing. She pushed the image of the Drowned Lady – a pale figure standing on the other side of the door, water dripping from her wet clothes – from her mind. This was no ghost. There had to be a rational explanation.

The whispers were louder here, but she couldn't work out what the voice was saying.

The protesting creak of a floorboard made Karen jump. Her heart rate spiked, and her breath caught in her throat.

She spun around, pressing a hand against her chest, feeling her heart thudding beneath her ribcage.

It was Ethan.

'What are you doing here?' Karen demanded. 'You're supposed to be at home.'

'I wanted to see how you were getting on. Have you found Natasha yet?'

'Why didn't you ask your dad?' Karen asked. 'I'm sure he'd keep you updated.'

'I'm grounded.' Ethan shrugged. 'He's not really talking to me.'

'If you're grounded, how come you're here? How did you get past the cordon?'

He shrugged again. 'I didn't tell my dad I was coming, and I told the officer at the gate that I left some belongings here and if he had an issue to call my dad, so he let me through.'

Unbelievable. Karen shook her head. She turned away as the whispering started up again. Quiet but definitely audible.

'Can you hear that?' Karen asked, pressing her hand against the flat wood of the door.

Ethan paused, but then shook his head. 'No. Hear what?'

'Whispers and dripping water.'

He looked at her oddly, tilting his head to one side, apparently listening, but then said, 'No, I can't hear anything.'

Karen rubbed her hands over her face. She wasn't imagining things. Maybe Ethan was hard of hearing, or maybe all the talk of ghosts was getting to her.

'Have you seen anyone enter this room?' Karen asked.

'No.'

Irritated, she tried to turn the doorknob again, but the door remained stubbornly shut. 'Have you seen Cressida or Ella?'

Ethan's eyebrows lifted. 'Cressida is here?'

'Yes, she is. But I don't think it's a good idea for you to see her.'

'Why not?'

'Because you shouldn't be here, Ethan. Your dad is right. You're in enough trouble. If you want to keep your nose clean you need to stay at home and keep out of this.'

'But I haven't done anything wrong. I'd never hurt Cressida or Natasha. And if I knew where they were, I'd tell you.'

'You have done something wrong, Ethan. You might not be involved in their disappearance, but you were smoking drugs with the girls.'

'It was only weed,' Ethan said dismissively.

'Your father's a police officer. You must have known how that would reflect on him.'

'He doesn't care about me. Why should I care about him?'

'Of course he cares about you.'

'Yeah, right,' Ethan said, folding his arms over his chest in a sulk that made Karen want to give him a shake.

'You could think of him now and again, you know,' Karen said, shocking herself by sticking up for the chief constable. Ethan pulled a face. 'He doesn't have an easy job. I'm not saying he's perfect, but your behaviour makes him look bad, and that's not fair.'

Ethan rolled his eyes. 'So I made a mistake. It's not like I set out to mess up his career. All he goes on about is his stupid job.'

Karen heard the noise again. She turned to look at Ethan. 'Can you really not hear that?'

Ethan shook his head. 'No, I can't. It must be the ghost, don't you think?'

Karen gritted her teeth. 'No, I don't.'

Looking bored, Ethan pulled his phone out of his pocket and turned his attention to the screen. It didn't make sense. Why couldn't he hear it? Abruptly, the noises stopped.

Karen sent Ethan downstairs, telling him to go straight home, and then knocked on Ella's door.

When Ella answered, she was smiling. 'Oh, hi,' she said, stepping back.

Cressida was sitting on Ella's bed. Her flaxen hair fell past her shoulders. The scratch on her cheek still looked angry and raw, but overall she looked much better today – healthier, with flushed cheeks. Definitely less traumatised. She stood up and linked arms with Ella, who looked surprised but pleased.

'Is there any news on Natasha?' Cressida asked.

'I'm afraid not,' Karen said. 'I was surprised you'd come back to Chidlow House today, but pleased. Have you remembered anything?'

Cressida looked down at the ground and tucked her hair behind her ear, and as she did so, Karen saw she'd been biting the skin around her fingernails. They were bleeding.

'I haven't. Not yet. I just thought maybe being back here, you know, might make me remember what happened. All I can recall is getting ready on Thursday night . . . but after that it's just blank until I remember sitting in the parlour yesterday, wet and cold and scared. The period in-between is just blackness, like someone reached inside my head and ripped out all the memories. Do you think I'll ever be able to remember?'

'I hope so,' Karen said. *For Natasha's sake*, she added silently.

'Ella's ever so brave for staying here on her own,' Cressida said, looking at the girl with the frizzy hair.

Ella beamed happily. 'Oh, I'm fine. Made of stern stuff. Takes a lot to scare me.'

'Did you sleep all right last night?' Karen asked.

'Yes, fine.'

'You didn't hear any noises or . . .'

Ella shook her head. 'No, nothing. I slept really well. I feel guilty for saying that, but I slept straight through.'

'Good,' Karen said. 'And your parents – when are they getting back? Tonight?'

'Tomorrow,' Ella corrected. 'Then they'll take me home.'

'You're okay staying here for another night?' Cressida asked, eyes wide.

'Oh, yes. I'll be fine.'

'Are you ready to have a chat?' Karen asked Cressida.

Cressida nodded. 'Yes. I mean, maybe in ten minutes or so. I just want to get my head together.'

'All right,' Karen said. 'I'll meet you back in the parlour with your parents in about ten minutes.'

CHAPTER NINETEEN

Karen left Cressida and Ella, wondering if she'd done the right thing by giving Cressida another ten minutes. She didn't want to pressure the young woman, not when she seemed to be turning a corner and appeared so much better than yesterday, but the clock was ticking.

The longer Natasha was missing, the less likely it was she would turn up safe and well.

Karen reached the top of the stairs just as PC Smith and Mike Harrington began to climb them.

Harrington saw her and lifted a bag of tools. 'I think these should work,' he said.

PC Smith cracked his knuckles. 'I'm a little bit rusty, but I should be able to get that door open.'

Karen walked with them, leading them along the corridor. 'This is the door that won't open. I keep hearing strange sounds coming from it, like whispering.'

'You think Natasha could be in there?' PC Smith's jaw dropped, and he made a grab for the tools in Harrington's hand. 'I didn't realise it was so urgent.'

'I don't think it's Natasha in there,' Karen said. 'In fact, it sounds so similar every time I hear it I think it must be a recording.'

'A recording?' Harrington scratched his head. 'Why would someone be playing a recording in a locked room?'

'I've got my suspicions, but I might be wrong. Let's just wait until you manage to open the door.'

PC Smith kneeled on the red carpet and peered closely at the lock. 'It might take me a few minutes. I don't want to damage the lock and land us with a bill from Lord Chidlow. I imagine he's not going to be very pleased when he gets home and finds out what we've done.'

Karen shrugged. 'He gave us permission to search the whole house, and we have a warrant now. His signature is on the paperwork.'

As PC Smith worked, Harrington stood beside him, handing him tools. Karen pulled out her mobile phone and walked to the other end of the corridor, planning to return Alice Price's call.

It rang for a long time before anyone answered.

'Yes.' It was a male voice.

'Oh, I was hoping to speak to Alice,' she said. 'It's Karen Hart, DS Hart.'

'Alice isn't here.' Karen recognised the voice now. It was Declan, Alice's husband.

'I'll call again later.'

'There's no point. She's gone away,' he said in a listless voice.

'Gone away? But she hasn't taken her mobile?'

'No, she does this quite a lot. Likes to go off on her own for a bit. It's her way of coping, I think. Being alone with her thoughts. Not being interrupted by frivolous phone calls.'

Karen frowned. 'I'm returning her call.'

There was silence on the other end of the phone and then Declan said, 'She called you?'

'Yes.'

'What about?' he asked, sounding suspicious.

'I'm not really sure,' Karen said, truthfully, 'but Alice asked me to call her back.'

Karen didn't mention Churchill's name. She wasn't entirely sure why, but she felt like it wasn't something Declan needed to know. Alice's husband wanted her to forget about the past and move on. Unsurprisingly perhaps, as his wife had had a breakdown. Maybe it was unfair, but Karen didn't feel like confiding in Declan.

'Do you want me to take a message?' he asked.

'No, that's all right. I'll catch up with her later. Do you know when she's coming back?'

'No.' He sounded shifty, evasive. 'I don't know. Probably a few days.'

'Right. I'll call her in a few days then. Thanks.' Karen hung up and looked at the phone, feeling uneasy.

That was odd. Sure, maybe Alice wanted to get away for a few days, but wouldn't she take her phone with her and just turn it off if she didn't want to be disturbed? In this day and age, most people kept a phone with them in case of emergency.

She put her own phone in her pocket and walked back to PC Smith, who was still hard at work on the lock. As she got closer, she heard the whispering and the dripping water.

'Tell me you hear that,' she said, pointing at the door.

'Yeah, I hear it,' Harrington said. 'And it's definitely coming from this room.'

At that moment there was a click followed by a loud clunk, as PC Smith finally managed to open the lock.

As the door swung open with a drawn-out groan, all three of them stood there staring. The room was absolutely jammed full of junk, and it looked like the door hadn't been opened for years. Dust and cobwebs coated everything. The wallpaper was yellowed with age, and the light fitting looked as though it was from the turn of the last century.

Then there was the sound of whispering again. PC Smith stood up and made to enter the room, but Karen put a hand out to stop him.

'Wait. Don't go in there yet.' She pointed to the floor, where she'd just noticed large footprints in the dust covering the floorboards. 'Someone's been in here.'

She scanned the area. There wasn't much space to walk between the stacked chairs, rolled-up rugs and old lamps and paintings. But Karen could see footprints in the dust – at least one person had been in here recently.

She was aware that both PC Smith and Mike Harrington were watching her. But she wasn't going to be hurried. She carefully took in the scene.

There was something odd about the whole situation. Chidlow had said he'd misplaced the key to this room, but Karen suspected he either hadn't wanted them to get in or someone else had taken the key, with or without his knowledge.

Someone had the key. Someone had been in here.

Her gaze travelled over a stack of gilt picture frames, and that's when she saw it. Something modern and quite out of place in a room stuffed with damaged, dusty antiques.

'There,' she said, pointing out a rectangular black box. 'That's a speaker, isn't it?'

As if on cue, the sounds started up again.

'I think we've found the source of the voices,' Karen said.

'Looks like a Bluetooth speaker,' PC Smith said. 'No wires. So we still don't know the source of the recording.'

'No,' Karen said, frowning. 'It could be coming from someone's phone.'

She glanced at Harrington.

'Don't look at me. I haven't got a mobile.'

'Or it could be coming from a computer nearby,' PC Smith suggested.

Karen nodded. 'I wonder if there's a way we can trace it.'

'Well, we could have a look ourselves first,' PC Smith said, taking out his phone. 'I'll see what other Bluetooth devices are in the vicinity.' He began to tap on the screen. 'Oh, there's quite a few phones. Looks like a MacBook as well.' He paused. 'But we can't tell which is connected to the speaker, not from my phone at least.'

'No. Maybe the tech team can help us with that. Can you get on to Forensics?' Karen asked. 'We're going to want the room fingerprinted, and we'll need photographs of these footprints as well.'

'Do you think it's related to Natasha's disappearance?' PC Smith asked.

'I don't know,' Karen replied honestly.

Harrington began to put his tools back in the bag. 'I wouldn't put it past Chidlow to be behind this. It's probably his way of trying to drum up business. Ghost tours on the estate. That sort of thing.'

'Maybe,' Karen said, but another idea had occurred to her.

'Do you think Chidlow's been trying to scare us?' PC Smith asked.

Karen wasn't sure. She wouldn't say she was scared by the noises, but they had unnerved her. Harrington had made a good point. It could be Chidlow trying to drive interest in his property and set the place up as some kind of haunted house for tours in the future. He'd probably prefer that to having a house full of students. But there was another explanation. One that, to Karen, made even more sense.

'I don't think this is down to Chidlow,' Karen said. 'In fact, I'm pretty sure someone else is behind it.'

'Well, don't leave us in suspense,' Harrington called as Karen walked off.

But she wasn't going to say anything until she'd confronted the culprit face to face. She only hoped she wasn't too late.

Karen was in luck. Ethan was in the parlour with Cressida and her parents. Karen was glad he hadn't done what he was told and gone home.

He didn't notice Karen enter the room. He was too focused on Cressida.

'Ethan, I'd like a word,' Karen said, before apologising to Cressida and her parents. 'I'll just be a few minutes. Sorry to keep you waiting.'

She escorted Ethan to Doyle's office.

'I was just about to leave,' he said as Karen shut the door and told him to sit down.

She folded her arms and remained standing, so she could look down at him. 'I know it's you.'

'What's me? I haven't done anything,' he said. 'I don't know anything about Natasha.'

'That's not what I'm talking about, Ethan, and you know it.'

Ethan's cheeks flushed, but he shook his head and kept up the denial. 'I don't know what you're going on about.'

'You said you couldn't hear it. Either you're very hard of hearing or you're a liar. Give me your phone.'

Ethan looked up and his jaw dropped. Did he really believe they wouldn't have found him out? That he'd get away with this in a house full of detectives?

Sometimes the arrogance of teenagers – or was it naivety – was staggering.

Karen held out her hand. 'Phone please, now.'

Grumbling under his breath, he reached into the pocket of his jeans and passed the phone to Karen.

She gritted her teeth and gave it back to him. 'Unlock it.'

With a scowl, he did so. Then he handed it to Karen.

She located the voice recording app. There were only two saved recordings. The first one was Ethan doing a terrible rendition of a recent pop song. His cheeks turned even redder. The second recording was the one Karen was looking for. The whispers and the sound of dripping water.

'You couldn't hear it?' Karen raised an eyebrow.

'It was just a joke.' He sank lower in the chair.

'Who is this? It sounds like a female voice.'

'I don't know. I recorded it from some TV show,' he said. 'I was just trying to lighten the mood. It was just a joke. We'd all been talking about the Drowned Lady and I thought it would be a laugh.'

'It's not the time or place for jokes, Ethan. Were you playing this so Miss King could hear?'

He looked down at his lap and then nodded. 'Yeah.'

'Is it your fault she fell from the roof?'

'How could it be my fault? It's just a recording of a dripping tap mixed with a voice whispering,' Ethan said. 'Talk about overreacting.'

'No, Ethan. I'm not overreacting. You don't seem to realise the seriousness of the situation. Natasha is still missing, and you were one of the last people to see her. That's serious. And now you're messing about with recordings, sneaking around, trying to scare people. And you've been taking drugs. It's almost as though you're trying to implicate yourself in Natasha's disappearance, trying to get us to focus on you as a suspect.'

Ethan paled. 'I'm a suspect?'

'Just because your father is the chief constable doesn't mean we're going to ignore the things you've done wrong here. We won't simply look the other way. You understand that, don't you?'

'Please don't tell my father,' he said.

'If you've done something wrong, Ethan, you need to take responsibility for it.'

The kid looked horrified at the idea. Did he think he was untouchable? That he was safe no matter what he got up to because of who his father was? The chance of a huge push forward on the corruption case was evaporating. Everything she'd hoped for was slipping through her fingers, thanks to a spoiled kid who couldn't see the damage he'd done. The chief constable wouldn't want to help her after this. But she couldn't ignore Ethan's actions. Her conscience wouldn't allow it. He'd said it was a joke, but could she believe that?

Would he ever take responsibility for anything if his father covered up his mistakes?

'I am going to have to tell your father about this. Not only because you coming back here makes you look guilty, but also the fact that you're wasting police time. You could be charged for that alone.'

He shifted awkwardly in his chair. 'Look, I'm sorry, all right? I'll leave.'

He still didn't get it. He thought Karen was being unreasonable. He didn't think of anyone but himself.

'Just give me the key and go, Ethan,' Karen said.

'And you're not going to mention it to my dad, right?'

'I am,' Karen said, unable to believe the audacity of the kid. 'I'll speak to him later today, so you'd better be waiting for him at home because you're supposed to be grounded.'

To Karen's surprise Ethan handed her two keys.

'What's the other key for?'

He shrugged. 'Don't know. Can I go now?'

Karen nodded and stared after him as he sloped off, taking her hopes of a successful investigation into the depths of Freeman's corruption with him.

CHAPTER TWENTY

Clutching both keys, Karen grabbed a pair of gloves and headed upstairs to solve the mystery. The larger key looked modern and very similar to the ones used for all the other rooms, but the smaller key was more delicate and well worn. It looked older.

She entered the girls' bathroom, pulled on the gloves and looked at the large bathroom cabinet. The keyhole was small. Promising. Karen smiled as the smaller key slid into the lock and turned easily. One mystery solved.

Stacks of towels and neatly arranged soap sat on the shelves. Nothing very exciting. She felt around the cupboard walls and used her phone to illuminate the wood to make sure she wasn't missing anything. But she found nothing out of the ordinary.

Finally, Karen made it back to the parlour.

'I'm really sorry to keep you waiting,' she said to the Blakes. 'How are you feeling now, Cressida?'

The young woman looked up. She looked much brighter today, but nervous. 'All right, thanks. I just want to help get Natasha back.'

Karen smiled and sank down into the armchair opposite Cressida.

'I'm not sure what the point of this is,' Ryan Blake said, gesturing around him. 'I don't think coming back here is a good idea. Cressida can't remember anything, and this is just upsetting for her.'

'I think it's very brave to come back,' Karen said. 'I know it must be very difficult for you.' She looked directly at Cressida. 'I was going to ask Lydia to show you some pictures this morning, but since you're here, I can show you now. We have some CCTV footage of Natasha on Monday evening.'

'Monday?' Ryan asked.

'But she went missing on Thursday,' Jasmine added.

'Yes, that's right,' Karen said, 'but she was having dinner in Harmston on Monday evening, with a man we want to identify. We'd like you to take a look at the images and see if you can recognise him.'

Cressida blinked. 'I . . . I didn't know she'd gone out on Monday.'

'It was about seven thirty,' Karen said. 'She went to the new Italian restaurant in Harmston. Could you have a look?' She opened the images on her phone and held it out for Cressida to see.

The young woman moved forward, elbows resting on her knees, hands clutched together, her face pensive.

As she flicked through the images, her father got up and stood by her side. They both looked down at Karen's phone.

'You can't really see very much of him,' Cressida said as she made her way through the collection of images.

'No,' Karen said. 'It was a bad camera angle.'

'This is from inside the restaurant,' Ryan Blake said. 'Is there a better view of them from the street, entering or leaving?'

'Unfortunately not,' Karen said. 'The restaurant owner didn't keep a copy of the security camera footage from the entrance. He didn't realise it would be important.'

'But he kept a copy of the recording from inside the restaurant – why?' Ryan rubbed his chin thoughtfully.

'It's on a different network. The outside security system only keeps the last forty-eight hours because the owner has to pay more if he wants to keep the recordings longer.'

'Oh, that's such a shame,' Jasmine said. 'Could I have a look?' She held out her hand for the phone, and Cressida passed it to her.

Jasmine went through the pictures in silence, then gave the phone back to Karen. 'I'm sorry, I don't have any idea who it is.'

'It's not the best picture. I thought Natasha might have told you who she was meeting on Monday evening.' Karen watched Cressida carefully. But the young woman maintained eye contact and didn't appear to be hiding anything.

'No. I'm sorry, Natasha didn't tell me anything about it. I spent Monday evening with some of the other students. We were outside, sitting on the terrace. It was freezing, but we had fun out there, chatting and joking around. But you're right, Natasha wasn't with us. She'd told me she was going to stay in her room and study.'

'Did you think that was unusual?'

'Maybe a bit, but she does work hard. She's a very good student. Her mother wants her to get top marks for her A levels this year, so she's under a lot of pressure,' Cressida said, plucking a piece of fluff from her skirt. 'They're pretty hard on her, I think.'

'You didn't go into Harmston on Monday evening?'

Jasmine cut in. 'No, we were both at home on Monday evening when Cressida called us, weren't we, darling?' She looked at her husband, who nodded.

'Sorry, I meant Cressida.'

'Oh, I see. Of course.' Jasmine put a hand up in apology.

Karen turned her attention back to Cressida. 'So you weren't in Harmston on Monday and have no idea who this man is? Natasha didn't mention seeing someone, a boyfriend?'

Cressida shook her head. 'No, not to me. I didn't think she was seeing anyone. She had a bit of a crush on the gardener.'

'The groundsman? Mike Harrington?' Karen asked. Perhaps that wasn't surprising. He was handsome in a rugged, moody way. He'd be more appealing to a teenage girl than a lad her own age, and certainly more attractive than Doyle or Lord Chidlow.

Cressida nodded. 'Yes.'

'Right. Maybe now we should focus on anything you can remember from Thursday night.'

Cressida gripped the edge of a cushion. 'I'm really sorry, but I don't think I can. I remember us getting ready to go out. I went to Natasha's room, and she was waiting for me. She got her coat . . .' Cressida's voice trembled. 'And then we . . . I think we went downstairs, but that's all a bit blurry now. I can't remember anything after that. It's all just nothingness.' She pressed a hand to her forehead.

Her mother rubbed her shoulder. 'It's all right, sweetheart.'

'Did you discuss your plans for the evening earlier in the day?'

'I'm not sure. I think we mentioned going to the pub, but I can't remember going there. I can't remember going anywhere.' Cressida's breathing quickened and her cheeks flushed. She was starting to get distressed.

'Okay. There's one more thing I wanted to ask you, and that's about last night, when you were leaving Chidlow House to go to the police station. You had a very strong reaction to something as we were walking to the car.'

Cressida nodded slowly.

'Do you know why?'

The young woman licked her lips and looked at Karen blankly, eyes wide.

'You walked down the steps towards the car. Was it something about the vehicle that made you panic?'

Cressida shook her head. 'I don't think so.'

'The dog barking?'

Cressida pushed her light blonde hair out of her eyes with a trembling hand.

'The light was on in one of the rooms in the house.'

Cressida stiffened.

'Did you see someone? Was that what upset you?'

She let out a sob.

'All right. No more,' Ryan Blake said. 'She's obviously very distressed now.'

'It's okay,' Cressida said tearfully. 'I don't know why I reacted like that, but I suddenly felt really scared and my heart was beating too fast. I couldn't breathe.'

'It was probably a panic attack, darling,' Jasmine said, wrapping her arm around her daughter and giving her a squeeze. 'We've booked Cressida an appointment with a psychologist this afternoon, to help her get over this trauma.'

'That's a good idea,' Karen said.

'Well, I think that's enough now. Come on.' Ryan Blake stood up and held out his hand before helping his daughter to her feet.

As the Blake family were leaving the room, Cressida turned and said, 'I'm really sorry I can't help.'

'You're doing your best,' Karen said. 'I know this is really difficult.'

When Cressida and her parents had left the room, Karen looked out of the window. It wasn't raining anymore, but the wind had picked up, sending yellow and gold leaves twirling over the patio.

The grey October sky was heavy with threatened showers. In the distance, the trees shook violently. Karen let out a frustrated sigh. She'd been holding out hope that Cressida would have remembered something today, something that could have led them to Natasha. There was still a slim chance they'd find her, but time was running out.

Morgan stared across the table at Mike Harrington.

There were piles of paperwork neatly stacked on the desk. Morgan had cleared an area for his own notes. He kept Harrington waiting for a few minutes, noticing how the man fidgeted. He clearly didn't like sitting still.

The dog was happy enough by the fire.

'How long have you worked here?' he asked Harrington.

'Isn't that in the file?' The groundskeeper nodded at the foolscap folder on the desk.

Morgan didn't respond, but waited patiently for an answer.

'Two years,' Harrington said.

'And before that?'

Harrington's mouth twisted in a grim smile. 'Why are we playing this game? You know what I did before.'

'I'd like you to tell me,' Morgan said.

'I had a "career break".' He made quote marks with his fingers. 'For eighteen months, before I started working here, I did nothing. Before that I worked for the Lincolnshire Police as a dog handler.'

'And Sandy was your dog?' Morgan nodded at the sleeping English Springer Spaniel.

'That's right.'

'You left the force early. Any reason for that?'

'I was sick of it,' he said. 'There didn't seem to be any point anymore.'

'Why do you say that?'

'Well, you have to admit it gets tiring seeing the bad side of life all the time. Depressing.'

'It's not easy at times,' Morgan replied.

'That's the understatement of the year,' Harrington said under his breath.

'You suffered a personal loss around the time you left the police service.'

Harrington's features tightened. 'I did,' he agreed, but didn't elaborate.

'Your son died.'

Harrington's hands tightened on the armrests of the chair. 'Yes.'

'I'm very sorry,' Morgan said. 'It must have been incredibly difficult.'

'It was. It is,' the groundskeeper said, clarifying. 'I almost didn't get through it.'

'Do you mind me asking what happened to your leg?' Morgan looked at Harrington's stick, which rested against the side of the armchair.

'I'm sure you could find out if you wanted to.'

'I'm sure I could, but I'm asking you.'

Harrington stared down at the floor for a moment, then sighed. 'I was in a pretty dark place when my son died. One night I'd had too much to drink and decided I'd had enough. I got in my car, drove it straight at a wall. I woke up in hospital with both legs broken. This one,' he tapped his left leg, 'came off worse. Needed metal plates and screws.'

Morgan waited a beat and then said, 'We're going to have to search your cottage.'

'Fine,' Harrington said. 'I don't have anything to hide.'

'Good,' Morgan said, making a note. 'Did you see Natasha Layton and Cressida Blake while they were staying at Chidlow House?'

'I saw them around.'

'On how many occasions?'

'I really don't remember. It may have been more than once, but I couldn't say for sure. I remember seeing them near the start of the week with a group of other kids. They were laughing and joking.

The lads were leaning back against the wall near Chidlow's study, trying to look tough, smoking spliffs and then trying to hide them when I walked past,' he said, rolling his eyes.

'You didn't report it to Doyle or Chidlow though?'

'Why should I? For all I knew, they were complicit. These kids aren't normal. Their parents are beyond wealthy and influential. They live by a different set of rules to everyone else.'

'They might think they do, Mr Harrington,' Morgan said, 'but if I have anything to do with it, they'll be held accountable to the law.' Harrington didn't look impressed. 'So when you saw the students, they were always outside? You never saw them in the house?'

'No. I'm hardly ever in the house. The place was full of teenagers this week. That's not my idea of fun, so I'd been making myself even more scarce than usual.'

'Did you hear anything on Thursday night? Any noises?'

'What sort of noises?'

'Screams, shouts, people talking. See any lights? Anything at all?' Morgan asked.

'No, I didn't hear anyone. You think they were by the lake?'

'Possibly,' Morgan said.

'I thought DS Hart was going to be interviewing me,' he said after Morgan thanked him for his time.

'She was, but she had to do something else this morning.'

Harrington stood up, called Sandy to his side, then turned and said over his shoulder, 'She's lost someone too, hasn't she?'

Morgan looked up.

'DS Hart, I mean,' Harrington continued. 'I can tell. She's got that look.'

Morgan said nothing, and Harrington turned to leave.

Then he paused again, this time with his hand on the door, and said, 'I hope the student turns up. I know people look on me

176

as odd, but I'm not a monster. I can't imagine what her parents are going through.'

'I would have thought you could,' Morgan said, 'after what happened to your son.'

'It was different in my case. There was no waiting, wondering or hoping. Nathan died by drowning,' he said, but he wasn't looking at Morgan. He was staring out the window. 'We were visiting friends. They had a swimming pool – it was all fenced off. Everything should have been safe. The gate was locked. But Nathan liked climbing things, you see. And he scaled the fence and went into the pool. I found him, face down in the water.'

'That must have been awful,' Morgan said, wincing at the understatement.

Harrington nodded. 'Yes . . .'

Morgan put his pen down on the desk, got up and walked out with Harrington and Sandy. 'I'll let you know when the search team is ready to come to your cottage. It will be soon.'

'Right.'

As they walked into the entrance hall, Morgan heard footsteps behind them. Cressida and her parents were heading towards them.

Cressida's gaze fixed on Mike Harrington as he carried on walking to the front door, his stick tapping on the flagstones. She tensed and grabbed her mother's arm.

What was that all about? Was she reacting to Harrington, the dog or simply the trauma of being back at Chidlow House?

CHAPTER TWENTY-ONE

After the Blakes left, Karen went to find Ella again. She had two reasons for doing so. She wanted to know if the girl was happy to stay here at Chidlow House with Graham Doyle and Edward Chidlow. Sophie had contacted her parents, who were still on holiday, to ask if they wanted to make alternative arrangements for their daughter in the circumstances. The parents of the other students hadn't been able to get their children away fast enough, and Karen thought it odd that Ella's parents had asked for her to stay at Chidlow House until they returned.

On the surface, Ella didn't seem worried about remaining here until her parents got home, but Karen had the feeling she wasn't someone who readily revealed her true feelings. Her confident voice contrasted with her shy, awkward body language.

She also wanted to ask Ella about her relationship with Cressida. The girls had seemed friendly earlier and that had come as a surprise. When Karen had first spoken to Ella, she'd said she wasn't close to Cressida and Natasha, even implying they were spoiled and cut her out of things.

Maybe Ella had sympathy for Cressida's plight. That could explain their cosy interactions today. She hoped talking to Ella would clarify things.

She rapped on the door and Ella answered, looking tired. She had crease marks on her cheek.

'Sorry, did I wake you?' Karen asked.

'Yes, although I shouldn't have fallen asleep really. I'm meant to be studying.' She smiled. 'Come in.'

She stepped back and Karen entered the room. 'How are you doing?'

Ella shrugged. 'I'm fine.'

'Funny you fell asleep when you had such a good night's sleep,' Karen said gently.

Ella gave a small, guilt-tinged smile. 'Well, maybe I didn't get quite as much sleep as I thought.'

'You know, if you feel more comfortable, we could make some arrangements for you. Just until your parents get back. Even if you don't want to stay at your family home, there must be a relative or friend you could stay with?'

'Honestly, I'm fine,' Ella said, sitting down on the edge of her bed. 'I'd prefer to stay here. I want to know what happens. I'd like to be here when Natasha returns.'

'Do you think she'll come back?'

'I hope so. Don't you?'

'I don't know,' Karen said. 'I hope she's all right and comes back here, like Cressida . . .' Karen trailed off. 'Anyway, we're doing our best to find her.'

'I know,' Ella said. 'I've noticed. You're a bit like me really.'

Karen was surprised. 'In what way?'

'Well, not you specifically, but detectives, you know. You watch people, don't you? Read their behaviour. Find out their secrets.'

Karen nodded slowly. 'I suppose we do.'

'Well, that's like me. I'm practically invisible here.' She plucked at a loose thread on the blanket. 'People just look through me.'

'I'm sure that's not true, Ella,' Karen said.

'It is. And don't get me wrong, it's not that bad really. I'm just plain – boring – but it means that people don't pay attention to me. They don't think I'm important and that gives me the chance to watch, to listen, to find out things.'

Karen sat on the bed beside her. 'What sort of things have you found out?'

'I don't know if it's anything important. I'm not saying I'm a detective or anything, but sometimes I hear things.'

Karen nodded, encouraging her to go on.

'Well, one thing that might be important happened on Wednesday evening. I overheard Cressida talking to Natasha. She was boasting that she'd been inside the gardener's cottage that day.'

'Cressida was inside Mike Harrington's cottage on Wednesday?'

A chill ran down Karen's spine. She'd felt sorry for him. How could she have been so stupid? She was glad she'd got Morgan to do the interview. Her instincts were off.

'Yes, that's what she said.'

'Was there anything going on between Cressida and the groundsman?'

'I don't know. I think she had a bit of a crush on him. Maybe he invited her back there.' Ella shrugged. 'But it seems a bit weird really, because earlier in the week, Cressida had been, you know, trying to flirt with him, get his attention when he was using the leaf blower underneath the oak trees near the house, and he'd completely blanked her. I thought it was quite funny, but she got really shirty about it. But then maybe he was putting on an act, you know? So that nobody suspected anything. Maybe he thought he'd get in trouble, lose his job. *Fraternising* with the students.'

'Thank you for telling me, Ella,' Karen said. 'I appreciate it.'

'Oh, you're welcome. While I'm here, I'll keep listening. See if I can find anything else out for you.'

'You don't need to do that, Ella. But if anything else occurs to you, then let me know, okay?'

Ella nodded happily.

'What about Ethan?' Karen asked. 'Are you friends with him?'

Ella shook her head. 'No, he's nice, but he only has eyes for Natasha and Cressida. Natasha especially. He doesn't even notice me.' She gave a small, sad smile.

Karen wondered if Ella knew anything about the recording and Ethan's involvement. 'Ella, did you ever hear the dripping water or whispering on this floor?'

Ella shook her head. 'No, I didn't . . . but I heard you talking earlier to Ethan.'

'You heard me?'

Ella flushed. Her hands fluttered nervously in her lap. 'Well, I just happened to be walking past Doyle's office at the time. Your voices were raised. I wasn't listening at the door or anything like that,' she added hurriedly.

It dawned on Karen that they'd underestimated Ella. The line between someone who paid close attention to the people around them and an eavesdropper was thin.

Disappointed with her own life, was Ella living vicariously through others? Getting excitement and thrills from finding out secrets?

'I see,' Karen said. 'You shouldn't really listen in on private conversations.'

'You didn't say that just now when I told you about Cressida being in Mike Harrington's cottage.'

'True,' Karen admitted. 'But that sort of thing can get you in trouble. You should make friends, Ella, create real bonds, have conversations with people. Don't spy on them.'

Two bright red spots burned in the middle of Ella's cheeks. 'I thought I was helping.'

She dipped her head and her frizzy hair fell forward, obscuring her face.

'You were. I'm sorry. I didn't mean to make it sound like I'm ungrateful for the information, because I'm not. It could be very important, and I'm glad you told me. I just think you'd be happier if instead of stepping back and observing, you took part.'

Ella shrugged. 'I'm not very good at that.'

'No, I know. It takes practice. And you're still young. You've got loads of time to learn.'

Ella smiled, but she still looked as though Karen had taken away her favourite chocolate bar.

Maybe Karen should have just thanked the young woman and left it at that. But she could picture Ella getting older, spying on people and becoming very unpopular and unhappy in the future.

'You'll let me know if you remember anything else you've overheard?'

Ella nodded stiffly.

Karen apologised again. 'I really do appreciate you telling me all this. Thank you.'

'That's all right,' Ella said, softening a little bit. 'I just hope it helps you find Natasha.'

So do I, Karen thought as she left the room, with Ella Seaton's watchful gaze following her.

Karen went downstairs and was crossing the entrance hall when she saw Mike Harrington standing with PC Smith at the door. Sandy was sitting beside his feet. The two men were chatting, evidently getting on like a house on fire.

'Going back to your cottage?' Karen asked coldly.

He nodded, frowning at her tone.

'We're going to send a team of officers to search your home.'

Harrington's frown deepened. 'So DI Morgan told me,' he said. 'It's fine. I've got nothing to hide. But if you could ask them to be careful when they . . . go through the boxes, I'd appreciate it.'

His voice broke. Karen gritted her teeth. He was talking about the boxes that held his son's possessions. Despite her suspicions, Karen felt her chest tighten. His loss weighed heavily on him still, and she could hear the grief in his voice.

She folded her arms, determined not to let the fact he'd lost his son have any influence over her. Ella had just told her that Cressida had been in Harrington's cottage, and he'd denied talking to her. The evidence suggested Mike Harrington was a liar.

'We've had some new information,' Karen said.

'About Natasha?' he asked. 'Have you found her?'

'No, about you actually. About the fact Cressida was in your cottage on Wednesday.'

To his credit, Harrington looked astonished. He was either a very good actor or really was surprised.

'That's rubbish,' he managed to growl out eventually. 'She was not in my cottage on Wednesday. Or any other day for that matter.'

'We have a witness who says otherwise.' Technically she didn't have a witness, only an overheard conversation. Maybe she should have waited until talking to Cressida before confronting Harrington. But the way she'd fallen for his vulnerable act grated on her.

'Then they're lying,' he said. 'I told you I've never even spoken to Cressida. I saw her around the grounds once, maybe twice. I never invited her into my cottage.'

Karen stared at him and he glared back.

'What time was she supposed to have been there?' he asked scathingly.

Karen said nothing. She didn't have that information and, until she'd spoken to Cressida, she didn't have much to back up Ella's story. She checked her watch. 'You'd better get home, open up for the search team, unless you want them to break down the door.'

He shot her a hurt look and then turned on his heel, marching out of Chidlow House. Sandy followed him down the stone steps.

Karen watched them go. Had he had a hand in Cressida and Natasha's disappearance? And if he had, then why didn't Cressida remember? Why hadn't she said something? Would he really stroll about so brazenly knowing that Cressida would see him and point him out?

'He seemed like such a nice chap,' PC Smith said.

Karen had forgotten he was there. 'Sorry?'

'Mike Harrington. He was just telling me about his time training up the detection dogs. Fascinating stuff.'

Karen didn't reply but kept watching as Harrington strode away, his limp barely noticeable, his stick hitting the ground hard each time he took a step. His whole frame was tense. She'd made him angry.

'Can't believe he was involved,' PC Smith said, tutting and shaking his head. 'He's got a dog.'

'Even Bill Sikes had a dog,' Karen said.

'Bill Sikes? Who's that? Another suspect?'

Karen put a hand to her forehead, then lifted her gaze to the sky and took a deep breath. 'Dickens, PC Smith. Dickens.'

She left a confused PC Smith standing in the doorway and headed back inside.

The most sensible thing to do now was to talk to Cressida, ask her to confirm Ella's story. She couldn't remember anything after Thursday night when she was getting ready to go out with Natasha. But she shouldn't have a problem remembering things that happened on Wednesday, and that's when Ella said Cressida was at Harrington's cottage.

Karen checked the time. Only twenty minutes had passed, so the Blakes probably weren't at home yet. She would have to wait a little longer before calling them.

With her hands in her pockets, feeling like she'd been played by Mike Harrington, she walked back into the main part of the house to find Morgan. He'd know what to do. He wouldn't be so foolish as to let personal feelings influence his opinion of a suspect.

CHAPTER TWENTY-TWO

Karen headed straight to the incident room they'd set up in the library. Sophie and Rick were hunched over their laptops.

Rick looked up, and after he'd seen the look on Karen's face, said, 'Is everything all right, Sarge?'

'I've just found out something from Ella Seaton, the student who's still here. She says that Cressida was at Mike Harrington's cottage on Wednesday.'

Rick's eyebrows lifted, and he exhaled a long breath as he leaned back in his chair. 'He didn't mention that earlier, I take it.'

'No,' Karen said, 'he didn't. In fact, he's denying it.'

'How did Ella know Cressida was in his cottage?' Sophie asked. 'Did she see them together? Was she there?'

'No, she overheard Cressida telling Natasha about it. I'm going to give Cressida another five minutes, then call her at home to see if she can verify.'

'What if she doesn't remember?' Rick asked.

'She can't remember what happened on Thursday or Friday, but there's no reason she shouldn't be able to recall events that occurred on Wednesday.'

'Good point,' Rick said.

'Sarge,' Sophie said, getting up and carrying her laptop over to Karen. 'I've been going over the areas we've looked at closely so far.

We've examined footage from CCTV cameras in Harmston and the nearby villages, both from private residences and businesses, but we're drawing a blank. I think we need to expand the perimeter and look at the larger villages.'

Karen nodded. 'Yes, I think you're right. It's like they vanished into thin air on Thursday night.'

'But Cressida came back,' Rick said.

'Yes,' Karen said, thoughtfully. 'But she came back walking across the lawns. She didn't come back via the main road.'

'That's right,' Sophie said. 'It bothered me that no one saw the girls on the road on Thursday. It's not a quiet road, someone should have spotted them – unless they didn't walk along the main road.'

Rick closed his laptop. 'Most of the houses are set well back from the road. Lots of trees and bushes around, so it's perfectly feasible the girls walked past all the residential places and no one saw a thing, especially at night.' He shrugged. 'When I checked on Friday, the staff at the pub in the village said they hadn't seen them the previous evening. I told them I'd go back tonight to see if I can catch any regulars, put the word out, ask if anyone saw them. But it doesn't look like they went there on Thursday night. The pub does have security cameras, and Cressida and Natasha weren't on them.'

'Well, they had to go somewhere,' Karen said. 'We just need to find out where.'

'It's a shame Cressida can't remember anything,' Sophie said. 'Do you think she's putting it on? The amnesia?'

'Why do you say that?' Karen asked.

'She seems scared. Do you think there's someone around here threatening her, making sure she doesn't talk?'

'She'd tell her parents if that were the case, wouldn't she?' Rick asked, turning around to look at Sophie.

'Unless she's hiding something herself. She was smoking weed. Maybe she got into something harder and doesn't want to admit to it.'

Karen pondered that for a moment. 'Maybe.'

'I don't know,' Rick said. 'She seems genuinely distressed. And trauma like that can do funny things to the mind.'

Karen nodded. 'That's true. I'll see what she has to say about Mike Harrington. That might give us more to go on.'

She spent a little more time with Rick and Sophie going over the future search plans, and then flipped through the file to get the home telephone number of the Blakes.

She dialled the number on her mobile while sitting in an armchair by the window. She looked out on to Chidlow's land as she waited.

Jasmine Blake answered with a flustered 'Yes?'

'Sorry to trouble you again so soon,' Karen said. 'This is DS Hart. I've just had a word with one of the students here and they told me Cressida spent time at Mike Harrington's cottage on Wednesday.'

'Who's Mike Harrington?'

'He's the groundsman here at Chidlow House.'

'I see. You think he might have had something to do with it?'

'I don't know, Mrs Blake. I'd like to talk to Cressida and ask her if she was, in fact, at the groundsman's cottage on Wednesday.'

'Oh, well, Cressida's very upset at the moment, and I don't want her to be distressed further. She's got an appointment with a psychologist in a few hours, and I'd like her to be in the best possible frame of mind for that.'

'I can appreciate that, Mrs Blake, but this is very important. I really do need to check whether Cressida has spent time with Mike Harrington.'

'I see. Can it wait until later this afternoon?'

'No, it can't,' Karen said, shaking her head in disbelief. 'Natasha is still missing, Mrs Blake. Time is key here.'

'Right. Well, the thing is, she's resting at the moment. I'll tell you what, I'll ask her and then I'll call you back.'

'Well, no, Mrs Blake, actually—'

But Karen was cut off when Jasmine Blake hung up the phone. Karen swore.

'What's wrong, Sarge?' Sophie asked.

'Apparently, Cressida is resting.' Karen checked her watch, wishing the FLO, Lydia, was still at the house. 'I'll give them a few minutes to get back to me, and if they haven't, then I'll call again.'

She grabbed two files from the desk and began to methodically go through them, looking for something they'd missed on Mike Harrington. Karen had empathised with his loss. She'd felt a bond, and she didn't like the thought that he'd pulled the wool over her eyes, that she couldn't trust her instincts when it came to judging his character. It was the same when the chief constable had told her his wife had died. She'd felt sorry for him and it had affected her ability to view him objectively. She wanted to trust him because she understood his pain, but that didn't mean he was beyond corruption.

With Chidlow on the other hand, she found it easy to imagine him tied up in all this. He was still high on her list of suspects. She rubbed her knee, trying to massage away the dull ache. It still gave her trouble now and then, thanks to Charlie Cook.

She sighed. She had suspects but no evidence a crime had been committed. They had one missing student. And another trauma-tised teenager, who would not or could not tell them what had happened.

A case like this required her to be objective, to look at all the angles, examine all the evidence and not jump to any conclusions just because she didn't like someone . . . or because she did.

Doyle was another interesting character. She couldn't see a motive, but he was a possibility. Here with the students overnight, he had the opportunity.

A few minutes later, Karen's mobile rang.

'Hello. Am I speaking to DS Hart?' It was Jasmine Blake.

'Yes, Mrs Blake. Have you managed to talk to Cressida? May I have a word with her?' Karen asked.

'Well, no, like I said, she's resting, but I did ask her if she'd been to that man's cottage, and she said no. She was boasting to her friends. It was just a silly story.'

Karen frowned. 'So she wasn't at Mike Harrington's cottage on Wednesday?'

'No, she wasn't.'

'Do you think I could talk to Cressida directly about this? I know she's resting, but this is really important.'

Jasmine paused and then said, 'Oh, very well, but do try not to upset her. She's been through such an ordeal.'

Karen rubbed the middle of her brow where the beginning of a headache was building.

'Hello?'

'Cressida, I'm sorry to bother you again. But there's an important question I have to ask you.'

'I know. My mum just told me you want to know if I spent time with Mike Harrington.'

'Yes, that's right,' Karen said. 'Did you? You're not in any trouble. We just need to know.'

'Um . . . I don't want to get anyone else in trouble. He didn't seem like a bad man.'

Karen's grip tightened on the phone. She hadn't thought so either. 'Did he hurt you or Natasha?'

'I . . . don't know. I can't remember.'

'Did you or Natasha spend time with him before Thursday?'

She paused before answering. 'No.'

'I spoke to Ella earlier and she recalls a conversation between you and Natasha where you were telling Natasha you'd been inside Mike Harrington's cottage. Is that true?'

Cressida hesitated. 'Well, I did say that, yes, but I was just trying to impress Natasha. She thought he was good-looking.'

'So you didn't go to his cottage?'

'No.'

Karen closed her eyes. This case was getting more and more confusing. Why would Cressida make something like that up? Was it just a matter of boasting to her friends, trying to make herself seem grown-up and important?

'Did you or Natasha have a crush on Mr Harrington?' Karen asked.

'Maybe. Natasha thought he was hot . . .' She trailed off.

'Okay. So just to get this clear, there was nothing going on between Natasha and Mike Harrington as far as you know?'

'No.'

'Did you see Mike Harrington on Thursday?'

'Um, not during the day, I don't think, but I'm not sure about the evening. I can't remember anything about that.'

'Okay, that's all right. Maybe the psychologist will help you remember.'

'Yes, maybe,' Cressida said quietly.

Karen asked a few more questions, trying to get more information from Cressida. Sometimes it wasn't so much what a witness said as the way they said it. That could provide just as much information.

But dealing with Cressida was like handling a closed book that refused to reveal its contents no matter how many times Karen tried to pry it open.

Karen was frustrated she couldn't get to the truth. Sophie's comment was still going around in her mind. Was Cressida's amnesia genuine, or was she hiding what had happened because she was scared?

191

CHAPTER TWENTY-THREE

Karen sat in a wingback armchair with a stack of files on her lap. A gust of fierce wind howled through the small gaps in the window frame. She looked out over the blustery scenery and wondered how Morgan was getting on.

He'd gone to liaise with Inspector Grant. The search team needed to extend the perimeter. They'd found nothing. No footprints, which wasn't really a surprise as the rain had been so heavy. No items of clothing, no discarded bags or phones. Maybe that was a good sign. It could indicate that Natasha was safe but hadn't wanted to return to Chidlow House.

Karen selected a file, ready to go back through the notes, when she heard footsteps. She turned and saw Edward Chidlow standing in the doorway.

He was scowling.

Karen said nothing but waited expectantly.

'When were you going to tell me?' he demanded.

'Tell you what, sir?' she asked.

'That you broke into one of the rooms, damaging my property.'

'Ah, you're talking about the lock?'

'Yes. You should have asked my permission before getting a locksmith in.'

'Actually, you'd already given us permission to search the premises. DC Shah requested the key. As you couldn't provide it, we had to gain access by other means.'

'You could have waited! I'm sure the key will turn up. I just hope you're prepared to fix any damage.'

Karen doubted he'd stormed into the library to tell her off without already inspecting the lock. PC Smith had done a very good job, and although the lock would need to be replaced, there was no damage to the door or the frame. He'd been very careful.

'Actually, we've found the key,' Karen said.

Chidlow blinked. 'What do you mean? If you'd found the key, why did you need a locksmith?'

'Because at the time we didn't know who'd taken the key and been using the room.'

'Hang on a minute. Someone's been using the room?' Chidlow was outraged. 'Who?'

Why was he having such a strong reaction to someone being in a room he used for storage?

'Are you all right, Lord Chidlow?' Karen asked. 'Would you like to sit down? You're very pale.'

He waved a hand at her. 'I'm fine. Just fine. Who's been in the room? What did you find in there?'

Karen watched him closely as beads of sweat broke out on his brow. The room was full of old junk, and she knew that Ethan was the one using the speaker, so why was Chidlow so anxious?

'I just want to know who was in the room and who's got the key,' Chidlow said.

'I've got the key.' Karen walked over to the desk and took the key from the drawer. 'Here you go.'

'Who had it? I demand to know. It's my property. I should be told who stole the key.'

'It was one of the students,' Karen said.

She couldn't tell Chidlow it was Ethan. That would drive the final nail in the coffin of Karen's hope that the chief constable would lend his support to the corruption investigation.

'What were they doing in there?'

Karen didn't answer his question.

Chidlow swore. 'That's the last time I'm having kids in my house, that's for sure,' he snarled. 'And you're not going to tell me what you found in there?'

'Not right now, sir, no.'

'But it's my house! How can you refuse to tell me what was in there?'

'Quite easily,' Karen said.

His face had flushed scarlet, and Karen thought that, any minute now, he'd stamp his foot and have a full-on tantrum.

Sophie walked into the library, announcing that the crime team had arrived to get to work on the room next to the bathroom.

Chidlow rubbed his neck. 'They're going to go through the storeroom? Whatever for? It's just full of junk.'

'We have a good reason, sir,' Sophie said, exchanging a look with Karen and then addressing Karen directly. 'Sarge, should I start the fingerprinting now?'

'Yes, please,' Karen said.

Sophie turned to Chidlow. 'We can start with you, sir, and take your fingerprints for elimination purposes.'

Chidlow scowled. 'I don't think—'

Karen interrupted. 'It would be very helpful. We'd expect to find your prints on your possessions. We are interested in fingerprints that aren't yours.'

They both stared at him, and eventually he let out a disgruntled huff and agreed.

'If you'd like to come with me, sir, we'll get started,' Sophie said cheerfully as Chidlow glowered at her.

After they left, Karen grabbed her coat and went outside to find Morgan. She saw him crossing the lawn at the side of the house.

'How's it going?' she asked as she reached him.

'They've found nothing.'

Karen sighed and looked over to the lake, where the divers were still hard at work. She told Morgan about Ella's claim Cressida had been in Mike Harrington's cottage.

Morgan shoved his hands in his pockets and frowned. 'And Cressida said she'd made it up? She denied being there?'

'Yes.'

'Did you believe her?'

'I'm not sure. What do you think of Harrington?'

'He seems to be a complicated character.'

Karen thought that summed him up well. 'Do you think he's got anything to do with the disappearance?'

'We can't rule it out.' He sighed. 'As far as we know, Natasha could have decided to leave of her own volition. Maybe she got sick of her overbearing parents and decided she wanted a bit of freedom.'

'But then Cressida coming back traumatised just doesn't make sense, does it?'

'No,' Morgan said. 'It really doesn't add up.'

'Sophie said something that made me think perhaps Cressida hasn't truly forgotten what happened. Maybe she doesn't want to tell us anything because she's scared.'

'Scared of who?' Morgan asked.

'I don't know. I really don't know.'

They gazed across Chidlow's land, taking in the russet- and gold-leaved woodland, the grey lake and the deep green of the lawns.

'Beautiful here,' Morgan said.

They both looked up as a hawk let out a harsh call. Fully opening its brown, rounded wings, exposing its pale speckled chest, it soared majestically above their heads, on the lookout for prey. A deadly predator for songbirds and small mammals. Karen shivered. A reminder that something beautiful could also be dangerous.

They both turned and walked back into Chidlow House.

◆ ◆ ◆

Karen had only been back in the house for ten minutes when she heard shouting coming from the entrance hall. She put down the file she'd been looking at and walked towards the source of the noise.

A shrill female voice was issuing demands. 'Don't you know who I am? Let me pass!'

When Karen made it to the entrance, she saw PC Smith trying to deal with a fiery woman who Karen judged to be in her forties. She was tiny and very petite – Karen guessed her to be less than five foot tall without her high heels.

PC Smith was trying to keep the peace, holding up his hands and attempting to reason with her.

'What's going on here?' Karen asked as she approached them.

PC Smith shot her a desperate look. 'She just turned up at the gate and demanded to be let in. I tried to explain that the house is closed to visitors due to the investigation, but she won't listen.'

'Who are you?' the woman demanded imperiously.

She had cool blonde hair, cut into a short bob. It looked sleek and elegant, but when she moved her head, Karen noticed that her hair didn't move. It was more like a helmet than a hairstyle. There had been a serious amount of product applied.

Her forehead was free of frown lines, but her nose scrunched up as she glared at Karen.

'I'm Lady Chidlow,' she said, hoisting her handbag higher on her shoulder, and Karen noted it was Chanel. And so was her suit, if the interlocking Cs on the buttons were anything to go by.

'Lord Chidlow's wife?' Karen asked. 'I thought he was divorced.'

'Well, yes, we are divorced, but I still have the right to come and visit my ex-husband if I want to.'

'I see,' Karen said. 'Did he know you were coming?'

'No.'

'And how did you get here?' Karen asked, wondering how she had bypassed the officer standing by the gates.

'My chauffeur,' she said.

'Did the officer at the gate tell you that only police and residents' vehicles are permitted access?'

'Well, yes, he did spout some nonsense like that, but I told him I'm visiting my husband.'

'Ex-husband,' PC Smith said, earning him a glare from Lady Chidlow.

'You're the detective in charge of the investigation, aren't you?' she asked Karen, a sly look passing across her features.

Karen nodded. 'Yes, I'm one of the team investigating.'

'A girl's gone missing, hasn't she?'

'A young woman. Do you know anything about that?' Karen asked.

Sophie had been trying to get in touch with Mrs Chidlow but hadn't had any luck after being fobbed off by the PA.

'I could tell you some stories that might interest you.'

'What kind of stories?' Karen asked, nodding at PC Smith to indicate he could go back to his position at the door now. She gestured for Lady Chidlow to follow her inside.

'I never thought I'd see the day when a detective led me around my own house,' she said.

'Is this your house?' Karen asked. 'You don't share the property with Lord Chidlow, do you?'

'Well, no,' she said. 'But I did live here for quite some time.'

'Of course,' Karen said. 'We're using Mr Doyle's office for interviews. Let's go in here and you can tell me some of these stories.'

She held open the door for Lady Chidlow.

'This used to be the secretary's room.' She looked at Karen disapprovingly. 'Who's Doyle?'

'He's the director of the student study programme. He was running the course here when the students went missing.'

'I told Eddie it was a bad idea.'

Karen found it strange to hear Lord Chidlow referred to as Eddie. 'You did?'

'Yes! He's hard up, but not that hard up, for goodness' sake. I don't see why he doesn't sell the place and buy a fancy pad abroad. Maybe a nice place in New York or Paris. He could afford it, if he sold this. Chidlow House is nothing but a drain on his finances.'

'Some people like old buildings,' Karen said. 'They like the sense of history a place like this holds.'

'Not me,' Lady Chidlow said. 'Besides, the history here is pretty dark.'

'It is?'

They took seats facing each other at the desk, and Lady Chidlow arranged her skirt and crossed her legs. 'Yes, really terrible things happened here.'

'I don't know much about the history of the house,' Karen said.

'There was a book published. It's out of print now,' she said. 'But it had some awful descriptions of the goings-on here over the centuries. I read it just after we got married. To tell you the truth, I wished I hadn't. It should be in the library somewhere. I think it's called *The History of Chidlow House*. Not the most imaginative title.'

'Thanks. I'll try to find it.'

'Some of the women who lived here drowned themselves.'

'Your ex-husband did mention it,' Karen said.

'Three of them in a row. Horrific stuff. Can you imagine how bad their lives must have been to do that?' She shuddered.

'Is there anything you can tell me pertaining to this investigation?'

'Actually, yes.' Lady Chidlow shuffled in her seat and leaned forward conspiratorially. 'I'm sure you're looking into my husband's past.'

Karen agreed that they were.

'Well, I can tell you that he left me for a young woman, and when I say young, I mean very young. He's always had a taste for young girls.' She gave Karen a meaningful look.

'How young?'

'Much younger than him,' she said. 'Anyway, I just thought you'd be interested.'

'How young was the woman he left you for?'

'He threw away ten years of marriage for a twenty-one-year-old.'

Karen nodded. Although not a great advert for Chidlow's fidelity, it didn't mean he had anything to do with Natasha and Cressida's disappearance.

Before Karen could ask any more questions, Lord Chidlow shoved the door open. Behind him was the simpering Graham Doyle.

'What are you doing here?' He glared at his ex-wife.

'I've come to help with the investigation,' she said, smiling smugly and sitting back in the chair.

'Thank you, Mr Doyle,' Karen said coldly. 'I see you took it upon yourself to let Lord Chidlow know his ex-wife was here.'

'It's only right he knows,' Doyle said. 'It is his house, after all.'

'You have no right to be here,' Chidlow growled.

'Maybe I should have pushed harder in the divorce.' Lady Chidlow smiled. 'I could have taken half of this place.'

Chidlow's face was scarlet. 'You were lucky to get what you did. You took me to the cleaners thanks to that cut-throat lawyer of yours.'

'Well, it was your fault for running off with a young girl!'

'She wasn't a young *girl*,' Chidlow said between gritted teeth. 'She was twenty-one.'

'Yes, but you were forty-five, and twenty-one is only four years older than the students who went missing.'

Chidlow's eyes widened. He glanced at Karen and then back at his ex-wife. 'Twenty-one is an adult, not a child.'

Before things descended into a screaming match, Karen stood and positioned herself between them. 'Okay, that's enough. Lady Chidlow, come with me.' She led the woman to the temporary incident room. 'Sophie?'

Sophie looked up from the desk. 'Yes, Sarge?'

'I'd like you to come and talk to Lady Chidlow.'

Karen heard footsteps and to her annoyance realised that Doyle and Chidlow had followed them. 'Lord Chidlow, is there a room we can use so DC Jones can talk to your ex-wife in private?'

'I really don't think it's appropriate,' Chidlow said. 'She wasn't here. She knows nothing about the case at all. All she wants to do is damage my reputation.'

'I have to agree,' Doyle said. 'It's most objectionable. Smearing a decent man like Lord Chidlow over this is a disgrace.'

'Thank you for sharing your opinions, gentlemen,' Karen said. 'All the same, DC Jones will be talking to your ex-wife, Lord Chidlow, so if you could provide a room for the interview, I'd appreciate it.'

Doyle turned to Chidlow. 'I'd rather they weren't in my office. They could go upstairs and use one of the guest rooms. There's plenty of space up there.'

Chidlow clenched his teeth and nodded. 'Very well, but I want it on record that this woman delights in making my life a misery, and I wouldn't put it past her to make up malicious lies purposely, to make me look bad.'

Karen took Sophie aside. 'Are you all right doing the interview?'

Sophie nodded. 'Absolutely.'

As Doyle escorted Sophie and Lady Chidlow upstairs, Karen turned back to Chidlow. It was easy to see that his ex-wife had been hurt and was still angry. Was this just malice from a scorned woman or was there something more to it?

'I really do have to object most strongly to this, Detective,' Chidlow said.

'Your objection is noted, sir, but we have to look into all allegations, no matter how unsavoury.'

Chidlow gave a curt nod and stalked off back to his own study.

CHAPTER TWENTY-FOUR

After Doyle left them in one of the rooms, Sophie pulled out the chair by the desk for Lady Chidlow and then sat on the stool beside the window. Not exactly the best environment for an interview, but it would have to do.

Sophie was determined to do a good job, because Karen had entrusted the task to her. But Lady Chidlow made her nervous. She had a pinched face and her eyes were very close together, quite like Chidlow's in fact. The couple reminded Sophie of birds of prey. Perhaps Chidlow would be a buzzard, with his long beak-like nose, and his ex-wife was like a sparrowhawk, with bright, glaring eyes.

Sophie shuddered and tried to collect her thoughts. 'Could I have your full name, please?'

'Selina Mary Chidlow.'

'So you kept your husband's name after the divorce?' Sophie asked, making a note.

'What's wrong with that?' she snapped.

'Nothing at all. I was just clarifying.'

'My maiden name was Pratt. I preferred Chidlow.'

Sophie wasn't quite sure what to say to that, so she smiled. 'I see. Now, how long were you married to Edward Chidlow?'

'Ten years.'

'And when were you divorced?'

'Two years ago,' Selina said.

'Would you say it was an amicable split?'

'I don't really see what that has to do with anything,' she said with a toss of her head.

Her sleek blonde hair gleamed but didn't move. The style remained impeccable.

Sophie was impressed. Her own hair, a mass of light brown curls, wouldn't behave like that no matter how much product she put on it.

Lady Chidlow watched Sophie closely. 'You're wondering how reliable my information is, aren't you? Wondering if my turning up today is down to sour grapes?'

'You must have been hurt by how the relationship ended.'

'Well, of course, but karma prevailed.'

'It did?'

Lady Chidlow gave a cat-like smile and leaned forward. 'It did. She only lived here for three months before leaving him for a pianist he'd hired for a party. Served him right!'

'Do you have the woman's details? I'd like to talk to her.'

'Her name's Veronica Didsley, but I've no other details. You'll have to ask my ex-husband.'

Sophie wrote down the name then tapped her pen against the pad in front of her. 'Lady Chidlow, do you have any reason to believe your husband was involved in the disappearance of Natasha Layton and Cressida Blake?'

'Cressida Blake has reappeared?'

Sophie nodded. 'That's right.'

'And did she say anything about my husband?'

'I can't disclose that information,' Sophie said, feeling suddenly that the interview was on the other foot.

Lady Chidlow looked thoughtful. 'You shouldn't underestimate him.' She leaned forward, her eyes no longer so sharp, an emotion in them Sophie couldn't quite place. 'He does have an interest in women far younger than himself.'

'Have you got any reason to think he would have hurt them or held either one of them against their will?' Sophie asked.

Lady Chidlow shrugged. 'I couldn't say.'

'Do you have any reason to think Edward Chidlow could be violent?'

'Are you asking if he used to hit me?' She raised an eyebrow. 'No. We screamed at each other. We threw a few pieces of porcelain around, perhaps a smashed wine glass from time to time during our marriage. We both had tempers, but no, he never hit me.' She lifted a hand to her neck. Her wrist was weighed down by a heavy gold bracelet. 'There's just something . . .' She broke off and shook her head.

'What is it?' Sophie asked.

'It's not just the woman he left me for. Granted, Veronica was twenty-one, well above the age of consent. I might disapprove of that, particularly because he was married to me at the time. But it's more . . . I'd noticed him watching younger women . . . girls, really. Let's not beat around the bush. Even when they were in school uniform. It made me uneasy.'

'I see,' Sophie said.

It was an uncomfortable subject and hard to determine whether Lady Chidlow was speaking out of spite or out of genuine concern for Natasha and a desire to help.

Sophie spoke to Lady Chidlow for a further twenty minutes but found it hard to judge what to do with the information she'd given her. It was nothing tangible.

Sophie offered to show her back downstairs after she said she had an appointment to get to, but the woman waved her off saying she was perfectly capable of finding her way around her own house. Sophie refrained from reminding her that it wasn't actually her house anymore.

After Lady Chidlow had left, Sophie gathered together her notes and put them in her bag, then went to use the bathroom on the girls' floor, passing the Forensics unit on the way. They were hard at work, methodically logging and photographing every item from the junk room. They'd already taken photographs of the footprints in the dust and told Sophie there was an excellent set of fingerprints on the Bluetooth speaker. That was good news, but she suspected that they already knew who they belonged to – Ethan, the chief constable's son. She was glad Karen had been quick to guess Ethan Grayson was behind the spooky noises when they'd found the speaker. The idea someone had been trying to scare them was unnerving.

She washed her hands, noticing that the cupboard that had previously been locked was now open and contained only towels and stacks of soap. After drying her hands, she looked at her reflection in the mirror, tucking her brown curls behind her ears in an effort to appear more professional. She was leaning forward to wipe away a tiny smudge of mascara just below her lower lash line when she noticed something very odd on the wall to the side of the mirror.

She stared at it for a moment, moving closer. There was a hole in the wall. It was small but definitely there. She quickly walked next door and asked to speak to one of the Forensics team. A large man in a pale blue coverall suit came forward.

'I've got a question for you,' Sophie asked. 'I know you're still at the front of the room at the moment, but could you check for a small hole in that wall?' She pointed at the general area she judged the tiny hole to be. 'It's about five feet up from the floor and two feet away from the corner of the room.'

He looked over his shoulder at the spot Sophie was pointing at. 'We haven't got that far yet, but I'll have a look. Why do you ask?'

'Because I've just seen a hole in the girls' bathroom wall. It's next to this room . . .'

'Right. I'll have a look,' he said, stepping over the debris on the floor, squeezing around two stacked chairs and passing an old frayed armchair wedged under the window.

'Yes, there's something here,' he called out. 'Just above the shelf. It looks like an old-fashioned peephole, not a freshly drilled hole. It's lined with brass. I've seen them in old houses before.'

'You have?'

'Yes, a few times.'

'So you don't think it's been used recently? To spy on the girls in the bathroom, I mean,' Sophie asked.

The other CSIs in the room had now turned their attention to Sophie.

'It's hard to say,' the officer said, staring at the wall. 'Someone could have been using it, I suppose.'

'Was there a set of footprints right up to the shelf?' Sophie asked.

'Yes,' he said. 'As a matter of fact, there was. That suggests someone has been using it, doesn't it?'

'Thank you,' Sophie said, and, feeling sick, turned and walked briskly towards the stairs. She had to tell DS Hart and DI Morgan that it was likely someone had been spying on the girls in the bathroom at Chidlow House.

Sophie found Karen in the library flipping through a tattered old cream paperback.

'How did you get on?' Karen asked. 'Chidlow is very upset we're talking to his ex-wife. I'm starting to think he has something to hide.'

'Oh,' Sophie said, momentarily distracted. 'Yes, she didn't give any firm evidence, but she did say she'd seen him watching girls in school uniforms,' she said.

Karen pulled a face.

'But it's her word against his,' Sophie said, 'and she's still very angry at him.'

'That's true,' Karen said. 'This is interesting.' She held up the paperback. 'A book about the Chidlow family over the generations. I'm not sure it will be much help, but—'

Sophie ignored the book, focusing on her more pressing concern. 'I went into the girls' bathroom upstairs and I noticed something pretty shocking.'

'What?' Karen closed the book.

'There's a peephole. I think someone's been spying on the female students when they use the bathroom.'

Karen's eyes widened. 'How could we have missed that in the search?' She held up the paperback. 'It talks about the spyholes in here. Says Chidlow's great-great-grandfather liked to watch his guests unawares as they moved about his house. It says all the holes have since been filled in, though.'

'Not this one. To be fair, it's a very small hole,' Sophie said, 'and it's right by the edge of the mirror. Easy to miss. The hole goes through to Chidlow's storage room next door. I asked a member of the crime scene team to take a look and he said he'd seen peepholes like it before in other old houses.'

'So it's old? Not one someone has made recently?' Karen asked.

'It's old, but there were footprints going right up to the shelf just below the hole.'

'Can they match the footprints?' Karen asked.

'I don't know. They've taken photographs but it's possible more than one person has walked back and forth, so getting a clear print isn't easy. There's not much room as you try to get around the furniture.'

Karen nodded. 'That's a shame, but it suggests someone has been using that spyhole recently, so we're looking for a peeping Tom.'

Sophie swallowed hard. 'I think so.'

'There wasn't any recording equipment on the shelf?'

'No.'

'That's something at least,' Karen said.

'Unless they removed it when we got here,' Sophie suggested. 'It's an awful thought, isn't it?'

'Yes, it is.' Karen held up the book. 'There's some horrible stuff in here as well. Apparently Edward Chidlow's great-great-grandfather enjoyed tormenting his wife. She wrote letters to her sister detailing the methods he used to frighten her.' Karen took a deep breath. 'We should tell DI Morgan about the spyhole and then see what Chidlow's got to say for himself.'

'It could be Chidlow spying on the female students,' Sophie said. 'It's his house, so he'd likely know about the peepholes, though the spy could be someone else.'

'You mean Ethan, the chief constable's son?'

'We know he was in that room.'

Karen nodded. 'We'll have to talk to him as well.'

CHAPTER TWENTY-FIVE

Karen found Morgan walking back and forth in front of the back staircase, looking at the paintings.

'Everything all right?' she asked.

He continued to pace, looking up at a bloody hunting scene. 'Yes, just thinking. There has to be something we've missed. I thought there could be a link between the death of the teacher and Natasha's disappearance, but I can't work out what it could be. Alison King enjoyed her job, she was close to her family, had plenty of friends and none of them said anything that might suggest she was upset or disturbed in the days leading up to her falling from the roof. And yet Doyle said she was disturbed. She was unnerved by the atmosphere of Chidlow House and the creepy noises.'

'The noises were Ethan's doing.'

Morgan met Karen's gaze. 'Yes.'

'Do you think he did the same to Cressida and Natasha? Scared them into leaving Chidlow House? We only have his word that they were dressed up, heading out for the evening. No one else saw them leaving.'

Morgan paused. 'That's true. The more I think about it, the more I'm convinced there's a connection.'

'But they were just noises. Would that really be enough to drive Alison King to jump from the roof and to cause Cressida and

Natasha to run away?' Karen sighed. Cressida had denied hearing the noises and so had Ella Seaton. It didn't add up.

When Karen mentioned the peepholes to Morgan, he stopped pacing and asked, 'Have any more been found around the property?'

'I don't think so.'

He frowned. 'We should have found the peephole during the search.'

Karen felt herself getting defensive, but Morgan was right. She had been in that bathroom but missed the peephole. She couldn't blame DC Shah and the rest of the search team for missing something so important when she had missed it too.

It had been a big slip-up on her part. 'I don't think there were any more in the rooms I searched,' Karen said. 'But I missed the one in the bathroom, so maybe we need to take a second look. I've asked the crime scene manager to send digital copies of the photographs to our emails.'

Morgan pulled out his mobile. 'I've got it.' He looked closely at the screen. 'Very small and well disguised. It's not like this house has perfectly smooth walls, and there are numerous rooms with patterned wallpaper that could disguise the holes. Easy to miss something like this.'

Karen nodded, appreciating his attempt to make her feel better. But the fact remained, she'd missed the hole.

She couldn't change that, but she could redouble her efforts now. Concentrate and work out if someone had been using these spyholes recently. Had someone been watching the female students undressing, bathing, getting into the shower? If so, who?

'Chidlow has to be top of our suspect list, but we can't rule out Ethan Grayson.' It pained her to admit it. Zeroing in on Ethan would not win her any favours with the chief constable.

'I agree. Do you want to talk to him, or shall I?'

'I'll do it.' Karen hoped talking to Ethan away from Chidlow House might get her some answers.

'Good,' Morgan said. 'I'm not sure how his father will react. I'll let the superintendent know about this development. I think she'll need time to prepare for the chief constable's bad temper.'

Karen couldn't help hoping Chief Constable Grayson wouldn't be there when she dropped in to visit Ethan at home.

'I can follow up with Chidlow,' Morgan said. 'He told me he hasn't been in there for years, but there were two sets of footprints in that room, weren't there?'

'It looked like there was more than one shoe print, but only one set were a good clear print. Maybe we could check all Chidlow's shoes and see if we get a match.'

'Do you think the crime scene team will be able to do that?'

'I'm not sure. It's not like an imprint made in the earth. Though the floor was dusty, it wasn't an even spread, but even a partial match could help us put the pressure on Chidlow.'

Morgan nodded thoughtfully. 'It's worth a try. I think it might be better if we both talk to Chidlow after his study has been searched. I'll check on the outdoor search, and when you get back from speaking to Ethan Grayson, we'll talk to Chidlow together, okay?'

It was early afternoon by the time Karen turned into School Lane in Washingborough. The chief constable lived with his son in a large Victorian house. The property was surrounded by a tall stone wall. There were iron gates at the entrance to the driveway, but thankfully they were open.

As soon as Karen got out of the car, she heard raised voices. She walked to the front door and paused, listening.

Chief Constable Grayson clearly had a temper. He was laying into Ethan about leaving home when he was supposed to be grounded. From the shouting, Karen gathered Grayson had come back home mid-morning and discovered Ethan wasn't there.

He was in a ferocious mood. Did Grayson believe Ethan was more deeply involved in this than any of them had realised?

Karen pressed on the doorbell and the shouting abruptly stopped. A moment later, Grayson opened the door with a face like thunder.

He blinked. 'DS Hart, has something happened?'

Karen had been hoping to get Ethan alone. She'd wanted to surprise him with what they knew, get him talking before he had a chance to prepare lies and concoct a story to cover up his involvement.

'Actually, yes, sir. I want to speak to Ethan. It's good that you're here. I can speak to you both together.'

Grayson shot a look over his shoulder, then stepped closer to Karen. 'Can you tell me first in private, before you speak to Ethan?'

In normal circumstances, Karen would have preferred to spring the news on both of them at the same time and judge their reactions. But Grayson was the chief constable.

'Of course, sir,' Karen said.

He ushered her into a large kitchen with a pine table in the centre of the room and retro carved wooden cupboards on the walls. The tiles above the countertops and behind the sink had tiny woodland animals painted on them. The kitchen had a surprisingly cosy feel. She hadn't expected that.

'Coffee?' he offered.

Usually Karen preferred to get down to business, but since the coffee Sophie had brought in early that morning, she'd had to make do with a choice between Doyle's watered-down coffee or nothing. Karen had opted for nothing. 'A coffee would be great. Thank you, sir.'

As he prepared the coffee, Karen filled him in. Summarising, she observed Grayson's face carefully as she said, 'So, as Ethan had a key to the storeroom, we'll need to examine his shoes to see if they match the prints. We think someone was using that peephole to spy on girls in the bathroom.'

Grayson ran a hand over his face. 'Good grief, you don't think Ethan would do that?'

Karen spoke with care. 'We don't know for sure that it was Ethan, but the evidence does point to him, sir. He had the key and we know he put the Bluetooth speaker in there. He admitted it.'

'What am I going to do with that boy?' he muttered under his breath as he put a mug of coffee on the pine table. 'Do you take milk?'

Karen nodded and waited in silence as Grayson got the milk from the fridge and added a small amount to her coffee.

Finally, he leaned heavily on the table, shaking his head. 'I can't believe he'd do that. Not Ethan.'

'Maybe he didn't. Why don't we ask him about it?'

Reluctantly, Grayson led Karen from the kitchen into the living room, where Ethan was sitting sulkily on an armchair. He had large, blue headphones clamped over his ears. Karen could hear the tinny music emanating from them.

On the mantelpiece behind him were various photographs. Childhood photos of a much happier Ethan, and a younger version of Grayson with a blonde woman that Karen guessed was Ethan's mother.

'Take those headphones off,' Grayson said, clicking his fingers at Ethan.

With an exaggerated sigh, Ethan did as he was told, then looked up at Karen. 'I suppose you've come to tell Dad about me turning up at Chidlow House earlier? Well, you can save your breath. He already knows. I told him.'

'Ethan, show some respect,' Grayson barked.

'Actually, Ethan, that's not why I'm here,' Karen said, and she sat on the sofa beside the bay window.

She stared at the boy for a moment as he shifted uncomfortably in his seat.

'Why are you here, then?' he asked.

'I wanted to ask you about the key to the junk room,' Karen said. 'How long have you had it?'

Ethan shrugged. 'A few days.'

'Right,' Karen said. 'And you went into the junk room to put the speaker inside and you've been connecting to the speaker with your iPhone, right?'

Ethan nodded. 'Yes, I already admitted that. But I wasn't doing anything other than trying to scare people a little bit.'

'Did you do anything else while you were in that room, Ethan?'

'Anything else?' His eyebrows lifted. 'What do you mean?'

'Look at anything else while you were in there?'

'Not really,' he said. 'I looked at a couple of the paintings but that was just . . .' He broke off and scowled. 'I didn't take anything, if that's what you mean.'

'No, that's not what she means,' Grayson snapped. 'Have you been spying on the girls, Ethan?'

'Spying?' His face scrunched up. 'What do you mean?'

'Exactly what I say. Tell me the truth.'

'No. I suppose I watched Natasha a bit, but I wasn't spying. She knew I was there. I don't know what you're getting at,' Ethan said, looking at Karen and then back to his father.

'I remember seeing you with a paperback, Ethan. It had a black-and-white photograph of Chidlow House on the cover and a red title.'

He nodded. 'Yeah, I was reading it. It was about the history of the house and the ghosts. What's wrong with that?'

'Did you read chapter twelve?' Karen asked.

Now it was Ethan's turn to look confused.

'Chapter twelve? I don't remember. I just flicked through it and only read the bits about the ghosts and the women drowning themselves. I didn't bother with the stuff about architecture. It goes into so much boring detail about how the gardens were designed.' His eyes narrowed. 'I didn't steal the book, if that's what you think.'

'In chapter twelve, the author describes spyholes around Chidlow House, one of which was in the storeroom on the girls' floor. The hole looked directly into the bathroom. You were in that room.'

Ethan's eyes widened as the implication dawned on him. 'I didn't know about the spyholes. Honestly. I didn't look through any holes.' His gaze darted between Karen and his father, his tone frantic.

'Do you promise you didn't spy on the girls, Ethan?' Grayson's voice was gruff but hopeful.

'I promise I didn't, Dad,' Ethan said. 'I didn't know about the holes.'

'Okay.' Grayson turned to Karen. 'I believe him.'

Karen was tempted to say that what Grayson believed was irrelevant, but managed to hold her tongue. Of course the chief constable didn't want to think the worst of his only child.

Karen didn't say anything for a moment but searched Ethan's face, looking for signs the kid was lying.

The chief constable may have believed him, but Karen wasn't convinced.

CHAPTER TWENTY-SIX

When Karen got back to Chidlow House, Morgan asked her to track down Lord Chidlow. She eventually found him lingering outside the storeroom where the crime scene technicians were still hard at work cataloguing individual items.

He craned his neck to see inside the room. 'Why is this taking so long?'

'I'll let you know when they're finished, Lord Chidlow,' Karen said, walking along the corridor towards him.

He turned and a flicker of irritation crossed his features. 'Oh, it's you. How long is all this going to take? I fail to understand why you're wasting time in here when you could be out there looking for the girl.'

'Natasha,' Karen said, putting a name to the missing young woman.

'Yes. I don't think you'll find her in there!' Chidlow said, waving a hand at the storeroom.

'We'd like to have a word with you again, sir, if you wouldn't mind coming downstairs with me. Another team is searching your office, so we'll have to make do with Doyle's for now.'

Chidlow huffed. 'This is getting to be quite unbearable.'

'If you'd like to follow me, please, sir,' Karen said, leading the way back down the corridor towards the staircase.

As they descended, Karen couldn't help looking at the portraits again, staring at the unhappy faces of the women. 'Why do they look so sad?'

'Well, rumour has it the previous Lord Chidlows weren't the kindest husbands. One of them, I think it was the sixth Lord Chidlow, did some awful things.'

'Such as?'

'Sadly, I only know my family history from the book I told you about. The family archives were lost when the cellars and basement flooded fifty years ago.'

Karen nodded. She'd read that book from cover to cover if she ever found the time.

Inside Doyle's office, Morgan was already behind the desk.

He looked up as they entered. 'Ah, good. Lord Chidlow. Please take a seat.'

Chidlow, annoyed at being told to sit down in his own house, clenched his teeth and sat stiffly in the chair opposite. Karen took the seat next to Morgan.

'We've made a discovery,' Morgan began, his gaze fixed on Chidlow. 'A small hole was found in the wall of your storeroom. It looks directly into the bathroom that was used by the female students. Did you know about that?'

Chidlow didn't even flinch. 'Yes. Well, I didn't know it hadn't been filled in like the others. There were peepholes all over this house, but during the refurbishment, when we renovated the guest rooms, the holes were covered up. We must have simply missed one. No harm done I'm sure. Nobody's been in that room.'

'Actually, they have,' Karen said.

'Oh, yes. The chief constable's boy, wasn't it?' Chidlow said with a sly look. 'I wonder if he'll get away with it. A bit of nepotism, eh? One rule for you lot, another for the rest of us.'

'He won't be getting away with it, sir,' Karen said, meeting his smug grin with a cold smile of her own. 'We only have your word the other spyholes have been filled in. Do you have a list of locations?'

'No, I don't have a list,' Chidlow said dismissively, stretching his legs and leaning back in his chair. 'But I can remember most of them, I think. I can tell you where they were from memory if that would help?'

'Thank you,' Morgan said, and made notes as Lord Chidlow looked up at the ceiling and began recalling the positions of the spyholes.

Karen watched him. She wouldn't be surprised to find he'd been spying on women. She tried not to take people at face value, but with Chidlow it was difficult. Arrogant, bad-tempered and self-ish, he was one of the most unlikeable men Karen had ever met.

When he finally finished reeling off the locations, she asked for the name of the company who'd done the renovation work. She wanted to check them out and make sure Chidlow hadn't told them to leave the one in the bathroom in place.

'Whatever for?' Chidlow said when Karen asked the question.

'We like to run a thorough investigation, sir.'

'I really don't see what this has got to do with that girl going missing,' he said, throwing up his hands.

'Natasha,' Karen snapped.

She was sick of him treating the girl like a nameless, faceless victim. She had a name. She was a young woman with a family and friends who loved her.

When Chidlow left them, Karen turned to Morgan. 'What do you think?'

'I'm not keen on him,' Morgan said. 'He'd say anything to save his own neck. But it doesn't mean he's lying about this. It's possible the spyhole was missed during the refurbishment.'

'And it just so happens to be the one that looks directly into the women's bathroom?' Karen raised an eyebrow.

'Yes, it does seem a bit of a reach, doesn't it?'

'It does.'

'Farzana and the rest of the crew are still working their way through Chidlow's study. We might find something. Though I doubt he'd be stupid enough to keep incriminating evidence in his personal office.'

'Maybe, but he's incredibly arrogant. He probably thinks we're no match for him.'

'Then he'll get a rude awakening.' Morgan smiled. 'How are Rick and Sophie getting on?'

'They're expanding the area and tracking down more CCTV. It's a big task.'

It was unusual in this day and age not to have a camera pick up something at some point. But in the rural villages, things weren't quite so easy. Officers had been using private cameras from homes, shops and restaurants too, but so far had come up blank.

Even Cressida's return had been stealthy. They hadn't picked her up on any cameras, no eyewitness sightings. The teenagers had gone out of their way not to be seen.

Karen left Doyle's office, planning to ask Rick to go down to the lake and check in with the underwater search unit. But before she entered the temporary incident room, she spotted Ella Seaton walking towards her.

Karen stared. Ella's face was chalk-white. Her frizzy hair sprang out in a mousey halo around her head. Her eyes were wide, and clutched in her right hand was an olive-green polo shirt.

When she got closer, Karen saw a small stain on the polo shirt, about the size of a five-pence piece. The circular stain was a rusty colour. Most likely blood.

'Ella, where did you find that?' Karen asked.

The young woman blinked. 'It was on the roof. I saw it lying on the floor. I thought it might be important.'

'So you picked it up? Ella, you should have left it where it was and told a police officer,' Karen said, her mind working overtime.

Why hadn't they spotted it before? The roof had been searched. Could they really have missed something so obvious?

'Stay there,' Karen ordered.

Ella did as she was told and remained frozen to the spot while Karen grabbed an evidence bag from the temporary incident room.

'Was it hidden away?' Karen asked, holding the bag open. 'Put it in there, please.'

'No, it was just left near the parapet. I'm sorry, I didn't think. You're right. I should have left it where it was. I thought it looked like blood.'

'It does,' Karen said. 'I need you to show me exactly where you found it.'

'Okay.' Ella nodded obediently.

'What's going on?' Edward Chidlow demanded, walking towards them. 'What's that?'

'A polo shirt I found on the roof,' Ella said.

Chidlow did a double take. 'What on earth were you doing on the roof? My insurance doesn't cover that. For goodness' sake, a woman died falling from that roof less than a week ago. Do you have a death wish?'

Ella bowed her head. 'I'm sorry. I didn't think. I just wanted to watch the search.'

Karen turned to Chidlow. 'Do you recognise the shirt?'

'Sadly, yes,' Chidlow said. 'It's very distinctive. Do you see?' He pointed to a small area where *The Chidlow Estate* was embroidered in yellow thread.

'So who does it belong to?'

He stroked his chin. 'My wife had uniforms made up. A job lot, a few years ago now. And we handed them out to staff. She was big on that sort of thing.'

It suddenly dawned on Karen where she'd seen that same olive-green polo shirt before. Not on Chidlow or Doyle, the driver or any of the catering staff. No, they wore white shirts. She'd only seen one person wearing an olive-green polo shirt at Chidlow House. Mike Harrington.

'The groundsman,' Karen said.

'Well, I don't like to point fingers,' Chidlow said hurriedly, 'but he is the only one who wears them now.'

'You said your wife ordered a job lot. Is it possible someone else could have access to one of the polo shirts?'

'I suppose it's possible, but quite unlikely. Green was for the outdoor members of staff, and since I've had to economise, I had to let the gardeners go.'

'I see. So as far as you know, Mike Harrington is the only person who wears this kind of shirt.'

'Yes,' Chidlow said. 'It doesn't look good for him, does it?' His eyebrows lifted as he leaned forward to look at the blood.

Karen transferred the bag to her other hand. 'Thank you for your help, Lord Chidlow.'

Before she went up to the roof, Karen asked a couple of the crime scene investigators, who were still working on the storeroom, for help. She wanted to make sure she took the appropriate path along the roof and didn't risk contaminating the scene further.

Greg Wainwright, a crime scene technician, volunteered to help.

Farzana, who'd been checking on the CSI team's progress, followed Karen, shaking her head. 'I can't believe it, Sarge. I checked the roof. Honestly, there was nothing there.'

'Ella found it,' Karen said. 'It's stained with blood. It could have huge implications for the case.'

Farzana rubbed her forehead. 'I don't understand. There was nothing there when I checked yesterday.'

It was unfair, but Karen was angry. Furious that they had evidence pointing to Harrington and she'd missed it. Maybe if she'd focused harder on him from the beginning, searched his property earlier, taken him in for proper questioning rather than letting him help them pick locks, they might have found Natasha by now.

Farzana looked hurt. She tried to catch Karen's eye as they walked up the stairs to the roof. 'I can tell you don't believe me, Sarge, but I promise you I did a proper search of the roof yesterday and that polo shirt wasn't there.'

'I missed the spyhole in the ladies' bathroom. I'd been in there, looked around, but I didn't spot it. We all make mistakes.'

'That's different. The hole was tiny. I'm telling you, I did not miss that shirt.'

Karen watched Ella lead Greg to the point on the flat roof area where she'd found the shirt, then turned to Farzana. 'If that's true, it means the polo shirt was planted.'

The wind was strong on the roof. Karen folded her arms over her chest, hugging herself to keep out the cold.

Farzana's hair whipped around her face as she nodded slowly. 'That's my guess. I searched that corner,' she said, pointing to where Ella was standing. 'It wasn't there yesterday, Sarge. I swear.'

'Who's had access to the house since yesterday?' Karen asked.

'Well, Lord Chidlow, Doyle, all of us officers, Chidlow's wife—'

Karen shook her head. 'No, she wasn't alone long enough to get up to the roof.'

'Ella?' Farzana whispered, nodding in the direction of the frizzy-haired girl.

'I'm not sure what to make of her,' Karen said. She took a deep breath. 'We need to test the bloodstain to see if it's Natasha's.'

Farzana tried to tuck her windblown hair behind her ears. 'I'll handle that.'

'Thanks.'

'What are you going to do? Talk to Harrington? Bring him in?'

'I think we're going to have to.'

They headed back down, glad to get out of the wind and into the house. Karen had missed the peephole during the search, but could they really have missed the polo shirt? The team was usually methodical and thorough. They wouldn't have missed such a vital piece of evidence, would they?

If what Farzana said was true and she hadn't missed the shirt, that meant someone had put it up there after the search – but why?

Did she want to believe it had been planted because the alternative was that Harrington was looking more and more guilty?

It was a large house and, despite the officer on the front door, it was possible someone had sneaked in. Ella was still living here, and Ethan had crept in earlier. Had he planted it to divert attention from himself? What about Chidlow? He definitely had the time and opportunity to plant the polo shirt and smear Mike Harrington in the process.

Karen ran a hand through her hair and watched Farzana head off to the crime lab back at the station, the evidence bag tucked under her arm.

CHAPTER TWENTY-SEVEN

In interview room two at Nettleham, Morgan made the necessary introductions for the benefit of the tape. He hadn't wanted to come back to the station. On a case like this, he preferred to be as close to the action as possible and that meant being on the ground near the search team or at the scene where Natasha was last seen. But the discovery of the bloodstained shirt had changed the direction of the investigation.

Harrington was now very much top of their suspect list.

Morgan had asked DC Rick Cooper to partner him for the interview. They sat on one side of the table, and Harrington sat opposite. The chair next to him was empty. He'd opted to go without legal representation.

Harrington was stressed, but not in a nervous, jittery way. He looked like he might explode at any minute. He was seething with anger.

All the better, thought Morgan. The more hot-headed the man was, the more likely he was to screw up and implicate himself if he was guilty. That would save them all some time.

Morgan shuffled his paperwork, leafing through it. His delay in asking the first question was a deliberate attempt to apply subtle pressure.

It worked. Harrington couldn't wait. He spoke first. 'This is a set-up! I've got nothing to do with those students.'

Morgan pushed a photograph of the shirt across the table. 'Do you recognise this?'

Harrington looked down, then pushed it away. He sat back in his seat, shaking his head. 'This is ridiculous.'

'Do you own a shirt like this one?' Morgan asked.

'I have five shirts like that,' Harrington said. He rested his clenched fist on the table. 'I wear them for work. Then stick them in the wash at the weekend.'

'Are you missing one?' Rick asked.

Harrington pushed back from the table and glared at Rick. 'I don't know. I haven't checked. Not that I've noticed. Where did you find it anyway?'

'It was on the roof at Chidlow House.' Rick moved the photograph back towards Harrington, pointing at the small rust-coloured stain.

'Is that blood?' the groundsman asked, looking up.

His anger seemed to melt away, his expression pure panic.

'It *looks* like blood,' Rick said. 'We'll have the results back from the lab soon. You surprised me, Mr Harrington. I thought you were going to spin us a story.'

Harrington just stared at him.

'You're not going to tell us you cut yourself while at work and accidentally left your shirt on the roof?' Rick asked. 'Good. That saves us some time.'

Harrington spoke slowly. 'I've never been on the roof of Chidlow House.' He looked away, towards the door and freedom.

Morgan said, 'This isn't looking good for you, Mike.' He paused, waiting until Harrington was looking at him. 'Maybe it was an accident. If you tell us what happened now, things will work out better for you in the long run.'

Harrington pressed his hands to his face. 'This can't be happening,' he muttered. Then he leaned forward, elbows on the desk, looking at them both beseechingly. 'You have to believe me. This is a stitch-up. I don't know how the blood got on my shirt . . . if it is my shirt.'

'The DNA evidence should be able to clarify that,' Rick said.

Harrington shook his head. 'It might be my shirt, but if it is, I don't know how it got to be on the roof. And I have no idea how it got blood on it.' He looked at the photograph again.

They went round and round, asking more questions, but despite his agitation Harrington didn't change his story. He kept insisting he was innocent and being set up by someone. When they asked him who might want to fit him up, he had no answer for them.

Morgan and Rick left him in the interview room to stew while they went back through to the main office.

'What do you think, boss?' Rick asked. 'Is he telling the truth?'

Morgan took a deep breath. 'I really don't know. The evidence against him is looking pretty strong. The lab results will be crucial. If it's Natasha's blood, then I think we have enough to charge him.'

'The technicians managed to get a DNA sample from the items provided by her parents.'

'Good. I've asked for a rush job but we're still probably looking at twenty-four hours.' Morgan glanced at his watch. 'I'm going to give Superintendent Murray an update. Then I think we should take Harrington back to his cottage. Let's see if he can go through his belongings and locate all five of his shirts.'

'You think one will be missing?' Rick asked.

'If that's Harrington's shirt, then yes, there must be.'

'So we have to wait for the lab results to charge him?'

'Yes, but we'll keep him close, maintain the pressure. He could have Natasha somewhere nearby.'

Karen took a step back from the whiteboard set up in the temporary incident room. The briefing with representatives from the search teams had just finished.

She focused on the names on the board and the lines linking them. Photographs of Natasha and Cressida were in the middle of the board.

Karen drew a thick, black line between the two students. Cressida had come back, but they still had no idea where Natasha was. Why? If someone had taken the students, why let one of them go? He or she couldn't have known Cressida wouldn't be able to remember what had happened. Unless Cressida was faking the amnesia and not speaking up because she'd been threatened.

Both sets of parents were wealthy, but there'd been no ransom demand.

She glanced down at the bottom right of the board, at Mike Harrington's name. Did he know where Natasha was? She'd felt *sorry* for him and now he was heading up their suspect list. She tightened her grip on the pen.

Was it Natasha's blood on the polo shirt? Farzana insisted the shirt hadn't been on the roof the day before it was found. So had it been planted? By who? Ella?

Karen sighed with frustration and slammed the whiteboard marker down on the table just as there was a rap on the open door. She looked up to see Chief Constable John Grayson standing there.

She straightened. 'Sir?'

She really hoped he hadn't come to try to persuade her to keep his son's name out of the official reports.

Just for once, she wanted to believe there were officers out there who were honest, who put the job before their own gain or that of their family.

But what did she really know about the chief constable?

Grayson walked into the room, looking down. His posture wasn't as straight now, and he moved tentatively. He clutched a reusable carrier bag. He seemed nervous, his face fixed in an expression you might expect a man to wear if he was about to ask a favour. A huge favour that would put her career on the line and save his son's reputation.

Karen swallowed the bitter taste in her mouth. If he tried to bribe her into keeping quiet about Ethan, what would she do? He'd already heavily hinted that if she did a good job here, he'd use his influence to push forward the Freeman investigation and make sure the case wasn't dropped.

But no matter what guarantees or promises he gave her, Karen couldn't keep quiet. She wouldn't omit evidence from a report, even if it earned her a demotion and she was stuck behind a desk for the rest of her career. She wouldn't hide the truth.

Ethan needed to take responsibility for what he'd done. The fact that he was the chief constable's son didn't mean he should go unpunished.

'DS Hart, I'm afraid I come to you about a rather delicate matter.'

Here it comes, Karen thought. *He's going to ask me to keep Ethan's involvement off the record.* For all she knew, the man in front of her could be suppressing the corruption investigation. He could be one of the ringleaders.

She faced him down, her hands curling into fists. If she accepted his offer of help in return for keeping his son out of trouble, then that made her no better than any of the corrupt officers she wanted to investigate.

She'd tell him no, no matter how he tried to bribe her.

Grayson had walked over to the desk, but now he looked over his shoulder. 'Actually, do you mind if I close the door? It's a sensitive subject, and I'd like to talk to you in private.'

'Go right ahead,' Karen said, shoving her hands in her pockets and lifting her chin at a stubborn angle.

Grayson shut the door, then lifted the carrier bag and dumped the contents on to the mahogany surface of the desk.

Karen stared down at the crumpled pieces of paper. 'What's this?'

'Letters, or aborted letters. I found them in Ethan's bag when I went to do his washing.'

Karen picked up one sheet, smoothed it to remove the creases and then began to read. Then she selected another, then another.

They were all letters to Natasha. Ethan clearly had strong feelings for her. They made awkward reading. She wasn't surprised he'd given up on the early drafts.

Karen grabbed her bag and pulled out her mobile, navigating to the evidence images. She zoomed in on the paper they'd found in the bin in Natasha's room. Could the note have been written by Ethan?

Two words. *Somebody knows.*

She laid her phone on the desk, next to one of the crumpled letters. It looked similar, but not identical. Karen was no expert, but if pushed, she'd have to say the note was not in the same handwriting.

'I wondered if Ethan sent this to Natasha.'

Grayson focused on the image. 'The writing looks different to me. What does it mean by "somebody knows"?'

She saw a war of emotions in his features. He was torn between wanting to protect his son and needing to do the right thing.

'I don't know. I wish I did. We found it in Natasha's room.'

Karen felt a pang of guilt for doubting him. She'd assumed the corruption ran so deep that even the chief constable could have been involved.

But here he was sharing information that could be detrimental to his son. What would she have done if this was her child? If this had been Tilly in trouble, would she have covered it up? She honestly didn't know the answer. She'd like to believe she was incorruptible, but was she? Was anyone?

'I know the letters make Ethan look bad, but I'm not going to hide anything from you, DS Hart. I know my son and he can be irritating and foolish, but I really don't believe he would hurt anyone.'

Karen didn't doubt Grayson saw the best in his son, but she couldn't take his word for it.

She turned her attention back to the words 'somebody knows'. 'I think someone may have been trying to warn Natasha,' Karen suggested, staring hard at the words, willing them to make sense.

'Possibly, but do we have any idea who "somebody" refers to?'

Karen had to admit she had no idea.

'Have you asked Ethan about the letters you found?' she asked.

Grayson sighed. 'Yes.' He put his hands up. 'I know you'd have preferred to talk to him first, but I had to speak to him about it. He's my son. I hoped he'd have an explanation.'

'Did he?'

'He refused to talk to me.'

Karen arranged the letters in a pile. 'This case would be a lot simpler if Cressida could remember what happened.'

'Her condition hasn't improved?'

Karen sighed and shook her head. 'She's seeing a psychologist this afternoon, and I hope to talk to her again after her appointment.'

'A delicate situation,' he said again. 'Well, it's up to you what you do with these letters. I've done my part by bringing them to you. I don't believe they show anything other than a lad with a crush.'

Karen could feel Grayson's gaze. He wanted her to agree with him, but she couldn't. Not yet. She wasn't willing to discount Ethan as a suspect.

'Is Ethan at home now, sir?' Karen asked.

'I hope so,' Grayson said. 'Though no matter what I do to try to protect him, the boy seems determined to implicate himself.'

'It must be difficult for you.'

Grayson looked down at the desk. 'How can I help him when he won't even listen to what I say? He won't talk to me.'

'You've done the right thing,' Karen reassured him. 'We're getting closer. We just don't have the final answer yet.'

'What if Ethan's done something stupid?'

'You should know that Ethan isn't the only suspect.'

She told Grayson they'd taken Mike Harrington into custody after finding the bloodied polo shirt on the roof.

'That's the most convincing evidence found so far.'

'You'd think so, sir, but the head of the internal search team is convinced it wasn't there when they searched the roof.'

'Planted, you mean?'

'Possibly. We're awaiting results back from the lab before we charge him.'

'The search team hasn't found anything else?' Grayson asked. He looked out of the French windows in the direction of the lake.

'No. Not yet.'

'I hope you get to the bottom of this soon, DS Hart. I have every confidence in you. The superintendent recommended you and DI Morgan highly, and I trust her judgement.'

'Thank you, sir.'

'I've been impressed with the job you've done so far. This hasn't been an easy case.'

'No.'

'I know you can't take my word for it, but I'm sure Ethan had nothing to do with this. He's just your typical teenager who doesn't want to listen to his father, but he's harmless really.'

Karen nodded politely, but said nothing. People could hide their secrets well, and even those closest to them could be fooled. She'd learned that lesson the hard way.

CHAPTER TWENTY-EIGHT

Karen was still with the chief constable when someone opened the French windows from the outside. It was Rick.

'You're back.' Karen was about to ask how the interview with Mike Harrington had gone when she noticed the look on his face.

He stepped inside the room. Something about the way he held himself, the way his shoulders slumped and his head was bowed, made her move past Grayson.

'Excuse me, sir. Rick, what is it?'

His face was sombre, quite a contrast to his usual cheeky expression. 'I'm sorry, Sarge. They found her. Natasha was in the lake.'

It felt like a physical blow. Karen inhaled sharply. They'd known there was a chance – that's why they'd ordered the search of the lake, but she'd hoped they were being overly cautious, hoped Natasha would return.

Rick wiped his feet on the mat. 'They're bringing her up from the lake now. I thought you'd want to be present.'

Karen swallowed the lump in her throat. 'Yes,' she said. 'I'll just get my coat.'

She swung around and almost walked into Grayson, who was standing behind her.

'Terribly sad,' he said.

Karen nodded and walked past him quickly to grab her jacket. There were multiple theories open to them, including accidental death, but the most likely was that someone had dumped Natasha's body in the lake.

She'd been doing this job long enough to know the longer a person was missing, the lower the chances of getting them back unharmed, but she'd hoped this case would beat the odds.

As she shrugged on her coat, Morgan entered the room. He lifted his head and met Karen's gaze with a sad smile.

'I'll leave you to it for now,' Grayson said quietly, then he left the library.

The three of them – Karen, Rick and Morgan – made their way down to the shore of the lake in silence. Divers were still in the water, their hooded wetsuits making their heads look like seals as they broke the surface.

'Do you think it could have been an accident?' Rick asked. 'Maybe she'd been drinking and went in of her own accord.' He shivered, looking at the grey water. 'Or stumbled and fell in.' He pointed at a spot along the lake that had no gradual sloping shoreline. The dark, murky water lapped at the reeds.

'It's possible,' Karen said, though she wasn't convinced.

They'd know soon enough if she'd been intoxicated. They'd take samples in the mortuary and get them processed for drink and drugs.

They'd been standing there for a couple of minutes, watching the vessel in the middle of the lake, when one of the underwater search team approached. It was Jed, the team leader Karen had spoken to earlier.

'It's her?' Karen asked.

He nodded. 'I think so. Bad news. The worst.'

'I was just thinking about the women in the Chidlow family who were said to have drowned themselves in the lake. Can you tell if Natasha drowned?' Rick asked.

Jed shook his head. 'I'm afraid I can't tell you that. But I can tell you that we found her body in the middle of the lake. Ropes had been tied around her waist and those ropes were attached to sandbags. I doubt she did that herself.'

Morgan blew out a breath and nodded slowly. 'Whoever did it didn't want the body to be found.'

'That's my conclusion.'

'They must have used a boat then,' Karen said, 'to get her body out that far.'

Jed nodded. 'Yes.'

'There is a rowing boat nearby,' Karen said. 'We'll need to have that examined by Forensics.'

She remembered seeing it when she walked to Mike Harrington's cottage.

Despite his limp, Harrington was tall and strong. He had access to the sandbags. It would have been easy for him to put Natasha's body in the boat, row halfway across the lake, then tie sandbags to her body and dump her over the side.

Karen hadn't believed him capable of that much evil. She raked a hand through her hair and nudged the toe of her boot against the thick red mud at the edge of the lake.

They stood silently, showing respect, as Natasha's body was removed from the water and put on the divers' vessel. As the diver closest to them struggled with the black body bag, Natasha's arm flopped free. Even from this distance, Karen could see the young woman's skin was mottled and swollen.

She looked away. 'Any injuries immediately apparent?'

'You'll have to ask the pathologist about that,' Jed said. 'He probably won't be able to get much from looking at her here, so we'll arrange for her body to be sent to the mortuary.'

'Thank you,' Morgan said. 'I'll liaise with the pathologist and get the post-mortem underway as soon as possible.'

All four of them turned to look as the vessel containing Natasha's body headed for the shoreline.

'So sad,' Morgan said. 'What a waste of a young life.'

'I . . . I can't believe it.' Tears were streaming down Cressida's cheeks as she sat on the sofa between her parents, who were trying in vain to comfort her.

Sophie and Rick had the unenviable task of going to inform Natasha's parents that their daughter's body had been found, and so Karen and Morgan had gone straight to the Blakes' residence to update them and also to try to get more information from Cressida.

'How did it happen?' Ryan Blake asked. His breathing was short and sharp. 'Did she drown? Was it an accident?'

'We don't know yet, sir. We'll have some more information after the post-mortem,' Karen explained. 'But it's unlikely to have been an accident, in my opinion. She was found in the centre of the lake.'

Karen paused. She didn't mention the sandbags. The fact that Natasha had been weighed down at the bottom of the lake was information they wanted to keep to themselves. It could prove important later when validating statements and witness reports.

'Have you remembered anything else, Cressida? Any memories of events on Thursday evening?' Morgan asked.

Cressida didn't speak, simply shaking her head as a tear dropped from her cheek and made a dark circle on the leg of her jeans.

'I can't bear to think about what must have happened to that poor girl,' Jasmine Blake said, stroking her daughter's hair. 'I'm almost glad Cressida can't remember.' She looked at Karen. 'Who would want to remember something like that?'

'It must be very traumatic,' Karen said, 'but if somebody hurt Natasha, we need to find out who it was and make sure he doesn't do it again to someone else.'

'He?' Mr Blake questioned.

'A slip of the tongue,' Karen said. 'We don't know who's responsible.' Though usually in these types of cases, it was a man.

'Well, I want you to catch whoever did this, of course. Unless it was an accident,' he suggested again.

'We're keeping an open mind until after the post-mortem,' Morgan said. 'Perhaps we could ask you to look again at the CCTV images of the man Natasha was with on Monday evening?'

'Again?' Ryan asked, looking up. 'Have you got better images now?'

'I'm afraid not, sir. They're the same ones. Just in case it rings any bells.' He pulled printed copies of the images out of the file and showed them to the Blakes.

Cressida refused to look. 'I don't want to see. I can't believe she's gone. Why would she go and see that man without telling me? We were supposed to be friends.' She turned to her father. 'Why would she do that?'

Her mother patted her arm and Ryan Blake put his head in his hands after passing the printout of the CCTV still back to Morgan.

'I'm afraid we don't recognise him,' Jasmine said. 'Sorry.'

'I understand,' Morgan said. 'It's not a very good picture. Cressida, can you think back to Monday evening for me? Was there anything Natasha said that made you think that she was planning to meet somebody later?'

Cressida rubbed her eyes. 'She didn't say anything about it.'

'What about on Thursday? What did you talk about?'

'I can't remember, except . . .'

'Yes?'

'We just talked about Lord Chidlow being back in the house and how ridiculous Ethan was, following Natasha and me around all day with puppy-dog eyes.' She wiped away a tear with the back of her hand. 'I just can't believe she's gone.' She broke down in sobs.

As carefully and sensitively as he could, Morgan asked more questions, but it was no good. Cressida couldn't talk through her tears.

'Right. That's enough,' her father said abruptly. 'I know you need to find the monster who did this, but not at the expense of my daughter's mental health. She's seeing the psychologist shortly, and this is only making her more distressed.'

'Cressida is our best chance of finding out who did this, Mr Blake.'

He shook his head stubbornly. 'No, I'm sorry, but I have to put my foot down. My daughter's needs come first.'

Sobbing, Cressida buried her head in her father's shoulder.

They drove back to Chidlow House in silence. The blustery autumnal weather continued. Trees leaned in the wind.

Karen stared out over empty brown fields. It was difficult when you had to deal with such a witness. After being through a serious trauma, Cressida was damaged. Now she'd found out her friend hadn't been as lucky as she had and hadn't made it out alive.

'What do you think about Harrington?' Karen asked as Morgan stopped at the crossroads.

'He's been through a traumatic period in his life. It's changed him.'

'But does that mean he's capable of something like this? Killing a teenage girl?'

'I don't know.'

'He just doesn't seem . . .'

'Sometimes you can't rely on instincts.'

'I know that.' As Morgan pulled away from the lights, Karen spoke again. 'What about Chidlow?'

'I don't know. He's a canny sort,' Morgan said. 'I'm sure his ex-wife was motivated to paint him in a bad light after what he did to her. But the peephole really makes me uncomfortable, I have to admit that.'

Karen agreed. 'I hope the post-mortem gives us more to go on.'

'I hope so too,' Morgan said, turning towards Harmston and Chidlow House.

CHAPTER TWENTY-NINE

As soon as Karen and Morgan entered Chidlow House, Doyle accosted them.

'Look at this,' he said, waving his mobile phone in their direction. 'It's a disgrace!'

'What is it?' Karen asked, finding it hard to focus on his ever-moving phone.

'There are now reports all over social media about the body in the lake. They make me sound terrible,' Doyle said, 'as though I just stood by and let it all happen.'

'I see,' Karen said.

'Is that all you have to say for yourself? You've handled this whole thing terribly.'

'What did you expect, Mr Doyle?' Karen asked. 'Your course was full of teenagers. Of course it's going to be all over social media.'

'You should have stopped it!'

'How?'

Doyle glowered at her before turning to Morgan. 'And do you have anything to say for yourself?'

'Only that we're in the middle of an investigation and have a lot to be getting on with.'

'Well, thank you very much,' Doyle said. 'The course is over; my reputation is ruined. I can give up any hopes of getting another programme like this off the ground. But you don't care about that, do you?'

'It's most unfortunate, Mr Doyle,' Morgan said. 'But right now, we're primarily concerned with getting justice for Natasha.'

'Oh, I see. Well, don't worry about me. You've only ruined my life.'

Karen and Morgan exchanged a look.

Karen could only put Doyle's outburst down to the shock of the situation. It was hard to believe anyone could really be that self-absorbed. Stress affected people in odd ways.

Just then, shouting at the end of the corridor made both Karen and Morgan move past Doyle to investigate.

It was Lord Chidlow. He was standing in the doorway of his study berating the officers inside.

'Be careful with that,' he said. 'And you can't take my computer! I don't give you permission. I need it,' he said, his arms folded and his lower lip protruding in a pout like a petulant child.

Farzana was standing behind him, and she turned and looked gratefully at Karen and Morgan as they approached.

She left Chidlow and walked towards them. 'The search of his office is finished,' Farzana said. 'We haven't found anything, but he's quite reluctant to give up his computer.'

'He doesn't have a choice,' Morgan said.

'No, I did try to explain that to him. We're packing it up now to take it back to the lab, but he's not happy. He's spent the last half an hour standing in the doorway telling us off for making a mess.'

'Leave it to me,' Karen said, leaving Farzana with Morgan and walking up to Chidlow.

She peered into the room. The study looked in pretty good shape. There was nothing dumped on the floor; everything from the drawers and filing cabinets had been returned.

'You can have your study back now, Lord Chidlow,' Karen said. 'But we will need to take your computer.'

'I don't see why. There's nothing on it.'

'It's procedure,' Karen said. 'I'm sure you have nothing to worry about.'

'I'm not worried,' he snapped. 'Besides, you won't find anything on it. I wiped it the other day.'

'You wiped it?' Karen raised an eyebrow. 'Why did you do that?'

'Because it had a virus,' he said, looking imperiously down his nose at Karen. 'I clicked a link on a spam email. The internet is full of scammers these days. So I had to reboot it and install a new operating system. You'll find nothing on it.'

'I see. The timing of that is quite suspicious.'

'Suspicious? I don't see why. Viruses are everywhere these days.'

'Just as we're taking your computer away to analyse the hard drive, you tell me that it's been wiped. That could be viewed as the behaviour of somebody with something to hide.'

'Well, think what you like,' Chidlow said with a shrug. 'I'm telling you the truth.'

'That's okay, sir. It's likely that our technicians can get information from the hard drive anyway,' Karen said.

'They can?' He looked surprised. 'Well, it doesn't bother me. Like I said, nothing to hide.'

'Good.'

They stood back as two officers brought out the computer. 'All done now, Sarge,' the last one said, holding a large cardboard box.

'So you're still taking it,' Chidlow said. 'After how accommodating I've been, how helpful.'

'Like I said, sir, we need to look at it. It's procedure.'

He pushed past her into the study. 'It's a disgrace how I've been treated. It really is.' He whirled back around to face her. 'It

242

shouldn't be me you're looking into. You need to look at Mike Harrington.'

'Why is that?' Karen asked.

'You know he's got a messed-up leg? It's because he tried to kill himself after his son died. He's not right in the head. He's the man you want.'

Chidlow's words and tone were full of spite. He couldn't have sunk any lower in Karen's estimation. As for Harrington, despite her best efforts to remain neutral, Karen felt a pang of sympathy for him.

As Chidlow continued to complain about his treatment, Karen caught a glimpse of Harrington and his dog Sandy on the lawns, walking towards the house.

Chidlow slammed the door, missing Karen's face by a few inches.

'He seems to have a temper problem,' Morgan commented as Karen returned to him and Farzana.

'He really does. I saw Harrington outside. Think I'll go and have a word.'

Morgan nodded. 'Good idea. We need to keep the pressure on until we can press charges.'

Karen slipped through the French windows and walked down the stone steps. On the patio, she called out to Harrington. He turned and saw her but made no effort to come any closer. Sandy bounded happily towards Karen.

She made a fuss over the dog and then walked up to Harrington.

With a sigh, Harrington frowned at the dog. 'Ungrateful wretch. You're supposed to be on my side. I'm the one who feeds you.'

'She's a friendly little thing.'

'Opposite of me, you mean?'

Karen said nothing.

'They're still searching my place. I had to get out of there.' He glared at Karen as though it was all her fault. 'They're going through all my stuff, the boxes . . .'

'The boxes containing your son's belongings?' Karen asked, although she already knew the answer.

He nodded stiffly.

'I'm sorry. I know that must be very difficult, but it is necessary.'

'I didn't put my shirt on the roof.'

He returned Karen's steady gaze. No fidgeting, no refusal to make eye contact. Her instincts told her he was telling the truth. But what had Morgan said? *Sometimes you can't rely on instincts?*

'Any idea how it got up there?' she asked.

'Someone must have put it on the roof to divert attention to me.'

'Who?'

He sighed and looked up at the grey sky. 'I don't have a clue. All I know is being your prime suspect and having officers turn my cottage upside down is a pretty awful experience.'

'If you've nothing to hide, we won't find anything.'

'No? Then how do you explain the shirt? How do I know one of your lot didn't plant it? How do I know they won't do the same again?'

'I know the team. They're trustworthy.'

'Really? You don't sound so sure.'

'Yes, really.'

'It goes on more often than you'd think. Bung an officer a few quid and they'll do you a favour.'

It was Karen who broke eye contact first. She was well aware of the possibilities.

He looked at her angrily. 'Anyway, that wasn't why I came up to the house. I need to show you something.'

'Oh really? What?'

'Something I saw last night. I think you'll want to see it.'

'Why? Is it relevant to the case?'

'It could well be.'

'Then why didn't you tell DI Morgan or DC Cooper about it during your interview?'

'Two reasons. I hadn't had a chance to check it out yet, and they were looking at me like they believed I was guilty. I didn't trust them.'

'And you trust me?'

He looked at her through narrowed eyes.

'All right. Where's this thing you want to show me?' she asked.

He pointed at a copse of trees on the right side of the property. 'Over there.'

Karen glanced back towards the house. She was still wearing her coat, and her bag, which contained a self-defence spray, was looped over her shoulder. That made her feel a little more confident, but it wasn't a good idea to walk off with a murder suspect alone.

'I'm trying to help,' Harrington said.

Karen pulled out her mobile, typed a quick message to Morgan, letting him know where she'd be and who she was with, and then nodded. 'All right. Let's go.'

He led her across the lawn, only leaning heavily on his stick when they headed through the trees. The leaves were damp and slippery underfoot. Sandy had no trouble. She scampered ahead before stopping by a stream to wait for them.

Harrington looked down at the fast-flowing water. 'It's not normally much more than a ditch, but after all the rain, it's swollen in size,' he said. 'We'll need to cross it. Will you be all right?'

Sandy jumped to the far bank, then turned back expectantly. Despite his bad leg, Harrington crossed with no trouble, his long limbs making it look easy. He held out a hand, as though it were nothing more than a muddy puddle Karen needed to step over.

She gritted her teeth. He wore boots that looked like they had thick, deep grooves in the soles. She wore boots too, but hers were not designed for outdoor pursuits.

Karen took a short run up, then jumped. She crossed the stream fine but stumbled as she landed, her knee bending awkwardly under her. Her *bad* knee, thanks to Charlie Cook, she thought, feeling a dart of pain as her knee hit the ground.

Harrington offered his hand again but Karen ignored it, pushing herself to her feet and testing her knee gingerly. 'I'm fine,' she said. Then she looked down at the slimy mud covering her trousers from knee to ankle and swore. 'This better be worth it.'

'Oh, I think it will be.'

'Are you going to tell me what it is, or are you going to keep up this enigmatic show until we get there?' Karen asked.

'I wasn't trying to be enigmatic. It's just not easy to explain because I don't really know what I saw.' He began walking again and Karen followed.

'That makes no sense,' she said.

'I'm trying to explain.'

'Well, try harder.'

'Fine. It was last night. I was out late, about two a.m. I couldn't sleep, so I went for a walk to clear my head.'

'Do you do that a lot?' Karen asked.

'Quite often,' he said.

'Thursday night?'

He turned, glaring at her stonily. 'No.'

'All right. I had to ask. What did you see?'

'Lord Chidlow,' he said. 'He was walking over here. I spotted the light from his torch and wondered what he was up to.'

'What was he up to?'

'He was carrying two boxes, roughly shoebox size, taking them away from the house. When he crossed the stream with them, I started to think he might be planning to bury them in the woods.'

'That wouldn't be a very intelligent move if he was trying to hide them, since there's a search team crawling over the entire estate.'

'No, and I underestimated him. He didn't bury them.'

'So what did he do with them?' Karen asked as they stopped in front of a hedgerow.

'He took them over here.' He nodded at the open fields.

'This isn't Chidlow land anymore, is it?' Karen asked as they slid between a gap in the hedgerow and began to walk along the edge of a field.

'No, it belongs to old Billy Dyer,' Harrington said. 'He's a nice old guy. His son runs the farm but lives over in Washingborough. Billy still lives in the old farmhouse. He's a stubborn character. He had a stroke a year ago, so I pop in now and then, to see if he's coping okay. And he usually is. He's pretty independent. Still makes all his own meals, even brews his own beer.'

As they reached the crest of the hill, he pointed out a small two-storey house on the far side of the next field. It had been hidden from sight before they'd reached this point. Next to it was a dilapidated barn and farm equipment that looked so old it could be antique. Long grass grew around the machinery. It hadn't been touched for a while. A fenced-in area at the side of the house made Karen wonder if animals were kept on the property, but she couldn't see any.

As they walked closer, Karen noticed the farmhouse could do with a bit of TLC. The paint was peeling from the wooden fascias. The door and window frames were cracked.

To the left of the property was a large chicken coop. Sandy bounded up to it, barking. The chickens clucked in panic and scattered.

Harrington called Sandy off, and she obediently returned to his heel.

'Is this definitely where Chidlow came last night?' Karen asked.

'Yes.'

'You think he asked Billy to look after the boxes for him?'

Harrington shook his head. 'No, I saw him stash them in the chicken coop.'

Karen frowned. 'In the chicken coop?'

'Yes, I thought it was weird. I was going to talk to Billy today, ask him about it. I thought maybe Chidlow had his permission, but I didn't get a chance after being taken in for questioning.' He gave Karen a pointed look.

'You should have mentioned this to DI Morgan. You're ex-police. We should be on the same side.'

'It didn't feel like DI Morgan was on *my* side during the interview.'

Karen stared at the chicken house inside the coop. It was constructed from wood, and the roof was covered with felt and bitumen paint to keep it watertight.

'I wanted to investigate last night,' Harrington said. 'But figured Sandy would spook the chickens. If they woke Billy, he'd have been out here with his shotgun. I wasn't confident he wouldn't mistake me for a fox.'

'Didn't you worry Chidlow might get shot?'

'Crossed my mind, that's why I stuck around. But Billy didn't come out. Chickens barely made a sound. They're used to humans, not dogs.'

'Right. Let's talk to Billy, then.'

Harrington rapped on the door. A small elderly man opened it. He had bright blue eyes, a flash of white hair and was wearing a chunky red jumper and blue trousers. He grinned at them.

'To what do I owe the pleasure?' He focused on Karen. 'Nice to see Mike hasn't cut himself off from civilisation completely.'

'You're one to talk,' Harrington said with his customary frown. 'You're not exactly a social butterfly yourself.'

Billy chuckled. 'I'm an old man. You're young. You shouldn't be on your own. Come in.'

As Karen walked in, Billy whispered, 'He's not as bad as he'd like you to think. Checked in on me every day after my stroke, he did.'

'Thanks, Billy, but she's not interested in my good points. She just wants to take a look in your chicken coop.'

The old man blinked. 'My chicken coop? Why?'

'She's a detective.'

Before Karen could show her ID, Billy guffawed. 'I don't think the chickens have broken the law, Detective.'

'We think someone put something in there last night,' Karen said. 'Edward Chidlow. Did you give him permission?'

The smile dropped from the old man's face. 'No, I didn't! He'd better not have hurt those chickens,' he said, stalking out of the house.

Karen and Harrington followed as he strode up to the coop. He put a hand on the gate but Karen stopped him.

She pulled a pair of latex gloves from her pocket. 'Let me do it,' she said. 'Just in case. Fingerprints.'

Billy stood back. 'Has this got anything to do with the girls who went missing?'

'I'm not sure.'

'He didn't put a body in there, did he?' Billy's eyes widened. He looked in horror at Harrington, who shook his head reassuringly.

'No, no. Nothing like that. I saw him with two boxes last night, about this big.' Harrington moved his hands to show the size.

Karen left them talking and entered the chicken coop. The chickens scurried away from her. The henhouse was at the centre of the coop, raised from the ground by stilts. A ramp led up to a small entrance so the chickens could come and go as they pleased. She peered in.

'You can take the whole roof off,' Harrington called out. 'Need a hand?'

'No, I've got it, thanks.'

As she pushed the roof, it creaked noisily, but it was easier to lift than she'd expected due to a hinge mechanism. It stayed open when Karen let go.

Two chickens squawked at the intrusion.

Nestled in a bed of straw at the centre of the henhouse were two cardboard boxes. Karen leaned in awkwardly. She could reach just far enough to lift one of the lids. Inside were unmarked DVDs and wires with what looked like tiny lenses at one end. Some kind of recording equipment?

And then it dawned on her. Small cameras. The perfect size to fit in peepholes. She pulled the first box towards her, then lifted it clear of the chickens.

'What is it?' Harrington asked.

'DVDs.' She didn't mention the miniature recording equipment.

'Are they labelled? What's on them?'

'No. I imagine it's something Chidlow didn't want us to find.' She set the box down, peeled off a latex glove and pulled out her mobile to call Morgan. He would be very interested in this discovery.

CHAPTER THIRTY

Morgan and Karen took the evidence to Nettleham station. They needed to find out what was on those DVDs as soon as possible, especially as recording equipment had been found alongside the discs.

While Morgan organised the paperwork, documenting the evidence, Karen checked a room was available and that they had all the equipment they would need, then went to grab coffee.

DC Farzana Shah was at the coffee machine when Karen approached. 'Have you checked the discs?' Farzana asked.

'Not yet. Morgan's processing them. It shouldn't be long though.'

'What do you think is on them?'

'I dread to think,' Karen said. 'Chidlow put in a great deal of effort to hide them.'

'Which moves him up our suspect list.' Farzana put a mug under the coffee machine spout.

As the machine buzzed into life, Karen nodded thoughtfully. 'It does. I'm not sure it proves he had anything to do with Natasha's death, but I'm hoping this is the start of the breakthrough we need.'

'How are the Laytons doing?'

'Sophie and Rick gave them the bad news, and they took it about as well as you'd expect. They're devastated and heartbroken.'

Farzana removed her steaming coffee mug and held her hand out for Karen's. 'I can't even imagine what they're going through.' She looked up. 'Actually, Sarge, I wanted to have a word.'

'Yes?'

Farzana pressed the button on the machine again, and steaming black liquid trickled into Karen's mug. 'It's about the polo shirt found on the roof. I just wanted to say . . .' She looked around to make sure nobody was in earshot and then continued. 'I know it must be really difficult for you to trust people after what Freeman did. To trust your colleagues, I mean.'

Karen had to admit she did find it hard. 'It is, but I should apologise because you're right. I should trust you. If you say you searched the roof thoroughly, then you did.'

Farzana offered a smile. 'I really did.' She picked up her own coffee and took a sip. 'I understand how it looks like we screwed up the search. But I went over that roof inch by inch and the polo shirt wasn't there.'

'I believe you.' Karen had doubted Farzana once before, but she'd come through and shown herself to be a good officer. If she said the polo shirt wasn't there yesterday, then it wasn't.

'Good; but it means the polo shirt has to have been planted,' Farzana said with a frown.

'Which suggests someone was trying to frame Mike Harrington. Have we got forensics back on the shirt yet? Do we know if it's Natasha's blood?'

Farzana shook her head. 'We've prioritised the request, but it'll be a few hours yet, I think.'

Karen nodded impatiently and reached for the milk, adding some to her coffee. 'I felt sorry for Harrington,' she said. 'Chidlow was pretty keen for us to look at him, so it's possible Chidlow planted the evidence.'

'It's a good theory. He was certainly quick to point the finger at Harrington. You're glad the groundsman is off the hook, aren't you?'

Karen struggled to find the words to answer. 'I suppose I am, really. Though he's not in the clear yet. I felt sorry for him after everything he's been through.'

'He *is* bad-tempered, a bit of a loner.'

'I agree,' Karen said, sliding another mug on to the chrome base of the machine for Morgan's coffee. 'And I know that my viewpoint is probably skewed because of what he's been through.'

'What you have in common, you mean?' Farzana asked gently.

Karen managed to nod and took another sip of her coffee, then set it back down on the counter, ignoring the tightness in the back of her throat.

'Your opinion means a lot to me, Sarge,' Farzana said, tucking her hair behind her ear. 'I don't want to let you down, but if I'd messed up that search, I would have been honest and told you.'

'I know,' Karen said, just as Morgan strode into the open-plan office area.

'Karen, everything's set up. Are you ready?'

'Yes.' She picked up both mugs of coffee and followed Morgan to the computer room she'd booked.

Morgan shut the door as Karen set the coffees down on the table. Then they both sat down, and neither of them spoke as Morgan inserted the first DVD.

Karen stared at the screen as he double-clicked on the DVD icon and a variety of files came into view, all labelled with different dates.

She took a shallow breath. Morgan clicked on one of the files. A video began to play. It was the bathroom on the first floor.

Karen had known this was coming, but that didn't make it any easier to watch. Morgan swore under his breath and said, 'He was using that peephole to record the girls' bathroom.'

Karen muttered a few choice words to describe Chidlow and leaned forward, resting her elbow on the desk and her chin in her hand.

'He was convincing when he nonchalantly brushed off the discovery of the peephole. When all along . . .' Karen said.

'Yes. Makes you wonder what else he's hiding, doesn't it?'

Morgan fast-forwarded the video until they saw someone enter the bathroom. He pressed play. It wasn't one of the students from the course. It was a woman of around twenty-five with long dark hair.

'This must be a guest from a previous course at Chidlow House,' Karen said. 'How are we going to identify her?'

'We'll have to get records from Lord Chidlow. Ask about all of the courses held at the property, and the names of the attendees. And then we're going to have to contact them individually, try to match up faces to the names.'

'That's not going to be an enjoyable job,' Karen said, watching the screen as the unsuspecting woman began to unbutton her blouse. She let it slide to the floor and then leaned over and turned on the taps to run a bath.

Morgan's gaze flickered away from the screen. 'It feels wrong to be watching this.'

'Yes,' Karen agreed. She looked at the rest of the DVDs, which had now been bagged and labelled as evidence. 'How many are there in total?' she asked.

'Thirty,' Morgan said.

'It looks like there's multiple recordings on each disc as well.' Karen shook her head in disbelief.

They watched the first DVD on fast-forward. Somehow it seemed less personal, less invasive to watch it that way. There were three women, and Karen wondered if there were three women on each of the other DVDs. That would make ninety women in total. The thought made her feel sick to her stomach.

'Right,' Morgan said, pushing back from the computer. 'I'll ask Sophie to go through these DVDs and take screenshots of the women's faces. Then we can create a database and crossmatch them against the IDs we get from Chidlow and the course organisers. Hopefully we'll be able to identify all the women who have been recorded without their knowledge.'

'Sounds like the most sensible method.' Karen glanced at her watch. 'I thought I'd go to the mortuary and talk to the pathologist, ask him if he's got any preliminary findings he can report on Natasha Layton.'

'All right,' Morgan said, getting to his feet, jaw clenched. 'You do that. I'm going back to the house to bring Lord Chidlow in for questioning.'

Karen picked up the mugs of cold coffee. They'd been so focused on the task they'd forgotten them. She paused. 'Actually, before I go to Raj, I'm going to get Ella Seaton. She's been staying at Chidlow House while all this has been going on. She can't stay there any longer.'

'You're right. Where are her parents?'

'They're on their way back from Africa, as far as I know. But she must have other family, or a friend she could stay with.'

Morgan nodded soberly. 'Wherever she stays tonight, it has to be better than Chidlow House.'

Karen left the station just after Morgan. She wanted to get Ella Seaton away from Chidlow House as soon as possible. As much as she'd like to see Lord Chidlow squirm when they presented him with the evidence, she'd have to leave that pleasure to Morgan. She had a list of tasks she needed to get through if they wanted to build a strong case against Chidlow.

She slipped behind the wheel and turned the car heaters on full. First task: find Ella. There was no way the young woman could stay where she was after what they'd found. Karen would bring her back to the station while they tracked down a friend or relative Ella could stay with until her parents returned. At least she'd be safe there.

Her second task would be speaking to Raj and finding out what she could from the pathologist. It was far too early to expect him to have completed the full post-mortem, but if he'd looked at the body, he might be able to give her some initial observations.

A light patter of rain hit the windscreen. Karen flipped on the wipers. Surely they'd used up their quota of rain for the month! The news had been filled with stories describing local flooding. She glanced at the dashboard clock. It seemed later than it was. So much had happened in a few short hours. This morning they'd still held out hope that Natasha would be found alive.

Karen focused on the road, her hands tightening on the wheel as a flurry of leaves swirled around the car.

Most of the rainwater had drained away from the roads, though huge puddles still spread across the small country lanes. When Karen finally pulled up outside Chidlow House, it was pouring. She ran inside, greeting PC Smith who was stood at the door.

'Everything all right, Sarge?' he asked.

'We're getting there,' she replied. 'I don't suppose you've seen Ella Seaton?'

'The student who hasn't gone home yet?'

Karen nodded.

'She was down here a few minutes ago, watching DI Morgan take Chidlow away. She's gone back upstairs now, I think.'

'Thanks.'

Karen headed to the staircase at the back of the house. As she reached the hallway, Graham Doyle appeared, carrying a large holdall and a small wheeled case.

'Ah, Doyle,' Karen said. 'Have you seen Ella Seaton?'

'No, I've not seen her for ages.'

Karen glanced at the holdall. 'Are you going somewhere?'

'Yes, as a matter of fact I am. I'm going home. The course was meant to end today anyway. The whole thing's been a disaster.'

'What about Ella?'

'What about her? She shouldn't be under my supervision now. Her parents are gadabouts. They left the girl here knowing that the course finished this afternoon at three p.m.' He shook his head. 'I'm sick of entitled parents expecting me to take care of their children.' He sighed. 'I suppose I could give her a lift to the train station or order her a taxi.'

Karen found it odd that Ella's parents hadn't rushed home when they were informed two students had gone missing. Now that Natasha's body had been found, she would have expected them to collect their daughter as soon as humanly possible.

'Before you go, Mr Doyle, were you aware someone was filming through a peephole in the women's bathroom?'

'Filming?' Doyle looked aghast. 'No, I was not. Who?'

'We're looking into it.' Karen studied him closely. He seemed genuinely shocked.

'That's why you took Chidlow off just now, isn't it? You think it was him?'

Karen braced herself, expecting a typical Doyle rant over her disrespecting a grand man like Edward Chidlow, who would never stoop to such a thing, but Doyle was silent.

'You didn't suspect anything?' Karen asked.

Doyle shook his head. 'No, I thought better of him. I have to admit this week has been an eye-opening experience.' He heaved his holdall on to his shoulder. 'If that's all, Detective, I'll be off.'

'I'll need your contact details.'

He nodded. 'You have them. DI Morgan already took them down.'

After Doyle left, Karen went to Ella's room.

When the young woman opened the door, her eyes were wide and her cheeks were flushed. She looked full of suppressed energy.

'Is everything all right?' Karen asked, wondering if she'd somehow found out about the recordings already.

Ella nodded, lifting her hand to run her fingers through her frizzy hair. Her silver charm bracelet slipped lower on her arm. 'Yes – I've just been watching all the action.'

'I need you to pack up your things, Ella. I have to take you home now, or I could take you to one of your relatives or a friend's house.'

'Can't I stay here a bit longer?' she asked. 'My parents should be back soon, and Mr Doyle will be here. I'm sure I'll be perfectly safe.'

'Graham Doyle's not going to be here tonight. He's leaving now.'

'He is?' Ella frowned. 'He told me he was staying until my parents got back.'

'I think he's had a change of heart due to the circumstances.'

Ella's shoulders slumped. 'Right. I suppose I should pack then.'

'Is there anyone you can stay with, just until your parents get back?'

'I'll be fine at home on my own.'

'I don't think it's a good idea to be on your own right now.'

Ella looked quizzically at Karen. 'I suppose I could go to my aunt's. She lives in Lincoln.'

'Perfect,' said Karen. 'I'll drop you there now. Do you want me to help you pack?'

Ella turned away. 'No, that's fine. I can do it.'

'I don't mind,' Karen said. 'And you'll get packed faster.'

Ella pulled out a suitcase from under the bed and began to empty the contents of the drawers into it. 'You could get my books together, if you don't mind?' Ella handed Karen a cloth book bag.

Karen slid the books, one by one, into the bag, as Ella finished packing her clothes. Then she gathered up the pens and pencils and slid them into the red pencil case on the desk.

Finally, Ella kneeled beside her and rescued her iPhone from its hiding place at the bottom of the heavy drapes. Karen had found it there when she'd searched Ella's room. She'd wondered then why Ella would have a phone hidden away like that.

'Why were you keeping your phone there?' Karen asked.

Ella shrugged. 'I didn't want it to be stolen. It's a good hiding place. I didn't unpick the stitching. It was already like that.'

'Fair enough,' Karen said, as Ella slid the phone into her pocket. 'Now, Ella, before we leave, I have to tell you something that's going to be quite difficult to hear.' Karen sat down on the bed.

Ella remained standing awkwardly by the desk. 'What is it?'

'We've discovered that someone in this house has been recording women in the bathroom.'

Ella's eyes widened. 'Did they record me?'

'We don't know yet. There are a number of recordings, and we haven't gone through them all.'

'I don't want you to! I don't want you to look at any videos of me.'

'We need to look at the recordings because they're evidence. No one's going to be looking at you specifically, Ella. We just need to identify all the women that were recorded so we can press the appropriate charges. A female officer will be reviewing the footage.'

'Do you know who made the recordings?'

'We're questioning someone at the moment.'

Ella's eyes widened further. 'Lord Chidlow? You took him in for questioning. You think he's been recording us?' Her face crumpled. 'That's disgusting.'

259

'We're investigating, Ella. I can't say more than that, but it's a horrible situation,' Karen said. 'I'm sorry this happened. We'll do our best to make sure the person responsible doesn't get away with it.'

Ella said nothing, just gripped the back of the chair.

'Come on. I'll take you to your aunt's. You might feel better if you talk to her about it.'

Ella looked at her doubtfully but leaned down and zipped up her suitcase. 'All right,' she said. 'I'm ready to go.'

CHAPTER THIRTY-ONE

Karen drove Ella into Lincoln. The young woman sat in the passenger seat, her fingers running over the smooth surface of the iPhone.

'I thought your parents didn't approve of expensive gadgets? You said you didn't have one.' Karen pointed at the phone.

'I didn't,' Ella said.

Karen thought that was going to be her final answer, but she tucked her tight curls behind her ear and gave Karen a sideways glance. 'My parents didn't buy it. One of my friends gave it to me.'

'Who?'

Ella didn't reply.

'That's an expensive gift from a friend,' Karen commented.

Ella sighed. 'Most of them are rich. It's not a big deal to them. Besides, it's just an old model.' She shoved it in her pocket. 'They didn't need it anymore. They got a new one.'

They drove in silence for the next few minutes, passing the sparse hedgerows dotted with red berries and occasional stubborn brown leaves that clung on despite the wind and the rain.

Karen took the main route into the city and was relieved to find the traffic flowing smoothly. Ella's aunt lived on Linton Street. It was a small terraced house just off Ripon Street with no front driveway, and parking was in short supply.

Karen managed to find a spot on the street, a few doors down. She got Ella's suitcase and bag out of the boot.

'It's fine. You don't need to come with me,' Ella said, grabbing the case.

'If you don't mind, I'd like to,' Karen said. 'I think your aunt might have some questions.'

Ella shrugged. 'All right, if you like.'

Karen carried the bag as Ella wheeled her case to number eight. The door was opened by a woman who had a clear resemblance to Ella. She had the same frizzy, springy hair. It suited her. It had been cut into a style that surrounded her face like a soft, puffy cloud and added extra height to her petite frame.

A scarf with an abstract print was tied around her neck, and she wore a long white tunic and navy-blue culottes. On her feet were a pair of wooden clogs decorated with painted flowers.

She beamed at Ella and then looked past the girl to Karen, a bemused expression on her face. 'What a lovely surprise,' she said.

'I thought you had telephoned your aunt?' Karen had asked Ella to call while she was putting the suitcase in the boot.

'I tried,' Ella shrugged, 'but there was no answer.'

'Sorry,' Ella's aunt said. 'I've been painting upstairs while listening to music. You're lucky you caught me. I just took a break for a cup of coffee. Come in.' She stood back and then eyed the large bag Ella was holding. 'Oh, you're planning to stay for a while?'

'No,' Ella said. 'Just until Mum and Dad get back.'

Ella started to walk past her aunt but the woman reached out and pulled her close, kissing her on the cheek before letting her go. Then she turned to Karen.

Karen held out her hand. 'I'm DS Hart,' she said. 'I don't know how much Ella has told you . . .'

'Not much. I haven't spoken to her since Christmas.'

'Right, then it's probably best if I fill you in. Were you aware Ella was attending an intensive study course this week?'

'No, I wasn't,' she said, ushering Karen in and shutting the door behind them.

She led Karen down a narrow hallway towards the kitchen, where Ella was already sitting at the table. It was a small room but there was good light from a large window and a double-glazed garden door at one end. The main part of the kitchen was long and thin, but at one end it opened up a little, leaving enough room for a table and four chairs.

'Can I get you a coffee?' she asked. 'I'm Millie by the way. Millie Cartwright.'

'A coffee would be lovely,' Karen said. 'Thanks. White, no sugar.'

As Millie set about making the coffee, Karen explained the circumstances that had led to her bringing Ella here. She told her that two young women had gone missing, and though one had returned, they'd discovered Natasha's body a few hours ago. Then she finally told a horrified Millie about the recordings.

'I don't think you should tell anybody about that,' Ella said, interrupting. 'Maybe I don't want people to know about the recordings.'

'I'm not just *people*,' Millie said. 'I'm your aunt.' She put the coffee on the table and then sat heavily on one of the chairs. 'What an awful thing to happen. That poor young girl.'

Karen sat too. 'Yes, so you can understand why I wasn't comfortable leaving Ella there this afternoon. As I understand it, her parents have been away on a safari trip and couldn't get back.'

Millie made a scoffing sound. 'It sounds like them.'

'Don't,' Ella said. 'It's not their fault. They were out of the country.'

'Well, I'm sure they could have arranged flights to come home early considering the circumstances.'

Karen diplomatically changed the subject. 'It's been quite a tough time for Ella, so I thought leaving her with you until her parents get back was the best idea.'

'That's fine with me,' Millie said. 'I was painting, but I could take the rest of the afternoon off. We could do something together,' she suggested to Ella. 'We could watch a film, if you like. I think I've got some popcorn somewhere.'

'It's fine,' Ella said. 'You don't have to interrupt your day for me. Carry on with your painting. I've got plenty of reading to do anyway. With everything that's happened I'm really behind with my studies.'

'You work too hard. You should take some time to relax,' Millie said.

'I've got too much to do. It's not easy. You wouldn't know because you didn't do A levels.'

'No, I didn't.' Millie turned to Karen. 'I went to art college. I was more of a free spirit. I didn't really get on with maths and English and all that sort of stuff. Would you like another?' She pointed at Karen's empty mug.

'No, I'm fine, thanks. I'll leave you guys to it. Ella, can I take your mobile number in case I need to get in touch?'

As Ella put her mobile number into Karen's phone, Millie asked, 'Will you keep us posted on those recordings? Someone will be prosecuted, I take it?'

'We hope so, yes.'

'Will Ella need to testify?'

'It's unlikely,' Karen said, 'but we will keep in touch with Ella and keep her updated on the investigation.'

Millie escorted Karen to the front door. 'It's awful, isn't it?' she said in a whisper. 'I mean, Ella seems to be taking it very well, but

I worry about her. She tends to keep everything bottled up. She doesn't talk to people or explain how she's feeling.'

'No.'

Millie's words made Karen think about a conversation she'd had with Ella. She looked back and saw the young woman standing by the kitchen door, silently observing.

Karen suppressed a shiver. Ella was good at watching people.

Karen's next stop was the mortuary.

Raj looked up when she entered the small vestibule and grinned.

Karen couldn't help smiling back. He was always so cheerful, despite his job. Raj's moustache curled up at the edges, emphasising his wide mouth.

He interlinked his fingers, resting his hands on his plump stomach. He wore navy-blue trousers, a bright white shirt and a purple bow tie.

'I've been expecting you,' he said, his eyes twinkling.

'Am I that predictable?' Karen asked.

'It's understandable. You want answers,' he said.

'I do. But the question is, do you have any to give me?' She walked up to his desk and looked down at the piles of paperwork.

The papers were neatly stacked but there were a lot of them. He was busy and extremely unlikely to have started the post-mortem already.

'I know I'm a pain,' Karen said, 'and you're not going to have a lot for me now, but I hoped you might have some preliminary findings to share.'

Raj tiptoed around the desk, pulled his chair out and sat down. 'I do have a few things to tell you,' he said, gesturing to the chair on the other side of the desk.

Karen sank into it. 'Right. You're going to tell me it wasn't an accident.'

'Most definitely not an accident. My preliminary judgement is that she'd been hit on the back of the head, a blow that stunned her. There was a lot of bruising, indicating she didn't die immediately. When I do the post-mortem, I'll know more, but I suspect she drowned. If I find water in her lungs, we'll have our answer.'

'So the blow to the head didn't kill her?'

'I can't say. Maybe it did, just not immediately.'

'Was the skin broken?' Karen asked, thinking about trace evidence.

'No, a great deal of bruising but no bleeding.'

'Isn't that unusual for a head wound?'

'Yes, but I've seen similar injuries before.'

Karen nodded. 'So the working theory is that she was struck on the back of the head and then somebody dumped her body in the middle of the lake, weighing her down with sandbags to make sure she had no chance of survival, as well as making the discovery of her body more difficult.'

Raj nodded.

'Were there any signs of a struggle?'

'Two broken fingernails. I've taken swabs from under all her nails, so if we get lucky and she scratched her attacker, we should get DNA.'

Karen blew out a breath, puffing out her cheeks. 'Let's hope we get lucky then.'

'Yes,' Raj said. 'I should be able to get to the post-mortem soon, but we've already sent off the swab samples.'

'Can you tell me when she died? Had she been in the lake a while?'

Raj gave a regretful smile. 'Yes, I think she died either late Thursday evening or the early hours of Friday morning.'

'So the whole time we were looking for her she was already dead?'

'I'm afraid so.'

Karen closed her eyes and leaned back in her chair, digesting the information before saying, 'I really appreciate you getting to this as soon as possible, Raj.'

'Of course,' he said. 'Post-mortems are never a pleasant job, but when they're so young . . .' He shook his head and swung around in his chair. 'Do you have any suspects in mind?'

'If I'm honest, I've got too many suspects.'

'Lots of motives?' he asked.

'Yes; I just have to narrow it down to the right one.'

'And that's why you get paid the big bucks,' Raj joked.

'I wish,' Karen said, standing up. 'I'll leave you to it. I really appreciate you giving me the information early.'

'Not a problem, as long as you don't build your whole case around it and then come back to chastise me if I've misled you.'

'I won't,' Karen called, already heading for the door. 'I promise.'

CHAPTER THIRTY-TWO

Karen grabbed a sandwich and a spiced latte from a café in the city centre. She ate the sandwich in the car before heading back to Nettleham.

At least Ella was safe now, and there were no more students at Chidlow House. Morgan and Rick would still be interviewing Lord Chidlow. She hoped they were getting somewhere.

At the station, she carried what was left of her latte into the main office, sat down at her desk and turned on the computer. She glanced at her watch as the machine started up. She wondered if Cressida was back from her appointment with the psychologist. *Only one way to find out*, she thought, reaching for the phone on her desk and dialling the Blakes.

'Hello.' Ryan Blake's tone was abrupt.

'Mr Blake,' Karen said. 'This is DS Hart. I was phoning to see how Cressida is doing after her appointment with the psychologist.'

'Oh, I see,' Ryan said, sounding distracted. 'She got on as well as can be expected. The psychologist said it's going to be a long process. We've made a follow-up appointment for next week.'

'I see. Did she remember anything more about Thursday night? Anything that could be relevant to the investigation?'

'No,' Ryan said shortly. 'And if that's all, Detective Hart, I've got things to be getting on with.'

'Actually, I was wondering if I could have a word with Cressida.'

There was a long pause and then Ryan said, 'No, I don't think that's a very good idea at all.'

'It could be very helpful, Mr Blake. We believe someone killed Natasha and we need to find out who that was.'

'Look, I said you can't talk to her. Why won't you take no for an answer? I've had enough of this harassment. Every time she speaks to you, she gets more upset. Please leave us alone.'

He hung up.

Karen put the phone down and sighed. They were getting precisely nowhere. Without evidence to the contrary, it was logical to believe Chidlow was behind the recordings. Had Natasha discovered what he was doing and confronted him? Was he so desperate to protect his dirty secret that he'd kill to keep it?

Karen leaned back in her office chair and drained the rest of the latte. Had Chidlow lost his temper? Lashed out at Natasha? She really didn't know.

She pulled a pad and pencil towards her, preparing to make some notes – a mind map of the case. She found putting it all down on paper helped her think.

She wrote a list of names. First, Chidlow. He was definitely high on the suspect list. They couldn't ignore the fact that Natasha had been found in the lake on *his* property. The lake held historical importance for the Chidlow family. Had the person who'd killed Natasha been purposefully imitating the past? Consecutive generations of Chidlow women had drowned themselves in that lake. Had it been some kind of sick, twisted fantasy for Chidlow to recreate the tragedy of his family's past?

Karen circled Chidlow's name. He'd been recording women in his house without their knowledge, so that was a strong mark against him. His wife said he had an unhealthy interest in young women. Another mark.

Karen made a note to check with his wife and make sure Chidlow hadn't been caught recording women without their consent in the past.

Then she wrote Doyle's name. A snobbish little man who put his own needs and wants before anyone else. But he had no real motive. There was no evidence to suggest he knew about the recordings. Nobody had spilled nasty stories about his past. Yes, he was aware of the book describing the drowning of the Chidlow women, but Karen didn't think he was a killer. He was upset about the murder, not because of the waste of a young life, but because it had ruined his business.

Stuart Blythe and *drugs* were the next words Karen wrote. Rick had followed up with Stuart's brother and was reasonably sure he'd never met Natasha. So drugs were unlikely to be the motive behind Natasha's murder. Karen drew a light line through Stuart's name.

Ethan? That was a can of worms Karen didn't want to open. Making an enemy of the chief constable was the last thing she needed. Grayson had come forward with the letters he'd found in which Ethan was confessing his feelings for Natasha. Had Natasha rebuffed him? Had he taken it badly and lashed out? Maybe she'd fallen, hit her head, and he'd panicked and dumped her body in the lake. Grayson had been honest and volunteered information instead of hiding it. Karen's suspicions of Grayson being corrupt had faded, but she couldn't remove his son's name from the list. He was still a possibility.

On the right of the paper, she wrote, *Monday night?* They still hadn't found out who Natasha had been with in the restaurant. It wasn't Chidlow. The man in the footage had dark hair and he wasn't as tall. So that left Doyle. Unlikely, because he was thinning on top and that would have been visible from the camera angle. Karen could rule him out, which left Mike Harrington.

She leaned heavily on the desk. Could it be Harrington?

He'd led her to the DVDs, but had he done that to take the heat off himself? Chidlow could be responsible for the recordings, but was he a killer?

Ella Seaton had said she'd heard Cressida say she'd been to Harrington's house. Cressida had denied it, but was that because she was embarrassed or scared?

With a sigh, Karen put her pencil on top of the pad and pushed it away. The case could be so easily solved if Cressida could remember what had happened on Thursday night. If Karen could just talk to her again, maybe more questions would jog her memory. But to do that, she'd need to get past Cressida's protective father.

She put her head in her hands.

'That bad, is it?' a familiar voice asked.

She turned and saw Harinder from the tech department approaching her desk.

'It's not good,' Karen said. 'I feel like I'm getting absolutely nowhere.'

'Well, I might have something that could change that,' Harinder said, pulling up a chair.

'Really? That's the best news I've had all day.'

'It's about the DVDs,' he said. 'Chidlow's wiped his computer, but the video editing software used gave the DVDs a digital signature. It takes information from the user file, so his name is attached to the recording, as well as the time and date they were processed. Resolution and screen dimensions also match the recording equipment. I'm confident the video files were recorded with the type of camera you found and then likely burned on to the DVDs by Chidlow.'

'So he was definitely recording the women?'

'Him or someone using his name and software, yes.'

'I'm sure it was him. I just hope Morgan and Rick find a way to prove it. Thanks, Harry,' Karen said as Harinder stood up. 'Appreciate it.'

'No problem. I thought you'd want to know as soon as possible, but I need to get back to the lab. We've got a lot of work queued up thanks to this case.'

'Sorry about that, but I know you'll work your magic as usual. We call you Harry for a reason.'

He winked at Karen and left her to her deliberations.

She pulled the notepad back towards her, then stared down at it. Tomorrow morning they'd have the post-mortem results. Maybe that would give them more answers. Or more forensic evidence, anyway. They hadn't had any luck with footprints around the lake. The rain had been too heavy, washing them away.

Perhaps they needed to go back to the start. They were missing something.

Doodling in the margin, she wrote Ella's name. She was an odd girl. There was something about her . . .

Karen reached for the takeaway coffee cup and then realised it was empty. Throwing it in the bin, she headed to the coffee machine. A little more caffeine might help her concentrate, and she needed all the help she could get.

Karen had her head bowed over piles of paperwork when Rick entered the open-plan office and made his way to her desk.

'I think we've got enough to charge Chidlow,' he said without preamble.

Karen looked up. 'For the recordings?'

'Yes.'

'That's great news. Where's DI Morgan?'

'He's with the CPS at the moment, but he's confident the evidence is going to be enough.'

'Finally, some progress,' Karen said, pushing back from the desk. 'I've called twelve of the women Sophie managed to identify from the recordings. Is she still making progress? I was about to check in with her again.'

Rick's face was grim. 'Yes, I think she's made her way through most of the DVDs. There's no evidence that the footage has been shared, so that's a small consolation.' He yawned and stretched. 'It's getting late. After we charge him, I'm going to head home.'

Karen glanced out of the rain-splattered window. The sky had been dark for hours. 'Yes, I'm not going to stay much longer either.'

'Coffee?' Rick asked.

Karen glanced at the empty mug on her desk, hesitated, then said, 'Better not if I want to get any sleep tonight.'

As Rick began to walk away slowly, Karen called after him, 'Good work, DC Cooper.'

Karen drove home. Her arms and legs felt heavier than usual, her bad knee ached and her eyes were sore. She was tired. Shattered, really. Thankfully, the traffic was light through Lincoln. She couldn't wait for the bypass to be finished. It should cut her commute in half.

She stopped at the traffic lights at the Ducati Garage junction. She glanced to her left towards the cemetery and felt a familiar tug of sadness.

'I'm sorry,' she whispered. 'I haven't given up.'

The lights changed and she accelerated, looking ahead to Canwick and the large memorial spire. She would never be able to look at that spot without remembering her previous case. Immediately her mind was filled with the other investigation that weighed heavily on her every day. DI Freeman's corruption. She hadn't managed to follow up on DCI Churchill, the name Alice Price had given her.

She needed to talk to Alice and get more information. Had she really gone away as her husband had said?

The most direct journey home was straight on the B1188, but Karen indicated left and turned on to Washingborough Road. She wanted to make sure Alice Price was okay. Her husband had said she wanted peace and quiet. That was fair enough, so why did it make Karen feel uneasy? Why did she feel the urge to check up on Alice? It went with the territory, she supposed. She was a police officer. It was her job to be suspicious.

She parked outside the Prices' house and saw only one car parked on the driveway. Maybe Alice *had* gone away.

When Declan Price opened the door, he didn't bother to hide his irritation. 'What are you doing here?'

'I wanted to see Alice. Make sure she's okay,' Karen said, looking over Declan's shoulder.

Everything seemed to be in order. No sign of a disturbance.

'I told you she's gone away.'

'I know what you *said*, Declan.'

His eyes narrowed to slits. 'You don't believe me?' He looked at her and laughed. 'I don't believe this. Do you think I've got her locked in a bedroom, or maybe you think I've bumped her off?'

'I'm concerned about her,' Karen said slowly.

He glared at Karen for a long moment. Then stepped back. 'Why don't you come in, search the place, satisfy your curiosity.'

Karen was tempted but she stayed on the doorstep. 'Why don't you just tell me where I can find her?'

He laughed again. 'You really have no idea what it's like, do you? I'll do better than tell you.' He reached for his keys on the telephone table. 'I'll show you. Follow me in your car.'

He marched past her, got into his car and began to reverse down the driveway. Karen got in her Civic and followed him out of the estate. Why was he being so cryptic? Why couldn't he just tell Karen where Alice was?

He drove to Branston via Station Road and turned on to the B1188 at the crossroads heading towards Metheringham. He then turned left, driving through Martin and finally into Woodhall Spa.

Karen was starting to think he was winding her up, when finally he indicated and turned on to a private road. A large sign was lit up by the entrance. Jubilee Park Caravan Site.

So this was where Alice was staying. Karen parked up behind Declan's car. He got out of the car and trudged over to one of the caravans. Karen followed him slowly and was relieved to see Alice open the door and come down the steps.

'She thought I'd done something to you,' he told Alice accusingly. 'Can you please tell her you're here because you want to be?'

'Sorry, Declan,' Karen said. 'I just wanted to make sure she was okay.' Maybe she had overreacted.

Alice walked up to Karen and took her hand. She'd lost weight since Karen had last seen her. Weight she couldn't afford to lose.

Her bony hand gripped Karen's. 'I'm sorry.'

'You've got nothing to be sorry about,' Declan said heatedly.

'I do, though. It's my fault Karen's here. I left a voicemail on her phone about a fellow officer, Churchill, and said I thought he was corrupt.'

Declan sighed and turned away, shaking his head.

Alice's dark gaze focused on Karen. 'I needed some time alone. I could feel myself slipping back to that confusing place where it all just seemed too much to handle.'

'I hoped you could tell me more about Churchill. Why you suspected him. I'll follow it up.'

She shook her head sadly. 'When I called you, I was so sure of it. So certain he was tied up in it all, but now I know I was wrong. It's hard to explain. I get episodes where everything adds up perfectly, it all makes sense. I feel like I've unravelled the whole mystery, but when I come back down to earth, I realise I was wrong. It's like working one day and thinking you've created a piece of art, but when you wake up the next morning to look at it, you see it's nothing but scribbles.'

'So Churchill isn't someone I should look into?'

Alice's hand was shaking. 'No. I want to help, to weed out officers we can't trust . . . but I've come to realise I can't trust my own mind.' Alice's eyes were sad. 'I think it's better if you do this on your own from now on, Karen. I'm sorry to let you down.'

Alice's experience had to be terrifying. Karen squeezed her hand. 'You haven't let me down. I understand how this must feel overwhelming. The most important thing is your health.' She glanced at Declan, who was staring miserably at the ground. 'Take care of yourself, Alice.'

Karen walked back to her car. Another setback. She'd always known Alice was troubled, but she'd hoped the woman might have useful information. However, no one from Internal Affairs had wanted to approach Alice for information, despite Karen's encouragement. The superintendent had been blunt, telling her Alice's involvement could only weaken the case. Unreliable evidence was the last thing she needed. An investigation was a balancing act. Bring in an element of doubt and the whole thing would come tumbling down.

It wasn't Alice's fault, of course, but Karen was bitterly disappointed.

She smothered a yawn as she travelled home. She considered dropping in on her old boss, ex-DCI Anthony Shaw, but decided against it. She wanted someone to talk to, but it was late and it wasn't fair to pile it all on Anthony.

He'd handed in his warrant card and had earned the right to a peaceful retirement. Maybe she'd pop in one day next week. Or take him to dinner to say thank you. Over the last couple of months he'd shown her a lot of support and had let her chew his ear off as she'd moaned about the lack of progress in the corruption investigation. She owed him.

Once home, she poured herself a glass of fizzy water, wishing it was wine but knowing she needed to keep a clear head.

She felt tired enough to fall asleep as soon as her head hit the pillow, but going on her nocturnal pattern over the last few months, she knew that wasn't going to happen.

Instead she went upstairs, ran herself a hot bath and tried to relax. She left her mobile on the bathroom cabinet.

She thought about calling Morgan just to decompress and go over the day's events, but he'd probably be with Jill again. She needed to be less reliant on people, to stop leaning on them. She could cope on her own. Anyway, it wasn't as though she had much choice.

CHAPTER THIRTY-THREE

The following morning, Karen was woken by her mobile's cheerful ringtone. Muffling a curse into the pillow, she reached for the phone.

She squinted at the caller ID. Harinder.

She answered, mumbling a hello.

'Karen, don't tell me you're still asleep. I've been slaving away for hours.'

She pulled the phone away from her ear and stared at the screen. 'Am I missing something? It's six a.m.'

'Is it? Thought it was later. Sorry. I came in early to set up the PCR for the repeat DNA test. Some of the results are back on the requests you filed. I thought you'd want them as soon as possible.'

Karen sat up. Now he had her attention. 'Go on.'

'The polo shirt,' Harinder said. 'You asked us to check for Mike Harrington's DNA, but we haven't found anything. There's a chance we could find low copy DNA, but it's likely been through a hot wash.'

'I don't understand,' Karen said, rubbing her eyes.

'When a person has worn an item of clothing, they leave behind skin cells, sweat. It leaves a trace. If someone had worn that shirt after it had been washed, there would be DNA left behind. But the test has come up negative. Now we can, as I mentioned, do more intensive experiments and get low copy number DNA, which could linger after a cycle through the washing machine. But that won't mean that person was wearing the shirt when Natasha was murdered. Or when the blood was transferred to the shirt.'

'So you're saying the polo shirt left on the roof was clean – that it hadn't been worn by Harrington?'

'Yes, not by Harrington or anyone else.'

'Then it *was* planted. So how did the blood get on the shirt?'

'Here's where it gets interesting. The blood was human, but almost certainly not Natasha's.'

'Not Natasha's?' Karen repeated.

'I'm running a duplicate experiment because it surprised me too, but no.'

'Right,' Karen said, frowning. 'So we've got blood on Mike Harrington's polo shirt, but it's not our victim's?'

'Right,' said Harinder.

'Okay,' Karen said slowly, trying to process the information. 'So it looks like someone was trying to frame Harrington. Why?'

'Luckily for me, figuring that out is your job,' Harinder said. 'I just give you the results.'

'Anything else for me?' Karen asked.

'Only that the fingerprints on the Bluetooth speaker belonged to Ethan Grayson, but I think you knew that already?'

Karen sighed. 'Unfortunately. Bad news for the chief constable.'

'Yes, but I do have some good news. We found Chidlow's fingerprints all over the DVDs.'

'Great. What about Natasha's phone?' Karen asked. It was a stroke of luck that Natasha's mobile had managed to stay wedged in the back pocket of her jeans.

'Nothing yet,' Harinder said. 'But we'll be looking at it again later today.'

'Okay,' Karen said, suddenly feeling more awake. 'Thanks for the update.'

She hung up and headed for the shower, her mind racing with possibilities.

◆ ◆ ◆

When Karen got to her desk, she found a note asking her to go to Superintendent Murray's office as soon as she got in.

It was only seven fifteen. Murray didn't usually get in until eight during the week. The early start on a Sunday wasn't a good sign.

Karen put her handbag in the desk drawer, draped her coat over the back of the chair and then headed upstairs. As it was Sunday, Pamela wasn't at her desk, so Karen rapped on the office door.

'Come in.'

Karen opened the door and entered. Superintendent Murray sat behind her desk. Her brow was furrowed, and her lips were pressed together, forming a thin line.

'Good morning, ma'am,' Karen said. 'Is everything okay?'

'Not really, Karen,' Murray said. 'Take a seat.'

When Karen sat, Murray asked, 'How do you think the investigation is going?'

'Slower than I'd like, but I feel we're close to a breakthrough. Lord Chidlow has been charged.'

'Do you believe he killed Natasha Layton?'

Karen hesitated. 'I don't know. We have no evidence to prove his involvement.'

'I see.'

'But we are making progress, ma'am. What's wrong? Is the chief constable making demands?'

'No,' Murray said. 'On the contrary, he's given us his full support and has been full of praise for the way you and DI Morgan have handled the investigation.'

Karen tried to hide her surprise. That was good news. She told the superintendent the information Harinder had passed on earlier, trying to convince her that they were making progress, albeit not as fast as they'd have liked.

'We need results quickly, Karen.'

'Of course, ma'am.'

Murray took off her glasses and rubbed the bridge of her nose. 'The Blakes have made a complaint through their lawyer. They're not happy with how the investigation has been handled. They say the way the police have hounded their daughter is equivalent to harassment. You can see the optics don't look good.'

'Harassment? I can assure you, ma'am, we've not harassed Cressida. We simply want to talk to her about what happened. We need to interview witnesses and the Blakes are trying to prevent us talking to their daughter again. I know it's difficult for the girl but—'

The superintendent put up a hand. 'I know. But the Blakes are upset, and angry. The situation could develop into something serious if their legal representatives press ahead with this harassment claim.'

'Well, they can't prove it, ma'am, because it simply isn't true.'

'Even if it isn't true, it will be a public relations nightmare.'

'I know this has been awful for their family, but the Blakes got Cressida back. Natasha's parents . . .' Karen met Murray's assessing gaze. 'They deserve answers, ma'am. And if talking to Cressida is the only way to get those answers, then that's what we have to do.'

'I take it you have no objection to having their legal representative and both parents present every time you speak to Cressida?'

'If that's what you think is necessary, ma'am, that would be fine,' Karen said stiffly, wondering why on earth the Blakes felt they were being harassed.

It was understandable the family wanted to be left alone to come to terms with what had happened, but when there was an ongoing investigation that wasn't possible. With every hour that passed, the case grew colder and their leads faded away.

'I'll suggest that and hope it calms the waters. Now, I'll let you get on,' Murray said.

As Karen reached the door, the superintendent said, 'I'm glad the chief constable has shown his support.'

'Shown his support, ma'am?'

'Yes. I had an internal memo yesterday. He's putting together a new team to look into Freeman's corruption and is planning weekly briefings.'

'Really, ma'am? I hadn't heard anything about it.'

'No, well, like I said, I only got the memo yesterday. But there's a good chance we'll get somewhere now that the chief constable is putting the pressure on.'

'That's great news,' Karen said. She refrained from adding, *It's about time.*

When she got back downstairs, she spotted Morgan entering his office.

She followed him in, and as he shrugged off his coat, said, 'Good result on Chidlow.'

'Yes. Now we need to get someone in the frame for Natasha's murder.'

'Harinder's working on her phone today, so we should find some communications on there if she didn't delete them. That could generate new leads.'

Morgan nodded. 'I hope it does. We could really do with them.'

'There's one piece of evidence I want to follow up on today. The CCTV. We haven't identified the man who was in the restaurant with Natasha on Monday night. I'm going to take a file of photos to the restaurant. Pictures of all the teachers who were on the course, Doyle, Harrington, Ethan and even Chidlow, though he doesn't have dark hair. I want to see if the owner recognises any of them as the man who had dinner with Natasha.'

'Yes, I think that's a priority,' Morgan said.

'I'll show the restaurant owner a photograph of Ryan Blake too. His hair is dark.'

'Ryan Blake. Cressida's father?' Morgan asked, raising an eyebrow.

'Yes, why not? He's got dark hair, and the young women were friends, so it's likely he came into contact with her.'

'His wife said he was with her on Monday evening.'

'Yes, and we all know that wives sometimes cover up for their husbands,' Karen said. 'Besides, his behaviour is suspicious. Did Superintendent Murray tell you the Blakes have claimed we're harassing them?'

Morgan sat behind his desk and frowned. 'No, I haven't spoken to the superintendent today.'

'They're not happy with the way we've been trying to get Cressida to open up. According to the Blakes, I've been calling too many times, making demands on their time.'

Morgan switched on his computer, his frown deepening. 'I suppose they have been through a very traumatic event.'

'Even so,' Karen said. 'It feels . . . like he's trying to keep us at arm's length, like he has something to hide.'

'Perhaps he's just trying to protect his daughter,' Morgan suggested.

'Maybe. Or maybe he's trying to protect himself. It can't hurt to include him among the photos.'

'I agree. Let me know how you get on.'

◆ ◆ ◆

Karen left Morgan and sat at her desk, sorting through the photographs. After she sent the files to the printer, she focused on a headshot of Ryan Blake. It was from the DVLA, his driver's licence photo.

Blue eyes, dark hair and a smug look on his face. He had every reason to be smug. No money worries, a happy home and multiple exotic holidays every year, which kept his tan topped up.

What was he afraid of? Could he be trying to protect Cressida, as Morgan had suggested? It was possible. Naturally a father would want to put his daughter first, but to go as far as to stop them questioning Cressida when the man who'd killed her friend and quite possibly abducted Cressida was still out there?

Material evidence in a case like this was crucial, but thanks to the weather conditions, it had been hard to come by. Karen liked behavioural evidence. It didn't hold up so well in court, but she had found it was often the key to a case.

She liked to focus on suspects whose actions didn't add up. Most behaviour could be explained when the full story was revealed.

Mike Harrington's surliness made sense when you considered the loss of his child.

Chidlow's attitude and pure creepiness was a tip-off to the fact he was a voyeuristic predator.

And Doyle's selfish, snobbish tendencies explained why he didn't care about anything but himself and how the incident would affect his business.

The reason for Ethan's odd behaviour had become clear once she'd realised he was a lonely kid who had a crush on Natasha and was trying to impress her. He had tried to scare people so that he would feel he mattered. That he wasn't being ignored. Though

Karen still wasn't completely sure he'd been working alone. He struck her as the easily led type.

Jasmine Blake wasn't as reluctant as her husband to let Cressida talk to the police. Karen believed she genuinely wanted what was best for her daughter.

Then they had the Laytons, Natasha's parents, and their behaviour. The mother, a history professor with an idealised view of her daughter, and a workaholic father – both devastated, shocked and horrified. All reactions she would expect.

But back to the Blakes, on the other hand . . . Jasmine Blake was concerned for her daughter, but also eager to cover up for her husband. Karen hadn't missed the way she'd been quick to say she and Ryan had been at home on Monday night.

It might be time to look at Mr Blake more closely. She could check his credit card receipts, track his vehicle over the past week.

Ryan Blake thought his family was being harassed when the police were actually treating them with kid gloves. They'd seen him as a victim. First as a father with a missing child, then as the parent of a traumatised victim.

He had no idea what harassment really was. Or maybe he did. This claim could be a ruse to stop them sniffing around him and his family. Was he worried about what they would find?

CHAPTER THIRTY-FOUR

Karen turned up at the restaurant clutching a file containing the images of all the men with dark hair who were known to have come into contact with Natasha recently, as well as a few stock photographs.

The restaurant was closed, but after she'd rung the bell three times, the door was finally opened by a bleary-eyed man of about forty.

Karen held up her ID. 'I'm sorry to bother you, Mr Clark.'

The man's eyes widened. 'Is this about the missing girls? I've spoken to one of your colleagues already.'

'Yes, that was DC Sophie Jones,' Karen said. 'Can I come in? I have a few more questions.'

'Of course. Sorry, it was a late night.' He stepped back, opening the large glass door for Karen to enter. 'I heard you found a body.'

News travelled fast in small villages.

'Yes, we did. Sadly we found Natasha Layton.'

'So young.' He shook his head. 'Can I get you a coffee?'

'That would be lovely, thanks.'

He made the drinks using the fancy chrome espresso machine near the bar area, and gestured for Karen to take a seat.

She sat at one of the dark wood tables.

He brought over two tiny cups of coffee and sat opposite her. 'Now, how can I help?'

'We want to identify the man who was dining with Natasha on Monday evening.'

'Yes, I thought he might be important. I let DC Jones look at the internal camera footage, but unfortunately the external recordings were wiped.' He put his elbows on the table, leaning forward. 'You haven't managed to identify him yet?'

'No.' Karen put the folder flat on the table. 'I've brought some photographs that I want you to look at. I'd like you to tell me if you recognise any of the men.'

'You think one of them was the chap with Natasha Layton on Monday?'

Karen laid the photos across the table. 'It's possible.'

She selected the first image and pushed it forward. It was Edward Chidlow.

'Oh, I know who that is,' he said, taking a sip of his espresso and nodding. 'Yes, that's Lord Chidlow. He's the owner of the hall, isn't he?'

'That's right. Has he been in here at all?'

Clark shook his head. 'No, unfortunately not.'

'Unfortunately?' Karen asked.

'Well, his presence might have generated some business. Things have been quiet since we opened. Word of mouth hasn't quite taken off. Speaking of which, if you could recommend us to any of your friends or colleagues . . .' He smiled at her hopefully.

'Sure,' Karen said, slightly thrown at the change of subject.

She pulled out another image, this time of Doyle.

Clark looked it over, his forehead creasing. 'I don't know. He kind of looks familiar, but I don't think I know him.'

'He wasn't here on Monday?' Karen asked.

'Not with Natasha, no.'

'Okay. And this gentleman?' Karen slid forward an image of Mike Harrington.

Harrington stared out from the picture, his dark eyes angry. The photograph had caught his mood well.

'I wouldn't like to meet him on a dark night,' Clark said, grimacing. He pulled the printout closer.

Karen held her breath as he stared at Harrington for a long time.

Finally, he said, 'No, he hasn't been here, and he definitely wasn't here with Natasha on Monday. The man was a bit younger and more . . . well groomed.'

Karen glanced at Harrington's photograph. Harrington was not the type to buff his nails or trim his eyebrows, unlike Chidlow and Doyle. She could picture Chidlow taking great care over his appearance, perhaps partaking in a weekly face mask, maybe a regular pedicure. And Doyle was a dapper chap. He was thinning on top, but she suspected he dyed his hair to hide the grey. He wore cravats, crisp white shirts and tailored trousers. Karen had never seen him in casual clothes.

'Okay, and this one,' she said, uncovering the image of Ryan Blake.

Clark grabbed on to it, pulled it towards him and then nodded. 'Yep, it's him. Definitely. I recognise the eyes and his hair. His hair was black, carefully styled. I asked him if he had Italian ancestry. He laughed and said not as far as he knew.'

'You're sure,' Karen said, leaning forward.

She'd known Ryan was shifty and suspected he was trying to hide something, but she hadn't anticipated this. Why would he be eating dinner with Natasha without his daughter?

'Were they alone?' Karen asked. 'Was there another young woman with them?'

'No, it was just the two of them.'

'Did they look intimate?'

'Well, they weren't exactly all over each other or anything, but they looked – yes, I'd say they looked like a couple. At first I thought he might be her father, but thinking back, they were pretty cosy.'

Karen exhaled a long breath. 'Thank you very much for your help,' she said, stacking the images, shuffling them back together and then putting them in the file.

That had certainly been a twist she hadn't seen coming.

'Would you like another coffee?' Clark offered as Karen stood up.

'No, thank you. I have somewhere to be,' she said, and then mentally added as she walked out of the restaurant, *and an arrest to make.*

◆ ◆ ◆

An hour later, Karen and Morgan knocked on the Blakes' front door. It was painted a shiny, cheerful red.

Ryan Blake opened it. His dark hair was neatly styled, combed back from his forehead. His youthful, expressive face was guarded, and he frowned when he saw them.

He tried to close the door. 'As I've already told your senior officers, I'm sick and tired of you harassing us.'

'We're not harassing you, Mr Blake. We're simply conducting an investigation, and we'd like your help with that. Your cooperation would be greatly appreciated,' DI Morgan said.

Ryan hesitated with the door half closed. 'Well, it's not a convenient time. My wife is out at the moment getting groceries, and Cressida is at a friend's house, trying to put this awful situation behind her.'

'So you're home alone, sir?' Karen asked.

He nodded stiffly. 'Yes, and it's a good job I am. If Cressida were here to witness you turning up on our doorstep, pestering us again, she'd be upset. Now, if you don't mind, please leave and telephone before calling on us next time. If you need to speak to Cressida, you must make an appointment through our solicitor.'

Morgan put up his hand to stop the door closing. 'It's not Cressida we need to see this time. It's you.'

Ryan Blake's hands fell from the door. He paled. 'Me? What do you want with me?'

Confusion played across his face. Half smiling, half frowning, as though he couldn't quite work out what facial expression to use to look innocent.

Nice try, Karen thought. 'Can we come in?'

He didn't reply.

She turned, looked over her shoulder and then back at Ryan. 'We could carry on this conversation on your doorstep, but it might give your neighbours something to gossip about.'

His face was now positively ashen. He gestured for them to come in.

'Fine. Come through to the living room.'

He didn't offer them a drink. Instead, he nervously paced in front of the marble mantelpiece. Karen and Morgan sat down on opposite ends of the huge cream sofa.

'Now, perhaps we could start with a fresh slate, Mr Blake. The last thing we want is for you to feel we're harassing you,' Karen said.

'Well, this isn't a very good start,' he said with a nervous laugh. 'You've turned up without invitation yet again.'

He was trying to keep up the outraged-parent act, but they'd rattled him.

'But surely you want us to catch the culprit. Whoever traumatised your daughter and killed Natasha is still out there.'

'Of course I want them caught. That doesn't mean I want my family disrupted and upset.'

'Perhaps you could tell us where you were on Monday evening,' Morgan said.

Ryan blinked. 'You already know. My wife told you we were at home all evening.'

'All evening, Mr Blake?' Karen asked, keeping her face blank and unreadable.

He swallowed hard. 'Yes, that's right. All evening.'

Karen leaned forward, placed the image of Natasha in the restaurant on Monday night on the coffee table and then tapped the shoulder of the unidentified man. 'We believe this is you, Mr Blake.'

'What? That's preposterous. It's not me.' He looked at Karen and then at Morgan, trying to judge how much they knew.

'There's no point lying anymore, Mr Blake,' Morgan said.

Ryan didn't say anything for some time. He scratched the back of his head, his eyes fixed on the pale cream carpet. Then he looked up. 'I need my solicitor.'

'You probably do, but we have some questions to ask you in the meantime,' Karen said. 'If you have nothing to hide, you have nothing to worry about.'

He paused with his hand halfway to his pocket. 'What do you want to know?'

'We have a witness who identifies you as the man dining with Natasha Layton on Monday evening. We would like to know the nature of your relationship.' Karen kept her gaze fixed on Ryan.

'The nature of our relationship?' He raked a hand through his hair. He was sweating. 'Look, I know this probably looks bad, but what happened to Natasha has nothing to do with me. You've got the wrong man.'

'Again, we have a witness. We know it was you at the restaurant with Natasha.'

'All right, all right,' Ryan said, putting his hands up. 'Yes, I did have dinner with Natasha on Monday. She was going through some tough times and I was talking to her.'

'Just *talking*, Mr Blake?' Karen asked.

Ryan's features tightened. 'Yes, just talking. She was a lonely young woman and she needed some guidance.'

'So you were guiding her. Would you mind explaining exactly what that means?'

Ryan's face flushed. 'She was having some trouble with her parents. They didn't accept the fact that she was grown-up, that she was an adult. We got talking on a couple of occasions when she was here visiting Cressida, and, well, we found we had a lot in common.'

'You had a lot in common with seventeen-year-old Natasha Layton?' Karen asked, emphasising the age.

'Yes, she was much more mature than you might think,' he snapped.

'Were you having a relationship with her?'

'That depends what you mean by "relationship", doesn't it?'

'Were you having an affair? Were you sleeping together?'

'That's none of your business! Look, she was seventeen years old. That's not illegal.'

'So what happened?' Karen asked. 'Did she threaten to tell someone about the affair? Or maybe she asked you to leave your wife? Did you get angry and lash out? Maybe you didn't even mean to hurt her.'

Ryan looked aghast. 'No, it wasn't me. I could never have hurt Natasha. I'm not a violent person. You have to believe me.'

'That's difficult for us to do, Mr Blake,' Morgan said, 'since you lied to us once before.'

'You know why I didn't come forward with all the details about me and Natasha. It would have looked terrible. I would have been top of your suspect list. Look, I could have called my solicitor and refused to talk to you now, but I was honest. That has to count for something.'

'It does,' Morgan said. 'It tells us you're prepared to tell the truth when it suits you.' He stood up. 'Ryan Blake. I'm arresting you for the murder of—'

'No!' the man roared, pushing past Morgan, trying to get out of the room.

He knocked into the coffee table, sending a porcelain vase tumbling to the floor. The carpet broke its fall, stopping it smashing into pieces. The only damage was a single crack along the length of the vase.

As Morgan restrained Ryan Blake and put him in handcuffs, the man howled. 'Do you know how expensive that vase was? It's a priceless heirloom from Jasmine's family,' he spat.

'Then you shouldn't have tried to run away, should you?' Karen said as Morgan led him out of the living room.

As they walked towards the front door, Ryan broke down in sobs, but Karen didn't feel any sympathy for him at all. It was lucky for him his wife and daughter weren't here.

'We haven't had the full post-mortem results back yet,' she said. 'Are we going to have any surprises?'

Ryan stopped crying for a moment and looked up. 'What do you mean?' he sniffed.

'Are we going to discover Natasha was pregnant? Is that why you killed her?'

His eyes widened and he shook his head vigorously. 'No, I didn't kill her. Please, you have to believe me. My wife isn't going to find out, is she?'

'All this time, we thought you were being protective of Cressida,' Karen said, 'but actually you were looking after yourself, Mr Blake. Making sure your secret didn't come to light.'

'No, you've got it all wrong,' Ryan said, dissolving into yet more self-pitying sobs.

CHAPTER THIRTY-FIVE

Back at the station, after Ryan Blake was processed, they gave him some time to collect himself. As he was talking with his solicitor, Sophie, Rick, Morgan and Karen discussed the case in the main office.

Karen leaned back in her chair, thoughtful. 'You know, something about this is bothering me.'

'Do you think we've got it wrong, Sarge?' Sophie asked. 'You don't think Ryan Blake killed her?'

Karen frowned and shook her head. 'I don't know. The restaurant owner positively identified Mr Blake, and Ryan has admitted to having a relationship with Natasha, but I'm not sure he's telling us the truth about everything.'

'I agree,' Sophie said, wheeling over a chair. 'I wonder how old Natasha was when this relationship started.'

Rick perched on the edge of Karen's desk. 'What if Ryan had something to do with Chidlow's recordings?'

'That's a possibility,' Morgan said. 'We'll ask him about that during questioning.'

Morgan was standing but leaning over Karen's desk, sketching out details on a pad and planning the interview strategy.

Karen fiddled with the pen on her desk, trying to work out the puzzle. Ryan Blake was a gift-wrapped suspect. Wanting to keep his affair with Natasha secret was a strong motive, so why didn't she believe they'd uncovered the whole story?

'So, what is it that's bothering you, Sarge?' Rick asked, turning to Karen.

'It's Ella Seaton,' Karen said. 'I don't understand how she fits into all of this, but I'm sure she does somehow.'

Sophie looked up, resting her chin on her interlinked fingers. 'Do you think Ryan Blake had a thing with Ella as well?' She looked at Karen doubtfully.

'No, I don't think so,' Karen said. 'Ella's an unusual girl. She observes rather than participates. I don't think she's been in a relationship with anyone.'

'There's the teacher's death too. Miss King. Maybe she found out something about Ryan and Natasha, and Ryan killed her?' Rick said, rubbing his chin.

Karen nodded, mulling it over. 'The two deaths could well be related. I think I'll check in with Ella and see how she's doing. She should be home by now.'

Sophie wheeled her chair back to her own desk to make the remaining calls to the women in the videos. Rick went with Morgan to his office to help with the interview questions, and Karen picked up her desktop telephone and called Ella's mobile number.

There was no answer, so she tried Ella at home, but again there was no reply.

She checked the file for any other contact details they had for Ella Seaton, and located Ella's mother's mobile number, but the mobile was switched off and she got a recorded message.

Karen frowned. This didn't make sense. Where was Ella? Concerned, she dialled the number she had for Ella's aunt.

The phone was answered on the third ring. 'Hello.'

'Is that Millie?'

'Yes, that's right. Who's this?'

'This is DS Karen Hart. I dropped Ella off at your house—'

'Oh yes, I remember.'

'I'm trying to get in touch with Ella. Has she gone home with her parents?'

'No,' Millie said. 'They were supposed to land this morning, but their flight was delayed again, so they're not getting back until this evening.'

'Oh, I see. Could I talk to her?'

'She's not here at the moment.'

'She's gone out?'

'Yes, about half an hour ago. She said she was meeting a friend in Lincoln. She mentioned the Bailgate Deli, near the castle.'

Karen thanked Millie and hung up. When she replaced the handset, she noticed Sophie was pale. She had her phone clamped to her ear and she was grimacing.

Karen waited until she'd hung up, then asked, 'Who was that?'

'Mrs Blake. She's very upset and demanded to know what was going on with her husband.'

'Did you tell her?'

'I said her husband was arrested in connection with the death of Natasha Layton. She was quiet for a moment, then began ranting and raving. Understandable really. This must have come as a terrible shock.'

Karen wondered if it really had. There was, of course, an outside chance Jasmine Blake had no idea what her husband was up to. But she'd been quick to say her husband had been home with her on Monday night when he hadn't. Had she suspected something?

Karen tried Ella's mobile again, but she didn't answer.

There was something wrong. Something she was missing.

Karen grabbed her coat and bag and stopped by Morgan's office, where he and Rick were still finishing off the interview plan.

'I'm heading out with Sophie for a little while; I'd like to talk to Ella Seaton – as long as you don't need me for the Ryan Blake interview.'

Morgan looked mildly surprised but nodded. 'Yes, we've got the interview handled. Keep me updated.'

'Will do.'

Karen loved the part of Lincoln near the castle and cathedral. There was so much history crammed into the area, from the old narrow houses to the cobbled streets. There were reminders of the past everywhere she looked.

Karen managed to nab a prime parking spot in the Cathedral Quarter and headed to the Bailgate Deli with Sophie.

'So what's your theory then, Sarge?' Sophie asked as they turned into Gordon Road.

'I don't really have one. Only that Ella's been acting oddly. She's hiding something.'

'Do you think she knows about Ryan and Natasha?'

Karen nodded. 'Yes, it could well be that. Ella said something to me once that stayed with me.'

'What was that?'

'She said she liked to watch people. She said sometimes it was nice being invisible because you got to watch people when they were unaware and find out their secrets.'

'So you think Ella's found out some secrets?'

'Yes, I suspect she has.'

They stepped under the blue and white awning and entered the small deli. It was immediately obvious that Ella wasn't there. Two women were enjoying coffees and delicious-looking brownies. A young man with purple-streaked hair was munching his way through a vegan fry-up, and the smell of fresh bread made Karen's stomach rumble.

'She's not here,' Sophie said. 'What do we do now?'

'We can have a quick look around the area and see if we can spot her.'

'Since we're here . . .' Sophie said, gazing at the menu. 'I might get something. A late breakfast. Anything for you, Sarge?'

'I'll have some plum bread. I'll wait for you outside; I'm going to try Ella's mobile again.'

Outside, Karen scanned the narrow road but couldn't see Ella. She looked through the window of the tea shop next to the deli, but drew a blank. Opposite and to the right was one of the doors to Gino's Italian restaurant, but that would be closed now.

She then walked to the end of Gordon Road, stopped in front of The Whisky Shop and dialled Ella's number again. No answer.

Sophie joined her and held out a paper bag containing the plum bread. Karen put it in her handbag for later as Sophie took a large bite of her chocolate brownie.

'No sign of her?' Sophie asked, wiping the crumbs away with the back of her hand.

'No. Let's take a quick look along Bailgate, then I'll give her mobile another try. If we still get nothing, I'll get a trace on her phone.'

Sophie paused, brownie halfway to her mouth. 'You think she's missing? Another victim?'

'I'm concerned about her.'

Sophie guiltily put the brownie away. 'Right. Let's go this way. I'll take the right side of the road, you take the left.'

CHAPTER THIRTY-SIX

They turned left and walked briskly along Bailgate, avoiding the puddles. They hadn't gone far when Sophie stopped dead.

'Hang on. Isn't that . . .'

Sophie had stopped just before the Thai restaurant, in front of an entrance to a narrow alleyway which divided the row of shops.

Karen quickly crossed the road. 'What is it?'

But Sophie's gaze was fixed on the alley. 'It's her. No!'

Ten feet or so into the alley were Cressida Blake and Ella Seaton.

'Stop!' Sophie shouted again, and began to run towards them.

Cressida held a small knife in her right hand. With the other, she gripped Ella's hair, tilting her head back and exposing the white of her throat.

Sophie's shouts distracted Cressida enough that Ella could pull back. The younger girl lashed out, desperately trying to defend herself. Her elbow connected with Cressida's stomach.

Winded, Cressida bent double. Sophie made an unsuccessful grab for the knife. Things seemed to progress in slow motion as Cressida raised the knife again in a long arc, this time aiming for Sophie.

Karen dived towards them, hitting the ground with a thud that sent a shockwave of pain down her leg.

Cressida inhaled sharply as Karen grabbed her wrist and twisted it until the girl cried out in pain and the blade fell, clattering against the cobbles.

Sophie kicked the knife away as Karen forced Cressida's arm up behind her back.

Cressida snarled, kicking and writhing furiously. Sophie helped Karen push her against the wall to subdue her. She was screaming like a banshee. Her breath was hot and sour against Karen's cheek.

'What's got into you?' Sophie shouted. 'Calm down. Have you got cuffs, Sarge?'

'Back in the car.'

'Great.' Sophie helped Karen hold on to Cressida as the girl snarled, turning the air blue with her imaginative swearing.

This was a side to Cressida that she'd kept well hidden.

Once they had Cressida relatively secure, pushed firmly against the wall, Karen looked over her shoulder. 'Ella, are you okay?'

There was a cut on the side of Ella's throat. A dribble of blood slid down to her collar, staining the white material a vivid red, but it wasn't a deep cut.

Ella put her hand against her neck and managed to nod.

'Can you call for backup?' Karen asked Sophie breathlessly as Cressida continued to struggle.

'You'd better let me go. You have no idea what you're doing. I'm the victim here,' Cressida shouted, panting with the effort of trying to wrench herself free.

She then delivered a well-aimed kick at Karen's knee. Her *bad* knee that was already throbbing. Pain shot up Karen's leg, stole her breath and made her feel sick.

Karen tightened her grip on Cressida, tilting her arm up higher until she squirmed with pain.

'You're hurting me. Let go. Help, help,' she cried. 'Police brutality!'

'That's not going to work,' Karen hissed. 'What were you planning to do to Ella? You could have killed her!'

'I was just defending myself,' Cressida insisted. 'She had a knife. She was trying to kill me!'

'We saw you, Cressida,' Karen said. '*You* had the knife to Ella's throat.'

Ella was badly shaken. She leaned against the wall, face pale, trembling.

After Sophie called for backup, she helped Karen with Cressida, and the two of them managed to restrain her more comfortably. But the teenager was still spitting with rage.

'You don't know who you're dealing with. You're going to regret this. You should've let me finish the job. She's nothing but a waste of space. You think you're protecting her but she's nothing but a blackmailer.'

'I know,' Karen said.

Ella looked shocked. 'You do?'

Karen nodded. 'That's where you got the charm bracelet from, isn't it?' she said, nodding to Ella's wrist. 'It used to be Cressida's.'

Ella hesitated, then nodded.

'And the phone as well?'

Ella sighed, leaned back against the brick wall and looked up at the narrow strip of sky above the alley. 'I'm going to be in a lot of trouble, aren't I?'

'Tell me what happened, and I'll see what I can do to help,' Karen said.

Ella tucked her frizzy hair behind her ears and bit her lower lip. 'I overheard something . . . but I didn't mean to be a blackmailer.'

'Yes, you did. You're a horrible, sly worm and I'm going to make sure you go to prison for a very long time,' Cressida shrieked.

'That's enough,' Sophie ordered.

'Carry on, Ella,' Karen said, and she leaned against Cressida, pushing her closer to the wall.

'Well, I was coming to meet Cressida today because she said she was going to give me some money. She had a secret that she didn't want anyone to know.'

'You shut up, you hear me? Just shut up,' Cressida roared.

Ella took a terrified step back.

'Go on, Ella,' Sophie said encouragingly.

But the girl shook her head, obviously scared of Cressida – and with good reason.

They kept trying to calm her, but the teenager was wild with temper. It seemed to take forever for backup to arrive. The disparity between the Cressida Blake standing in front of Karen now and the sobbing, fragile girl who had staggered into Chidlow House on Friday was astonishing.

Cressida glared at Karen, her blue eyes like pieces of ice.

'Cressida, do you want to tell me why we caught you holding a knife to Ella's throat? She's bleeding.'

'It was only a scratch.'

'Speaking of scratches,' Karen said, 'was that mark on your cheek made when Natasha scratched you?'

The girl scowled and tried to yank her arm away.

'You may as well tell us because we're going to have the DNA results soon. We'll find your skin cells under Natasha's fingernails if she did make that scratch on your cheek.'

Cressida seethed silently. Her body shook beneath Karen's hands. But it wasn't down to fear. It was fury.

'And what about the polo shirt. The one on the roof. Did you plant that?'

Cressida was silent for so long that Karen started to think she wasn't going to answer, but then she lifted her chin and gave Karen a mocking look. 'You can't prove anything. Maybe Ella did it. Maybe Ella needed a fall guy. You have to admit, it almost worked.'

'A fall guy?'

Cressida's smile widened. Karen shook her head as she studied the skin around Cressida's fingernails. Though still red and inflamed, the skin had started to heal and was no longer bleeding. She thought back to when Ella had found the shirt . . . Just after Cressida had returned to Chidlow House, saying she had come because she wanted to help find Natasha. She'd been so believable. Her grief had seemed genuine. 'You tried to frame Mike Harrington because it was *you* who killed Natasha.'

Sophie sucked in a sharp breath. 'Why?'

'Because she thought Natasha was going to ruin her life,' Ella said quietly.

'Shut up!' Cressida spat, trying to pull away from Karen.

'Lord Chidlow would have been a better scapegoat,' Ella said with a sigh. 'Lord Chidlow would have been more believable – easy to believe a sicko like that who recorded women getting undressed and showering could have killed a teenager.'

'Hang on, you've lost me,' Sophie said, staring at Cressida. 'Why would you kill Natasha? She was your friend.'

'She wasn't my friend. She was an evil cow who was trying to ruin my life,' Cressida said.

The raging energy had left her now, so Karen loosened her grip. Just a little though. She had started to believe the pretty blonde teenager in front of her was a psychopath.

Sophie shot a confused glance at Karen, then looked back at Cressida. 'What did she do to you?'

'She wanted to destroy my family. Her parents were a nightmare, and she was jealous of mine.'

'So you killed her?' Sophie looked dumbfounded.

'I didn't say that! If you're trying to trick a confession out of me, it won't work.'

'We won't need your confession, Cressida. Your blood is on Mike Harrington's shirt that you planted on the roof. Did you think we wouldn't check and find out it wasn't Natasha's blood?'

Cressida swallowed hard and hesitated before replying. 'That's because he hurt me. He killed Natasha. He would have killed me too if I hadn't got away. I remember now.'

'That's not true,' Karen said. 'You planted the shirt.'

'You can't prove anything,' Cressida said calmly.

They weren't making any progress, so Karen tried another angle. 'Where does Ethan Grayson fit into this?'

'Ethan?' Cressida scoffed. 'Nowhere. He just followed instructions. All he did was play those stupid recordings on his phone when I told him to. He'd do anything I asked. He's pathetic.'

'You lured Ella here in order to kill her. You promised her money so she would turn up?'

'No matter how hard you try, I'm not going to say anything to incriminate myself.' Cressida rolled her eyes. 'Although I will say Ella was supposed to meet me in the park. It's quieter there.' Her eyes glinted as she gave the other teenager a cruel smile.

Ella turned away, hugging her long wool coat around her.

Karen straightened and looked at Sophie. 'Cressida killed Natasha because she found out she was having an affair with her father.'

'You know about that?' Cressida asked, the cold smile slipping from her lips.

'We do. He's in custody.'

'Why?'

'For the murder of Natasha Layton,' Sophie said.

Cressida burst out with a high-pitched laugh, tinged with hysteria. 'Oh, that's just classic. Typical police. You couldn't find your way out of a paper bag.'

'But he didn't murder Natasha, did he?' Karen said. 'You did.'

Cressida gave a sly smile. 'Whatever I tell you now won't be admissible. I'll get an expensive lawyer, and they'll get me off. It's the way the system works.'

'No, it doesn't,' Sophie snapped.

Cressida gave her a patronising look. 'So naive,' she said in a sing-song voice. 'And to think you're a police officer.'

'So tell us what happened,' Karen said.

'No, you tell me what you think happened.'

'All right,' Karen agreed. 'You were furious with Natasha. She was seeing your father behind your back. She lied to you. She was one of your closest friends, and she'd betrayed you like you meant nothing. So you lured her to the lake. You hit her over the head, put her in the boat and then threw her into the water.'

'Close,' Cressida said, tilting her head and nodding. 'But if I'd killed her, I'd have waited until she got into the boat before I hit her. There'd be no point exerting myself unnecessarily.'

She laughed. It was sickening to watch her describe the murder as though it was an amusing memory.

Karen breathed a sigh of relief when she saw four uniformed police officers enter the alleyway.

'They've sent four?' Cressida said. 'For little old me? I'm impressed.'

As one of the officers approached, Cressida spotted the taser in his hand.

She pulled back, yanking Karen's arm. 'They'd better not use that on me. I'm not resisting arrest. I swear I will sue you for everything you're worth!'

'Calm down. Nobody's going to shock you if you just behave yourself,' Karen said, handing Cressida over to the other officers.

'I'm really glad to see you guys,' Sophie said before she briefed the uniformed officers on the situation.

As they began to lead Cressida away from the alleyway, Karen put a hand on Ella's shoulder. 'Are you okay to walk?'

'Um, yes. I think so. My legs feel a bit shaky, but I'm okay.'

They walked together. 'How did you know about Natasha and Ryan Blake? Did she tell you?'

Ella shook her head. 'I found out by accident. I was about to walk down the stairs on Tuesday evening before dinner and I saw Cressida peering through the banisters. She was spying on Natasha and Miss King.

'I wondered why so I stopped and watched them. I overheard the conversation. Miss King saw Cressida's father and Natasha together on Monday evening in Harmston. Miss King said she was going to tell Mr Doyle.'

Karen closed her eyes and took a breath. Alison King had discovered the affair, and unfortunately for her, Cressida was prepared to do anything to stop that becoming public.

Ella continued in a shaky voice. 'Then Cressida sensed me behind her and turned. When she saw me watching her, she smiled. She said we were friends and I should keep the secret because that's what friends did for each other. I . . . I wanted to believe her. I wanted to have a friend like Cressida. She's so popular. Everything I'm not.'

'That's when she started giving you things to keep you quiet?' Karen asked.

'Yes, she told me they were gifts, and friends were supposed to give each other presents. It wasn't really wrong. It's not like I asked for the phone or the bracelet.'

Karen wasn't that easily swayed. 'But you came here today for money?'

Ella looked sheepish. 'Yes.'

'I hope that's a lesson in what greed can do, Ella. If we hadn't arrived when we did—'

Ella shuddered. 'I know. I've been really stupid. I'm sorry.'

As things fell into place, Karen recalled the handwritten study notes she'd seen on Ella's desk.

'Did you write Natasha a note?'

'A note?'

'Yes, we found one in Natasha's room that said "Somebody knows".'

'Oh, yes, that was me. I wanted to warn Natasha that Cressida knew, but didn't want Cressida to find out, so I put the note under her door.'

'Did you know what Cressida was planning to do?'

Ella's eyes filled with tears as she shook her head.

Tourists and locals gaped as they walked to the police cars. Cressida scowled at everyone they passed.

Sophie helped Ella into one of the marked cars, and Karen walked over to the other car just as Cressida got into the back.

Karen put up a hand to stop the officer shutting the door and asked, 'Miss King didn't commit suicide, did she?'

'I don't know what you mean.' A smile twitched at the corners of Cressida's mouth.

'She didn't just fall from the roof.'

Cressida giggled, then leaned over to Karen and said in a whisper, 'Well, just between you and me . . .' She pulled an exaggerated sad face. 'I was so confused about what was happening with my dad. I was so upset and had no one to talk to.' Then the sad expression evaporated and she grinned.

Karen shuddered. It was scary the way Cressida could easily switch between moods. She was terrifyingly believable. She'd managed to fool them all.

'You pushed Miss King off the roof,' Karen said simply.

'I don't know what you mean.' Cressida smiled with menace.

Karen swallowed her distaste, turned and gave the signal to the officer to close the door and take the teenager to Nettleham.

Then she walked to the other car, where Sophie was speaking to Ella.

'Did you know what had happened to Natasha?' Sophie asked.

Ella shrugged. 'No. I thought maybe Mr Blake lost his temper and killed her. I thought that was why Cressida had disappeared too. Maybe she'd seen or suspected what he'd done and hid away for a while.'

Karen looked at Ella's pale face as the teenager clutched her trembling hands together.

Ella Seaton had been way out of her depth. The silly girl had had a lucky escape.

CHAPTER THIRTY-SEVEN

'Do you want to fill me in?' Morgan asked when he met Karen and Sophie in the custody suite.

'I suspected Ella knew more than she was letting on,' Karen said. 'Rather than tell us what she knew, Ella used the information to her advantage, gaining a bracelet and a mobile phone. She was meeting Cressida today to receive another little gift. Money, this time. But Ella's plan backfired. Cressida held a knife to her throat.'

'Do you think she was just trying to scare her, to stop the blackmail?'

'Possibly. But we saw a side of Cressida today that was very different to the young woman we'd previously seen.'

Morgan looked away for a moment, thinking. 'So Ella was extorting her? And we *really* think Cressida killed Natasha?'

Karen nodded. 'Looks that way.'

'It's hard to believe.'

'Wait until you talk to her. She's . . .' Karen shook her head. 'It's hard to explain, but it's like her carefully constructed façade has fallen away.'

'So how did Ella find out what we couldn't?'

'She saw Cressida eavesdropping on Miss King when she was talking to Natasha about her relationship with Ryan Blake.'

Morgan frowned as Karen explained what she'd managed to piece together from Cressida and Ella's stories.

When Karen finished talking, Morgan rubbed his hands over his face. 'So we're looking at a double murder?'

'Yes – we are,' Karen said.

'She's dangerous,' Sophie said. 'At first Cressida was content with buying Ella off, telling her that they were friends and friends kept each other's secrets, that sort of thing. But when we found them today, I really thought Cressida was going to kill Ella.'

'In the middle of Lincoln?'

'Well, they were in an alleyway, but yes, there were people shopping within shouting distance. Cressida has no fear. She doesn't think she's going to be punished. She believes she'll get away with everything.'

Morgan raised an eyebrow. 'Not if we have anything to do with it.'

Later, Karen sat in the viewing room, watching Cressida Blake being interviewed by Morgan and Rick. Cressida sat between her solicitor and her father. As she was seventeen, Ryan Blake was permitted to be present during the questioning.

Superintendent Murray and Sophie were on either side of Karen, watching the screen.

'It's not going well, is it?' Sophie said when Cressida refused to comment for the tenth time. 'She won't talk.'

'We've still got the physical evidence,' Karen said. 'We have her DNA under Natasha's fingernails.'

'But look at her face. It's like butter wouldn't melt.'

Sophie was right. Cressida looked like an angel. Her freshly brushed blonde hair glimmered like a halo around her peaches-and-cream complexion. She looked sweet. Vulnerable. The perfect little actress, Karen thought.

They'd had the post-mortem results back now and knew that Natasha Layton had not been killed by the blow to her head. She'd drowned, which meant that when she went into the lake, she was still breathing. But with the sandbags tied around her waist, she didn't stand a chance. Karen hoped she hadn't regained consciousness.

Cressida's solicitor began to read from a sheet of paper. He recited details of the psychologist's report, describing Cressida's mental crisis, which he said was brought on by extreme stress after her abduction.

Karen rolled her eyes. Cressida hadn't been abducted. But by presenting their case this way, the solicitor was providing a reason for Cressida's attack on Ella. No matter how good Cressida's legal team was, they couldn't deny Cressida had held a knife to Ella Seaton's throat. Not when both Karen and Sophie had witnessed it.

Karen's gaze fixed on the teenager. She kept her hands together on the table. A puzzled frown creased her forehead, and her eyes were wide as she glanced between her solicitor and Morgan. Anyone watching her without knowing the history of this case would be sure to give her the benefit of the doubt.

Not once had Cressida lost her temper during questioning. She'd kept up the innocent, little-girl-lost routine since her attack on Ella. She was so convincing.

Karen was glad Sophie had been with her when Cressida spilled her fury, otherwise she might have started to think she'd imagined it.

Superintendent Murray's mobile rang. She spoke for a few moments, then sighed and hung up before turning to Karen. 'That was the front desk. Jasmine Blake is here, demanding to know what's going on. Would you mind coming with me, Karen?'

312

'Not at all,' Karen said, standing up.

They made their way to the front desk, where Mrs Blake was standing. The woman looked more dishevelled now than she had during the time Cressida was missing.

She wore an oversized, tan wool coat and a mustard scarf. Her usually smooth, gleaming hair looked greasy and tangled.

Jasmine slammed her palm hard against the surface of the desk, sending a pile of leaflets flying to the floor. 'I demand to know what's happening!'

She was shouting at the officer behind the desk. When he spotted the superintendent and Karen approaching, he gave them a relieved smile.

Jasmine turned to face them and pointed a finger at Karen. 'You've destroyed my family. You've ruined our lives.'

'I'm sorry you feel that way, Mrs Blake. Your husband has been released. He's staying with your daughter during her questioning, but he'll soon be able to collect his personal possessions, and you'll be able to take him home.'

She looked incredulously at Karen. 'I don't want to take him home. I want to know what you're doing with my daughter. You were supposed to help her. She was the *victim*.'

Karen shook her head slowly. 'No, Mrs Blake. Cressida was never the victim.'

Jasmine's face crumpled, and Karen wasn't sure whether she was about to cry or become violent.

'Why don't you come to the visitors' room? You can wait for your husband there,' Superintendent Murray said.

Jasmine shook her head, gripping the front of the desk. 'This isn't fair. You've got it wrong.'

'No, I don't think we have,' Karen said softly. 'We're interviewing Cressida now. She's safe. Her solicitor is with her, as well as her father.'

She looked at Karen with hatred. 'How could you do this to her? She's just a child.'

Karen looked into her eyes. Had this woman lived with Cressida all this time and not realised? Had Cressida's evil not once broken the surface? Did she believe that the front Cressida showed to the world was the true version of her daughter? Karen found it hard to believe that in seventeen years there had been no hint of the wickedness lurking beneath the surface.

Jasmine broke eye contact and looked down at the floor, smothering a sob.

The woman knew the truth. It just hurt her too much to admit it.

The following week, there was an odd mood among the team. Though the evidence they'd gathered was strong, and they were reasonably confident of a conviction, Cressida had been assessed by an independent psychiatrist and it appeared she would plead diminished responsibility.

Karen was polishing off some paperwork when she got a call from Superintendent Murray, asking Karen to come to her office.

She entered and saw Chief Constable John Grayson.

Grayson smiled. 'Ah, DS Hart. I'd like to congratulate you. I was very impressed by your and DI Morgan's work on this case. It was certainly not a straightforward investigation.'

'Thank you, sir.'

'Have a seat, Karen,' Superintendent Murray said warmly, and Karen took the chair beside the chief constable.

'How's Ethan, sir?'

Grayson frowned. 'Subdued. It was a harsh lesson for him.'

'He wanted to fit in, to impress them.'

Grayson nodded. 'He thought they were everything he wasn't. Popular, happy. He had no idea what Cressida Blake was really like. A lesson for us all in there somewhere, I think.'

'The chief constable has some good news related to the corruption investigation,' the superintendent said.

Karen felt a spark of hope. 'You do?'

He smiled. 'Yes, I believe Superintendent Murray told you we've got a new team looking into it now. Two full-time officers and one part-time civilian admin assistant. And that's not all. They're going to give the assistant chief constable weekly updates. We need results. We need accountability.'

'I agree, sir,' Superintendent Murray said.

Karen shifted in her chair. It sounded good. Actually, it sounded great. Finally, some forward momentum, and someone with a drive to get to the bottom of the corruption. There was one thing that worried Karen though. Updates to Assistant Chief Constable Kenneth Fry. She had dealt with him before and his attitude towards the corruption case didn't fill Karen with confidence.

A moment later there was a knock, and Pamela opened the door for the assistant chief constable.

He strode in and offered a smile to Grayson and a nod to Murray. He ignored Karen. Not a good start. A woman with red curly hair and freckles followed him in.

'Ah, Kenneth, DS Grace,' Grayson said. 'Glad you could make it. I've just been telling DS Hart and Superintendent Murray that we've made new plans for the corruption inquiry. We're determined to get to the bottom of it, aren't we?'

Fry nodded. 'Absolutely, sir.'

'And we're going to get results this time. You've met DS Hart before?'

'Yes, I have.' Fry's eyes narrowed slightly as he glanced at Karen.

'I haven't,' DS Grace said, offering Karen a warm smile and her hand to shake.

'DS Grace will be the lead on this investigation, Karen,' Grayson said. 'She's from Boston.'

'Good to meet you.' Karen shook her hand. 'Let me know if there's anything I can do to help.'

'Will do.'

'Excellent.' Grayson stood. 'With proper accountability, we'll get results. The important thing is absolutely no drifting,' he said, prodding the desk as he spoke.

DS Grace looked a little confused but nodded and went along with it. 'Absolutely, sir. No drifting.'

Karen was smiling as she left the superintendent's office. She followed DS Grace to the stairwell. The woman had an open and friendly face, and Karen hoped she was the right officer for the job. She'd found it hard to trust her colleagues after Freeman's betrayal. People could be very deceptive, and this latest case and Cressida Blake had driven that point home.

It was hard not to wonder, if it came down to it and her life was on the line, could she trust her fellow officers, or would they turn their backs on their morals to earn a bit of extra cash?

DS Grace gave Karen a conspiratorial smile. 'What was all that about drifting? I hope it made sense to you.'

'Grayson was concerned that the previous corruption investigation was drifting on without direction.'

'Ah, that makes sense. I'll be coming to talk to you next week, if that's okay?' DS Grace said. 'I know I've got the events detailed in the reports, but I'd like a one-on-one meeting.'

'No problem. If it helps get to the bottom of this then I'm on board.'

'Great.'

As Karen made her way back to her desk, she felt hopeful for the first time in a long while that they might finally get to the truth.

'Sarge?'

Karen turned and headed over to Sophie's desk. The young officer sat in front of her computer, hair tucked behind her ears, cheeks flushed and eyes shining with excitement.

'What is it? Found something?'

'I think so.' Sophie turned her screen so it faced Karen.

'What is it?'

'We've been trying to track down where Cressida was on Thursday night after she killed Natasha.'

Karen nodded. 'Yes, you were looking at the outbuildings in the area.'

'I was, but then I thought, Cressida would have been cold and wet. When she returned on Friday, she didn't have a coat.'

'Right.'

'So I thought she'd need to be somewhere warmer than an outbuilding.'

'A B&B?'

'I thought about that, but then I remembered my conversation with Mrs Jackson.'

'Mrs Jackson?'

'The old lady who Natasha and Cressida helped when she fell on her drive. She had a video doorbell that recorded them helping her, and on it, Mrs Jackson was telling them about her annexe. Her son was away so it wasn't in use.'

'You checked it?' Karen asked.

Sophie beamed. 'I did. Someone had been using it. Food was taken from the freezer, a dirty plate was in the sink. And I found Cressida's coat, soaking wet in the wheelie bin.'

'Well done, Sophie. Great work, and another part of the mystery solved.'

CHAPTER THIRTY-EIGHT

On Saturday morning, Karen knocked on the door of Mike Harrington's cottage. He didn't answer straightaway, but she heard Sandy barking inside.

It had felt odd to walk on Chidlow land after everything that had happened. Lord Chidlow had been released on bail and was staying in London. As his flat in the capital was the address he'd given the court, he wouldn't be at the house today, but Karen couldn't help glancing over her shoulder as she walked down the lawns to the lake.

The edge of the lake had shown signs of the search. Flattened reeds, footprints, churned-up mud. But the lake itself was calm and peaceful. Karen had thought of the bright young woman, full of promise, heading out for a fun night with her friend – with no idea what lay in store for her.

Karen had lingered by the shore of the man-made lake for a moment, feeling desperately sorry that the only way they could help Natasha Layton was by ensuring her killer was held to account.

When Harrington opened the door abruptly, Karen was so lost in her thoughts again that she jumped.

Sandy greeted her, enthusiastically wagging her tail. Karen reached down to pet her.

Harrington's surly face was a little brighter this morning. His usual moody frown had almost disappeared.

'I wasn't expecting visitors,' he said bluntly.

'I would have called first, but you don't have a phone.'

'Actually, I do now. Got it a couple of days ago.'

'You've rejoined society? Next you'll be on social media.'

He pretended to shudder. 'Don't even joke about it.' He smiled. 'Come in. Sorry about the state of the cottage.'

Karen stepped inside, and her eyes widened. The place was a mess. Every counter was stacked high with Harrington's belongings, and the floor was covered with cushions, folded blankets and various possessions.

'Did the search team leave it like this?'

'Oh, no,' Harrington said. 'I'm moving, packing up.'

Karen took in the crates and the items that had been stuffed into them at odd angles. *Inefficient use of space*, she thought, but managed to keep that to herself.

'How can I help?' he asked.

'Sorry?'

'Did you come for a specific reason or were you just after that cup of tea you missed out on the last time you were here?'

It was Karen's turn to smile. 'Yes, I had a reason.' She dug around in her handbag and pulled out an envelope. 'Official letter, explains how you can retrieve your property after the trial. Could be a while yet, though.'

Harrington frowned and took the envelope. 'What property?'

'The polo shirt.'

'Oh, I don't want that back.'

'No? But I thought you had five shirts, so you didn't need to do washing until the weekend.'

'You remember me saying that?' He looked amused.

'I read DI Morgan's interview notes. Washing your work shirts once a week is an efficient way to operate. That, on the other hand' – she pointed at the haphazard items in the crates – 'is not an efficient method.'

He grinned. 'No, I suppose I could have done a better job. Want to help?'

'So you get free labour? I don't think so. I'm acting in a purely advisory capacity.'

'Oh, I see. Well, to thank you for the advice, the least I can do is offer you the cup of tea you turned down last time you were here. You couldn't get out of here fast enough.'

As he made the tea, Karen looked out of the window at the woods. The weather was much better today and the weak sunlight filtered down through the bare branches.

'Sorry if I scared you last time,' Harrington said. 'I was angry.'

'You were . . . but it wasn't because I was scared.' Karen took a deep breath. 'It was the boxes, I think. The ones you had by the door.'

Harrington handed her a mug of tea. 'Ah, I thought so.'

Karen frowned, watching him closely as she sipped the tea. 'You thought so?'

'You lost someone too? A child?'

Karen had to look away. His gaze was unsettling; she didn't like the way he was able to read her so easily. Or had someone told him? Morgan? But Karen couldn't imagine Morgan sharing details of her private life with a man who was a suspect during an investigation.

'Am I that transparent?' she asked, warming her hands around the mug.

'No, not at all, but I can see something of my own pain reflected in you, I suppose.'

Karen said nothing.

'Well, this is all getting a bit deep for a Saturday morning.' He ran a hand through his dark hair and turned to inspect the crates.

'So, where are you moving to?' Karen asked before taking another sip of her tea.

'Not far. Still Lincolnshire. Got a new job offer. I can't stay here and work for a man like Chidlow now I know what he's been doing.'

'No, I wouldn't want to either. What's the new job?'

'At a rescue centre for dogs. It's a volunteer role.'

Karen wondered what he would do for money without a salary coming in, but decided that was none of her business.

'I'm sorry about the search and everything,' she said. 'It can't have been easy to have officers going through your son's possessions.'

'No, and you were a bit judgy too.'

'Judgy? That's not even a word.'

He laughed. 'All right. Judgemental, then. You thought I was guilty.'

Karen put her mug down on the draining board and folded her arms. 'It's my job.'

'I know, and thanks to you doing your job well, I was exonerated.'

Karen glanced at Sandy, who was looking at Harrington and Karen in turn like she was watching a tennis match. 'Luckily I don't do this job expecting to get thanked.'

'I suppose I should thank you. I could cook you dinner one night?'

Karen hesitated. She liked him. The moodiness took some getting used to, but when he smiled his eyes were warm, and he was smiling now.

'You could help me celebrate a new beginning,' he continued.

Still Karen didn't answer.

'Why don't I call you when I've settled into my new place?'

'You'd need my number to do that,' Karen said.

'Yes, I would.' He smiled again. It suited him.

'All right,' Karen said. 'But you should know it's mainly because I want to see Sandy again.'

He laughed. 'Don't worry. I know where I stand in the pecking order. I like to think Sandy's my dog, but sometimes I think it's the other way around. I'm her human.'

After leaving the cottage, Karen walked back across the lawns. When she reached her car, she realised she was still smiling.

On Monday, at six p.m., Karen shut down her work computer. Things were progressing well. Natasha Layton's body would be released back to the family tonight and they could make plans for the funeral. The case against Cressida Blake was complicated, but Karen was hopeful. She believed the evidence was strong enough to withstand Cressida's legal team, her youth and her talent for manipulation.

Karen reached for her handbag and spotted Morgan leaving his office, shrugging on his jacket.

'Fancy a drink?' he asked. 'Butcher & Beast?'

'Sounds good,' Karen said.

The mention of a drink caused Rick to lift his head and grin at Karen. 'A beer is just what I need. It's been a long week.'

Sophie, who was sitting opposite Rick, laughed. 'But it's only Monday!'

'Then I *really* need a drink.'

'No Jill tonight?' Sophie asked Morgan, as all four of them left the office.

Morgan still hadn't introduced Jill to the team – not that he needed to, but Karen couldn't help wondering what she was like.

He'd said he and Jill had a lot in common, so Karen had imagined her to be a female version of Morgan. Serious, sensible and a stickler for the rules.

'No, not tonight. As things have been so hectic here recently, we decided I'd call her when things calmed down.'

As they headed out of the main door, Rick and Sophie walked to one side of the car park and Karen and Morgan went to the other.

The air was cold, and Karen wrapped her scarf around her neck, then rummaged in her bag for her car keys.

'I'm here if you want someone to talk to, you know,' Morgan said.

'I know,' Karen said, stepping around a puddle on the tarmac.

'After the other night, I thought you might think I was fobbing you off.'

'You were busy. You have every right to relax with Jill and enjoy yourself. I didn't think you were fobbing me off.'

'All right. I just don't want you to think you can't rely on me if you need help.'

Karen smiled. 'Thanks, Morgan. I know I can rely on you, but I'm fine.'

'Really?'

Karen's smile widened as she nodded. She really did feel okay. 'I'm more positive about things now. The new team looking into the corruption is working hard. I spoke to DS Grace this morning and she's fully focused and hugely determined. Now the chief constable is on board, pushing for results, we have a real chance of finding out who else was involved with Freeman.'

'Did you ever find out the significance of DCI Churchill?'

Karen shook her head as she unlocked her car. 'No, but I think that might have been a red herring. Alice Price wants to help, but she doesn't always give reliable information. Her mental health has suffered since she left the police.'

'That must be hard for her.'

'I think it is. One moment she was convinced DCI Churchill was involved, the next she couldn't remember why she ever suspected him.'

'Then you should carefully assess any information she provides in the future.'

'I will, but I'm hoping with DS Grace on the case, we'll soon have more reliable sources of information than Alice. We're moving in the right direction.'

'That's good news.'

Karen smiled. 'It is. The best news I've had for a long time.'

'Then we'd better get to the Butcher & Beast to celebrate,' Morgan said, heading to his own car.

Karen drove out of the station car park and headed towards Lincoln. The road through the city was clogged with rush-hour traffic. She put some music on, a cheerful pop song, and hummed along, determined not to let traffic dampen her mood.

The line of cars slowed near the crossroads by the cemetery. Karen glanced across and said, 'It won't be much longer now.'

This time next month, with DS Grace digging into the corruption, they should have some real results.

Finally, they would have justice.

ACKNOWLEDGMENTS

A huge thank you to my fantastic editor, Jack Butler, and all at Amazon Publishing for their hard work and enthusiasm for the Karen Hart series.

Special thanks to Russel McLean for his insightful input and invaluable attention to detail.

Heartfelt gratitude to Jane, Lesa and all the people at Branston Community Library for generously spreading the word about my books.

To my family, a special thank you for things too numerous to mention, after a very difficult year for us all; and, as always, thanks to Chris for his belief in me and unwavering support.

And finally, most importantly, thank you to all those who have read and recommended my books. Your kind words and encouragement mean the world to me.

ABOUT THE AUTHOR

Born in Kent, D. S. Butler grew up as an avid reader with a love for crime fiction and mysteries. She has worked as a scientific officer in a hospital pathology laboratory and as a research scientist. After obtaining a PhD in biochemistry, she worked at the University of Oxford for four years before moving to the Middle East. While living in Bahrain, she wrote her first novel and hasn't stopped writing since. She now lives in Lincolnshire with her husband.

Printed in Great Britain
by Amazon